I0749444

Jean Vanmai's
CHÂN ĐĂNG
The Tonkinese of Caledonia in the Colonial Era

Translated and with a critical introduction by
Tess Do and Kathryn Lay-Chenchabi

UTS
ePRESS

UTS ePRESS
University of Technology Sydney
Broadway NSW 2007 AUSTRALIA
epress.lib.uts.edu.au

This work includes a full translation into English of Jean Vanmai's original book, *"Chân Đăng" les Tonkinois de Calédonie au temps colonial* first published in 1980 by the Société d'Études Historiques de la Nouvelle-Calédonie.

Publication Details
DOI citation: https://doi.org/10.5130/aai
ISBN: 978-0-6453713-0-7 (paperback)
ISBN: 978-0-6453713-1-4 (eBook pdf)
ISBN: 978-0-6453713-2-1 (ePub)
ISBN: 978-0-6453713-3-8 (mobi)

Peer Review
This work was peer reviewed by disciplinary experts.

Declaration of conflicting interest
The authors declare no potential conflicts of interest with respect to the research, authorship, and/or publication of this book.

Funding
The authors gratefully acknowledge the funding support by The University of Melbourne, Faculty of Arts Internal Grant Schemes (FIGS).

UTS ePRESS
Manager: Scott Abbott
Books Editor: Matthew Noble
Designer: Megan Wong
Enquiries: utsepress@uts.edu.au

For enquiries about third party copyright material reproduced in this work, please contact UTS ePRESS.

OPEN ACCESS

UTS ePRESS publishes peer reviewed books, journals and conference proceedings and is the leading publisher of peer reviewed open access journals in Australasia. All UTS ePRESS online content is free to access and read.

To the Chân Đăng and their descendants

Aux Chân Đăng et à leurs descendants

Contents

Preface

I came to be aware of the history of the Chân Đăng through a series of meaningful coincidences. In the summer of 2014, I was sitting in a stuffy office at La Trobe University, in Woiworrung land, where I was working as a research assistant on "*Decolonisation and the Pacific*" (Cambridge University Press, 2016) for the pathbreaking historian of the Pacific, Tracey Banivanua Mar, having recently completed a doctorate about the politics of languages and Asian migration in 1890s Victoria. There, I was making summaries of Australian Security Intelligence Organisation (ASIO) files that had recently been made public. In the midst of these files, I came across a surprising report. ASIO officials were observing Vietnamese New Caledonians marching down to the Noumea port, waving flags sporting the Red star, evidently full of hope and joy at returning to their much-missed homeland.

I had had a long-held interest in Vietnamese history. After living in Vietnam in my early twenties, I'd wanted to do a doctorate on the French colonisation of Vietnam but could find no supervisor willing and tenured enough to support this. What, I wondered now, were Vietnamese people doing living in New Caledonia, and why were they now returning to Vietnam with such excitement?

After following Chân Đăng trails, I would learn that, for many Viet-Caledonians, news that the north had fallen filled them not so much with hope of New Caledonian independence from French rule, but rather with a hope to return home. The Viet Minh's victory at Điện Biên Phủ spurred

Viet-Caledonians to embark on a seven-year campaign to gain permission from the French government for their departure from New Caledonia, with the first ship leaving Noumea for Hà Nội in 1961. With more reading, and vitally, after reading work by Dr. Tess Do, one of the translators of this book, these surprising twists of history began to make sense to me. This was a transnational history that connected people across landmasses, languages and colonial and national regimes and polities. Eventually, I reimaged Melbourne as a city at the oceanic edge of the French empire, its people and politics entangled with Vietnamese history for decades earlier than the Colombo Plan of the 1950s, the era often chronicled as the beginning of any significant Vietnam-Australia connection.

I would meet Jean Vanmai, the son of former indentured labourers and author of *Chân Đăng*, on a 2016 research trip to New Caledonia inspired by those glimpses of Chân Đăng history in ASIO files. Vanmai found it somewhat amusing that an Anglo-Australian historian was so interested in Chân Đăng history. While my limited Vietnamese and scarce French, as well as Vanmai's limited English, left some gaps in our mutual understanding, this admixture of languages perfectly reflected the entwined histories and geographies of colonialism (and anticolonialism) that had brought us to the same room. I was born in a settler colony, where English had been planted to usurp over 250 Indigenous languages. Vanmai was born in New Caledonia, where he had his Vietnamese, the language of his parents' homeland, and French, the language of the settler colony of New Caledonia. Rather than think in conventional "colony/metropole" binaries, I began to think of my research, and of Chân Đăng history, as a significantly triangular formation involving Vietnam (formerly Indochina), Australia and New Caledonia—territories and cultural spaces historically connected in the first instance by the South China and Coral seas, and in the second by British and French colonial regimes.

The translators of *Chân Đăng*, Kathryn Lay-Chenchabi and Tess Do, are both French scholars with interests in the Francophone world. Lay-Chenchabi is a scholar in Francophone postcolonial studies and a French and English translator. Do is a lecturer in French Studies at the School of Languages and Linguistics at the University of Melbourne. She specialises in Francophone literature and has a long-standing interest in the history of French Indochina and the Vietnamese diaspora. A transnational migrant, Do has lived in Vietnam, Canada, New Zealand, and Australia and is fluent in Vietnamese, French and English. She became interested in the Chân Đăng history when, by a fortunate coincidence, she was introduced to Jean Vanmai and his literary work in 2001 during one of her conference trips to Noumea.

In December 2016, an event at the University of Melbourne, "Rencontres: A Gathering of Voices of the Vietnamese Diaspora," brought together Vietnamese scholars, artists and writers from Australia, France, Canada and New

Caledonia. When the sole Caledonian participant, Jean Vanmai, recounted parts of his Chân Đăng parents' story, it became startlingly clear how little the Australian and French participants knew of the history of Vietnamese indentured workers in New Caledonia, as well as of New Caledonia generally. It also became clear that Australia—located between France, Vietnam and New Caledonia—was a fertile meeting ground for conversations about the ongoing impact of French colonialism in and beyond New Caledonia and Vietnam. The hyphens between Australia, Asia and the Pacific, the liminal spaces that live across the so-called Australia-Asia-Pacific region, became alive and locatable within a human history of labour migration. It was also here that I met Dr Tess Do, whose translations and readings of Vanmai's *Chân Đăng* I had read and been impressed and moved by, in particular her book chapter titled "Exile: Rupture and Continuity in Jean Vanmai's *Chân Đăng* and *Fils de Chân Đăng*."

It is in this thick context that Anglophones now have the opportunity to read more about the Chân Đăng and their history and self-understanding. In her translation of Georges Baudoux's *Jean M'Baraï The Trepang Fisherman* (University of Technology Sydney ePress, 2015), historian Karin Speedy has written of "the dearth of earlier francophone Pacific literature in translation," which means that Anglophone readers "lack a context against which they can read francophone Pacific literature as part of an ongoing dialogue within their own literary tradition." Also, the dearth of Francophone and Vietnamese historical accounts in translation means that Anglophone historians are missing and misreading the entwined British and French histories of colonialism and indentured labour. This translation of *Chân Đăng* counters the urgent problems of redressing Anglocentric perspectives of history, enabling the building of bridges between Anglophone, Francophone and Vietnamese historians and histories. As well as enabling new scholarly insights and opening conversations between historians of the British and French empires, this translation enables Vietnamese Australians forming part of the Vietnamese diaspora living across the Pacific Rim to gain knowledge about one lesser-known story of Vietnamese migration.

Chân Đăng is invaluable both as a work of literature and a work of historical record. This is an account of the past that draws on memory and communal knowledge—one that completes the experiences of the Chân Đăng, permitting us to enter the violent operation of French colonialism as it came to bear on Vietnamese lives, all while honouring the complexity and richness of love, hope and desire and the ways in which Chân Đăng families made their lives as "twice-colonised" people.

The publication of this translation is extremely timely. A page is about to be turned, as the second generation of Chân Đăng, the Niaoulis, are now in their mid-eighties. At a time when it is urgent for their heritage be passed on to the younger generation, this translation signals the preservation of and strengthening engagement with Chân Đăng stories. In May 2021, the Niaoulis commemorated the 791 Tonkinese workers who were on board the first boat to arrive in Noumea in 1891, "celebrated," or so the New Caledonian press reported, "in the purest Vietnamese tradition, with firecrackers, dragon dance and conical hat, and incense." At the same time, the advent of a global pandemic has seen the reassertion and hardening of national borders—overlaid as they are on colonial ones—making the translation and increased accessibility of this history that crisscrosses and collapses such borders even more precious and poignant.

Nadia Rhook
University of Western Australia

Sources

Do, Tess. 2008. "Exile: Rupture and Continuity in Jean Vanmai's Chân Đăng and Fils de Chân Đăng". In: Paul Allatson and Jo McCormack (eds.), *Exile, Cultures, Misplaced Identities*. Rodopi, Amsterdam, 151–172.

Speedy, Karin, trans. 2015. *Jean M'Barai: The Trepang Fisherman*, (Sydney: University of Technology Sydney ePress).

"130 ans de présence des Chân Đăng," Radio Rhythm Bleu, Noumea. https://rrb.nc/article/130-ans-de-presence-des-chan-dang. Accessed 1 August 2021.

List of Figures

Acknowledgements

We gratefully acknowledge the funding support by The University of Melbourne, Faculty of Arts Internal Grant Schemes (FIGS), without which the writing of the critical introduction and the translation of *Chân Đăng* into English would not have been possible.

We are also indebted to friends and colleagues who have supported us at different stages of our translation project.

We would like to express our deep gratitude to the author Jean Vanmai for his incredible generosity, both with his time and his knowledge of the Chân Đăng history; Dr. Nadia Rhook (The University of Western Australia) for her insightful preface and comments on our project; Professor Véronique Duché (The University of Melbourne) for her thorough re-reading of our French introduction; Christophe Dervieux and the Archives of New Caledonia for their generous welcome and the precious documents provided for our research; Nina Kurzman and the Archives of New Zealand for the permission to publish images held in their collections; Joe Chuvan for kindly allowing us to use the photos from his private collection; Dr. Paul Allatson, Matthew Noble, Scott Abbott, Helen Chan, Duncan Loxton, Julie-Anne Marshall, the reviewers and the editorial team at the University of Technology Sydney ePress for their helpful advice and support throughout the publication process; and last but not least, French graphic author Clément Baloup for his stunning creative book cover.

Remerciements

Nous tenons à remercier l'Université de Melbourne et la Faculté de Lettres pour leur généreux appui financier. C'était grâce au fond de recherche *Faculty of Arts Internal Grant Schemes (FIGS)* que notre projet de traduction en anglais du roman *Chân Đăng* a pu être réalisé.

Nous sommes également très reconnaissantes pour les nombreux témoignages de soutien que nous avons reçus tout au long de notre projet.

Nous remercions l'auteur Jean Vanmai pour son soutien sans faille et ses renseignements inestimables sur l'histoire des Chân Đăng; Dr. Nadia Rhook (The University of Western Australia) pour sa préface et ses commentaires judicieux sur notre projet; Professeur Véronique Duché (The University of Melbourne) pour sa relecture attentive de notre introduction française; Christophe Dervieux et les Archives de la Nouvelle-Calédonie pour l'accueil généreux et les précieux documents fournis; Nina Kurzman et les Archives de la Nouvelle-Zélande pour la permission de publier des images de leurs collections; Joe Chuvan pour son aimable permission de publier des photos de sa collection privée; Dr. Paul Allatson, Matthew Noble, Scott Abbott, Helen Chan, Duncan Loxton, Julie-Anne Marshall, les évaluateurs et l'équipe éditoriale à UTS ePress (University of Technology Sydney ePress) pour leurs excellents conseils et soutien au cours du processus de publication; enfin, Clément Baloup, auteur de bande dessinée et illustrateur, pour la magnifique couverture de notre livre.

A Critical Introduction to *Chân Đăng*

The Historical and Literary Context of *Chân Đăng*

The historical novel *Chân Đăng*,[1] by Jean Vanmai, was published by the *Société d'Études Historiques de la Nouvelle-Calédonie* (New Caledonia Historical Studies Society) in 1980, in the midst of the Cold War and at the height of the Indochinese refugee crisis. With hundreds of thousands of Vietnamese boat people taking to sea in makeshift boats, only to meet a tragic end by drowning or crowding into refugee camps in Southeast Asia, their stories became headlines around the world, particularly in France, where the rescue operation *Un bateau pour le Vietnam* (A Boat for Vietnam) had just been launched the previous year by Bernard Kouchner, supported by French intellectuals and celebrities such as Jean-Paul Sartre, Raymond Aron, Michel Foucault, Yves Montand and Simone Signoret. Given this fraught context, it is not surprising that despite the fact that the novel won the prestigious *Prix de l'Asie* (Asia Literary Award) in 1981,[2] the story of the Chân Đăng, the Tonkinese indentured workers in colonial times,[3] went virtually unnoticed by Vietnamese readers both in the diaspora, where they were too busy dealing with their own traumatic accounts of exile, and in Vietnam, where they were still cut off from the outside world due to the U.S. embargo.

That *Chân Đăng* was written in French and published in Nouméa (rather than in Paris) has also contributed to its limited readership. Although the story of the Chân Đăng was given high praise by the French jury, who immediately recognised its historical importance, it took Francophone readers, including Vietnamese outside New Caledonia, much longer to discover Vanmai's first novel. According to Yannick Fer (2014: 7), even within the South Pacific communities, Asian diasporas and their histories have often been overlooked in the representation of Oceania in the social sciences and literature, even though their presence in the region dates to the end of the 19th century. In the confrontation between the West and the indigenous peoples, 'ces personnages de coolies agricoles, petits commerçants et commis de magasin' (these coolie farm labourers, small shopkeepers and shop clerks),[4] like the Chân Đăng, are mere 'ombres chinoises' (shadow puppets)—shadowy figures moving silently in the background. Within the Vietnamese diaspora itself, largely formed by post-1975 refugees, the Vietnamese Caledonian community is less visible than other Vietnamese diasporic communities in the United States, Canada and Australia because of its small size.[5] Although France took in a fair number of Vietnamese refugees—128,531 in 1979 alone, according to Pierre Haski (2015)—only about 700 people came to resettle in its island territories between 1975 and 1985 (Angleviel: 79; Crocombe 2007: 75).

Parallel to the low visibility of the Vietnamese community in New Caledonia is the fact that *Chân Đăng* cannot be easily placed within the Vietnamese Francophone literary tradition that goes back to the 1920s.[6] Marked by a peak period in the 1950s, the publication of novels in French slowly declined in the decade preceding the fall of Saigon, with the last being Lý Thu Hồ's *Au milieu du carrefour* (In the Middle of the Crossroads) in 1969. Vanmai's book came out in the period between the pre-1975 publications and the post-1975 revival of this literary tradition, which saw the emergence of a young generation of diasporic Vietnamese Francophone writers, one of whom is the prolific Linda Lê, who debuted with the novel *Un si tendre vampire* (A Very Sweet Vampire) in 1987. Compared to the majority of the colonial and pre-1975 Franco-Vietnamese novels, which deal mainly with the impact of colonisation and French education on the Vietnamese elites and the culture shock of the East-West encounter, often represented in failed colonial romance tropes,[7] *Chân Đăng* presents a completely different context and topic. Set neither in France nor in Vietnam, but rather in the unfamiliar New Caledonia, its strange title raises questions as to its roots and meanings. Among them, the explanation given by Vanmai is the most widely accepted: *Chân*, meaning 'feet' in Vietnamese, and *Đăng*, 'to enlist' ('*d'engager*' in French), the combined term *Chân Đăng* is a name invented by the Tonkinese indentured workers themselves to reflect the fact that they were bound ('*pieds liés*' or 'bound feet') or worse, shackled ('*pieds enchaînés*' or 'chained feet'), by their contract of either three or five years[8] (Figures 1 and 2).

In addition, with its portrayal of the Chân Đăng as the main characters, rather than middle-class Vietnamese Francophones or Francophiles, Vanmai's book seems to occupy a place of its own in Vietnamese Francophone literature. Yet nothing could be further from the truth because the Chân Đăng story, in revealing how the colonial relations between France and Vietnam played out in New Caledonia throughout the anticolonial war until well after the decolonisation of Indochina in 1954, not only sheds light on the indentured workers' past, but also makes an essential contribution to the understanding of the history and formation of the Vietnamese diaspora in the South Pacific.

Until the publication of Vanmai's novel there had been no public or written account, let alone from an insider's perspective, that documented the life of these contract workers. No one from the Chân Đăng side had ventured to break the silence (Do 2008). This was partly due to the feeling of shame associated

PAIEMENT
PAR MENSUALITÉ
entière

NOUVELLE-CALÉDONIE
et
DÉPENDANCES

IMMIGRATION

N° 624 d'enregistrement

CIRCONSCRIPTION
de

ACTE D'ENGAGEMENT

Le 26 novembre 1941

Entre le Chef du Service de l'Immigration d'une part,

Et Madame E. Rousseau

habitant à Nouméa d'autre part,

il a été arrêté et convenu ce qui suit :

A la demande de Madame Rousseau

il lui est confié l'Immigrant Nguyen Van Thuy

N° M^{le} 2-1844 pour la durée de son contrat initial, telle qu'elle reste à accomplir à ce jour,

Madame Rousseau, qui l'accepte, s'engage, en outre, à verser trimestriellement, au Service de l'Immigration, les redevances et le pécule du travailleur, fixés par les arrêtés en vigueur.

Madame Rousseau, qui a versé le montant des frais d'inscription, ne supportera aucune charge pour le rapatriement anticipé du travailleur et de sa famille, il aura droit, au surplus, au remplacement de l'Engagé ci-dessus mentionné si celui-ci ne pouvait terminer à son service son contrat quinquennal, et si la maladie ou l'accident ne sont pas imputables au travail.

Madame Rousseau reconnaît avoir pris connaissance des dispositions du dernier contrat en vigueur et s'engage à les respecter.

Le présent acte aura son effet à compter du 26 Novembre au point de vue des salaires et du 1° Décembre 41 au point de vue des mensualités.

L'employeur — Rousseau

LE CHEF DU SERVICE DE L'IMMIGRATION, p.i.

NOUVELLE-CALÉDONIE ET DÉPENDANCES — SERVICE — IMMIGRATION

Les mensualités partent du 1er ou du 16 de chaque mois, toute période de 8 jours accomplie par le travailleur compte pour la quinzaine entière.

Figure 1 Engagement contract and identification number (Archives of New Caledonia, 332 W 17)

with the image of the colonised 'coolie', the slave-like conditions they had had to endure and the need to forget and to spare their descendants the traumatic memories, and partly due to the fear that they and their families might get into trouble if they exposed the injustice and physical abuse they had suffered at the hands of their 'masters', both the white men and the Kanaks, the indigenous inhabitants of New Caledonia, some of whom were still alive in the 1980s. Even

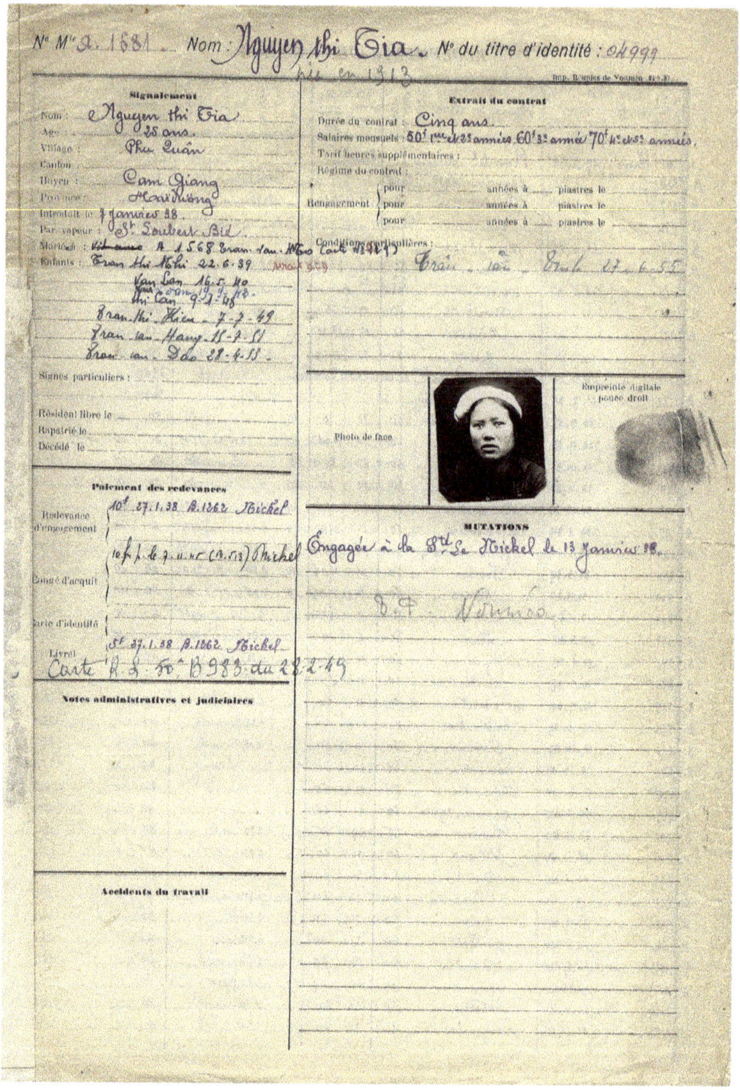
N° Mle A. 1681 Nom: Nguyen thi Tia. N° du titre d'identité: 04999

Née en 1913

Signalement

Nom: Nguyen thi Tia

Age: 25 ans.

Village: Phu Quan

Canton:

Huyen: Cam Giang

Province: Haiduong

Introduit le 7 janvier 38.

Par vapeur: St. Joubert Bil

Marié à: A 1568 Tran van Nho

Enfants: Tran thi Nhi 22.6.39

Van Lan 16.5.40

Thi Can 9.7.48

Tran thi Hien 7.7.49

Tran van Hang 18.7.51

Tran van Dao 28.4.53

Signes particuliers:

Résident libre le

Rapatrié le

Décédé le

Extrait du contrat

Durée du contrat: Cinq ans.

Salaires mensuels: 50f 1re et 2e années 60f 3e année 70f 4e et 5e années.

Tarif heures supplémentaires:

Régime du contrat:

Rengagement: pour ... années à ... piastres le

Conditions particulières:

Tran van Tinh 17.6.55

Photo de face

Empreinte digitale pouce droit

Paiement des redevances

Redevance d'engagement: 10f 27.1.38 B.1262 Michel

Congé d'acquit

Carte d'identité

Livret: 5f 27.1.38 B.1262 Michel

Carte A.L. 50f B 983 du 28.2.49

Mutations

Engagée à la Sté Le Nickel le 13 janvier 38.

Notes administratives et judiciaires

Accidents du travail

Figure 2 Identity document and identification number (Archives of New Caledonia, 332 W 15)

those who had already left New Caledonia and had no reason to worry about the reaction of their former employers or foremen did not care to tell their stories. Repatriated to North Vietnam in the early 1960s at the height of the Vietnam War, they had no time to dwell on the past, as they had to face the reality and hardship of resettling and surviving in a poor, war-torn country.

On the French side, there was understandably little interest in unearthing this story of slavery and exploitation in which France's role as the dominant colonial power was hardly flattering. Furthermore, in the 1980s, France was dealing with its difficult withdrawal from the newly independent Vanuatu (ex-French condominium of New Hebrides), an event that deeply unsettled its Caledonian territories, which were caught up in a nationalist fervour and struggle for independence (Aldrich 1993).

The Genesis of *Chân Đăng*

Given this context, it was a brave and remarkable achievement for Jean Vanmai, a 'son of Chân Đăng'[9] who until then had not pursued a literary career, to write his debut novel and have it published. Born on 3 August 1940 in the small town of Koumac near the Chagrin mine in the north of New Caledonia, Vanmai was the eldest son of a family of nine siblings.[10] His father, Nguyễn Văn Khảo, was an indentured worker who came to the islands in 1937, where he met and married Nguyễn Thị Hảo, a native of Tonkin just like him.[11] Vanmai attended school in his hometown before going to technical college in Nouméa. He was in his early twenties when his entire family boarded the *Eastern Queen* on 30 December 1960 to return to North Vietnam. Their trip, departing from Nouméa and taking on board repatriates from New Caledonia only (Figures 3 and 4), was the first in a series of nine that were arranged by the French government between

Figure 3 *Eastern Queen* on the first repatriation trip back to Hải Phòng, December 1960 (Jean Vanmai's collection)

Figure 4 *Eastern Queen* embarking at the port of Nouméa, December 1960 (Jean Vanmai's collection)

1960 and 1964, during which 3,553 Vietnamese workers and their families left New Caledonia and New Hebrides (Mohamed-Gaillard, 2010).

Although long awaited, the repatriation was met with ambivalence by the Chân Đăng, many of whom had spent over twenty years in New Caledonia. It was a real cause for celebration for some, but for others, especially those who were born and had grown up in New Caledonia, it was difficult to tear themselves away from a land to which they had become attached.[12] Vanmai was one of these. In love with his Futunian fiancée, Helena Wendt, who later became his wife, he decided not to accompany his parents and siblings, but he kept his decision a secret to avoid causing them too much pain—a situation that he developed in *Chân Đăng* through the character Hồng. On the day of departure, Vanmai was nowhere to be found. For the distressed mother, it was shameful for the eldest son to abandon his ageing parents and, after searching in vain, the family had no choice but to leave without him. Little did they know that he was hiding, not among their Vietnamese friends and relatives, but with a Kanak friend.[13] It would take another fifteen years for the whole family to be reunited when Vanmai travelled to Vietnam with his wife in 1975 to visit his parents. He would make several more trips back to the country to see them, and over the years, he provided them with substantial financial support. According to Vanmai, as a result, his mother came to realise how fortunate they were that he had stayed in New Caledonia.[14]

After his family's repatriation, Vanmai pursued a successful career in Nouméa as a radio technician and businessman in the audiovisual and home appliance industry. An influential figure in the Vietnamese community in New Caledonia, he was elected a member of the *Rassemblement pour la Calédonie dans la République du Congrès du Territoire* (the RPCR of the Territorial Congress) from 1988 to 1995 and was one of the main forces behind the foundation of the *Amicale Vietnamienne de Nouvelle-Calédonie* (Vietnamese Association in New Caledonia) in 1974. Vanmai's strong bond with his diasporic community dates to his youth when, struck by the sudden realisation that with the repatriation of four-fifths of the Vietnamese population and fewer than 1,000 Vietnamese remaining in New Caledonia, he became acutely aware of the need to save the little-known experience of these workers from oblivion. In an interview with Christiane Terrier (2016) on the *New Caledonian* radio program, Vanmai revealed how Peter Viertel's novel *Chasseur blanc coeur noir* (White Hunter Black Heart) (1954), which he saw in a bookshop in Nouméa a few months after his family's departure, made him realise the power of the written word to preserve memories:

> En voyant ce livre, je pense qu'il faudrait bien que quelqu'un de chez nous se décide, un jour ou l'autre, à écrire l'épopée des Vietnamiens en Nouvelle-Calédonie. Il est inconcevable de laisser disparaître cette période dure, pénible, difficile, vécue par tous les nôtres, sans laisser la moindre trace écrite.[15] (Seeing this book made me realise that one of us should, someday, finally decide to write the saga of the Vietnamese of New Caledonia. We can't allow this harsh, difficult, painful period that our parents experienced to disappear without a single written trace.)

However, at twenty-one years of age, Vanmai felt that the task of writing the story of the Chân Đăng was beyond him, and it would take him another fifteen years before he could put pen to paper after taking a French course on creative writing at *L'École française de rédaction* (French School of Writing) in Paris during one of his business trips to the capital. A whole new world opened up for him as writing became his passion. Drawing heavily from stories he had overheard from his parents, as well as those he collected from friends and other Vietnamese workers, who told him their personal experiences in their native tongue, Vanmai finished the manuscript of *Chân Đăng* within six months in 1976. Asked by Terrier why he had chosen to write a novel rather than a factual historical account of the Vietnamese indentured workers, he explained that rather than produce scientific research on this subject, he wanted to focus on the feelings and suffering of the characters involved, in order to make this saga feel more real:

> J'ai effectué un travail de conteur et de romancier afin de rendre plus 'réelle' cette épopée. Ainsi l'ouvrage a l'avantage d'être présenté comme un véritable témoignage, un vécu, voire comme un 'grand film' de cinéma.

> Ce qui contrairement à un livre historique donne aussi la possibilité de mettre l'accent plutôt sur les sentiments et les souffrances de nos parents en ce temps dit colonial. (As a storyteller and novelist, I could make this saga more 'real', make the work seem to be a real testimony, a lived experience, like a 'great film'. Unlike a historical book, working in this way also allowed me to focus more on the feelings and suffering of our parents during this so-called colonial period.)

Driven by what Hamish Dalley (2014: 9) identifies as the realist imperative, which characterises the contemporary postcolonial historical novel, Vanmai made a conscious effort to report true events and respect historical dates to give his novel strong credibility in the eyes of his first intended readers, the New Caledonian people. Concerned, however, that his book might stir people up even before it was published because it reminded them of the abuse suffered by the Chân Đăng, their fight for the right to be free men and the hostility they had attracted when they celebrated the Việt Minh victory in the aftermath of the French defeat at Điện Biên Phủ in 1954, Vanmai disclosed to Terrier why he purposely avoided any archival research: 'Ne voulant absolument pas éveiller les soupçons de l'administration tatillonne de l'époque sur mon projet d'écriture, je me suis bien gardé d'aller consulter les documents officiels de l'administration coloniale ou même des archives territoriales'. (Not wanting to raise the suspicions of the meddlesome authorities at the time about my writing project, I deliberately avoided consulting not only the official documents of the colonial authorities, but even the local archives.) While this lack of scientific research results in some involuntary and minor geographical inaccuracies[16] on the part of the author and the older Chân Đăng who told him their stories, the fiction genre allows him more freedom to build his plot and characters in a way that highlights their feelings and suffering without sacrificing literary realism and the veracity of the often very violent facts he related. Thus, Vanmai's account of the Chân Đăng can be read as a serious interpretation of the past that allows what Dalley (2010: 10) called 'a dynamic interplay between novelistic invention and historical claims'.

The Reception of *Chân Đăng* in New Caledonia

This historico-fictional approach explains the warm reception that the New Caledonian readers gave to a book that had the potential to ruffle feathers, and also attests to the author's remarkable achievement in striking the right balance between the need to reveal the indentured workers' true and painful experiences, and thus have these recognised by the wider Caledonian society, and the importance of maintaining social harmony and friendship among the various ethnic groups in a country that he and other descendants of Chân Đăng now called their own. It is to Vanmai's credit that several descendants of the 'white' foremen who read his book even found that the violence he described was understated—they were aware of much worse stories. As the author explained, he knew that if his descriptions of violence were excessive, rather than producing the sympathy and recognition he was seeking, the story of the suffering of the Chân Đăng would have had the opposite effect: 'En écrivant, c'est comme si je . . . 'marchais' en équilibre sur les 'lignes de crêtes'. . . pour ne pas tomber soit sur un côté soit sur l'autre de la montagne . . .'[17] (Writing was like trying to keep my balance while walking along the ridge of a mountain . . . if I lost my balance, I could fall on one side or the other.)

This comparison between the act of writing and tightrope-walking exposes two major interrelated aspects of *Chân Đăng*. First, the extreme physical and mental violence perpetrated by those in power against the Tonkinese indentured workers lies at the core of the novel and has to be told. This raises the question of how Vanmai presents violence in the novel, a theme that we will return to later in more detail. Second, and consequently, the author faced great difficulty in reclaiming and recovering, even in fictional form, the minority history of the Chân Đăng workers. In practical terms, this meant finding sufficient support for the publication of their story at a time when Vanmai was a first-time novelist. Understanding this primary necessity allows us to recognise the unequal power relationship between Vanmai and the author of the foreword, Georges Pisier, and to call for a rereading of Pisier's patronising comments and mixed assessment of *Chân Đăng* in its proper context. The chief administrator of overseas affairs in Indochina (1943–1950) and New Caledonia (1950–1966), as well as a historian and director of the *Société d'Études Historiques de la Nouvelle-Calédonie*, Pisier was a powerful and influential editor whose foreword would not only lend enough credibility to Vanmai's book for it to be published and potentially boost sales,[18] but also 'protect' its author from possible criticism.

Today, reading *Chân Đăng* reveals the tension between the official historical account, as expressed in Pisier's preface, and the unofficial recollection of the colonial history of indentured labour from Indochina in New Caledonia. Backed up by figures and quotations from national historical sources, such as the report on the Asians in New Caledonia published in 1974 by historian Janine Moret, Pisier's official narrative reframes and freezes the Chân Đăng story in a colonial discourse by confining it to the past: 'Le récit de Jean Vanmai, intitulé "Chân Đăng" (les engagées sous contrat) évoque *une page d'histoire, aujourd'hui tournée*, celle de l'immigration des travailleurs tonkinois en Nouvelle Calédonie (et accessoirement aux Nouvelles-Hébrides).' [Jean Vanmai's account, 'Chân Đăng' (indentured workers), evokes *a page of history which has now been turned*, that of the immigration of Tonkinese workers in New Caledonia (and also in New Hebrides).][19] The relegation of the Chân Đăng story to the dustbin of history right from the beginning of the preface not only ignores Vanmai's attempt to revive and save their memories from oblivion, it also undermines the author's voice, as Pisier points out errors that need to be corrected, thus casting some doubt on the book's authenticity: 'Son récit *semble* suffisamment authentique pour mériter de figurer dans les archives de l'Histoire. Cependant, il nécessite des correctifs'[20] (His account *seems* to be authentic enough to deserve a place in historical records. However, some corrections need to be made.) The defensive stance taken by Pisier in the name of a fair judgement clearly exemplifies what Toby Green (2018: 62) describes as the impact of the intrusion of postcolonial subaltern voices on the official narrative, causing it to '[fray] at the edges when confronted by the multiplicity of voices and evidence pointing to alternative narratives'.

The Sublimation of Violence through Martyrdom

Any reader of *Chân Đăng* would not fail to notice that extreme physical and mental violence is at the core of the novel and cuts across gender, age and race divides. Most of this violence targets the indentured workers from the moment they set foot on the ship taking them to New Caledonia and is dealt out by the French colonial masters (both men and women, such as the rich landowner Chauvedin, the foremen Mainote, Missard and Watard, and the Frenchwoman Madame Lucas), and their Kanak employees (such as the guard John). Jean Vanmai's account in no way exaggerates the harsh working and living conditions of the Chân Đăng in colonial times. Often described as slavelike and similar to those previously imposed on convicts (Merle 1995: 317; Devambez-Armand 1994: 215), these conditions can be seen in the photos of the laborers at work. Equipped with the most basic tools, the men had to break rocks to extract ore and minerals (Figures 5, 6, 7, 8, and 9), while the women, dressed

Figure 5 Digging in an open-cut mine (Jean Vanmai's collection)

Figure 6 Working with picks and shovels (Private collection)

Figure 7 Entrance to a chrome mine, mid-20th century (Private collection)

Figure 8 Underground chrome mine gallery (Private collection)

in their traditional tunics, were not spared the hardship of digging and clearing the land (Figure 10). Those who were parents had no choice but to leave their children to their own devices, sometimes in a makeshift cage, while they worked in the mines and on the land (Figure 11). Often living in rickety huts on the mine site in small camps or villages, they also had to make do with the barest minimum (Figures 12, 13, 14, 15, and 16). On Sunday, the women would spend time with their children, while the men took to selling wood or fishing to increase their daily income (Figures 17, 18, 19 and 20).

Jean Vanmai was intent on giving a true account of the Chân Đăng's experiences, of the horrific corporal punishment,[21] public whippings, floggings, beatings, mental and sexual abuse, arrests and imprisonment at the hands of their white and Kanak torturers, but, as mentioned earlier, he knew that he was walking on eggshells, so to speak. Needless to say, whereas this brutal treatment of these workers had been considered in the past to be an imposed and widely accepted social norm at that time (Chêne 2016), no one in New Caledonia today would want to be reminded of this brutality, and Vanmai's descriptions of the foremen's cruelty might indeed offend their powerful descendants. The only way that he could get his novel published was to achieve some degree of balance in his fictional presentation of violence, which would protect those on both sides. One example is how he portrays violent incidents among the Chân Đăng themselves, such as Ngạch's attempted sexual assault of Lan, Năm's horrific plot to murder his wife's lover or Thắng's fistfight with Trần. We argue, however, that it is essentially through a single character, the young Tonkinese worker Thắng, that Vanmai manages to attenuate the violence, and thus achieve this balance.

Figure 9 Digging a tunnel (Private collection)

Figure 10 Female Tonkinese labourers on the work site (Private collection)

Figure 11 Child left in his cage on his mother's work site (Archives of New Caledonia, 148 Fi 33-35, Collection Serge Kakou, Album J. O. Haas)

Figure 12 A Chân Đăng camp at the end of the 19th century (Archives of New Caledonia, 135 Fi 316, Album Sinclair)

Figure 13 Chân Đăng children at the end of the 19th century (Archives of New Caledonia, 135 Fi 317 Album Sinclair)

Figure 14 Chân Đăng village at the beginning of the 20th century (National Archives of New Zealand)

Figure 15 Kitchen in a Chân Đăng house in Koumac, 1960 (Jean Vanmai's collection)

Figure 16 Inside a small shop in Koumac circa 1950 (Jean Vanmai's collection)

Unlike the other Chân Đăng characters, such as Cung, Toán, Pháp and Bích—victims of relentless physical abuse and exploitation in the mines and plantations that lead to an unending spiral of hatred, revolt and revenge against their white masters—the construction of the character of Thắng allows Vanmai to speak of the violence while providing a way of transcending it through martyrdom. As Thắng's character develops, so too does his perspective of violence. Initially a victim, he suffers severe mental anguish as a result of everything he has lost: the country he has left behind, his name and identity—which are replaced by a matriculation number—the new friends he had made and, most painfully, his beloved Liên, a fellow passenger on the ship with whom he falls madly in love and from whom he is forcibly separated as soon as they arrive on Nou Island. The agonising description of the separation of the lovers shows

Figure 17 The new generation in the mid-20th century (National Archives of New Zealand)

how callous the foremen are and how quickly they resort to violence to establish their absolute power over the poor workers. Yet it also reflects a reality where only families (i.e., those registered as legally married couples) were allowed to stay together.[22] Overwhelmed with grief, anger and despair as he realises that, given the ratio of one woman for every five men amongst the workers, Liên will soon be married off to someone else, Thắng almost inevitably becomes a rebel, subjected as he is, along with his fellow indentured workers, to physical abuse on a daily basis. Meeting violence with violence, Thắng soon acquires the status of hero amongst the Chân Đăng because he is the first 'coolie' who dares to strike a white foreman. As the colonial masters retaliate with more ferocious corporal punishment, Thắng's body becomes the locus of violence in a situation

Figure 18 Sunday, the only day that workers could rest with their children (National Archives of New Zealand)

Figure 19 Selling wood with a smile on Sunday (National Archives of New Zealand)

Figure 20 Return from a fishing trip (National Archives of New Zealand)

where self-harm is the only means of defense available to the voiceless and powerless against ruthless maltreatment. By pouring a bowlful of tobacco juice into his eyes, which makes them swell up horribly, and chewing and ingesting red peppers, which induce a high fever, Thắng resorts to what Chêne (2016) describes as a form of personalised struggle against authority rather than collective rebellion. Rendering his body incapable of work for two consecutive days, he forces his masters to accept his absence while earning himself some much needed rest for his recovery.

Yet Thắng's first taste of hatred and vengeance does not cause him to spiral into further violence and madness that could lead to murder, as happens with Pháp, Bích and the workers at the coconut farm in New Hebrides. On the contrary, the savage beating incident is a turning point for Thắng, a gentle man who, during his childhood of deprivation and poverty, had always been against violence: 'Il se rappelait sa jeunesse d'enfant déshérité et sa vie passée, une vie de misère; mais il ne se souvient pas d'avoir été méchant et brutal avec quiconque, ayant toujours été contre la violence.' (Vanmai 1980: 218) (He recalled his childhood of deprivation and poverty, but he had always been against violence and he didn't remember ever being brutal or nasty). Surprised at how easily he has been caught up in the spiral of violence, Thắng decides that he will fight his colonial masters not by striking back when they hit him, but by giving up his own life for the benefit of others, if necessary: '"il a toujours voulu sacrifier sa liberté et même sa vie si c'était nécessaire, pour combattre l'injustice et les méthodes féodales qui nous accablent dans cette partie du monde" (235) (he has always been willing to sacrifice his freedom, and even his life if necessary, to combat injustice and the feudal methods we endure in this part of the world).

Thus, by developing the fictional character of Thắng into the figure of a saviour and martyr who readily takes upon himself the guilt of others and their punishments, Vanmai manages to put a less brutal end to the confrontation between the white masters and the Vietnamese workers. In the first incident involving the theft of dynamite by the young boy Yến, Thắng steps in to protect the culprit. Consequently, he is sent to prison, and then to New Hebrides to work on Chauvedin's coconut farm. In the second incident, the crime involved is no less than death and murder. Here, Vanmai pushes the violence to a climax by relating two fatal incidents involving two contrasting figures: a baby, the very figure of vulnerability and innocence, and the fat landowner Chauvedin, described as 'un tyran, le diable en personne' (235) (a tyrant, the devil in person). Similar tragedies occurred amongst the Vietnamese indentured workers in New Hebrides: the French reports quoted by Đồng Sỹ Hứa (1993: 64) relate how, as a punishment for having broken her French employer's tea set, a Vietnamese woman worker was left to die in the sun on a red ant nest with her hands and feet bound.[23] As for the assassination of Chauvedin by his workers, this incident evokes a real crime against a French master, which was widely known in the media at that time as 'l'affaire Malo-Pass' (the Malo-Pass case).

In *Chân Đăng*, Vanmai links the two deaths in a cause-effect relationship to exemplify the brutality of the colonists and the violent revenge of the workers. Although he portrays the boss and foremen as cruel and inhumane, he is careful not to turn them into real murderers. Chauvedin, who forbids the baby's parents to stop work to go and check on their son, despite the child's desperate cries as he is stung by red ants, is only indirectly responsible for the death of the infant, unlike the master mentioned previously, who purposely used these dangerous insects as a means to torture his employee to death. Vanmai does not let the workers take the full force of the ferocious retaliation of their masters either. When, not long after the baby's death, Chauvedin mysteriously disappears and is eventually found buried under the hearth of the workers' canteen by sniffing dogs, the author reveals in an ellipsis that the sadistic landowner has been killed in an act of collective revenge. However, unlike the horrific description of the baby's swollen corpse, neither the details of this gruesome killing nor the description of the victim's remains are given. In fact, the murder of the Frenchman takes place completely offstage, and the reader is spared the details of his violent demise. Furthermore, by depicting his death as the result of a collective assassination and letting Thắng, the innocent man, willingly take the punishment for the others in an act of supreme self-sacrifice, Vanmai avoids drawing a direct correlation between the criminal act and its consequences before the law. In this way, he does not accuse anyone in particular for this murder and manages to protect the Chân Đăng from their own crime, although he suggests via one of his characters that they will have to answer for their act before God.

In this perspective, the fictional rendering of a true event allows the novelist to create a different ending for his martyr character. Whereas in the Malo-Pass case, four Tonkinese male workers were found guilty of murder and guillotined in Port Vila in 1931 following the death of a French landowner named Chevalier on a plantation in Santo (Đồng 1993: 65; Bonnemaison 1986: 72; Chêne 2016), in *Chân Đăng*, only Thắng is arrested, and he is spared the death penalty. Similarly, no one is killed under Vanmai's pen when he relates another true event, the miners' rebellion in New Caledonia. Indeed, the Tonkinese indentured workers became politically active as the anticolonial war intensified in Vietnam, especially after Hồ Chí Minh proclaimed the independent Democratic Republic of Vietnam in 1945. They organised themselves in a workers' union, arranged meetings at their headquarters, the *Việt Nam Công Nhân Hội Quán* (the Vietnamese Workers Clubhouse), signed petitions and called for strikes to demand more humane conditions for themselves and their fellow men (Figure 21). If Vanmai included true historical details in *Chân Đăng*, such as the workers' strike and the raising of the communist flag, he omitted other more violent events, such as the fatal shooting of a striker by French gendarmes (Đồng 1993; Chêne 2016).

Thắng's courageous and selfless act to protect the powerless indentured workers in the face of colonial brutality and oppression is expressive of what

Figure 21 Meeting place of the Vietnamese Workers Union circa 1955 (Private collection)

Sophie-Grace Chappell (2018) identifies as the five aspects that characterise Jesus's political and personal sacrifice on the Cross: solidarity, protest, defiance, hope and imitation. Indeed, Thắng's transformation into a Christ-like figure is complete when he fulfils his role as savior one last time. Finally released after a twenty-year prison sentence, he is one of the many Chân Đăng who opt to return to their homeland. Just as he is boarding the ship that will take him back to Vietnam, Thắng is reunited with the love of his life, Liên. To the now lonely and childless widow, he offers the love and protection that she will need to face the new challenge of resettling in her country after more than two decades of exile.

By bringing the two lovers together at the end of his novel, Vanmai offers his reader more than just a happy, romantic outcome to a story of long-lost love. Indeed, the heavy luggage that Thắng helps Liên carry up the gangplank is highly symbolic of the weight of all the memories and suffering of not only their life, but the life of all Chân Đăng in New Caledonia. Thắng's return to Liên (and to life) also points to redemption through suffering and hope for the future. In summary, we argue that through the character of Thắng, Vanmai is able to present the theme of violence through the lens of martyrdom, and thus breaks the cycle of brutality that pervades his novel. In a clear-sighted view of the future of New Caledonia as a harmonious multiracial and multicultural society, he has succeeded in creating a historical fiction that honours the memory of the Chân Đăng while protecting all of those implicated in this colonial chapter of New Caledonian history.

The Growing Scholarly and Popular Interest in the History of the Chân Đăng

Some fifty years after the repatriation of the Chân Đăng and their families to Vietnam, their little-known story has started to attract growing interest amongst scholars working in the field of postcolonialism, subaltern studies, labour history, slavery, transnational migration and collective memory, both in the Asia-Australia-Pacific region and globally. The history of the Indochinese indentured workers in New Caledonia and the former New Hebrides has been the focus of several books by French historians, such as Claudy Chêne's doctoral research *Les engagés Tonkinois sous contrat en Nouvelle Calédonie. 1891–1964. Vivre, Subir et Résister*, Sarah Mohamed-Gaillard's *L'Archipel de la puissance: la politique de la France dans le Pacifique Sud de 1946–1998* (2010), or Paul de Deckker's edited volume *Le peuplement du Pacifique et de la Nouvelle-Calédonie au XIXe siècle. Condamnés, Colons, Convicts, Coolies, Chân Dang* (1994). In addition, the French journalists Anne Pitoiset and Claudine Wéry published *Mystère Dang* (2008), a biography of Đặng Văn Nha, a Vietnamese Caledonian mining magnate and descendant of Chân Đăng.

Closer to home, a growing number of academics from universities across Australia and New Zealand have been interested in histories that cross the boundaries of the British and French imperial worlds. For example, the historian Nadia Rhook (2017) has located connections between Chân Đăng and Australian history and investigated the way in which colonial powers operated through a geopolitical triangle of French Vietnam, Australia and New Caledonia. Other scholars, such as Peter Brown, Karin Speedy, Jean Anderson, Raylene Ramsey and Deborah Walker, have long devoted themselves to the translation of Pacific Francophone authors. Their scholarship has been instrumental in 'bridg[ing] the linguistic distance between the literary islands' (Speedy 2015: 14) and has inspired our efforts to translate Vanmai's *Chân Đăng*.

There has also been a great deal of curiosity amongst Vietnamese people, especially from the younger generations both in Vietnam and overseas, who wish to find out about the historical events recounted by Jean Vanmai in *Chân Đăng*. This need was made clear at the symposium 'Rencontres: A Gathering of Voices of the Vietnamese Diaspora'[24] organised by Tess Do and Alexandra Kurmann at the University of Melbourne in December 2016, where Vanmai was one of the six French and Australian guest writers of Vietnamese origin. Vanmai was the only speaker to deliver his paper in French, and his emotional reading of an extract from his novel *Chân Đăng*[25] was deeply moving for the audience, especially the Anglophone Vietnamese. Their questions and his discussion with them after his talk showed how the language barrier has prevented the transmission of a collective memory of the Vietnamese colonial past, and how urgent it is for them to access his writings. In view of this interest, the translation of Vanmai's novel constitutes an important new historical resource that enables this story to enter the collective memories of Anglophone Vietnamese diasporic communities, in Australia most immediately, but also in England and other Pacific-Rim sites, such as New Zealand, Canada and the United States.

While for Jean Vanmai, the symposium highlighted the importance of sharing the Chân Đăng memory, it should be noted that one of the earliest documentaries on the Chân Đăng was made in 2005 by the very popular Vietnamese American entertainment company Vân Sơn as part of their DVD life-show *Vân Sơn in Australia—Down Under*. Two years later, it was from Vietnam that the first large-scale documentary on New Caledonia came, as the Hồ Chí Minh City Television Film Studios launched an impressive thirty-episode documentary telefilm entitled *Ký Sự Tân Đảo* (2007).[26] In fact, the Vietnamese government itself can be said to have played a leading role in putting the Chân Đăng story on the map as an integral part of Vietnamese history, and their descendants in New Caledonia as an inseparable part of the Vietnamese nation. In 2004, it passed Resolution 36, the first official policy in favour of Vietnamese living overseas, with the aim to create 'favourable conditions and provision of support' for them, and most importantly, to maintain and strengthen their ties with the homeland (Koh 2015:185). The five-year visa exemption certificate for

Vietnamese overseas, introduced on 1 July 2007, was instrumental in prompting the first official visit to Vietnam a year later, after more than a hundred years of Vietnamese presence in New Caledonia, by some twenty Vietnamese delegates from the *Amicale Vietnamienne* (Vietnamese Association) in New Caledonia and Vanuatu (*Gần lắm quê hương* 2008). It must be noted that since its creation, the association has played an active role in preserving Vietnamese traditions in New Caledonia, such as organising the annual celebrations of the Lunar New Year, the traditional lion dances (Figure 22), the Centennial Festival of the Chân Đăng's arrival in New Caledonia (Figure 23), and the dragon float parade at a festival in Nouméa (Figure 24). It also played an important role in supporting the community, as can be seen in a photo of the young Vietnamese women of the association performing a traditional fan dance during a visit to the Little Sisters of the Poor aged care home in Nouméa (Figure 25).

In 2012, the French director Jacques-Olivier Trompas (2012) released *Chân Đăng, 50 ans après*, a fifty-two-minute French documentary that was two years in the making, marking the anniversary of the repatriation of the Chân Đăng in 1960. In the same year, a commemorative statue representing a Chân Đăng family in colonial times was commissioned from Vietnam by the *Amicale Vietnamienne* in New Caledonia, who were keen to honour the memory of their Chân Đăng forefathers and their contribution to the economic development of the island. Made in Vietnam, the life-size bronze statue was then shipped to Nouméa, where it was installed in the Asian district (Figure 26) and unveiled on 17 October 2013 (Hoàng Hoa 2013; Như Quỳnh 2013).

Figure 22 Lion dance at the old Town Hall in Nouméa (Jean Vanmai's collection)

Figure 23 Centennial Festival at the hall of the Vietnamese Association of New Caledonia (Jean Vanmai's collection)

Figure 24 Dragon float at a festival in Nouméa (Jean Vanmai's collection)

Two years later, on 27 December 2015, the Vietnamese government organised on a grand scale a fifty-fifth-anniversary reunion in Hà-Nội, bringing together the Chân Đăng and their descendants from both sides of the Pacific (Lan Phương 2015). Another documentary on the Chân Đăng, *The Roots* (or, in Vietnamese, *Biết đâu nguồn cội*), came out in the same year and was telecast by

Figure 25 Young women from the Amicale Vietnamienne in New Caledonia performing a fan dance at the Little Sisters of the Poor aged care home in 1991 (Jean Vanmai's collection)

the Vietnamese international channel TVT World (VTV4). Besides these main sources, numerous personal blogs, such as *Tân Đảo Xưa và Nay* (New Hebrides past and present) (Vanson 2013), and video clips on the internet are evidence of the popular interest generated by the Chân Đăng whose story has inspired many curious Vietnamese from both within and without Vietnam to crisscross the Pacific to capture the *témoignages* (oral stories) of the few remaining nonagenarians in New Caledonia.[27] More recently, the graphic novel *Les engagés de Nouvelle-Calédonie*, the fourth volume of the series *Mémoires de Viet-Kieu*[28] by the Eurasian artist Clément Baloup (2020), gives new life to the history of generations of Vietnamese men and women who have tirelessly taken up the challenges of migration against all odds, and with their heart full of hope: 'des générations de Vietnamiens qui, contre vents et marées, et le cœur rempli d'espoir, relèvent inlassablement les défis de la migration' (Do, 2020: 64). In the eyes of their descendants, the courage, sacrifice and resilience that they showed in their exilic life as indentured workers have earned them the respectful title of 'Chân Đăng elders' ('các cụ Chân Đăng' in Vietnamese) (Figures 27 and 28). It was in front of the Chân Đăng statue that on 15 May 2021 the whole community, young and old, gathered to celebrate 130 years of Vietnamese presence in New Caledonia (Figures 29 and 30). Today, they do, indeed, have much to be proud of in their Vietnamese roots and cultural heritage.

Figure 26 Statue of Vietnamese Chân Đăng, Nouméa 2019 (Tess Do's collection)

Jean Vanmai, 'the Translated Man', and the Translation of *Chân Đăng*

In his famous essay *Imaginary Homelands* (1991), Salman Rushdie makes a much-cited statement in relation to diasporic colonial writers: 'The word "translation" comes, etymologically, from the Latin for "bearing across". Having

Figure 27 Chân Đăng elders, Nouméa 1991 (Jean Vanmai's collection)

Figure 28 Fiftieth anniversary of the Christ-Roi Church, Vallée du Tir 2005 (Jean Vanmai's collection)

Figure 29 Celebration of the 130 years of Vietnamese presence in New Caledonia 2021 (Joe Chuvan's collection)

Figure 30 Little girls from the Amicale Vietnamienne performing a lantern dance to celebrate the 130 years of Vietnamese presence in New Caledonia (Joe Chuvan's collection)

been borne across the world, we are translated men. It is normally supposed that something always gets lost in translation; I cling, obstinately, to the notion that something can also be gained'. The term 'translated man' is indeed apposite in the case of Jean Vanmai, who was 'borne across' from the Vietnamese language and culture into the Pacific Francophone world of New Caledonia.

In translating this text, we became aware that we were working with a text that had already been translated, since Vanmai had translated the shared oral narratives of the Chân Đăng that he had received in Vietnamese from often illiterate fellow countrymen into written form in French. In this sense, it was not only a translation but also a transliteration, a transformation of fluid oral narratives into a fixed text. Certain aspects were inevitably lost in the process, and in addition, the written text had to be manipulated to some extent to ensure readability for French-speaking readers. Whereas in some circumstances this could be seen as a misuse of a position of power, in this case the dual process of transliteration and translation was not carried out by an outsider to the marginalised group of the Tonkinese indentured workers. Thus, what is left out or added during the process of translating these oral histories told in the 'secondary' language of Vietnamese and recast in the 'dominant' language of French is the choice made by a true insider. In writing *Chân Đăng*, the 'translated man' Vanmai, has become the cultural mediator and voice of the subaltern.

Translation into written form was a way for Vanmai not only of preserving knowledge of this history, but also of making cultural advocacy. In his role as advocate, the author speaks on behalf of the Chân Đăng; on behalf of those whose voices have not been heard, thus giving a voice to the subaltern. Spivak (1988: 275) points to the double meaning of the term 'representation': 'speaking for' as used in politics, and 're-presentation' as used in art. Vanmai both speaks for and re-presents the Chân Đăng, the minor actors who, as we mentioned earlier, have been excluded from the discourse on the conflict between white colonisers and the indigenous Kanaks. This is why Vanmai's account is so significant. Translating the Chân Đăng experience not only into written form, but into French, a major global language, puts it on the world stage, making this community visible and allowing their voices to be heard through the French text, thus reaching a readership extending beyond the region to mainland France.

This English translation has been completed in a very different context from that of the original text, and for a very different readership. When Vanmai wrote *Chân Đăng*, French rule in New Caledonia was still firmly in place and, as we have seen, the author did not feel at liberty to reveal the full extent of the brutality meted out to the Chân Đăng. Nearly thirty years later, this English translation will be read in a context informed by the last of the three referendums on independence held in December 2021, which arose from the 'événements', as the uprisings against French rule have been called. In addition, it will allow the text to break out of the fixed category of Francophone literature and acquire a more visible life in a new context. Our translation provides a way for the text to be 'reincarnated' and thus to survive, as suggested by Jacques Derrida, who sees the translation as the 'after-life' of the source text—its reincarnation (cited by Bassnett 1998: 25).

The work of translation did not present many linguistic challenges, no doubt because there is little evidence of foreignisation in Vanmai's text, such as that advocated by Venuti (2008) as a way of keeping the 'foreign flavour' in the translated text, and thus performing a 'resistant' translation that does not appropriate the source culture through domestication. In *Chân Đăng*, the process of domestication was carried out by Vanmai himself, as we have mentioned, through his transliteration of oral testimonies from Vietnamese into French. However, this was clearly not done at the expense of the Chân Đăng. Indeed, Vanmai's novel, by its very existence, can be seen as a resistant text in the same way as the miners' strike is a public act of resistance. Writing most of the novel in dialogic form, Vanmai has preserved the orality in which the testimonies were first passed on to him. The Chân Đăng, divested of their names, had become mere numbers in the eyes of the masters and were thus deprived not only of their voice, but even of their individual identity. In the dialogues, which reflect the oral form in which these stories were transmitted to the author, the individual voices of the Chân Đăng characters can be heard. The apparent transcription extends through to the use of the punctuation marks '?' and '!' as emotional but silent reactions to what has been said. This stylistic quirk is perhaps a further instance of Vanmai's attempt to retain the flavour of the conversations and discussions—a way of transcribing the oral telling of the story.

At the level of translation from French into English, questions of foreignisation and domestication did not arise as the two languages are equal in status and power and one culture is not appropriated in favour of the other. The dominant feature of the text, its dialogic form, could therefore be easily transferred from the source to the translated text, retaining the author's voice and style. Naturally, the translation is a result of the translator's interpretation of both linguistic and cultural differences, but it is also a rewriting, and the choices made by the translator necessarily reflect a personal style. As Liddicoat (2013: 14) states, language is a 'living expression of the self, with each choice from the language repertoire a portrayal of personality'. As both formal and thematic mediator, the translator, who makes the ultimate decision on the form and content to be transferred, enjoys a position of power that could be viewed as a form of dominance. The punctuation, for example, was changed considerably; however, aware of the pitfalls inherent in ennobling the style, as Antoine Berman (1992) puts it, we did not feel that this was in any way reductive of the original text. Rather than benefiting from an instance of power and dominance, we have kept foremost in mind who is to gain from this translation. Indeed, any manipulation occurring through this act of translation is undertaken with the sole idea of enabling the subaltern to be heard—the voices of both the Chân Đăng, whose stories can now reach an English-speaking readership, and Jean Vanmai. To return to Rushdie's quote at the beginning of this section, rather than something being lost in translation, something is clearly gained. The translation itself, as a reincarnation of Vanmai's text, gives it new life and allows it to survive beyond the boundaries imposed by the French language to create knowledge of this page in history for a new readership.

The Contemporary English Readership of *Chân Đăng*

The readership of the English translation of *Chân Đăng*, whether it be an Anglophone Pacific readership (including Australia and New Zealand) or a wider audience, will no doubt receive the translated text differently from Vanmai's original French readers. Indeed, the significance of this historical novel for a new readership unfamiliar with the history of this particular part of the Pacific can be understood only if it is contextualised. This introduction has provided information about the historical context, as well as insights into Vanmai's motivations in writing this novel. In addition, correspondence with the author has shed light on his approach to the portrayal of violence, allowing us to develop a critical analysis that helps in the understanding of the difficult position in which Vanmai found himself as documenter of the drama of the Chân Đăng experience in colonial times. These explanations are not only enlightening but essential for the reader, who undoubtedly would otherwise have perceived the book as unbearably violent. Similarly, readers in the 21st century will probably find the romantic scenes dated and sentimental. However, they need to be understood as not only a way of providing relief in the context of the unrelenting physical hardships endured by the workers, but also as a reflection of the fact that love and romance were all these young men and women had to fuel their hope and dreams for a better future as they struggled to survive in a harsh environment.[29]

Speaking from our Australian perspective, we believe that the average Australian reader would undoubtedly be shocked by the violence that pervades *Chân Đăng*. As our analysis here has shown, Vanmai downplayed the actual violence on both sides for fear of reprisals against himself, but also against all others implicated in the historical events he recounts. Vanmai's explanation of his approach allows for a better understanding of the novel, thus showing how important it is to contextualise the work for a new, English-speaking readership. Despite the author's elucidations, however, for most readers the novel remains extremely brutal, and the undercurrent of violence that runs through *Chân Đăng* is testimony to the fact that, although slavery had been outlawed in 1848, the practice of indentured labour, particularly in the case of the colonised Tonkinese in New Caledonia and New Hebrides, was in many ways akin to forced labour and slavery (Angleviel 2000; Bougerol 2000: 86; Merle 1995: 317).

Introduced by British colonists after the banning of slavery, indentured labour provided a system in which 'coloured' labourers were imported to work for the white settlers who had displaced the indigenous population in countries such as Fiji and South Africa, but also Australia. Just as the colonisation of New Caledonia mirrored the colonisation of Australia, with both countries shifting from penal colony to settler colonialism, the practice of using indentured labour in the French Pacific was modelled on the Australian experience (Rhook 2017; Neilson 2018). Over 50,000 people were brought into New South Wales and Queensland from the Pacific Islands in the 1800s to work in Australia as indentured labourers, a practice known as 'blackbirding', where islanders were often kidnapped or coerced into coming to Australia. Although it is true that, at least as a general rule, the Chân Đăng were not coerced, but rather signed up willingly to become contractual labourers, they had no inkling of the slavelike conditions, nor of the violence and brutality that awaited them at the end of their sea crossing.

It is well documented that Australia and New Caledonia have intertwined labour histories, but it is a less well-known fact that Australia has links to the Chân Đăng story. As Rhook (2017) has shown, the arrival in Townsville of the French ship *Ville d'Amiens*, transporting 'coolie' labour, and the appalling conditions on board triggered disgust and moral outrage in Australia at the cruelty of 'the French'. However, Australians were quick to forget the role played by their own country in this page of history; and still today, there is little acknowledgement of Australia's use of South Sea islanders for indentured labour, although 2,500 remained in the country after the majority were deported (Higginbotham 2017). In addition, at the time, the fear of the 'Yellow Peril' and communism in the region was exacerbated by the large presence of Indochinese indentured workers in the Pacific region in the aftermath of World War II. According to Mohamed-Gaillard (2010), as early as 1946 the Australian consul in New Caledonia saw them as a source of potential trouble due to their fight for better pay and working conditions, which took the form of violent brawls and strikes. The Australian press also reported how the news of the French defeat at Điện Biên Phủ had given rise to jubilation among a number of the Vietnamese workers in New Hebrides, particularly in the Anglo-French Condominium of Santo, where these workers were concentrated. The concern that this region could turn into another Indochinese battlefield had thus led to a hostile view of the Vietnamese community in these Pacific islands.

Jean Vanmai's historical fiction of the Chân Đăng in New Caledonia, which offers a rare insight into the experience of Vietnamese workers in New Caledonia and Vanuatu, comes as a stark reminder that Australia was implicated in similar practices in the not-so-distant past. This account of the personal and emotional complexities of the experience of indentured labourers and their descendants, therefore, is highly relevant to Australian readers and of profound intellectual and ethical significance for scholars concerned with the interconnected histories of Australia and the Pacific. It is significant not only for Australia-Pacific history, as it is unique in allowing the voices of Vietnamese indentured workers to be heard and understood. This translation into English, together with our critical introduction that contextualises it, thus allows the text to take on its full significance for an English-speaking readership, whether it be in Australasia, the Pacific or further afield.

Tess Do and Kathryn Lay-Chenchabi

Notes

[1] In italics, *Chân Đăng* refers to the novel; in normal typeface, to the Tonkinese indentured workers.

[2] Vanmai was the second writer of Vietnamese origin to be honoured by the Association des Écrivains de Langue Française (French-Language Writers' Association) since the creation of the prize in 1971. The first laureate was Nguyễn Văn Phong, in 1972, and the last to date was Hoài Hương Nguyễn, in 2013.

[3] Tonkin was a French protectorate encompassing today's northern Vietnam. It was one of the five territories (Tonkin, Annam, Cochinchina, Laos, and Cambodia) that formed French Indochina (1887–1954).

[4] All translations are our own unless otherwise noted.

[5] According to the census of the Institut national de la statistique et des études économiques census (National Institute for Statistics and Economic Studies), the Vietnamese made up 0.93% (2,499 people) of the total population of New Caledonia (268,767 people).

[6] See Selao (2011).

[7] See Britto (2004); Trouilloud (2006); Nguyễn (2003).

[8] The name "Chân Đăng" is used solely to refer to Tonkinese indentured workers. Their descendants—in particular, those who were born in New Caledonia or New Hebrides—are called "niaoulis," a name they share with the descendants of Javanese indentured workers. There are two explanations for this term. The first refers to the way that Javanese mothers used to wrap their babies in their sarongs and suspend them on the branches of the niaouli—a large, emblematic tree of the myrtle family—so their youngsters could be protected from animals or insects and they could keep an eye on them while working in the fields. The second explanation draws on the comparison between the Javanese great power of resilience and adaptability and the robustness of the niaouli. See Maurer (2002); Bouan (2003).

[9] Jean Vanmai's second novel published in 1983 is titled *Fils de Chân Đăng* (*Son of Chân Đăng*)

[10] Jean Vanmai has three brothers and five sisters.

[11] Both of Vanmai's parents worked at the chrome mine in Chagrin, which belonged to the prominent family of Jacques Lafleur, leader of the Rally for Caledonia in the Republic, one of the two anti-independence parties in

New Caledonia. Lafleur was a signatory to the Matignon Accords in 1988 and the Nouméa Accords in 1998.

12 One listener, on hearing Jean Vanmai's interview with Michel Voisin (2012), recalled that just as the ship was leaving port, people were jumping overboard and swimming back to Nou Island.

13 This incident may explain why there were two different statistics regarding the number of repatriates in this first trip: 550 passengers according to Vanmai in *Centenaire de la présence vietnamienne en Nouvelle-Calédonie* (1991: 79) and 551 according to Mohamed-Gaillard (2010: 207). The missing passenger was Vanmai himself.

14 Private email to Tess Do (2 July 2021).

15 The transcription of the interview, entitled 'La vie des engagés vietnamiens d'autrefois' (The life of the former Vietnamese contract workers), broadcast on 12 April 2016 on the episode 'Terre d'histoire(s) et de partage(s)', No. 53, was provided by Jean Vanmai. In an earlier interview conducted by Michel Voisin for the New Caledonian radio program (NC 1ère) on 29 September 2012, Vanmai had also mentioned this incident.

16 One example is the location of the lodgings where the indentured workers were sent after their arrival in New Caledonia. In Vanmai's novel, it is situated on Nou Island, but in reality, the workers first arrived at Freycinet Island for their quarantine and were then transferred to the Dépôt de l'Orphelinat, where they were picked up by their employers. See Angleviel (2000); Boyer (1996); Merle (1995).

17 Private email to Tess Do (17 January 2019).

18 According to Vanmai, *Chân Đăng* had a sales circulation of 3,000 copies in its original publication in 1980 (in a country with a population of 200,000 inhabitants), and 1,000 copies in its reprint in 1993. The novel is currently out of print.

19 Emphasis added.

20 Emphasis added.

21 According to an anonymous source dated 1882, the commissariat of immigration kept a cat-o'-nine-tails behind his door and used it on stubborn New Hebridians brought to him (Angleviel 2000: 71).

22 Indeed, Article 15 in the worker contract states that families cannot, under any circumstances, be separated (Angleviel 2000: 74).

23 Apparently, this cruel form of discipline was also found in New Caledonia. A Frenchwoman from the small town of Témala remembers how her neighbour, a French colonist, punished his Javanese workers: He stripped them naked before forcing them to kneel on an ant nest with their hands on their heads. See Merle (1995: 396).

24 A symposium volume was later published in *Portal Journal of Multidisciplinary International Studies*; see Kurmann and Do (2018).

25 The audience was provided with an English translation of the extract.

[26] According to Vanmai, the Vietnamese broadcasting channel HTV7 in Hồ Chí Minh City contacted him in 2007 with a project to make a thirty-episode television series on the Chân Đăng. However, he declined their offer because he was concerned that in such a large project, the television adaptation of scenes of the abuse and mistreatment of the Chân Đăng would backfire on the Chân Đăng and their descendants, as well as on New Caledonia and its people. Per Vanmai web document (n.d.).

[27] See Từ Bốn Phương Trời (2013); Voice of America (2016); Bà Bán Phở Channel (2018).

[28] To date, this series includes the following titles: *Quitter Saigon* (Leaving Saigon) (2013), *Little Saigon* (2012), *Les mariées de Taiwan* (The Brides of Taiwan) (2017) and *Les engagés de Nouvelle-Calédonie* (The Bound 'Coolies' of New Caledonia) (2020).

[29] For some female Tonkinese indentured workers, young girls in their late teens and early twenties, the decision to leave their families and villages to work in a distant, unknown country where they did not speak the language was motivated by a desire to escape unwanted marriages arranged by their parents. For them, finding love in New Caledonia would be a happy outcome. Vanmai gives a few examples of these happy couples in his book, such as Minh and Lan and Hiếu and Thế.

References

Aldrich, Robert. 1993. 'The Crisis in New Caledonia in the 1980s'. In: *France and the South Pacific since 1940*. Palgrave Macmillan, London, 240–284.

Angleviel, Frédéric. 2000. 'De l'engagement comme "esclaves volontaires". Le cas des Océaniens, Kanaks et Asiatiques en Nouvelle-Calédonie (1853–1963)', *Journal de la Société des Océanistes*, vol. 110, 65–81.

Baloup, Clément. 2020. *Les engagés de Nouvelle-Calédonie, Mémoires de Viet-Kieu, volume 4*. La Boîte à Bulles, Paris.

Bassnett, Susan. 1998. 'When is a Translation not a Translation?'. In: Susan Bassnett and André Lefevere (eds.), *Constructing Cultures: Essays on Literary Translation*. Multilingual Matters, Clevedon, UK, 25–40.

Berman, Antoine. 1992. *The Experience of the Foreign: Culture and Translation in Romantic Germany*. State University of New York Press, Albany.

Bonnemaison, Joël. 1986. 'Passions et misères d'une société coloniale: les plantations au Vanuatu entre 1920 et 1980', *Journal de la Société des Océanistes*, vol. 42, 82–83.

Bouan, Marc. 2003. *L'écharpe et le kriss*. Publibook, Paris.

Bougerol, Christiane. 2000. 'Chronique d'une crise coloniale et son contexte: les Vietnamiens de Nouvelle-Calédonie (1945–1964)', *Journal de la Société des Océanistes*, vol. 110, 83–95.

Boyer, Sylvette. 1996. 'La main d'oeuvre asiatique sous contrat en Nouvelle Calédonie', *Archives Territoriales*, Nouméa, Nouvelle Calédonie.

Britto, Karl. 2004. *Disorientation: France, Vietnam, and the Ambivalence of Interculturality.* Hong Kong University Press, Hong Kong.

Chappell, Sophie-Grace. 2018. 'The Cross' [in Special Issue 'Sacrifice and Moral Philosophy'], *International Journal of Philosophical Studies*, vol. 26, no. 3, 478–498.

Chêne, Claudy. 2016. 'Domination et résistances des engagés tonkinois en Nouvelle-Calédonie et dépendances, 1891–1960', *Transversales*, Université de Bourgogne, accessed 15 June 2020, https://hal-univ-bourgogne.archives-ouvertes.fr/hal-02059087.

Crocombe, Ron. 2007. *Asia in the Pacific Islands: Replacing the West.* IPS Publications, University of the South Pacific, Suva, Fiji.

Deckker, Paul de. 1994. *Le peuplement du Pacifique et de la Nouvelle-Calédonie au XIXe siècle: condamnés, colons, convicts, coolies, Chân Dang.* L'Harmattan, Paris.

Devambez-Armand, Véronique. 1994. 'Les recrutements: chronologie de la main-d'œuvre immigrée sous contrat en Nouvelle-Calédonie (1869–1939)'. In: P. de Deckker (ed.), *Le peuplement du Pacifique et de la Nouvelle-Calédonie au XIXe siècle: condamnés, colons, convicts, coolies, Chân Dang.* L'Harmattan, Paris, 208–217.

Do, Tess. 2008. 'Exile: Rupture and Continuity in Jean Vanmai's *Chân Đăng* and *Fils de Chân Đăng*'. In: Paul Allatson and Jo McCormack (eds.), *Exile, Cultures, Misplaced Identities.* Rodopi, Amsterdam, 151–172.

Do, Tess. 2020. 'Postface'. In: Clément Baloup, *Les engagés de Nouvelle-Calédonie, Mémoires de Viet-Kieu, volume 4.* La Boîte à Bulles, Paris, 1–64.

Fer, Yannick. 2014. *Diasporas asiatiques dans le Pacifique: histoire des représentations et enjeux contemporains.* Les Indes Savantes, Paris.

Green, Toby. 2018. 'Challenge or Opportunity? Postcolonialism and the Historian'. In: Anne Maerker, Simon Sleight, and Adam Sutcliffe (eds.), *History, Memory and Public Life: The Past in the Present.* Routledge, London, 48–64.

Hồ, Lý Thu. 1969. *Au milieu du carrefour*. Peyronnet, Paris.

Koh, Priscilla. 2015. 'You Can Come Home Again: Narratives of Home and Belonging among Second-Generation Việt Kiều in Vietnam', *Journal of Social Issues in Southeast Asia,* vol. 30, no. 1, 173–214.

Kurmann, Alexandra and Tess Do. 2018. 'Rencontres: Transdiasporic Encounters in Việt-Kiều Literature', *Portal Journal of Multidisciplinary International Studies*, vol. 15, nos. 1–2.

Lê, Linda. 1987. *Un si tendre vampire*. La Table Ronde, Paris.

Liddicoat, Anthony J. and Angela Scarino. 2013. 'Languages, Cultures and the Intercultural'. In: *Intercultural Language Teaching and Learning.* Blackwell Publishing Ltd., Oxford.

Maurer, Jean-Luc. 2002. 'Les Javanais de Nouvelle-Calédonie: des affres de l'exil aux aléas de l'intégration'. In: Rosita Fibbi and Jean-Baptiste Meyer (eds.), *Diasporas, développements et mondialisations*. L'Aube, La Tour-d'Aigues, 67–90.

Merle, Isabelle. 1995. *Expériences coloniales: la Nouvelle-Calédonie (1853–1892)*. Belin, Paris.

Meyerhoff, Miriam. 2002. 'A Vanishing Act: Tonkinese Migrant Labour in Vanuatu in the Early 20th Century', *Journal of Pacific History*, vol. 37, no. 1, 45–56.

Mohamed-Gaillard, Sarah. 2010. *L'Archipel de la puissance: la politique de la France dans le Pacifique Sud de 1946–1998*. Peter Lang, Brussels.

Moret, Janine. 1974. 'Les Asiatiques en Nouvelle Calédonie'. *Bulletin de la SEH*, no. 19.

Neilson, Briony. 2018. 'Settling Scores in New Caledonia and Australia: French Convictism and Settler Legitimacy', *Australian Journal of Politics and History*, vol. 64, no. 3, 391–406.

Nguyễn, Nathalie. 2003. *Vietnamese Voices: Gender and Cultural Identity in the Vietnamese Francophone Novel*. Southeast Asia Publications, Center for Southeast Asian Studies, Northern Illinois University, DeKalb, Illinois.

Pitoiset, Anne and Claudine Wéry. 2008. *Mystère Dang*. Le Rayon Vert, Nouméa.

Rhook, Nadia. 2017. 'Annamese Coolies' at Australian Ports: Charting Colonial Geographies of Emotion, and Settler Memory, from French Vietnam to New Caledonia via Interwar Australia', *Australian Historical Studies*, vol. 48, no. 3, 399–415.

Rushdie, Salman. 1991. *Imaginary Homelands: Essays and Criticism 1981–1991*. Granta, London.

Selao, Ching. 2011. *Le roman vietnamien francophone*. Les Presses de l'Université de Montréal, Montréal.

Spivak, Gayatri. 1988. 'Can the Subaltern Speak'. In: Cary Nelson and Larry Grossberg (eds.), *Marxism and the Interpretation of Culture*. University of Illinois Press, Chicago, 271–313.

Trouilloud, Lise-Hélène. 2006. 'The Genesis of Vietnamese Literature Written in French: 1920–1942', *Contemporary French and Francophone Studies*, vol. 10, no. 2, 141–148.

Vanmai, Jean. 1980. *Chân Đăng, les Tonkinois de Calédonie au temps colonial*. La Société d'Études Historiques de la Nouvelle Calédonie, Nouméa.

Vanmai, Jean. 1983. *Fils de Chân Đăng*. Éditions de l'Océanie, Nouméa.

Vanmai, Jean. 1991. *Centenaire de la présence vietnamienne en Nouvelle-Calédonie 1891–1991*. Centre Territorial de Recherche et de Développement Pédagogique, Nouméa.

Venuti, Lawrence. 2008. *The Translator's Invisibility: A History of Translation*. Routledge, London.

Web documents

Bà Bán Phở. 2018a. 'Gặp người Chân Đăng cuối cùng ở New Caledonia', accessed 27 February 2019, https://www.youtube.com/watch?v=A1b052eTbA8.

Bà Bán Phở. 2018b. 'Gặp người Việt thành đạt ở New Caledonia', accessed 27 February 2019, https://www.youtube.com/watch?v=gF9oolbuuQY.

Café Sáng CFV3. 2013. 'Người Việt ở Tân Đảo', accessed 15 January 2019, https://www.youtube.com/watch?v=BTaSGNnLitc.

Haski, Pierre. 2015. 'Quand la France ouvrait les bras à 120 000 réfugiés sauvés en mer', *Le Nouvel Obs*, accessed 20 January 2019, https://www.nouvelobs.com/rue89/rue89-monde/20150424.RUE8808/quand-la-france-ouvrait-les-bras-a-120-000-refugies-sauves-en-mer.html.

Higginbotham, Will. 2017. 'Blackbirding: Australia's history of luring, tricking and kidnapping Pacific Islanders', accessed 4 March 2019, https://www.abcnews.net.au.

Hoàng, Hoa. 2013. 'Nouvelle-Calédonie: les Chân Đăng immortalisés par une statue', *Le Courrier du Vietnam*, accessed 22 January 2019, https://www.lecourrier.vn/nouvelle-caledonie-les-chan-dang-immortalises-par-une-statue/112333.html.

Hoàng, Mai, Như Quỳnh. 2008. 'Gần lắm quê hương', accessed 22 March 2019, http://avnc1974.blogspot.com/2008/09/.

Hồ Chí Minh City Television Film Studios TFS. 2007. 'Ký Sự Tân Đảo', accessed 28 February 2019, https://www.youtube.com/watch?v=a9VdLeOeM2Q.

Lan Phương. 2015. 'Kỷ niệm 55 năm Việt kiều Tân Thế giới hồi hương', accessed 22 January 2019, https://vovworld.vn/vi-VN/nguoi-viet-muon-phuong/ky-niem-55-nam-viet-kieu-tan-the-gioi-hoi-huong-396832.vov.

Phạm Trung Thành, Vũ Lệ Trung. 2015. *Biết đâu nguồn cội—The Roots*, accessed 15 January 2019, https://www.youtube.com/watch?v=3JYsInKlZu4.

Trompas, Jacques-Olivier. 2012. *Chan Dang, 50 ans après*, accessed 22 January 2019 https://www.lnc.nc/article/coco-tv/chan-dang-50-ans-apres.

Từ Bốn Phương Trời. 2013. 'Con cháu người "Chân đăng" xưa tại Nouvelle Caledonie', HTV9, accessed 15 January 2019, https://www.youtube.com/watch?v=fHZ4TLh_0Ds.

Từ Bốn Phương Trời. 2013. 'Con trai của người Chân Đăng', HTV9, accessed 15 January 2019, https://www.youtube.com/watch?v=KSfjpLXo-6Y.

Vân Sơn. 2005. 'Vân Sơn in Australia Down Under', accessed 28 February 2019, https://www.youtube.com/watch?v=DxMplgrmrhU.

Vanson, Jean. 2019. *Tân Đảo Xưa và Nay*, accessed 15 January 2019, http://jeanvanjeanchandang.blogspot.com/.

Vanmai, Jean. n.d. 'Présentation de Chân Đăng en français à Hanoi', accessed 28 February 2019, https://www.ecrivains-nc.net/publications/chan-dang-2/.

VOA Tiếng Việt. 2016. 'Người Chân Đăng cuối cùng', accessed 22 January 2019, https://www.youtube.com/watch?v=SIEWhmEUAYA.

Voisin, Michel. 2012. 'Jean Vanmaï, auteur de Chan Dang', Nouvelle Calédonie 1, accessed 22 January 2019, https://www.dailymotion.com/video/xquw97.

Introduction critique à *Chân Đăng* de Jean Vanmai

Le contexte historique et littéraire de *Chân Đăng*

Le roman historique *Chân Đăng*[1] de Jean Vanmai est publié par la Société d'Études Historiques de la Nouvelle-Calédonie en 1980 en plein milieu de la guerre froide et de la crise des boat people d'Indochine. Quelque cinq ans auparavant, en avril 1975, la prise de Saigon par les forces communistes du Nord avait mis fin à la longue guerre du Vietnam (1946-1975) et déclenché le plus grand exode de l'histoire vietnamienne contemporaine. Des dizaines de milliers de Vietnamiens fuyaient chaque jour leur pays dans des embarcations de fortune en mer de Chine pour aller grossir rapidement le nombre des réfugiés dans les camps en Asie du Sud-Est ou périr en haute mer dans des conditions horribles, de faim et de soif, ou aux mains des pirates. Leurs histoires tragiques faisaient la manchette des journaux du monde entier, en particulier en France. Une opération de sauvetage, nommée *Un bateau pour le Vietnam* et soutenue par des intellectuels et célébrités, tels que Jean-Paul Sartre, Raymond Aron, Michel Foucault, Yves Montand et Simone Signoret, a été lancée l'année précédente par Bernard Kouchner, homme politique français et co-fondateur de Médecins du Monde. Dans ce contexte d'urgence, il est peu surprenant que l'histoire des Chân Đăng, travailleurs tonkinois sous contrat en Nouvelle-Calédonie à l'époque coloniale,[2] soit passée inaperçue auprès des lecteurs vietnamiens, en dépit du prestigieux Prix de l'Asie que son auteur a remporté en 1981.[3] Ceux de la diaspora étaient trop préoccupés par leurs propres exils traumatiques, alors que ceux au Vietnam restaient encore virtuellement coupés du monde à cause de l'embargo américain. Le fait que *Chân Đăng* ait été écrit en français et publié à Nouméa, et non à Paris, a également limité sa diffusion auprès d'un large lectorat. De plus, selon Yannick Fer (2004 : 7), parmi les communautés du Sud Pacifique, les diasporas asiatiques et leurs histoires ont été souvent négligées dans les représentations de l'Océanie en sciences sociales et littérature bien que leur présence dans la région date de la fin du 19ème siècle.

Dans le face à face entre l'Occident et les peuples autochtones, ces 'coolies agricoles, petits commerçants ou commis de magasins', comme les Chân Đăng, ne sont que des 'ombres chinoises' se déplaçant silencieusement à l'arrière-plan. Dans la diaspora vietnamienne largement formée par des réfugiés d'après 75, la communauté calédo-vietnamienne est moins visible que les autres communautés vietnamienne, américaine, canadienne ou australienne, en raison de sa petite taille[4] : environ 700 personnes seulement sont venues s'installer sur le territoire entre 1975 et 1985. Bien que la France ait accueilli un bon nombre de réfugiés vietnamiens – 128 531 rien qu'en 1979, selon Pierre Haski (2015) – seules quelques 700 personnes sont venues s'installer sur ses territoires calédoniens entre 1975 et 1985 (Angleviel 2000-1 : 79 ; Crocombe 2007 : 75).

Outre la faible visibilité de la communauté vietnamienne en Nouvelle-Calédonie, l'ouvrage *Chân Đăng* ne se plaçait pas facilement dans la tradition littéraire francophone vietnamienne, qui remontait aux années 1920.[5] Après une recrudescence dans les années 1950, la publication des romans d'expression française par les auteurs vietnamiens a progressivement décliné dans la décennie précédant la chute de Saigon, pour s'arrêter avec le roman de Lý Thu Hồ *Au milieu du Carrefour*, en 1969. C'est entre cette période de pointe d'avant 1975 et l'émergence d'une nouvelle génération de jeunes écrivains de la diaspora vietnamienne francophone, à commencer par *Un si tendre vampire* de Linda Lê en 1987, que le livre de Jean Vanmai a vu le jour. Comparé à la majorité des romans franco-vietnamiens publiés à l'époque coloniale et pré-75 dont le sujet est centré sur l'impact de la colonisation et l'éducation française parmi les élites vietnamiennes, ainsi que sur le choc culturel de la rencontre entre l'Occident et l'Orient, souvent représenté à travers l'échec des relations coloniales amoureuses,[6] *Chân Đăng* présente un sujet et un contexte tout à fait différents. Placée ni en France ni au Vietnam, mais sur cette île peu connue qui est la Nouvelle-Calédonie, l'histoire des Chân Đăng étonne par son titre étrange. D'après l'explication de Vanmai, qui est le premier à utiliser ce terme à l'écrit, *Chân* signifie 'pied' en vietnamien, et *Đăng* vient du verbe '[d']engager'. Chân Đăng est donc un nom que les travailleurs tonkinois sous contrat ont inventé pour s'identifier et pour refléter leur condition d'engagés, aux 'pieds liés', ou pire, aux 'pieds enchaînés' par leurs contrats de trois ou cinq ans[7] (Figures 1 et 2).

En outre, la représentation de Chân Đăng, plutôt que de bourgeois vietnamiens francophones ou francophiles, comme personnages principaux, semble destiner le livre de Vanmai à une place à part dans la littérature franco-vietnamienne. Or, rien ne saurait être plus loin de la vérité. En révélant comment la relation coloniale entre la France et le Vietnam se manifeste en Nouvelle-Calédonie tout au long de la guerre anticoloniale jusque bien après la décolonisation de l'Indochine en 1954, l'histoire des Chân Đăng ne fait pas que jeter la lumière sur le passé des travailleurs contractuels : elle apporte une contribution essentielle à la compréhension de l'histoire et de la formation de la diaspora vietnamienne dans la région du Pacifique Sud.

Avant la publication du roman de Vanmai, aucun livre n'avait été écrit sur la vie de ces travailleurs engagés, et encore moins de leur point de vue. Personne du côté des Chân Đăng n'a osé briser le silence autour de ce qu'ils ont vécu, en partie à cause du sentiment de honte associé à l'image des 'coolies', aux conditions de vie et de travail, proches de celles des esclaves, et du besoin d'oublier et d'épargner à leurs enfants leurs histoires traumatisantes (Do 2008). Aussi, la révélation des maltraitances qu'ont subies les travailleurs tonkinois aux mains de leurs 'maîtres', qu'ils soient blancs ou kanak (terme désignant les premiers habitants de Nouvelle-Calédonie) – peut être vue comme un acte offensant et transgressif qui aurait froissé nombre d'anciens patrons et contremaîtres encore vivants dans les années 1980. Même les travailleurs rapatriés au Nord Vietnam dans les années 1960 n'en ont soufflé mot alors qu'ils n'avaient plus rien à craindre de leurs ex-employeurs. Débarqués au beau milieu d'une guerre civile, dans un pays appauvri et ravagé par des années de conflits militaires, confrontés à des conditions de vie particulièrement dures auxquelles il fallait s'adapter rapidement, ils ne tenaient guère à ressasser le passé. Du côté des Français, il y avait peu d'intérêt, bien entendu, à dénicher cette vieille histoire d'exploitation de la main d'œuvre coloniale dans laquelle la France n'avait pas eu le beau rôle. De plus, dans les années 80, la France avait à gérer à la fois son retrait difficile des Nouvelles-Hébrides, devenues un pays indépendant au nom de Vanuatu et la répercussion de ce bouleversement politique sur ses territoires calédoniens pris par la fièvre nationaliste kanak (Aldrich 1993).

La genèse de *Chân Đăng*

Sur ce fond historique et du fait que l'auteur n'a jamais, jusque-là, poursuivi de carrière d'écrivain, le projet et l'accomplissement littéraires de Jean Vanmai, un fils de Chân Đăng, s'avèrent aussi courageux que remarquables. Né le 30 août en 1940 dans un petit village de Koumac, près de la mine Chagrin, au nord de la Nouvelle-Calédonie, Vanmai est le fils aîné d'une fratrie de neuf enfants.[8] Son père, Nguyễn Văn Khảo, faisait partie des engagés sous contrat qui étaient venus sur le Caillou en 1937 et c'est là qu'il avait rencontré et épousé sa future femme, Nguyễn Thị Hảo, originaire elle aussi du Tonkin.[9] Vanmai avait vingt ans quand ses parents ont pris la décision de se rapatrier avec toute la famille le 30 décembre 1960. Ils étaient parmi les premiers travailleurs tonkinois à quitter Nouméa et à s'embarquer sur *The Eastern Queen* (Figures 3, 4). Le rapatriement, organisé par la France, s'était déroulé sur une période de trois ans. Entre 1960 et 1964, neuf convois partant des Nouvelles-Hébrides et de Nouvelle-Calédonie ont ramené 3 353 Chân Đăng et leurs descendants au pays (Mohamed-Gaillard, 2010).

Bien que très attendu, le rapatriement a provoqué chez les Chân Đăng et leurs familles des sentiments ambivalents. Les uns l'ont fêté, les autres l'ont pleuré, surtout ceux qui étaient nés sur le territoire, tant il leur était difficile de quitter une terre à laquelle ils s'étaient attachés[10]. Amoureux de sa fiancée futunienne, Helena Wendt, qui deviendra plus tard son épouse, Vanmai a décidé de ne pas accompagner ses parents et sa fratrie. Afin de ne pas trop les faire souffrir, il a gardé cette décision pour lui-même. Il a raconté dans *Chân Đăng* ce déchirement familial à travers le personnage de Hồng. Le jour du départ, Vanmai a disparu et tous les efforts de ses parents pour le retrouver sont restés vains. En effet, ils l'ont cherché chez des connaissances vietnamiennes, ignorant que leur fils aîné s'était caché chez un ami kanak[11].

Aux yeux de la mère en détresse, c'était un déshonneur pour un fils aîné d'abandonner ses vieux parents. Il a fallu attendre encore quinze ans avant que Vanmai ne soit réuni avec sa famille lors de sa première visite au pays ancestral avec sa femme en 1975. Il y est retourné plusieurs fois par la suite et, au long des années, a apporté une forte aide financière à ses parents. Ceci a fait reconnaître à sa mère que c'était après tout un bonheur que son fils soit resté en Nouvelle-Calédonie.[12]

Resté seul à Nouméa après le rapatriement des siens, Vanmai a poursuivi avec succès une carrière de technicien radio et d'entrepreneur dans le secteur audiovisuel et de l'électro-ménager. Personnage influent dans la communauté vietnamienne en Nouvelle-Calédonie, il a été élu membre du *Rassemblement pour la Calédonie dans la République du Congrès du Territoire* de 1988 à 1995. Il était également l'un des principaux moteurs de la fondation de l'*Amicale Vietnamienne de Nouvelle-Calédonie* en 1974. Le fort attachement de Vanmai à sa communauté diasporique remonte à sa jeunesse. En voyant s'effacer lentement les dernières traces des Chân Đăng sur le Caillou, suite à leur rapatriement massif laissant derrière eux une poignée de moins de mille Vietnamiens, il s'est vite rendu compte du besoin de préserver leur mémoire et de sauver de l'oubli l'histoire de leur vécu en Nouvelle-Calédonie. Dans un entretien avec Christiane Terrier (2016) à l'émission radiophonique 'Nouvelle-Calédonie La Première', Vanmai a raconté comment la vue du roman *Chasseur blanc cœur noir* (1954) de Peter Viertel dans une librairie à Nouméa quelques mois après le rapatriement de sa famille lui a révélé le pouvoir des mots dans la préservation de la mémoire :

> En voyant ce livre, je pense qu'il faudrait bien que quelqu'un de chez nous se décide, un jour ou l'autre, à écrire l'épopée des Vietnamiens en Nouvelle-Calédonie. Il est inconcevable de laisser disparaître cette période dure, pénible, difficile, vécue par tous les nôtres, sans laisser la moindre trace écrite.[13]

Pourtant, à l'âge de 21 ans, Vanmai ne se sentait pas capable d'assumer la tâche de raconter l'histoire de ses parents et de tant d'autres travailleurs tonkinois sous contrat. Il lui faudra attendre encore quinze ans et l'achèvement d'un cours d'écriture créative à *L'École française de rédaction*, pris sous l'impulsion du moment lors de l'un de ses voyages d'affaires à Paris, avant de pouvoir mettre sur papier le vécu des Chân Đăng. Recueillies en vietnamien auprès de ses amis et d'autres engagés, puis réécrites en français sous forme de fiction, ces histoires ont rempli des centaines de pages d'un manuscrit que Vanmai a rédigé en l'espace de six mois en 1976. Lorsque Terrier lui a demandé pourquoi il avait choisi d'écrire une fiction, plutôt qu'un ouvrage de recherche scientifique, Vanmai a expliqué son désir de se concentrer sur les sentiments et les souffrances des personnages, de manière à rendre leur saga plus vivante et plus réelle:

> J'ai effectué un travail de conteur et de romancier afin de rendre plus 'réelle' cette épopée. Ainsi l'ouvrage a l'avantage d'être présenté comme un véritable témoignage, un vécu, voire comme un 'grand film' de cinéma. Ce qui contrairement à un livre historique donne aussi la possibilité de mettre l'accent plutôt sur les sentiments et les souffrances de nos parents en ce temps dit colonial.

Motivé par ce que l'historien Hamish Dalley (2014 : 9) identifie comme 'l'impératif réaliste' [realist imperative] qui caractérise aujourd'hui le roman historique postcolonial, Vanmai a fait consciemment l'effort de rapporter des événements réels et de respecter les dates historiques afin de rendre son roman encore plus crédible aux yeux des Calédoniens de tous bords. Craignant toutefois que bien avant sa publication, son livre puisse provoquer les lecteurs, du fait qu'il leur rappelle les abus subis par les Chân Đăng, les luttes qu'ils ont menées pour réclamer le droit d'être des hommes libres, l'hostilité qu'ils ont attirée pour avoir célébré la victoire des forces Việt Minh et la défaite des Français à Điện Biên Phủ en 1954, Vanmai avait intentionnellement évité toute recherche archivistique : 'Ne voulant absolument pas éveiller les soupçons de l'administration tatillonne de l'époque sur mon projet d'écriture, je me suis bien gardé d'aller consulter les documents officiels de l'administration coloniale ou même des archives territoriales' a-t-il confié à Terrier. Si ce manque de recherche scientifique a pour conséquence quelques inexactitudes géographiques mineures et involontaires[14] de la part de l'auteur et des vieux Chân Đăng qui lui ont narré leurs histoires, le genre romanesque a donné à Vanmai la liberté de créer son intrigue et ses personnages de sorte à mettre en lumière leurs émotions et afflictions, sans toutefois sacrifier le réalisme littéraire et la véracité des faits souvent violents qu'il relate. Son roman serait ainsi vu comme une interprétation sérieuse du passé permettant ce que Dalley (2010 : 10) qualifie 'd'interaction dynamique entre l'invention littéraire et les revendications historiques'.

La réception de Chân Đăng en Nouvelle-Calédonie

Cette approche historico-fictionnelle explique la réception chaleureuse que les lecteurs calédoniens ont réservée à un livre qui aurait pu être troublant et qui atteste l'équilibre que l'auteur a pu atteindre, entre d'une part, le besoin de révéler et de faire reconnaître au grand public calédonien des expériences réelles et pénibles des travailleurs tonkinois, et l'importance de maintenir la bonne entente entre les différentes communautés composant le pays, devenu aujourd'hui le sien et celui de ses enfants et petits-enfants. Que les descendants des contremaîtres aient trouvé plutôt modérés les incidents violents décrits par Vanmai par rapport à ceux qui avaient eu lieu dans le passé, témoigne du mérite de l'auteur qui était bien conscient que sa description des incidents violents pourrait provoquer un effet inverse à la sympathie, si les lecteurs la trouvaient excessive : 'En écrivant, c'est comme si je . . . marchais sur les 'lignes de crêtes' . . . pour ne pas tomber soit sur un côté soit sur l'autre de la montagne . . .'[15]

La comparaison entre l'acte d'écriture et le funambulisme expose deux aspects majeurs interconnectés de *Chân Đăng.* D'abord, l'extrême violence physique et mentale perpétrée par les détenteurs de pouvoir à l'égard des travailleurs engagés tonkinois, qui est au cœur du roman et qui devrait être racontée. Cela pose la question de la mesure prise par Vanmai pour aborder la violence dans son livre, thème auquel nous retournerons en plus de détail ultérieurement. Ensuite, c'est la difficulté de l'auteur à récupérer et réclamer, même à travers une forme fictionnelle, l'histoire des minorités qu'étaient les Chân Đăng. En pratique, cela signifie trouver suffisamment de soutien pour la publication de leurs histoires à une époque où Vanmai n'était qu'un romancier débutant. La reconnaissance de cette nécessité première nous permet de reconnaître le rapport de force déséquilibré entre Vanmai et le préfacier Georges Pisier, ainsi que le besoin de réexaminer dans son contexte les commentaires évaluatifs mitigés et condescendants de celui-ci sur *Chân Đăng.* Chef administrateur des Affaires étrangères en Indochine (1943-1950) et en Nouvelle-Calédonie (1950-1966), historien et directeur de la *Société d'Études Historiques de la Nouvelle-Calédonie,* Pisier était un éditeur puissant et influent dont la préface conférait non seulement la crédibilité au livre de Vanmai en vue de sa publication et ses ventes,[16] mais aussi la 'protection' à son auteur contre d'éventuelles critiques.

Lire *Chân Đăng* aujourd'hui dévoile la tension entre la version historique officielle de la préface de Pisier et la version non-officielle de l'histoire coloniale des travailleurs engagés d'Indochine en Nouvelle-Calédonie. S'appuyant sur des chiffres et citations provenant des sources historiques nationales, telles que le rapport 'Les Asiatiques en Nouvelle-Calédonie' publié par l'historienne Janine Moret dans le Bulletin de la Société des Études Historiques et cité par Pisier, l'histoire officielle recadre et fige le récit des Chân Đăng dans un discours colonial en le confinant au passé : 'Le récit de Jean Vanmai, intitulé 'Chân Đăng' (les engagés sous contrat) évoque *une page d'histoire, aujourd'hui tournée,* celle de l'immigration des travailleurs tonkinois en Nouvelle-Calédonie (et accessoirement aux Nouvelles-Hébrides).'[17] La relégation du passé des Chân Đăng aux oubliettes de l'histoire dès le début de la préface ignore tout l'effort de Vanmai de faire revivre et sauvegarder leur mémoire. De surcroît, en pointant les erreurs à corriger, Pisier affaiblit la voix de l'auteur et jette le doute sur l'authenticité du récit qui '*semble* suffisamment authentique pour mériter de figurer dans les archives de l'Histoire', mais qui 'nécessite des correctifs.'[18] L'attitude défensive adoptée par Pisier au nom d'un jugement impartial illustre parfaitement ce que Toby Green (2018 : 62) décrit comme la conséquence de l'intrusion des voix subalternes postcoloniales dans l'histoire officielle : 'confrontée à la multitude de voix et d'évidences qui indique d'autres histoires alternatives', celle-ci 's'effiloche et se découd.'

La sublimation de la violence à travers le trope du martyre

Nul lecteur ne saurait ignorer l'extrême violence physique et mentale qui forme le noyau du roman de Vanmai et qui dépasse les divisions de genre et de race. La plupart de cette violence est dirigée contre les travailleurs engagés. Dès le moment où ils débarquent en Nouvelle-Calédonie, ces derniers sont livrés aux mains des maîtres coloniaux français (tels que le riche propriétaire terrien Chauvedin, les contremaîtres Mainote, Missard et Watard, et la patronne française Madame Lucas) et de leur employé kanak (tel que le gardien John). Jean Vanmai n'exagère guère les conditions de vie et de travail extrêmement dures des Chân Đăng à l'époque coloniale. Souvent décrites comme proches de l'esclavage et semblables à celles imposées aux bagnards (Merle 1995 : 317 ; Devambez-Armand 1994 : 215), ces conditions se voient dans les photos des laboureurs au travail. Munis d'outils les plus élémentaires, souvent exposés à un environnement de travail dangereux, les hommes avaient pour tâche l'extraction de minerai et minéraux à force de bras dans les mines ouvertes et souterraines (Figures 5, 6, 7, 8, 9), alors que les femmes, vêtues de leurs tuniques traditionnelles, s'échinaient à creuser et défricher la terre avec pelles et pioches (Figure 10). Les parents n'avaient pas d'autres choix que de laisser leurs enfants à eux-mêmes, parfois dans des sortes de cages improvisées, pendant qu'ils travaillaient dans les mines ou les champs (Figure 11). À la fin d'une longue journée éreintante, ils rentraient fourbus à leurs pauvres cabanes regroupées dans des petits villages ou camps au pied des mines (Figures 12, 13, 14). Ils devaient se débrouiller avec le strict nécessaire et ces conditions de vie difficiles ont perduré jusqu'au milieu du vingtième siècle (Figures 15 et 16). Le dimanche, leur seul jour de repos, ils se réunissaient avec leurs familles et amis, les femmes passaient du temps à s'occuper de leurs enfants (Figures 17, 18) tandis que les hommes allaient vendre du bois coupé ou pêcher pour améliorer leurs revenus (Figures 19, 20).

Dans son roman, Vanmai vise à relater une histoire réelle du vécu des Chân Đăng, sans chercher à cacher les sévices corporels,[19] les fouettages publics, les violences psychologiques et sexuelles, les arrestations et les emprisonnements que leurs patrons leur ont infligés. Or, Vanmai sait qu'il marchait sur des 'lignes de crête' car si dans le passé les traitements brutaux des travailleurs étaient une norme acceptable (Chêne 2016), en 1980, personne en Nouvelle-Calédonie ne voulait se rappeler cette brutalité. En effet, sa description de la cruauté des contremaîtres aurait pu offenser leurs puissants descendants. Afin d'éviter de froisser les familles des agresseurs et celles des agressés, et d'assurer la publication de son livre, Vanmai a dû recourir à cette stratégie littéraire afin de protéger les deux partis : il répartit de façon équilibrée les incidents violents entre les deux camps, et relate des agressions et meurtres commis par les travailleurs tonkinois dans leur propre communauté : la tentative de viol de Lan par Ngạch, l'horrible complot de Năm pour tuer l'amant de sa femme ou la bagarre à coups de poing entre Trần et Thắng. Toutefois, nous postulons que c'est essentiellement à travers un seul personnage, Thắng, jeune travailleur engagé célibataire, que Vanmai parvient à la fois à concentrer et à atténuer toute la violence coloniale ciblée sur les Chân Đăng.

À l'encontre des autres personnages Chân Đăng tels Cung, Toán, Pháp et Bích, dont l'exploitation perpétuelle dans les mines et plantations mènent à une spirale de haine, de révolte et de vengeance sans fin envers leurs maîtres blancs, Vanmai développe son protagoniste Thắng de manière qu'il puisse transcender la violence à travers le trope du martyre. Il fait évoluer son personnage au long du récit, de même que sa perspective de la violence. Victime de violence dès le début du roman, Thắng est construit comme l'image même de la souffrance mentale et physique. Comme ses autres compatriotes, il souffre affreusement du manque du pays qu'il a quitté, de la perte de son identité et de son nom vietnamien, remplacés par un numéro de matricule français. Mais la perte la plus traumatisante pour Thắng est celle de Liên, une jeune co-passagère de bateau rencontrée pendant le voyage en Nouvelle-Calédonie, dont il est follement amoureux et de qui il est séparé aussitôt après le débarquement des Tonkinois à l'île Nou. La description déchirante de la séparation des amoureux montre la brutalité des contremaîtres et la rapidité avec laquelle ils recourent à la violence pour établir leur pouvoir absolu sur les pauvres travailleurs. C'est pourtant une réalité historique car seules les familles, c'est-à-dire, les couples inscrits comme légalement mariés, avaient le droit de rester ensemble[20]. Fou de douleur et sachant qu'au ratio d'une femme pour cinq hommes, Liên sera sous peu mariée à quelqu'un d'autre, Thắng devient inévitablement un rebelle, à force d'être soumis quotidiennement, comme ses camarades, aux mauvais traitements d'ordre mental et physique sur le lieu du travail. Répondant à la violence par la violence, Thắng acquiert rapidement le statut de 'héros' parmi les Chân Đăng pour avoir été le premier 'coolie' à oser frapper un contremaître blanc. La punition féroce que lui admet son maître en retour transforme son corps en un lieu de violence, l'automutilation s'avèrant être le seul moyen de défense dont il dispose contre les maltraitances impitoyables. C'est ainsi que Thắng recourt à des mesures extrêmes qui traduisent, selon Chêne (2016), une forme de lutte personnalisée contre l'autorité coloniale plutôt qu'une révolte collective. En versant du jus de tabac dans ses yeux pour les enflammer et en ingurgitant une grande quantité de piments rouges pour provoquer une forte fièvre, il rend son corps incapable de travail pendant deux jours de suite, obligeant son maître à accepter son absence et gagnant pour lui-même un repos nécessaire pour se remettre de ses blessures.

Cependant, ce premier goût de haine et vengeance n'a pas entraîné Thắng dans la spirale de violence et folie qui pourrait mener au meurtre, comme dans le cas des travailleurs de la plantation de cocotiers en Nouvelles-Hébrides. Au contraire, le tabassage sauvage annonce un point tournant chez Thắng, un homme doux qui, durant 'son enfance pauvre et démunie, a toujours été contre la violence' et qui ne se souvenait pas avoir été brutal ou méchant (Vanmai 1980 : 218). Surpris de s'être laissé si facilement pris dans le cycle infernal de la violence, Thắng décide de répondre aux attaques de ses maîtres coloniaux quand ils le frappent, par le sacrifice pour ses compatriotes Chân Đăng : 'il a toujours voulu sacrifier sa liberté et même sa vie si c'était nécessaire, pour combattre l'injustice et les méthodes féodales qui nous accablent dans cette partie du monde' (235). Ainsi, en développant le personnage fictif de Thắng en une figure de martyre et de sauveur, prêt à prendre sur lui le fardeau de la culpabilité des autres et leurs châtiments, Vanmai parvient à créer une fin moins brutale à la confrontation entre les maîtres blancs et les travailleurs tonkinois. Lors du premier incident impliquant le vol des bâtons de dynamite, commis par le jeune Yến, Thắng intervient pour protéger le coupable. Par conséquent, il est d'abord envoyé en prison, puis en Nouvelles-Hébrides pour travailler dans la cocoteraie de Chauvedin. Lors du deuxième incident, il ne s'agit plus de vol mais de mort et de meurtre. Ici, Vanmai intensifie la violence en relatant deux tragédies, celle d'un bébé, figure par excellence d'innocence et de vulnérabilité, et celle du colon Chauvedin, décrit comme 'un tyran, le diable en personne' (235). Des tragédies similaires avaient lieu parmi les travailleurs sous contrat vietnamiens en Nouvelles-Hébrides : les rapports français cités par Đồng Sỹ Hứa (1993 : 64) racontent comment, pour punir une travailleuse vietnamienne d'avoir brisé un service à thé, le patron lui a ligoté les mains et les pieds, l'a placée sur une fourmillière puis l'a laissée mourir à petit feu au soleil[21]. Quant à l'assassinat de Chauvedin par ses employés tonkinois, il s'agit d'un vrai crime commis contre un maître français, connu dans les médias à de l'époque sous le nom de 'l'affaire Malo-Pass'.

Dans *Chân Đăng*, Vanmai relie ces deux morts pour en faire une causalité susceptible d'exemplifier la brutalité des colons et la violente vengeance des travailleurs. Bien qu'il brosse un portrait cruel et inhumain du maître et de ses contremaîtres, Vanmai prend soin de ne pas les transformer en vrais meurtriers. Chauvedin qui interdit à un couple tonkinois d'arrêter leur travail au champ pour aller vérifier la sécurité de leur fils, malgré les cris désespérés de ce dernier, n'est qu'indirectement responsable du décès de l'enfant dû aux piqûres de fourmis rouges. Vanmai ne laisse pas non plus les travailleurs subir les terribles représailles de leurs maîtres quand peu après cet accident fatal, les chiens renifleurs ont retrouvé le corps de Chauvedin. Porté disparu, celui-ci a été assassiné et enterré sous le foyer de la cantine chez ses travailleurs tonkinois. Utilisant une ellipse narrative, Vanmai révèle ainsi l'assassinat du colon aux mains de ses coolies, mais au lieu de décrire l'horrible mort comme il l'a fait avec le cadavre tuméfié de l'enfant, il nous épargne les détails choquants du meurtre et la description des restes de Chauvedin. De plus, en reliant la mort de Chauvedin à une tuerie collective, et en laissant Thắng, l'homme innocent, payer le prix du crime des autres dans un acte de sacrifice suprême, Vanmai évite d'établir une corrélation directe entre le crime et sa punition devant la loi. De cette manière, il n'accuse personne en particulier de ce meurtre et parvient à protéger les Chân Đăng de leur propre crime, quoiqu'il suggère à travers l'un des personnages que les coupables auront à rendre compte de leur acte devant Dieu. Dans cette perspective, la fictionalisation d'un fait réel permet au romancier de créer une fin alternative pour son martyre. Alors qu'en réalité, dans l'affaire Malo en Nouvelles-Hébrides en 1931, quatre travailleurs tonkinois ont été guillotinés après avoir été jugés coupables de l'assassinat de Chevalier, propriétaire d'une plantation à Santo (Chêne 2016 : 3; Meyerhoff 2002 : 51; Đồng 1993 : 65; Bonnemaison 1986 : 72), dans *Chân Đăng*, seul Thắng est arrêté et celui-ci a échappé à la peine capitale. Similairement, personne n'a trouvé la mort sous la plume de Vanmai quand il relate un autre événement réel, celui de la révolte des miniers tonkinois en Nouvelle-Calédonie. En effet, les travailleurs sous contrat devenaient politiquement actifs au fur et à mesure que la guerre anticoloniale s'intensifiait au Vietnam, surtout après la déclaration de l'indépendance de la République Démocratique du Vietnam en 1945 par Hồ Chí Minh. Ils se regroupaient en syndicat, organisaient des réunions à la Maison des Travailleurs vietnamiens (Việt Nam Công Nhân Hội Quán), signaient des pétitions et appelaient à la grève afin d'exiger des conditions de travail plus humaines pour eux-mêmes et leurs compatriotes (Figure 21). Si Vanmai inclut dans son livre des incidents historiques réels, tels que la grève des miniers et le lever du drapeau rouge à l'étoile d'or au camp des Vietnamiens, il omet des événements plus violents, telle la fusillade des gendarmes français qui a coûté la vie à l'un des grévistes (Đồng 1993 ; Chêne 2016).

L'acte courageux et altruiste de Thắng pour protéger ses compagnons face à l'oppression et la brutalité coloniales fait de lui un sauveur. Sa métamorphose est complète quand il remplit une dernière fois ce rôle. Libéré après vingt ans de prison, Thắng choisit le retour au pays natal. Au moment où il embarque sur le bateau qui le ramènera au Vietnam, il retrouve Liên, veuve et sans enfant, seule parmi les passagers. Réuni finalement avec la femme de son coeur, Thắng lui apporte l'amour et la protection dont elle aura besoin pour surmonter les difficultés que comporte sa réinstallation au pays natal après plus de vingt ans d'exil. La réunion des amants à la fin du roman offre aux lecteurs bien plus qu'une conclusion romantique et heureuse d'une histoire d'amour perdu. En effet, le retour de Thắng à Liên, et à la vie, souligne la rédemption par la souffrance et l'espoir dans le futur. Ainsi, à travers le personnage de Thắng, Vanmai a trouvé le moyen de présenter le trope de la violence coloniale sous l'angle du martyre, brisant le cercle vicieux de la violence et la contre-violence. Dans une vue clairvoyante de l'avenir de la Nouvelle-Calédonie, en tant que société multiraciale et multiculturelle harmonieuse, Vanmai a réussi à créer une fiction historique qui honore la mémoire des Chân Đăng tout en protégeant les partis qui sont impliqués dans ce chapitre colonial de l'histoire calédonienne.

L'intérêt grandissant de l'histoire des Chân Đăng

Une cinquantaine d'années après le rapatriement des Chân Đăng et leurs familles au Vietnam, leur histoire méconnue a commencé à attirer un intérêt grandissant parmi les spécialistes du post-colonialisme, des 'subaltern studies', de l'histoire du travail et de l'esclavage, de la migration transnationale et de la mémoire collective dans la région Asie/Australie/Pacifique et globalement. L'histoire des travailleurs contractuels tonkinois en Nouvelle-Calédonie et l'ex-Nouvelles-Hébrides a été le sujet central de plusieurs livres écrits par des historiens français. Citons, par exemple, la recherche doctorale de Claudy Chêne intitulée *Les engagés Tonkinois sous contrat en Nouvelle-Calédonie. 1891-1964. Vivre, Subir et Résister* ; l'ouvrage *L'Archipel de la puissance : la politique de la France dans le Pacifique Sud de 1946-1998 (2010)* de Sarah Mohamed-Gaillard ; le volume édité *Le peuplement du Pacifique et de la Nouvelle-Calédonie au XIXe siècle. Condamnés, Colons, Convicts, Coolies, Chân Dang* (1994) de Paul de Deckker. En 2008, Anne Pitoiset et Claudine Wéry ont publié *Mystère Dang* (2008), une biographie de Đặng Văn Nha, un magnat des mines d'origine vietnamienne calédonienne et descendant de Chân Đăng. Plus près de nous, de nombreux universitaires en Australie et Nouvelle-Zélande se penchent sur les histoires qui transcendent les frontières des mondes impériaux britanniques et français. Par exemple, l'historienne Nadia Rhook (2017) a localisé des connexions entre les Chân Đăng et l'histoire australienne et a examiné la façon dont les puissances coloniales opéraient à travers un triangle géopolitique reliant le Vietnam français, l'Australie et la Nouvelle-Calédonie. D'autres érudits, tels Peter Brown, Karin Speedy, Jean Anderson, Raylene Ramsey and Deborah Walker, se sont dévoués à la traduction des auteurs du Pacifique francophone. Leurs travaux étaient essentiels pour 'combler le fossé linguistique entre les îlots linguistiques' (Speedy 2015 : 14) et ils ont inspiré nos efforts pour traduire *Chân Đăng* de Jean Vanmai.

Les Vietnamiens, surtout ceux des jeunes générations, se montrent particulièrement curieux d'en savoir plus sur les événements historiques relatés par Jean Vanmai dans *Chân Đăng*. Ce besoin s'est clairement fait ressentir lors du symposium 'Rencontres : A Gathering of Voices of the Vietnamese Diaspora'.[22] Organisé par Tess Do et Alexandra Kurmann à l'Université de Melbourne en décembre 2016, il a réuni six écrivains français et australiens d'origine vietnamienne, dont Vanmai. Seul conférencier à communiquer en français, Vanmai a ému l'audience, particulièrement les Vietnamiens anglophones, avec une lecture touchante d'un extrait de son roman *Chân Đăng*.[23] Leurs questions et sa discussion avec eux après son intervention ont montré que la barrière linguistique avait empêché la transmission d'une mémoire collective du passé colonial vietnamien et souligné à quel point il était urgent pour eux d'accéder à ses écrits. Vu cet intérêt, la traduction du roman de Vanmai constitue une nouvelle ressource historique importante qui permet à cette histoire d'intégrer les mémoires collectives des communautés vietnamiennes anglophones diasporiques, en Australie d'abord, mais également en Angleterre et dans les autres pays riverains du Pacifique, tels la Nouvelle-Zélande, le Canada et les États-Unis.

Quoique pour Jean Vanmai le symposium souligne l'importance du partage de la mémoire des Chân Đăng, il convient de noter que l'un des premiers reportages sur les Chân Đăng a été réalisé en 2005 par la très populaire entreprise de divertissement vietnamien américain *Vân Sơn*, qui l'a inclus dans leur DVD tourné en Australie *Vân Sơn in Australia – Down Under*. Deux ans après, c'est au Vietnam qu'a vu le jour le premier documentaire de grande envergure lorsque le studio Hồ Chí Minh City Television Film Studios a sorti *Ký Sự Tân Đảo* (2007),[24] un téléfilm impressionnant en trente épisodes. En effet, on pourrait dire que c'est le gouvernement vietnamien qui a joué un rôle phare dans la reconnaissance de l'histoire des Chân Đăng comme partie intégrante de l'histoire vietnamienne et de leurs descendants en Nouvelle-Calédonie comme partie inséparable de la nation vietnamienne. En 2004 il a adopté la Résolution 36, la première politique officielle en faveur des Vietnamiens résidant à l'étranger, en vue de créer 'des conditions favorables et des modalités de soutien' à leur égard, et surtout, de maintenir et de renforcer leurs liens avec le pays d'origine (Koh 2015 : 185). L'exemption de visa d'une durée de cinq ans pour les Vietnamiens d'outremer, introduite le 1er juillet 2007, a ouvert la porte l'année suivante, à la visite officielle d'une vingtaine de délégués de *L'Amicale Vietnamienne*, marquant le retour des Vietnamiens de Nouvelle-Calédonie et du Vanuatu après plus d'un siècle depuis leur débarquement dans ces îles (*Gần lắm quê hương* 2008). Il est notable que depuis sa fondation, l'Amicale a toujours joué un rôle actif dans la préservation des traditions vietnamiennes en Nouvelle-Calédonie, par exemple, l'organisation des fêtes du Nouvel An lunaire, des danses du lion (Figure 22), du Festival du Centenaire de l'arrivée des Chân Đăng en Nouvelle-Calédonie (Figure 23), ou la participation du 'Char du Dragon' à un festival de Nouméa (Figure 24). Elle a aussi apporté un soutien important à la communauté, comme le montre la photo d'une danse d'éventails traditionnelle exécutée par de jeunes femmes vietnamiennes de l'Amicale lors d'une visite à la maison de retraite 'Petites Soeurs des Pauvres' à Nouméa (Figure 25).

En 2012, après deux ans de gestation, le réalisateur français Jacques-Olivier Trompas (2012) a sorti *Chân Đăng, 50 ans après*, un documentaire français de 52 minutes marquant l'anniversaire du rapatriement des Chân Đăng en 1960. Dans la même année, une statue commémorative représentant une famille Chân Đăng au temps colonial a été commandée au Vietnam par l'*Amicale Vietnamienne de Nouvelle-Calédonie* qui tenait à honorer la mémoire de leurs aïeux Chân Đăng et leur contribution au développement économique de l'île. Fabriquée au pays, de grandeur nature, la statue en bronze a été ensuite expédiée à Nouméa où elle a été installée au quartier asiatique et inaugurée le 17 octobre 2013 (Hoàng Hoa 2013 ; Như Quỳnh 2013) (Figure 26). Deux ans après, le 27 décembre 2015, le gouvernement vietnamien a organisé à Hà Nội et à grande échelle la 55ème réunion des Chân Đăng et de leurs descendants venant des deux rives du Pacifique (Lan Phương 2015). Dans la même année, un autre documentaire sur les Chân Đăng, *The Roots*, ou en vietnamien *Biết đâu nguồn cội* (2015), a été diffusé sur la chaîne vietnamienne internationale TVT World (VTV4). Outre ces principales sources, de nombreux blogs personnels, tels *Tân Đảo Xưa và Nay* [*Nouvelles-Hébrides, hier et aujourd'hui*] (Vanson 2013), et plusieurs clips de vidéo sur internet sont la preuve de l'engouement populaire pour les Chân Đăng et leur histoire au fur et à mesure que les Vietnamiens du Vietnam et d'outremer sillonnent le Pacifique pour filmer les témoignages de quelques derniers nonagénaires résidant en Nouvelle-Calédonie.[25] Plus récemment, le roman graphique de l'artiste eurasien Clément Baloup (2020), *Les engagés de Nouvelle-Calédonie*, quatrième volume de la série *Mémoires de Viet-Kieu*,[26] a donné une nouvelle vie à l'histoire des générations d'hommes et femmes vietnamiens qui 'contre vents et marées, et le cœur rempli d'espoir, [ont su relever] inlassablement les défis de la migration' (Do, 2020 : 64). Aux yeux de leurs descendants, le courage, le sacrifice et la résilience dont ils ont témoigné tout au long de leur vie de travailleurs sous contrats exilés leur ont conféré le titre respectueux 'd'anciens Chân Đăng' ou 'các cụ Chân Đăng' en vietnamien (Figures 27, 28). C'était devant leur statue commémorative que le 15 mai 2021, les jeunes et les vieux de la communauté se sont rassemblés pour célébrer les 130 ans de présence vietnamienne en Nouvelle-Calédonie (Figures 29, 30). Aujourd'hui, ils ont en effet de quoi être fiers de leurs racines et leur héritage culturel vietnamien.

Jean Vanmai, 'l'homme traduit', et la traduction de *Chân Đăng*

Dans son célèbre essai *Imaginary Homelands (Patries imaginaires, 1991)* Salman Rushdie énonce sa notion maintenant bien connue de 'l'homme traduit' :

> le mot 'traduire' vient étymologiquement du latin 'transporter'. Ayant été transportés à travers le monde, nous sommes des hommes traduits. Généralement on suppose qu'il y a toujours quelque chose de perdu au cours du processus de traduction; or, je tiens, obstinément à l'idée qu'il peut y avoir aussi quelque chose de gagné.

En effet, cette notion 'd'homme traduit' est pertinente pour parler de Jean Vanmai qui fut 'transporté' d'un monde, celui de la culture et de la langue vietnamienne, à un autre monde, francophone celui-là, de la Nouvelle-Calédonie, île située dans le Pacifique. En fait, en traduisant ce texte, nous nous sommes rendu compte que nous avions affaire à un texte qui avait déjà été traduit, puisque Vanmai, pour sa part, avait traduit en français les témoignages oraux partagés qui lui avaient été transmis en langue vietnamienne par ses compatriotes souvent illettrés, les Chân Đăng. Or, il s'agit non seulement d'une traduction, mais aussi d'une translitération, puisque ces récits oraux, donc fluides, ont été transformés par le biais de l'écriture en un texte fixe. Inévitablement la transformation de l'oral en écrit entraîne la perte de certains éléments; de plus, le texte écrit a dû, dans une certaine mesure, être manipulé pour assurer sa lisibilité par un lectorat français. S'il y a des circonstances où on peut considérer cette manipulation comme l'abus d'une position de pouvoir, ici le processus double de translitération et de traduction n'a pas été effectué par quelqu'un d'étranger au groupe marginalisé d'engagés tonkinois. Au contraire, les décisions concernant les omissions et les ajouts lors de la traduction de ces témoignages racontés dans la langue vietnamienne 'secondaire' et remaniés dans la langue française dominante ont été prises par quelqu'un dont les parents appartiennent à ce groupe et qui, par conséquent, en fait partie lui-même. Ainsi, 'l'homme traduit', Vanmai, en écrivant *Chân Đăng,* devient le médiateur culturel et la voix du colonisé.

Cette 'traduction' de l'oral à l'écrit était, pour Vanmai, une manière non seulement de faire connaitre cette histoire et de la préserver, mais aussi d'adopter le rôle de défenseur des intérêts des Chân Đăng, parlant *en leur nom,* au nom de ceux dont la voix n'a jamais été entendue. Il donne ainsi une voix au 'subalterne', pour utiliser le terme de Spivak (1988 : 275), qui signale le double sens du mot 'représentation' : l'usage en politique, 'parler au nom de' et l'usage dans les arts, 'la re-présentation'. Les deux sens du mot s'appliquent à Vanmai puisqu'il parle au nom des Chân Đăng mais aussi il les re-présente, ces acteurs mineurs de l'histoire qui, marginalisés dans le discours sur le conflit entre les colonisateurs blancs et les Kanak indigènes, ont fini par en être exclus. D'où l'importance du roman de Vanmai. La traduction de l'expérience des Chân Đăng non seulement en une forme écrite, mais, de plus, en français, une des principales langues mondiales, la met sur la scène internationale, rend les acteurs visibles, et permet que leur voix soit entendue à travers le texte français, atteignant ainsi un lectorat qui s'étend au-delà de la région du Pacifique jusqu'à la France métropolitaine.

Cette traduction en anglais de *Chân Đăng* s'est effectuée dans un contexte bien différent de celui dans lequel le texte original est apparu et elle sera lue par un lectorat tout aussi différent. Au moment où Vanmai écrivait *Chân Đăng*, la France était encore solidement installée au pouvoir en Nouvelle-Calédonie et, comme nous l'avons vu, l'auteur ne se sentait pas libre de révéler l'ampleur réelle des brutalités infligées aux Chân Đăng. Presque trente ans après la sortie du livre de Vanmai, cette traduction anglaise sera lue dans un contexte où on doit tenir compte du dernier des trois référendums sur l'Indépendance de la Nouvelle-Calédonie (décembre 2021), l'aboutissement des 'événements', comme on appelle les soulèvements contre le pouvoir français. En outre, notre traduction en langue anglaise permettra au texte d'échapper à la catégorie fixe de littérature francophone pour acquérir une nouvelle vie plus visible dans un nouveau contexte. Dans ce sens, le nouveau texte traduit pourrait être considéré comme une 'réincarnation' du texte original, pour utiliser la notion de Jacques Derrida, qui voit la création d'un nouveau texte par la traduction comme un moyen de faire survivre le texte source (cité par Bassnett 1998 : 25).

Au cours de ce travail de traduction nous n'avons pas rencontré beaucoup de défis linguistiques, sans doute parce qu'il y a peu d'instances dans le texte de Vanmai de ce que Venuti (2008) appelle 'foreignisation' (en français, étrangéisation) une démarche qu'il préconise comme moyen de retenir 'le caractère étranger' dans le texte traduit et de réaliser ainsi une traduction 'résistante' qui n'approprie pas la culture d'origine en la 'domestiquant'. Dans *Chân Đăng*, c'est Vanmai lui-même qui effectue le travail de 'domestication', comme nous l'avons mentionné, à travers sa translitération des témoignages oraux du vietnamien en français. Cependant cette domestication n'est manifestement pas faite aux dépens des Chân Đăng. Au contraire, l'existence même du texte de Vanmai peut être considérée comme un acte de résistance, de la même manière que la grève des mineurs est un acte de résistance publique. En écrivant la plupart du roman en forme dialogique, Vanmai tente de garder l'oralité des témoignages qui lui avaient été transmis. Dépourvus de leur nom, les Chân Đăng étaient devenus de simples numéros aux yeux de leurs maîtres et furent ainsi privés non seulement de leur voix mais de leur identité individuelle même. C'est à travers les dialogues, qui reflètent la forme orale dans laquelle ces histoires furent transmises à l'auteur, que les voix individuelles (et donc le caractère des personnages) du livre sont entendues. La transcription va jusqu'à l'emploi des '?' et des '!', pour indiquer des réactions émotionnelles mais silencieuses des travailleurs. Il s'agit sans doute d'un exemple de plus de la tentative de Vanmai de faire entendre le caractère des conversations et des discussions : une manière de transcrire la narration orale.

Au niveau de la traduction du français en anglais, les questions d'étrangéisation et de domestication ne se sont pas posées, puisque les deux langues bénéficient d'un statut égal et donc il n'y a pas de rapport de force entre elles qui verrait l'appropriation d'une des cultures au profit de l'autre. Pour cette raison, la forme dialogique du texte s'est transférée sans difficulté du texte d'origine au texte traduit sans perte de la voix et du style de l'auteur.

S'il est bien entendu que la traduction effectuée est le résultat de l'interprétation des différences culturelles et linguistiques par la traductrice, il s'agit en fait d'une réécriture et les choix faits par la traductrice reflètent forcément son style personnel. Comme l'affirme Liddicoat (2013 : 14), la langue est 'une expression vivante du soi, et chaque choix pris du répertoire de la langue révèle le caractère du locuteur.' En tant que médiatrice formelle et thématique, c'est la traductrice qui prend la décision finale de la forme et du contenu à transférer et, à ce titre, elle bénéficie d'une position privilégiée qu'on pourrait qualifier de dominante. Or, même si nous avons changé certains aspects du texte, la ponctuation, par exemple, nous l'avons fait en pleine connaissance du piège que pose le désir 'd'ennoblir' le style, comme le dit Antoine Berman (1992), et par conséquent nous avons évité une approche qui soit en quelque façon réductrice du texte d'origine. Plutôt que d'exploiter une position de pouvoir et de domination, nous ne perdons pas de vue à qui profite cette traduction. En effet, toute 'manipulation' effectuée lors du processus de transfert est entreprise dans le seul but de faire entendre la voix du subalterne, que ce soit celle des Chân Đăng, dont les histoires sont maintenant accessibles à un lectorat anglophone, ou celle de Jean Vanmai lui-même. Pour revenir à Rushdie, cité au début – plutôt que de perdre quelque chose au cours de la traduction, il est indéniable que quelque chose est gagné. La traduction elle-même, en tant que 'réincarnation' du texte de Vanmai, donne à celui-là une nouvelle vie et lui permet de survivre au-delà des limites imposées par la langue française, créant ainsi le moyen de faire connaître cette page d'histoire à un nouveau lectorat.

Le lectorat contemporain anglophone de *Chân Đăng*

Les lecteurs de la traduction anglaise de *Chân Đăng*, qu'ils soient de la région du Pacifique, y compris l'Australie et la Nouvelle-Zélande, ou d'un public anglophone plus large, recevront sans doute le texte traduit bien différemment des lecteurs francophones au moment de la sortie du livre de Vanmai. D'ailleurs, l'importance de ce roman historique pour un nouveau lectorat peu familier avec l'histoire de cette région du Pacifique ne peut prendre son sens que s'il est contextualisé. Cette introduction fournit ce contexte historique, ainsi que des observations sur les motivations qui ont poussé Vanmai à écrire ce récit. De plus, notre correspondance avec l'auteur nous a permis de comprendre son approche de la représentation de la violence, et par la suite, de développer une analyse critique qui aide à la compréhension de la position difficile dans laquelle Vanmai s'est trouvé en tant que chroniqueur du drame de l'expérience des Chân Đăng à l'époque coloniale. Ces explications sont non seulement instructives, elles sont essentielles pour le lecteur qui sans elles, aurait sans doute trouvé la violence du livre insupportable. De la même façon, les lecteurs du 21ème siècle auraient perçu les scènes romantiques comme démodées et trop sentimentales. Or, il faut plutôt les comprendre comme une manière pour ces travailleurs de trouver du répit dans le contexte d'une souffrance physique sans relâche. De plus, l'amour romantique tel qu'il est exprimé dans ces couples plutôt innocents, produits de leur culture traditionnelle, représentait le seul espoir pour ces jeunes gens qui aspiraient à un meilleur avenir que la vie de survie qu'ils menaient dans cet environnement hostile.[27]

Du point de vue australien qui est le nôtre, nous croyons que le lecteur ordinaire serait choqué par l'omniprésence de la violence dans *Chân Đăng*. Comme le révèle notre analyse, Vanmai a minimisé la violence réelle des deux côtés de peur des représailles envers lui, mais aussi envers tous ceux qui étaient impliqués dans les événements qu'il décrit. Les explications de Vanmai à ce sujet permettent une meilleure compréhension du roman, démontrant ainsi l'importance de la contextualisation de l'œuvre pour un nouveau lectorat anglophone. Or, malgré les élucidations de l'auteur, pour la plupart des lecteurs, beaucoup d'incidents décrits dans le roman apparaitront comme extrêmement cruels et ce fond de violence qui parcourt *Chân Đăng* témoigne du fait que, bien que l'esclavage fût interdit en 1848, la pratique du travail sous contrat – surtout en ce qui concerne les Tonkinois colonisés de Nouvelle-Calédonie et des Nouvelles-Hébrides – fut à plusieurs égards semblable au travail forcé et à l'esclavage (Angleviel 2000 ; Bougerol 2000 : 86 ; Merle 1995 : 317).

Introduit par les colons britanniques suite à l'interdiction de l'esclavage, le travail sous contrat a fourni un système permettant l'importation de main-d'œuvre de couleur pour travailler pour les colons blancs qui avaient déplacé les populations indigènes dans des pays tels que Fidji, l'Afrique du Sud et l'Australie. Tout comme la colonisation de la Nouvelle-Calédonie répliquait celle de l'Australie, où les deux pays passaient de colonie pénale en colonie de peuplement, la pratique de se servir d'engagés sous contrat dans les territoires français du Pacifique fut modelée sur l'expérience australienne (Rhook 2017 ; Neilson 2018). Au 19ème siècle, plus de 50 000 personnes furent transportées des îles du Pacifique pour travailler sous contrat dans les colonies australiennes de Nouvelles-Galles du Sud et du Queensland – une pratique appelée 'blackbirding' – où les habitants des îles du Pacifique furent souvent kidnappés, dupés ou forcés de travailler en Australie dans des conditions misérables pour un paiement minime (Speedy 2015 ; Higginbotham 2017). S'il est vrai que, en principe au moins, les Chân Đăng ne furent pas contraints de s'engager, dans la réalité ils n'avaient aucune idée des conditions d'esclavage ni de la violence brutale qui les attendaient au bout de leur voyage en mer.

C'est un fait bien documenté qu'il y a des liens historiques entre l'Australie et la Nouvelle-Calédonie qui partagent une histoire du travail similaire, mais il est moins bien connu qu'il existe des liens entre l'Australie et l'histoire des Chân Đăng. Comme l'a révélé Rhook (2017), l'arrivée à Townsville en 1927 du bateau français, *Ville d'Amiens,* qui transportait des 'coolies' vietnamiens dans des conditions épouvantables a provoqué le dégoût et l'indignation en Australie face à la cruauté 'des Français'. Or, les Australiens oubliaient un peu vite le rôle similaire joué par leur pays pendant cette période de l'histoire. Encore aujourd'hui il y a peu de reconnaissance du fait que l'engagement des habitants des îles du Pacifique fut exécuté de manière malhonnête, bien que quelque 2 500 d'entre eux soient restés dans le pays après la déportation de la majorité (Higginbotham 2017). En outre, en Australie les vieilles craintes du 'Péril Jaune', et la menace perçue de la propagation du communisme dans la région, furent exacerbées par la forte présence de travailleurs sous contrat indochinois dans la région du Pacifique au lendemain de la Deuxième Guerre Mondiale. Selon Mohamed-Gaillard (2010), dès 1946 le Consul australien en Nouvelle-Calédonie les considérait comme une source potentielle de troubles, à cause de leur volonté résolue d'obtenir une meilleure rémunération et des conditions de travail correctes, ce qui prit la forme de disputes violentes et de grèves. Par ailleurs, la presse australienne signala que la nouvelle de la défaite de la France par les forces révolutionnaires vietnamiennes à Điện Biên Phủ en mai 1954 donna lieu à des scènes de jubilation parmi certains travailleurs vietnamiens dans les Nouvelles-Hébrides, en particulier dans le Condominium anglo-français de Santo où étaient concentrés ces travailleurs. Ainsi, le souci que cette région pourrait devenir un autre champ de bataille indochinois entraîna une attitude hostile envers la communauté vietnamienne dans ces îles du Pacifique.

Pour conclure, s'il est clair que cette description de l'histoire des Chân Đăng en Nouvelle-Calédonie par Jean Vanmai nous donne un rare aperçu de l'expérience des engagés vietnamiens en Nouvelle-Calédonie et au Vanuatu, elle nous rappelle de plus que cela ne fait pas si longtemps que l'Australie était aussi impliquée dans des pratiques similaires. Pour cette raison, ce récit, qui révèle les complexités et personnelles et émotionnelles de l'expérience des travailleurs sous contrat et leurs descendants, est d'une grande pertinence pour les lecteurs australiens, et d'une importance intellectuelle et éthique capitale pour les chercheurs intéressés par les histoires qui relient l'Australie et le Pacifique. Cependant, l'importance du livre dépasse l'histoire entre ces deux régions, en faisant en sorte que, pour la première fois, les voix des engagés vietnamiens sous contrat soient entendues. Cette traduction en anglais, ainsi que l'introduction critique qui la contextualise donnent donc au texte d'origine toute son importance pour le lectorat anglophone, qu'il soit en Australasie, au Pacifique ou au-delà.

Tess Do and Kathryn Lay-Chenchabi

[1] Écrit en italique *Chân Đăng* fait référence au roman et en caractères romains les travailleurs tonkinois sous contrat.

[2] Le Tonkin fut un protectorat français qui englobe aujourd'hui le Nord du Vietnam. Avec quatre autres territoires dont l'Annam, la Cochinchine, le Laos, le Cambodge, il faisait partie de l'Indochine française (1887-1954).

[3] Jean Vanmai fut le deuxième écrivain d'origine vietnamienne à être couronné par l'*Association des Écrivains de Langue Française* depuis la création du Prix en 1971. Le premier lauréat fut Nguyễn Văn Phong en 1972 et la dernière lauréate à ce jour fut Hoài Hương Nguyễn en 2013.

[4] Selon les données du recensement de l'INSEE en 2014, les Vietnamiens constituaient 0, 93% (2 499 personnes) de la population totale de la Nouvelle-Calédonie (268 767 habitants).

[5] Voir Selao (2011).

[6] Voir Britto (2004) ; Trouilloud (2006) ; Nguyễn (2003).

[7] Le nom 'Chân Đăng' est seulement utilisé en référence aux travailleurs tonkinois sous contrat. Leurs descendants, particulièrement ceux qui sont nés en Nouvelle-Calédonie ou aux Nouvelles-Hébrides, sont appelés 'niaoulis', un nom qu'ils partagent avec les descendants des travailleurs javanais. Deux explications existent pour ce terme : la première se réfère à la manière dont les mères javanaises se servaient de leur sarong pour envelopper et suspendre leurs nourrissons aux branches du niaouli, un grand arbre emblématique de la famille des myrtes, afin de les protéger contre les animaux ou insectes et de les surveiller pendant qu'elles travaillaient dans les champs. La deuxième explication s'appuie sur la comparaison entre la résilience des Javanais et la solidité du niaouli. Voir Maurer (2002) ; Bouan (2003).

[8] Jean Vanmai a trois frères et cinq sœurs.

[9] Les parents de Vanmai ont travaillé à la mine de chrome Chagrin qui appartenait à la grande famille de Jacques Lafleur, leader du *Rassemblement pour la Calédonie dans la République*, l'un des deux partis anti-indépendantistes en Nouvelle-Calédonie. Lafleur fut le signataire des Accords de Matignon en 1988 et des Accords de Nouméa en 1998.

[10] Un auditeur, en écoutant l'entretien de Jean Vanmai avec Michel Voisin (2012), s'est rappelé qu'au moment où le bateau quittait le port, des gens ont sauté à l'eau pour rejoindre l'île Nou à la nage.

[11] Cet incident explique peut-être pourquoi il y avait deux statistiques différentes concernant le nombre de rapatriés du premier voyage : 550 passagers selon Vanmai dans le *Centenaire de la présence vietnamienne en*

Nouvelle-Calédonie (1991 : 79) et 551 selon Mohamed-Gaillard (2010 : 207). Le passager qui manquait ne fut autre que Vanmai lui-même.

[12] Communication envoyée au courriel privé de Tess Do (2 juillet 2021).

[13] La transcription de l'interview intitulée 'La vie des engagés vietnamiens d'autrefois' transmise le 12 april 2016 dans l'émission 'Terre d'histoire(s) et de partage(s)', Numéro 53, a été fournie par Jean Vanmai. Dans un entretien accordé auparavant à Michel Voisin pour l'émission radiophonique 'Nouvelle-Calédonie La Première', le 29 septembre 2012, Vanmai avait aussi mentionné cet incident.

[14] Parmi ces inexactitudes géographiques, on peut citer l'exemple de la localisation du logement où étaient envoyés les engagés dès leur arrivée en Nouvelle-Calédonie. Dans le roman de Vanmai, ce logement se situe sur l'île Nou, mais en réalité, les travailleurs furent d'abord placés en quarantaine sur l'île Freycinet, puis transférés au Dépôt de l'Orphelinat où leurs employeurs venaient les chercher. Voir Angleviel (2000) ; Boyer (1996) ; Merle (1995).

[15] Communication envoyée au courriel privé de Tess Do (17 janvier 2019).

[16] Selon Vanmai, *Chân Đăng* a été tiré à 3 000 exemplaires vendus lors de sa sortie en 1980 (dans un pays d'une population de 200 000 d'habitants) et à 1 000 exemplaires lors de son retirage en 1993. Le roman est aujourd'hui épuisé.

[17] C'est nous qui soulignons.

[18] C'est nous qui soulignons.

[19] Selon une source anonyme datant de 1882, le commissariat d'immigration gardait derrière sa porte un martinet qu'il utilisait sur les fortes têtes des Nouvelles-Hébrides qu'on lui amenait. (Angleviel 2000 : 71).

[20] L'article 15 du contrat de l'engagé stipule que les familles ne peuvent, en aucun cas, être séparées. (Angleviel 2000 : 74).

[21] Il parait que cette forme de punition cruelle existait aussi en Nouvelle-Calédonie. Une Française de la petite ville de Témala se souvient de la manière dont son voisin, un colon français, punissait ses employés javanais. Il les forçait à se déshabiller avant de les mettre à genoux sur une fourmilière les mains sur la tête. Voir Merle (1995 : 396).

[22] Un volume basé sur ce colloque fut publié dans *Portal of Multidisciplinary International Studies.* Voir Kurmann and Do (2018).

[23] Une version anglaise de l'extrait a été fournie au public.

[24] Selon Jean Vanmai, la chaîne de télévision vietnamienne HTV7 à Hồ Chí Minh Ville l'a contacté en 2007 pour collaborer à un projet de production d'une série télévisée de 30 épisodes sur les Chân Đăng. Or, il a dû refuser leur offre de peur que dans un projet de cette ampleur, l'adaptation pour la télévision des scènes de mauvais traitement se retourne contre les Chân Đăng et leurs descendants, ainsi que contre la Nouvelle-Calédonie et son peuple. Voir le document Web de Vanmai (n.d.).

[25] Voir Từ Bốn Phương Trời (2013); Voice of America (2016); Bà Bán Phở Channel (2018).

[26] Cette série contient à ce jour ces volumes: *Quitter Saigon* (2013), *Little Saigon* (2012), *Les mariées de Taiwan* (2017) et *Les engagés de Nouvelle-Calédonie* (2020).

[27] Pour certaines engagées tonkinoises, des jeunes filles âgées d'une vingtaine d'années ou moins, la décision de quitter leur famille et leur village pour aller travailler dans un pays lointain inconnu où elles ne parlaient pas la langue, fut motivée par le désir d'échapper à un mariage non-voulu arrangé par leurs parents. Donc, trouver l'amour en Nouvelle-Calédonie serait un bon résultat pour elles. Vanmai donne quelques exemples de ces couples heureux, tels que Minh et Lan, Hiếu et Thế.

Jean Vanmai's
CHÂN ĐĂNG
The Tonkinese of Caledonia in the Colonial Era

The Arrival

Lan, pale and thin, held on to the ship's rail with her shaking hands to stop herself losing her balance. Her head spun dizzily as soon as she tried to take even a tiny step; her legs felt wobbly and could barely support her slight body any longer. And yet the boat was anchored, immobile, in front of the isle of hope, her immense hope.

Lan, so frail and young, had crossed the Pacific Ocean, fleeing the hardship of her miserable life as a peasant farmer. She was alone on board, without family or relations amongst the hundreds like herself, her compatriots, all dressed in the same way, in trousers and the brown jacket of a Tonkinese "nhà quê."[1]

"What a terrible journey!" she murmured, her face tense at the thought of the bad memories of the long crossing. "Now I have to get off this ship . . . we're here."

She gathered her strength, tried to step forward, but had to grip the rail again to hold herself up.

"I can't. I'll never be able to—willpower alone is not enough to get me there," she said to herself, as she looked anxiously down at the dizzying descent of the gangplank to the flat surface of the water.

Meanwhile, a constant stream of the ship's passengers, silent and grave, was making its way along the only exit off the ship, a gangplank which swayed slightly under their feet, the strongest amongst them supporting the sick in order to reach the barges waiting for them far below.

"I feel like I'm going to fall flat on my face," thought Lan, unable to take her terrified eyes off the unsteady ladder.

Two young men, who had been lucky enough to have escaped seasickness, were walking towards the young girl.

"Come with us, miss. We'll help you." Without waiting for her answer, they grabbed her arm and pulled her along. At the top of the ladder, Lan's feet hesitated for a moment, she closed her eyes and let herself be carried along by the strong arms which held her tightly. When she opened her eyes again, she was already on a barge. Lan thanked her saviours with a broad smile.

"Hold on to me if you're too tired," suggested the taller of the two young men.

"The barges are overcrowded now. We'll soon be on dry land," said the second.

"This young man, with his direct gaze and distinguished manner, seems really out of place in his peasant's garb," thought Lan as she admired the emerald colour of the water below the tug which, using long ropes, was pulling the barges filled with their human cargo.

"My name's Minh," said the young man. "We don't know each other yet, but I hope we'll become good friends!"

"I hope so too. I'm Lan."

"My name's Toán," said Minh's companion. "Let's try to keep together from now on," he added without raising his head, his gaze lost in the silver wake of the tug.

"We're heading for the island opposite the port. We don't get off at Nouméa," remarked Minh, frowning slightly. "What a pity, the town looks beautiful, nestled against the slopes of the hills." His eyes carefully scanned the port, where a motley crowd was bustling around warehouses with gaping entrances, the better to swallow up the cargo taken off ships coming from all corners of the world, but mainly from France. Wagons painted bright yellow, overloaded with boxes and barrels, pulled by powerful horses, were leaving the port and heading for the centre of town. Through the gaps between the buildings in the port, Minh could make out wooden houses with shady verandas like the houses of the American Far West that he had seen in picture books. Raising his head, Minh was struck by the rugged relief of the mountains in the distance, eerily carved out against the luminous sky.

One by one, the barges berthed at the jetty of the island. A moment later Lan was able to touch the solid ground—nothing could be more precious to her. She closed her eyes, a slight smile on her lips which were chapped by fatigue and entire days spent without the tiniest morsel of food.

"At last! At last, land," she murmured happily. "Such a dreadful two-week sea voyage is really too much for a daughter of rice farmers like me."

But, alas, her satisfaction only lasted a brief instant as, exhausted, she was once again overcome by seasickness and had to sit down on the ground. Giving in to the call of her exhausted body, Lan stretched out on the soft grass at the edge of the path.

The image of her father, then of her mother, appeared all of a sudden in her mind and her face darkened immediately.

"My beloved parents," she murmured. "Can they really imagine how far away I am at the moment?" She remained pensive, her face tense.

"Just one more effort, I beg of you, Lan. When we get to our camp you'll be able to rest as much as you want." Minh was leaning over her, holding out his hand to help her up. He grabbed hold of the young girl's things and they followed the human column, made up of men and women who were heading for the buildings that could already be seen near the rounded shapes of the hills ahead. The sharp stones of the path cut into their bare feet which were more used to wading in the mud of rice fields.

Gathering her strength, Lan tried to keep moving forward at an even pace so that she wouldn't hold up her companion. Escorted by hard-faced guards wearing pith helmets to protect them from the heat of the sun, the column stretched along the winding track. Once in front of the administrative buildings, they had to show their identity papers to the authorities at the official immigration checkpoint. The sun was beating down harder and harder, and, after registering at the reception centre, Lan and the other young women assembled in the courtyard hurriedly put on their conical hats.

At the stroke of noon, a bell rang and their very first meal in this new land was brought to them. Then, each of them had to go up with the bowl they had received on the day of departure. Lan hastened to open her bundle, which consisted of a mat wrapped around her entire fortune: two spare trousers and two spare jackets, a comb, her identity papers and a few piastres which she had been given as a bonus when she was hired in Hải-Phòng.

Trembling, she said, "I've lost my bowl, my bowl! Maybe I lost it when we disembarked this morning, or did I leave it on the ship?"

"How will I get my food ration? I'll need it if I want to recover my strength quickly enough," she thought anxiously.

Minh, who was standing near the young girl, could see what was going on.

"Don't worry," he said, "I'll work something out. Why don't you give me your hat?"

Without really understanding, Lan took off her hat and gave it to him.

"Stay here quietly and wait for me to get back," Minh said, getting up. He made his way towards the kitchen table at the end of the courtyard, holding in one hand a bowl and in the other the young girl's hat. A few moments later, Minh and Lan met in the shade of a veranda.

That day Minh had lunch from one of the biggest bowls on earth, Lan's upturned hat. After the meal, the camp manager, Monsieur Bordos, showed them, through an interpreter, the dormitories which were set up around the central courtyard.

"Come with us, Lan. Let's stay together in a group. It'll be much better," suggested a young couple she'd shared a cabin with for a few hours during the crossing. Lan looked over to Minh and Toán, inviting them to join the group.

"I don't see why not," replied Minh. "Let's go."

"I've had a look around," said Toán, "The building with the most ventilation is the one at the back, over there on the eastern side. It's the farthest away."

"We trust you. My name's Thắng and this is Liên, my fiancée. Let's head for the building on the eastern side!"

The small group rushed over to the dormitory. It was a huge room, bare of any furniture, with no ceiling and stiflingly hot inside because of the corrugated iron roof. Fortunately, from time to time, a slight breeze brought a bit of relief from the heat. They put their mats on the ground, as close as possible to the doorways, to stake out their spot. Then, as there was nothing else to do but try to recover a little, they fell asleep next to each other, only waking up at the end of the afternoon. When they woke, they were surprised to discover that the floor of the dormitory was completely covered in mats on which many young people were sleeping, while others outside chatted peacefully under the big veranda.

The sound of a bell rang out from the centre of the courtyard, calling them all to assemble there once again. The head of the immigration service wanted to come and see them in person. Through the interpreter he announced, "Welcome to New Caledonia. You are now in quarantine and you will have to have medical checks and compulsory vaccinations in accordance with the regulations of the colony. Your employers will come to fetch you within a week or ten days. In the meantime, as you have nothing much to do, we will hand out food and cooking utensils. Get yourselves into groups. It will make our work easier if you do your own cooking. Organise yourselves as you wish and, if you respect the rules, everything will run more smoothly."

The small community received this news with great satisfaction. Lan, astonished at the size of the enormous, three-legged cooking pots, set about learning how to use them, while Liên planned a delicious meal for them and the men chopped wood for the fire.

Note

[1] Nhà quê means "Vietnamese peasant."

Memories of the Crossing

In the evening, human clusters formed around the fires in front of each building. Liên and Thắng laughed at the way Minh fed himself with his giant bowl. Indeed, they laughed often, happy as they were to be together, carefree, and madly in love.

The night was hot and uncomfortable. Lying so close to each other, they let their minds wander freely to thoughts and memories of their past. Lan noticed with great apprehension that there were more men than women. So far there had not been any problems, at least as far as she knew. During the crossing, the young people who had never known anything but the rice fields of their native land, had almost all got seasick.

In the dark of night, she had a clear picture in her mind of the ship sailing steadfastly away from the beloved country where she was born. She could see the port of Hải-Phòng disappearing gradually, leaving behind a dark line, the coast of Tonkin which, in turn, vanished from sight. She remembered, too, the vast ocean that had rocked the boat, battering it with giant waves during the first days when the seas were rough. During the crossing, Lan had her spot in one of the ship's holds which was being used as a dormitory, a horrendous dormitory, filled with confident young men and women, determined to accept any type of work, even the most unpleasant or difficult, so that one day they could go back home rich and powerful.

But their ambition waned with the passing of the days on the boat. The sea made them sicker and sicker. There was not enough air for all these people who were pinned to their mats. The heat became unbearably stifling, and the weakest vomited their food up onto the floor. The smell sickened even the most resilient. The worst-affected got so weak that they were unable to get up and had to urinate in their bedding. But the fear of losing their strength completely made them swallow a few balls of rice which, unfortunately, they brought up straight away as their stomachs refused any food at all.

Lan too felt overcome by seasickness but, driven by an iron will, she gathered all her strength, rolled up her mat and the few things she had and crawled towards the ladder. Her head spun at the slightest movement of her body, and her stomach, having emptied itself of its contents long before, rumbled agonisingly.

Fresh air could no longer get into the hold as it was immediately diluted and pushed away by the sickening smell. Lan almost fainted from her efforts. A much stronger breeze rushed in at that moment through the opening just above the ladder, entering her lungs like an electric shock, spurring her on. She made the most of this moment of clear-headedness and climbed up a few steps leading to the exit, but her temples ached and her head spun. She closed her eyes. When she got to the last rung she stopped, unable to go a step farther and almost let go. A sailor who was passing by saw her just in time and managed to pull her up onto the bridge. The smell coming from the hold reached his nostrils and the man grimaced in disgust, leaving hurriedly to get on with his work.

The fresh air whipped Lan's face, filling her lungs, and her body gradually came back to life. Feeling revived, she sheltered under a tarpaulin. She did not go back down to the dormitories again.

Thắng and Liên, who had shared her cabin, often came to visit her under her tarpaulin shelter. They would remain still and silent for hours on end because Thắng and Liên were happy, while Lan would often think of the beloved parents she had abandoned back home in her village. The image of her two young brothers crying desperately the day she left distressed her even more.

Lan got up, then moved towards the ship's railing to gaze at the sea swirling below her. From time to time, a small flying fish emerged on the surface of the water, propelling itself over a short distance like a silver arrow, before disappearing again into the depths of the ocean. But Lan was too weak. Her legs felt like jelly and she had to go back to her spot. With her head on her knees she began to wonder if, in the end, she had been right to venture away on her own, at the age of twenty, so far from her country and her loved ones.

"It's much too early to have regrets," she said to herself. Sometimes, Liên's loud laughter comforted her. Indeed, Liên had no regrets at all. She could only praise the heavens for guiding her on the wonderful pathway to love. In Hải-Phòng, just before their departure she had met Thắng at the recruitment office. From that moment, nothing else existed for them; they were in love and happy.

Liên felt the cold in her bones and couldn't get to sleep on the bridge. And she was frightened of the noise of the sea which sounded even louder in the dark of night. So, at nightfall, Liên and Thắng went down to their dormitory, amongst the sick and the suffocating odours.

"How can they love each other, spending entire nights in such nauseating conditions?" Lan wondered, shuddering. "Love is indeed blind and . . . oblivious too."

She pinched her nostrils closed, then immediately tried to take her mind off these unwelcome thoughts.

Minh, who was staying in one of the holds at the back of the ship, was astonished to find that neither the sea, nor the smells bothered him. He spent most of his time looking after his fellow travellers to avoid remaining idle. His regular features and frank manner reassured them. He spoke little, devoting himself to the task tirelessly all day, his movements as precise and caring as those of an experienced nurse. At times in the evening, he was especially silent, staring into the distance and, at these moments, his face became grave and mysterious, as if he was meditating deeply.

"Don't sit there like that. Come with me. Let's go and look at the stars," Toán would often say.

"You're right. I'll come with you, Toán!"

And Minh would put on a smile, although he was not able to completely remove the small frown from his worried brow and would follow his friend. Thus, the two friends walked every night on the bridge. Often, they slept under the stars, and at these times, Toán had a big advantage over Minh—once he was in a horizontal position, he fell asleep immediately.

And yet Toán, too, suffered on this boat, but in his own way. Having lived a large part of his life on the rivers of Tonkin on sampans of all sizes, he had no problems with the sea. But his misfortune on the ship now was that he found only people who were either sick or weakened, unable to gamble. He could gamble night after night, at any game, as long as there was money to be won! Even so, he was a charming little man, a little surly perhaps, but very obliging. One evening, as they were taking a walk on the rear deck, he suddenly asked his friend, "Why are you on this boat? Why did you sign up?"

"To be free," answered Minh, slightly irritated.

"You don't act like a farmer. I've been watching you, you know."

"You've worked things out," said Minh with a slight smile on his lips. "Actually, my parents have a small shop in Hà-Nội and . . . I'm the only child."

"So, what are you doing here, you wretch?" cried Toán in astonishment.

"My father wanted me to marry, as is the custom, the daughter of one of his friends. The engagement had been made between the two families when I was only four years old. The young girl's now eighteen and corresponds perfectly to my parents' ideal of beauty: she's strong, plump, you could even say squat—perfect for carrying heavy loads, apparently. She works tirelessly from morning until night and never says anything wrong, since she only knows one thing—how to obey. I can't imagine having a single interesting conversation with her; she wouldn't know how to respond. You know, Toán, for me, total happiness is. . . remaining single for ever!"

"Wasn't there anything else you could do?" asked Toán, intrigued.

"No, it wasn't possible. Just a few hours before the boat set sail, I wrote a letter to my parents to tell them I was leaving and why. I didn't have a choice: if I stayed in Hà-Nội, in the country, I'd have to respect the promise my parents had made."

Minh remained still for a moment and then said, "What about you? Why did you leave?"

"I happened to meet a traveller who was returning from Nouméa, I think it's the capital city of the island. He returned to his village, almost a year ago now, a wealthy man. Apparently, it's a real paradise in New Caledonia. That's what gave me the courage to leave behind my wife and two children, a beautiful boy of seven and a little girl aged two."

Then he said, softly, "I've signed up for five years. It's not too long, five years," he added, as if to convince himself. "And when I go home, I'll buy sampans, a fleet of sampans, and set up a river transport business."

His face was shining.

"Your optimism's comforting," murmured Minh. "I don't really know what I'm doing or where I'm headed at the moment."

"Let's sleep," said Toán, "rest calms the mind."

And he lay down on the bridge. Minh hardly had time to look at the stars before he heard the loud, regular snoring.

Life on the Island

The whole community recovered their strength and energy after a few days of rest on Nou Island. Minh observed this idle group, waiting somewhat apprehensively for the day they would meet their employers. They had endured, in the meanwhile, the regulatory vaccinations and medical checks. The officials found their names too long and complicated, for example, Nguyễn Văn Khảo or Trần Trọng Vạt, and so graced each one of them with a registration number.

Toán had broken out into a cold sweat when an official questioned the validity of his identity papers.

"Phạm Văn Toán!" said the man, "You seem a lot older than what's on these papers, twenty-six. I'd say you're more like thirty-three or thirty-five years old."

Toán had managed to remain calm and convince the interpreter, after long and exhausting explanations, to act in his favour. When everything was settled and he could finally go back to his dormitory, he collapsed onto his mat among his friends who were now very worried for him.

"I'm thirty-six," he confided to them. "I was too old to join, so I had to buy a false identity card in Hải-Phòng. It cost me a fortune."

Minh shook his head, saying, "You're a real character, really smart. You'll manage, I'm sure of it!"

That afternoon the wind forgot to blow its refreshing little breeze. A torrid heat settled over the island, and, without ceilings, the buildings became real ovens, forcing the inhabitants to seek refuge on the verandas or under the flamboyant trees whose leaves spread over a part of the courtyard like huge parasols. Lying under one of these trees, Minh could see some young people, bolder than the others, venturing out of the camp, drawn by the temptation of the cool water of the sea. When they got to the small beach strewn with dead coral which formed a thick, dazzling white carpet in the sun, Yến, the youngest boy in the gang, hesitated briefly, then, unable to wait any longer, jumped into the water. A smile of satisfaction lit up his boyish face.

"He must be sixteen or seventeen at the most," thought Minh without taking his eyes off him. "He can't be twenty, which was the minimum age to be hired. Another one who managed to register with false papers."

Meanwhile, the young man jumped happily through the water, waving to his friends on the beach to come and join him. The water came up to his hips. He kept going deeper, and then, when a fresh wave reached his chest, he dived suddenly to cool down his young body. But he did not reappear. One of his hands emerged from the water, flailed around wildly, then disappeared immediately. A few seconds later his head emerged suddenly, and he let out an unintelligible shriek.

Minh, still lying in the shade of the flamboyant, noticed that Yến's eyes were convulsing. With a sinking feeling he rushed towards the beach as fast as he could. The boy appeared once more, letting out a desperate scream. Then his head went under as he swallowed a large amount of salty water through his nose and mouth. His friends remained petrified on the beach, not knowing what to do, then suddenly they began to yell out together, completely panic-stricken, "Help! Yến's drowning. We can't swim. Do something."

Once he got to where the unfortunate boy's companions were standing, Minh grabbed a stick that was lying on the carpet of coral. Bravely, he entered the water, watching closely to try to make out the potential enemy moving around under the water. Minh immediately felt the mud under his bare feet. Nevertheless, he continued as quickly as he could towards the poor boy who was desperately gasping for air whenever he could get his head out of the water. Minh was terrified, but he had decided to save the child's life, even if it meant risking his own. Finally, he reached Yến, who was now surrounded by a reddish liquid.

"It's blood!" he yelled, his eyes wild with fear.

With one hand, Minh grabbed the shirt of the wounded boy and pulled him back towards the beach, keeping his head out of the water all the while. He swam backwards as fast as he could. With the other hand he held the stick firmly, ready to defend himself. When they were out of danger, Minh lifted the injured boy and realised that he was losing a lot of blood from a deep wound, the width of a finger, on the top of his left foot, near his toes.

At that moment the guards from the camp arrived, distraught.

"Watch out!" they cried, "This place is infested with sharks." Minh looked over at the small puddle of blood that they'd just left behind them. Black, sinister fins appeared on the scene.

"Sharks! Sharks!" he heard shouting all around him. One of the guards, a giant with ebony skin and dazzling white teeth, came to help Minh get the wounded boy out of the sea. They put him down on the beach. Bordos, the camp manager, put a tourniquet on the wound to stop the flow of blood before transporting the boy to the island clinic.

The black guard explained, "The boy must have disturbed a stingray that was resting under the mud. It must have thought it was in danger, so to defend itself it stung the boy in the foot with the venomous spinal blade beneath its tail."

The nurse came along to inspect the wound and said, "It's spectacular, but there's no cause for concern. He'll have to wear shoes or boots to avoid infection. Fortunately, the sting was just between the two metatarsal bones. Nothing's broken. He'll recover quickly!"

On the way back, Minh realised that his stick would have been useless against any enemy under the water. He was a little scared at the thought.

"Well, it gave me the courage to go and help young Yến. Without the stick, I would've felt completely exposed and vulnerable, and I may not've dared to rush to his aid without a second thought."

Bordos gave a severe warning to the foolish young people, but also to Minh. "You left the camp without my authorisation; that could cost you a lot. I'm warning you, if there's another escapade you'll spend the rest of your stay here in prison. And you," he said, looking sternly at Minh, "I should put you under arrest immediately for your irresponsible action."

"But sir, I went to the aid of this child without hesitation. If I hadn't intervened, he would either have drowned or been eaten by sharks," protested Minh in impeccable French, which surprised everybody, including the interpreter.

Embarrassed by this logic, Bordos turned scarlet.

"First of all, you will not answer without permission. Second, the rules are the rules. You left the camp and you risked your life to save this poor kid. Imagine if you hadn't been successful and the sharks had come when you were out there. I would've had two deaths on my conscience plus all the problems that could cause. Don't forget that I'm also accountable."

Minh was furious. "It's incredible," he thought. "This man has gone mad. Perhaps he would've preferred me to let the kid be devoured by sharks. Or maybe he doesn't know what he's saying."

Minh went pale. He was about to give a sharp response to Bordos and tell him what he thought of his peculiar attitude when he felt a small hand grab his and drag him back, gently, as if to say, "Calm down, Minh! Don't lose your temper."

Minh realised that Lan was behind him, with him. She murmured in his ear, "He's the boss, Minh! Whatever he may do or say, don't forget that he'll always be right. It's pointless to waste your time on sterile discussions. Consider the incident over, Minh. This man's capable of anything. If he wanted to, he could give you a disastrous report and you would have all sorts of problems, including getting the worst jobs with your future employer."

Minh remained still as he considered this advice. With anger in his heart, he lowered his head. Without a word he and the young girl moved away.

"I can't stand men who are full of their sense of power," he said once they were alone. "Deep down, this man's pleased that I was able to save Yến. Otherwise, he would've had a lot of problems, given he's the boss. But his pride won't allow him to acknowledge it."

"And this way he doesn't need to thank you," added Lan. "Actually, we should pity him rather than criticise him. There are people like this man, and a lot more than we think, who always have to have the last word, even when they're wrong!"

***

The sound of the cathedral bells ringing out over the sky of Nouméa reached the island, transported by the ocean breezes. Toán retired to his dormitory, kneeled down on his mat and began to pray in silence. The sun's rays were so harsh, on this first Sunday after Easter in 1939, that the town opposite them, Nouméa, the capital of the colony, was completely drowned in a mist which was like a thick bluish fog.

Despite his morning prayers, Toán was the most disappointed and dissatisfied of them all at the end of the day, even though he had managed, with much gusto, to organise a card game, a game using curious little cards with Chinese characters. But misfortune had pursued him all day long and, at sunset, all that was left were regrets and bitterness.

"Being beaten like a beginner. It's really too much. I've never lost like this before," he grumbled. Then, thinking it over for a few seconds he said to Minh, "You see, all this has happened because I'm out of practice. I'm going to have to get back all the money I've lost!"

He added, feeling both worried and a little embarrassed, "But I don't have a cent to my name. I've lost everything."

"Don't worry Toán, I'll lend you the money, but not today. Another day, maybe tomorrow," said Minh to reassure his friend.

Immediately, Toán felt happy again, confident he would win. That evening, as was his habit, he stretched out on his mat and fell peacefully into a deep sleep.

***

Cocooned in their intense happiness, Liên and Thắng liked to be alone, away from the crowds of people. More than three hundred had been temporarily brought onto the island. The young couple, unbeknownst to the others, often came to admire the magnificent garden surrounding Bordos' house. They were in awe of this tropical paradise. At the entrance was a hedge of crotons with their beautiful rainbow-coloured leaves. On the right, a bougainvillea hung from the top branches of the trees showing off its brilliant jewels which fell to the ground in purple bunches, sprinkled with tiny white dots. At the end of the courtyard, near the outbuildings, the perfumed honeysuckle grew all over the trellis, covering it with its many delicate tendrils and filling the air with its sweet fragrance. The terrace was bordered with canna lilies, yellow and scarlet, speckled with vermilion. Above their heads, the coconut palms, moving in the wind, reflected the bright dappled sunlight. They were in rapture.

"Oh, how I'd love to have such a wonderful place one day, a house with a little paradise like this," exclaimed Liên. Then she turned to Thắng and said, "We'll have a house like this, won't we?"

"Yes, Liên. As soon as we have work, we'll ask the boss to get us the papers we need to get married, as soon as possible."

"Are you really in such a hurry?" she asked, laughing.

"Oh yes, Liên. I'm in a hurry. Maybe because I'm madly in love with you, but also because of all these men here with us. They're all so young and I've noticed that there are five times more men than women. So that means that four men out of five will remain single on the island and, as I'm realistic and . . . very jealous, I wouldn't want any other boys to come and try to court you. Just thinking about it makes me sick. You understand, don't you?"

"You have nothing to fear Thắng. You know that I love you, that you are my first and only love. For the first time in my life, I'm happy. And I'll do anything to make you satisfied with your little woman. Yes, let's get married, as soon as possible!"

Her voice was shaking with emotion and her sincerity unsettled the young man. They remained still and silent, their faces shining with ineffable joy.

The dark night isolated them from the rest of the world, their only witnesses the stars.

Separations

Quarantine finished on the morning of the tenth day. Most of the young people were declared fit to work, although a few of the sick had to stay in the camp until they had recovered completely. They were called into the main courtyard with their personal belongings. Their faces showed some apprehension, as it was now that the serious work was beginning. Nevertheless, they were determined. The representatives of different contractors were there. Immobile under their pith helmets, they looked them up and down, these barefoot "nhà quê."

"I need fifty workers," said one of the men.

The immigration authorities followed the order promptly, respecting the rules of hiring one woman for every five men. Minh was shocked that their names weren't being used any more. They were called up only by their registration numbers.

"From now on, like everyone else, I won't have a name anymore, just a number," he murmured sadly. Suddenly he remembered his father's shop, his simple life in Hà-Nội, with its wide streets shaded by large trees all along the pavements.

"What have I rushed into?" Mechanically, he took out his immigration papers and saw that he had the number 3141.

"What's your number, Lan?"

"Mine's 3140," said Toán.

"I have number 3142," replied Lan.

To their astonishment, Toán was the only one taken on by the first employer. They were dismayed.

"My God!" cried Toán, looking distraught, "I'm in this group without you. No! Minh, you speak French—talk to these people so that I can stay with you. I beg of you!"

Alas, the immigration official remained intractable, and Minh's efforts were useless.

"There will be no favouritism. I'm applying the rules of one woman to five men and there is no exception. Number 3140 will go with his employer. I'm sorry for you and your friend, but I'm following the rules!" repeated the man unwaveringly.

Toán had to leave, a lump in his throat, without a word, for his pain was too great to express. He glanced for the last time at his friends before walking away, towards his new destiny.

Lan's eyes were full of tears, "I hope I'll see him again, he's a good man," she murmured, "but will we ever see him again?"

She paled suddenly. With the back of her hand she wiped away her tears and then, nervously, she took Minh's arm before whispering in his ear, "I'm afraid Minh . . . afraid of being separated from you. I don't know why," she continued, without any embarrassment, "but I feel safe with you."

"I hope so too, Lan. I hope so with all my might. We've become great friends and it would be terrible if these people separated us. Look at me, I'm just as nervous as you."

Liên and Thắng were extremely worried. As they weren't legally married yet, they could be separated for ever. Thắng had gone white with fear. He grabbed Liên's hand and squeezed it tightly in his, as if this simple gesture would make them inseparable. The young girl was quite pale, her throat was dry and, shaking, she gazed silently at the man she already considered to be her husband, for ever. After an interminable, unbearable lapse of time, the man announced the numbers for the second group.

Minh was relieved to hear his, Lan's and then Liên's number.

"Just Thắng now and the four of us will be together—that'd be wonderful!" said Lan.

"Yes, but without Toán," said Minh, pensively.

"My God, I hope Thắng will be on our team," mumbled a frightened Liên anxiously.

The official had just finished reading his list. Thắng was not on it.

"No! No!" cried Liên frantically, "No, I want to be with my husband!" she screamed, clinging to Thắng as tightly as she could.

Thắng was in a daze, unable to make the slightest movement, so great was his dismay. He stayed like that for a moment without a word. Liên understood suddenly how unhappy she was and despaired of ever having any joy in her life again. She felt unwell and her legs crumpled under her. Minh managed to catch her just in time. He rushed towards the official.

"Sir," he said, "please excuse me for insisting, but please be indulgent, be a good man. Allow this young couple to be together. Look how they're suffering. They need each other. Help them, please!"

The man remained unfazed.

"They aren't married. According to the rules, I can do nothing for them, and I would ask you to mind your own business, or else you'll be in trouble yourself. Do you understand?"

Minh was outraged at the official's attitude. He felt like hitting him, whatever the consequences. But at a sign from the man, two guards seized Minh immediately by the arm and dragged him behind them, towards the official from his new company, who was heading for the pontoon. A boat awaited them.

Lan and the small group of about sixty followed them. Liên had refused to leave, but her resistance, alas, was short-lived. She fought off one of the guards but, despite her tears, she too was taken away.

Young Yến, having recovered from his wounds, with the help of his friends tried to hold back the furious Thắng, to stop him from doing something stupid. Any act of revolt would be severely punished, and Yến knew it. They all knew it.

The small boat sailed away from the island with its passengers; some were crying, others looked glum. They crossed the bay, then tied up next to a coastal vessel moored in the port. Minh and Lan helped the devastated Liên onto the vessel's oily deck which was cluttered with ropes and all sorts of goods.

The boat sailed away from the dock early in the afternoon. The air was humid, stifling. The sky suddenly turned grey, like the souls of those leaving for a mysterious unknown destination. The sea was calm, smooth as a mirror. Lan could see her reflection gliding along on the water, at the same speed as the boat.

They had just sailed across the small bay. The island of Nou was to starboard.

"That's the island where we spent so many enjoyable and relatively carefree days. Are they to be our last days of peace and quiet?" wondered Minh, very worried now.

He had a premonition that everything would get more and more difficult and uncertain.

"Ah! There's the little beach where Yến almost drowned."

He gaped, his eyes wide open. "Sharks! It's infested with sharks here! The guard was certainly right about that."

Flabbergasted, Minh watched in dismay the black fins swimming about a hundred metres from the beach, like dangerous guards jealously protecting their underground territory. The coastal vessel continued on its course in the lagoon where the jade-coloured water dazzled even those who were the most accustomed to seeing it—the crew.

"Oh, look Minh," said Lan, leaning over the rail and pointing to the bottom of the sea. "The water's so clear you can easily see the underwater rocks. Oh, it's marvellous. There are dark ones, light ones and even ochre-coloured ones!"

The rocks were of particular interest to the captain, a debonair little man who was staring at the light-coloured rocks with expert eyes, "Ah," he murmured, "There must be lots of lobsters under these yellow 'potatoes.'"

His mouth watering, he squinted as if he could already see them cooked, red and steaming, on his dinner table.

"Fins, over there, at the back of the boat," cried some young people.

"They're following in our wake. They're catching up with us. They're sharks. They're chasing us, for heaven's sake!"

Lan was terrified. Only Liên remained removed from all the agitation.

The captain was jubilant. Observing their distraught faces, he said, "No, they're our friends. They're having a party for us. Look how much fun they're having. Look over there on the right, there are two leaping out of the water, look how beautiful they are. They're dolphins. Enjoy the show—it's quite rare."

The captain's words reassured them. The dolphins, about ten of them, kept them company for more than twenty minutes, before disappearing out into the open sea.

The boat continued at a regular pace over the still surface of the sea. Minh kept a lookout and watched as a small round animal came out of the water and observed him with big astonished eyes before returning quickly into the depths of the sea. The water was crystal-clear and Minh could see the animal clearly; he recognised it as an enormous turtle that had come up to the surface for air.

A bit farther on, the noise of the propellers disturbed a giant ray, speckled with black dots, which had been sleeping on the sand near a rock. Its wild movements made the fish—both big and small—that were living in the gaps of the underwater rock flee in all directions. Minh broke out into a cold sweat thinking about Yến's foot. "The ray's huge, more than six metres in diameter; it could easily have broken his foot with its powerful tail."

The captain was getting worried; towards the northwest, the clouds on the horizon were turning as black as ink and looked ominous. The boat was now half an hour from the narrow channel which joined the open sea. The air was humid, but for the passengers, this impressive spectacle was no cause for alarm.

"This calm, this stifling heat and those dark clouds on the horizon are signs of strong westerlies," said the captain.

A moment later, torrential rain poured from the black sky over the sea. The drops hammered the smooth surface of the water, forming tiny liquid craters which then disappeared, to be replaced by bigger ones. Then the wind rose, shattering this fleeting scene. Waves formed rapidly, strong gusts lifted the water, and the heavy rain turned into an opaque liquid fog all around the ship. The passengers had to seek shelter in the depths of the holds which were crammed with goods.

The ocean waves, menacing and furious, broke against the coral reef, making huge fountains of foam which sprayed high into the sky before falling back into the lagoon with a loud roar. The rain, the wind and the smaller waves came together and crashed onto the old vessel, but it was not in danger. Wisely, the captain had slowed down so that they would stay inside the lagoon.

After a quarter of an hour, all the elements suddenly relented and calmed down, the wind and the rain gradually disappeared, the sky cleared, and the sea returned to normal. The danger had passed, and the captain took the ship through the channel and then steered in the direction of the north of Grande Terre.

At Work

A boat was anchored in front of the small port of Kunéo. Barges laden with minerals were coming up next to its rusty sides as the old coastal vessel sailed into the bay. The passengers observed the small village built up against the mountain.

"Is that where we're going to have to spend five years?" wondered Minh, his eyes full of disappointment.

"It's so mountainous and there's hardly any vegetation!" he observed. "The soil's red and because of the erosion there isn't a single plant left on the slopes and mountains. Even the village laneways are covered with a thick layer of dust."

Lan had noticed the same things. "The village was built on a block of red earth," she said, frowning. "What a desolate landscape. I'll miss the rice fields of Tonkin."

The captain berthed his ship at the small port, built with enormous solid wooden beams. Minh and Lan had to help Liên down onto the gangway. She seemed to be floating along the quay; her body was present on this new land, but her soul was absent, drifting towards the island where she had spent such happy days.

Despite Lan's insistence, Liên had refused any food since leaving Nouméa. She had not slept a single minute, and she was now walking on the dusty ground, barefoot, her eyes vacant, like a robot, a poor, helpless creature, wandering aimlessly towards her sad fate.

Liên had spent her time on board mulling over the same questions, "My dear Thắng, my husband, where are you now? Where have they taken you? Will we ever be able to see each other again, my husband?"

Other thoughts consumed her. "Why didn't we meet earlier? We could've married legally, before leaving. We'd be husband and wife today, and no one could've separated us! But what can I do now?" she lamented. "Must I die, throw myself into the water, let myself drown?"

Liên's head ached, but her tormented soul would give her no respite. "Die, yes, die, not have to think about anything anymore."

Then in the middle of her frenzy she pulled herself together, “No, Thắng would never forgive me if he were to find out one day. Yes, maybe one day, for there’s always hope. I just need to learn to wait, but is that possible?”

An odd light shone in her eyes and her face was serene again. “Yes, it’s possible, with patience,” she said to herself. Weak and wretched, Liên, supported by Minh, made her way towards the reception centre. “I just need to get a grip on myself, to fight, to continue to live and wait for Thắng,” she thought.

Suddenly she trembled, “Oh, Heavens! I’d forgotten the whole point of my voyage. I’m here to work to support my parents. My own problems almost made me forget my duty.” Her face was grave again, as if she had woken up from a bad dream.

The small group gathered in front of a wooden house where a notice above a door indicated: OFFICE. Inside were two men.

“Well, here’s some backup!” said the man sitting behind the desk. Then, addressing himself to the giant in front of him,

“Mainote! You can use these extra hundred and twenty arms. That’ll make two hundred and forty for you in all. I got you to come down from the mine especially, so that we could make up the delay caused by the disastrous weather conditions in the area these last few days. We have to fill up the holds of the ship as quickly as possible. Every idle day costs us money, a lot of money.”

Mainote moved towards the door, glancing distractedly at the men and women.

“Put your things here in the courtyard and get to work,” he commanded suddenly.

Minh, surprised, translated this order straight away for his compatriots. There was a general outcry from the group.

“Get to work!” yelled Mainote again.

“We’ve been travelling for over forty hours, sir. We’re tired, exhausted.” said Minh to the giant. “We know we’re here to work, but please allow us just a short rest.”

Mainote turned purple.

“I’m warning you that I will not be disobeyed, ever. Any resistance will be severely punished. Are you going to get to work, yes or no?”

Minh’s face hardened, but he continued, “We men are at your disposal, but at least allow these young women a moment to rest so that they can recover their strength.”

He pointed to Liên who, white as a sheet, was resting her head on her friend’s shoulder.

“Look at them, I’m not making it up. They’re completely worn out.”

Mainote would have none of that and began to threaten them.

“Get to work,” he yelled, “you’re making us waste time, it’s already nine o’clock. Anyone who refuses to pick up a shovel or a pickaxe will lose a month’s wages. I can assure you that I mean it; you wouldn’t be the first to lose your wages!”

Then he added with obvious pleasure, "And you'll have no way of defending yourselves. To convince you, we can even use . . . other methods. Don't even think of complaining to the authorities," he concluded with a smile full of innuendo.

"We can't do anything against them. They're in charge," sighed Liên in a tired voice, then with a stern, determined look on her face, she said more loudly, "Come on, let's get to work. We all need this money. Let's not lose it. When we came here, we told ourselves we were prepared to put up with anything and everything. So let's get to work!" she repeated.

They were taken to the ore deposit about five hundred metres from the sea where they were delighted to find other compatriots, their faces blackened by the dust, busily digging out the ore from a huge hill. Out of the corner of their eyes the men observed the new arrivals with extreme interest without stopping their work for a moment. They would have liked to be able to rest a few minutes to come and greet them, chat, get news of home. It was written all over their faces.

Minh went up to one of the men to talk to him, but Mainote's voice rang out threateningly, "It is strictly forbidden to talk during working hours!"

Then he went over to join a group of foremen who, from the shelter of a wooden hut, were keeping an eye on the women and men working in the blazing sun. The women had been given pickaxes, the men had to wield heavy shovels, and the new arrivals had to push the wagons, overloaded with ore, as far as the port.

Minh worked like a maniac for hours. He observed with dismay that to fill up one barge they had to make many return trips. By midday he felt dizzy from the heat and fatigue. They were given food, and the men from the work site could at last join the new workers and get to know them. They were by then all just as exhausted and filthy as each other. The ten young women were crying silently, wiping their tears with their shirtsleeves, not realising that they were making white patches around their eyes.

For almost an hour Minh and his friends were inundated with questions; they all had so much to learn from each other. They got on so well together that those who had lived in the same town or village in Tonkin already considered themselves to be closely related.

"Now I understand why you were so excited when you saw us this morning," said Minh.

"We're completely isolated from the rest of the world here," said one of the men, Phúc, "so we're always really pleased to welcome any new people. It's as if you've brought us a breath of fresh air from home."

"What's this strange black ore that the big ship comes all this way to get?"

"It's chrome. Once it's transformed in the blast furnaces it turns into a stainless metal. They also use it to make bumper bars for cars, apparently. But here we just extract the ore from the heart of the mountain."

There was a loud ring of the bell.

"Let's go. We'll have to wait until this evening to catch up," said Phúc flatly. "Here we're seen only as tools for work."

The sky was an intense blue, perfectly cloudless, and the sun took advantage of this to send out its harshest rays. The ground released all the heat that had been stored there since the morning and they got so hot that they sweated even more. The sweat mixed with the black dust irritated their skin and stung their eyes which were already exhausted from so much effort.

"How small these wagons are, how tiny these shovels next to those huge holds in the ship! How many shovelfuls will we still have to lift? How many wagons will we still have to push?" wondered the newcomers, distraught, as their strength faded.

Lan's hands were covered in blisters and the insidious black dust easily managed to get into the affected parts of her skin, sticking to the fragile, bloody flesh and causing searing pain as she worked.

Liên was in an equally deplorable state, but her rage and fury against her fate gave her a haughty, insolent, hard expression.

As for Minh, he talked himself into controlling his anger and desire to put up a fight.

Work only stopped at nightfall. By then they had become nothing more than a silent, dazed group, moving like sleepwalkers towards their quarters, a short distance from the work site.

Without much appetite they ate their ration of rice and dried fish. Then the most valiant went to have a bath, in an area set up behind the buildings. The others, the majority, black with filth, unable to move, slept on the bare ground as if dead.

Work started again at the same fast pace the next morning at six o'clock. The sun had just sent its first rays from the other side of the mountains, towards the southeast.

Lan and Minh, like all the new recruits, were aching and stiff, unable to make the slightest movement without grimacing in pain. The muscles of their bodies were not yet used to lifting tons of ore in one day.

"Working in rice fields isn't as bad as this," sighed Lan, her face twitching. She felt as if her shoulders were so heavy that they were ready to separate from the rest of her body.

"I feel like I weigh a ton. My hands are so sore that I can't even feel the handle of my pickaxe!"

The new recruits were all in the same state and it was extremely difficult for them to keep up the pace of those who had been there some time. It was only at noon the next day, when the sun was high in the sky, that Minh and one of his companions who had come back from the port covered in dust and sweat, pushing an empty wagon towards the mound of ore could at last announce the good news: "It's almost finished . . . just one more hour . . . or two . . . and then the boat can leave."

To the women, even blacker and dirtier than before, these words were like a pleasant, cool shower. They let out little cries of satisfaction. And they all decided together that the work should be completely finished before going over to the old hangar, now called "the canteen." They had their first meal of the day at about two thirty, after eight hours of uninterrupted work. Even so, they were happy to have come to the end.

The sounds of the siren could be heard in the bay, like cries of joy.

"It's the ship leaving," said Minh.

"Go away, go away and never come back again," murmured Lan, sulking, looking at her blistered hands.

"I hope that the next load won't be for a few days," said a young woman with a worried look on her face.

"Oh no," said Phúc, quick to reassure her, "there won't be another for a month or two. We now have to extract the ore from the mountain until we have a big enough stock for the next boat."

"Where's the mine?" they asked anxiously.

"At the top of the mountain, quite far from here. I think we'll be going there tomorrow," said Phúc. "We only came here to load the ship. The rest of the time we work at the mine. And this is the first time there were so many workers in the port to load a single ship."

"We don't regret it!" said another, smiling, without taking his eyes off the young women. "It allowed us to meet you."

Too tired to react, the young women got up without a word as if they were deaf and made their way to the shower to flush away the sweat and the dirt sticking to their bodies.

They were afforded a few hours of rest and then all fell asleep, the men in one dormitory and the women in another much smaller room, until the bell announced the evening meal.

"They aren't very generous here," remarked Minh at the table.

"Alas, no. As we've finished the work, they consider what they're giving us now should be enough. It's based on performance," said Phúc bitterly.

Liên had not slept all afternoon. She had folded a corner of her mat over her face and cried in silence. Lan only realised it when she had gone to fetch her for dinner and Liên refused to go to the canteen. She wiped away her tears discreetly, saying, "I'm not hungry. I want to sleep."

Minh had to intervene to persuade her to join the small community. Liên's behaviour worried Lan a lot. She had become a true mother to her friend.

The conversations continued long into the night, as everyone got to know each other better. Minh enquired about the conditions at the mine, and what he discovered in no way comforted him. He remained pensive, lost in vague and troubling thoughts. Then, waking suddenly from his stupor, he said, blaming himself, "I didn't talk to Lan and Liên all last night, that wasn't very nice of me."

The two friends were over in a corner of the building, away from the other girls who found themselves surrounded. Most of the men were single and had not been near women for months and, in some cases, for years. The young women gathered together, smiling and joyful, were for them a spectacle, and a wonderful if unlikely opportunity. Overexcited by this unexpected presence they tried hard to be as attractive and witty as possible, and then they spent the rest of the time wondering how successful they'd been.

But none of them managed to strike up a conversation with Lan and her friend. The two had adopted a singular attitude of defence. They stayed in their corner looking stern and threatening, like two tigresses ready to pounce. When Minh came near them, Lan's face was even more sullen.

"Ah, there you are, at last!" she said haughtily. "You abandon Liên who is in such need of comfort and friendship at the moment. You leave us alone, just like that."

"I haven't abandoned you, I'm standing here in front of you," replied Minh with his direct smile, which unsettled the young girl and, without realising it, she dropped her fierce look, and retracted her claws, becoming conciliatory,

"We don't know anyone else apart from you, Minh. We trust you."

She hesitated a moment and then finally implored him.

"Protect us, Minh. We're afraid of these men, we know that most of them are single."

Minh nodded, "Yes, you're right. I hadn't thought about this problem, I'll admit, but from now on, we'll be even more united than before!"

Minh seemed to be thinking it over, then he continued, "We don't know this country, we don't know exactly what awaits us at Pimboé, which is where I think we'll all be sent. The team we're now part of is specialised, they come down to work in the port of Kunéo every time the ship has to be loaded. The men have explained the living conditions in this country to me, but it's still very difficult for us to imagine exactly what happens in a place we still don't know. So, we should expect anything, even the worst. I've been asking myself for the last few hours the same question: Have we already experienced the worst, or was that just the beginning, a small taste of what is to come? My fears, alas, also concern you, Lan and Liên, as I'm sure that women are granted no special treatment in this place. I'm really sorry to be so brutally frank, but there's a proverb which says, 'Forewarned is forearmed'. We have to be vigilant and ready for anything. We can't go back now!"

Caledonian Panorama

The next day, they had to climb up the mountain. The new ones carried their packs on their backs, but their bare feet were torn to shreds by the sharp stones on the winding track. The old hands, gallantly, wanted to give their shoes to the young girls, but they had to give up the idea, as the girls had never worn shoes in their lives and were unable to take a single step in them on the rocky pathways.

The slopes were so steep in some places that it was only with Minh's help that Lan and Liên managed to climb them.

Minh observed the mountainous terrain surrounding them and from time to time contemplated the deep valleys below. The column stretched over a long distance, following the route of the overhead cables, which were supported by evenly spaced metal pylons. Hanging from these cables, bins filled with ore were going down while empty ones were going up to the top.

"It's the overhead conveyor," said Phúc. "It takes the ore from the top of the mountain down to the port of Kunéo for the new stock."

The sun was beating down, its hot rays sparing no one. Lan, sweating profusely, was having difficulty keeping up with her companions, as one of the toenails on her right foot had broken on a stone. Each step was painful as her toe got more and more swollen. Whenever her injured toe hit something on the track, she turned pale, as the intense pain shot through her leg, spread through her body and exploded inside her head.

Minh managed to ease Lan's pain somewhat by putting the young girl's arm around his neck, above his tall shoulders. This slightly raised position helped Lan continue her climb.

Phúc considerately offered to carry their things. From time to time he helped Liên get through the most difficult and dangerous spots. When they got to the top of the mountain, they decided to stop to wait for the stragglers and rest a moment. Minh put Lan down on a bed of branches Phúc had prepared for them. He was still worried.

"What I find particularly strange is that we're unaccompanied, unsupervised; it's as if they've abandoned us," said Minh, continuing, "We're completely alone, almost free, without a single guard or supervisor."

"Alas, they're a lot smarter than we are," said Phúc. "We've got a certain amount of time to get to the mine. Up there they must know what time we left Kunéo, and they also know what time we're due to arrive. We can't spend more than a quarter of an hour here as we've already wasted a lot of time; the sooner we arrive at the village the better. Up here the sun's extremely fierce around noon."

Minh had slept well the night before and felt in good form and, unlike his initial reaction on the boat when he had looked on this desolate terrain with dismay, at present he seemed captivated by the mountain. He felt elated by this semi-desert country where the bare rocks and the red soil seemed to want to conquer the mountaintops, leaving little space for the stunted vegetation. He took a few steps off the track, pulled himself up onto a mound overhanging a precipice. What he discovered enchanted him: the sea, intensely blue, extending as far as the eye could see, blended into the luminous sky dotted with puffs of milky-white clouds. A short distance from the coast and the port of Kunéo, which he could make out down below at the foot of the mountain, was a big sparkling white line which lay parallel to the length of the coast, just opposite the port.

Phúc had joined Minh.

"It's extraordinary!" exclaimed Minh.

"That silver line you can see over there," explained Phúc, pointing his finger at the sea, "is the foam produced by the ocean waves as they break on the coral reefs. It's a natural barrier that surrounds the coastline of New Caledonia, providing perfect protection. And the gap you see there is the channel the boats come through to get to the port of Kunéo. Feast your eyes on this lagoon, Minh," continued Phúc, "it's one of the most beautiful in the world."

Minh, immobile, gazed at the lagoon which, from the reef to the shore was several kilometres wide and extended in a parallel strip along the coastline. He suddenly remembered his voyage on the coastal vessel, when they left the port of Nouméa and sailed for several hours in the lagoon. He could see, as if he were still there, the clear jade-coloured water, the rocks under the sea, the giant ray and the multicoloured fish, then the tortoise with its bewildered eyes, and the dolphins that had enchanted them.

From the top of the mountain, Minh could almost feel the fresh water flowing over his body. He imagined he was swimming in the clear water, discovering this fascinating unknown world. But he was jolted out of his daydreaming by Phúc's hand on his shoulder.

"We have to go now. We still have almost an hour to go."

With regret, Minh left this extraordinary magical landscape which nature offered up free of charge to the passersby. He helped Lan get up from the ground where she had been lying, and they continued to climb the mountain without a word.

As he was supporting Lan, his mind turned to Toán, to the young Yến and to poor Thắng.

"Where are they now? What's become of them?" he wondered.

From time to time he glanced furtively over at Liên. Glumly she continued, with Phúc's help, following the human column as it moved along the mountainous path.

Lan leant against Minh's shoulder and with clenched teeth made a superhuman effort not to cry out in pain whenever her foot knocked against a stone or roots sticking out of the ground.

An hour later they reached the top. Lan and Liên took refuge in the shade of a tree.

"You know the way like the inside of your pocket!" said Minh, smiling despite the fatigue and the heat.

"It's my sixth year on the mine," replied Phúc.

"Sixth year? I don't understand," said Minh, intrigued.

"Well, my contract ended last year. Now I've started the second one; I've signed up again. I'm a Chân Đăng[1] and I want to remain one. A hardened Chân Đăng, if you like . . ."

"So, you like it here?"

"I've got no one back home. No family, so it doesn't worry me to stay on five more years."

He added in confidence, "I can tell you that you need to be tough to be able to handle ten years working in this country. Above all, you have to be able to take the beatings and the punishments."

Seeing Minh's puzzled expression, he grabbed his arm, pulling him along.

"Come on! Let's change the subject! I'm going to show you the Caledonian panorama. It's really worth seeing, especially as I've noticed you appreciate beauty."

Minh nodded. He was still mulling over Phúc's latest revelations. "You have to be able to take the beatings and punishment," he muttered, "What does he mean?"

"Are you coming, Minh?" said Phúc, who had reached the top of the mountain about thirty metres ahead. Minh joined him and his face lit up as his eyes took in the scene that spread out beneath his feet.

"We're almost at the northern tip of the island. For your information, New Caledonia is also known as 'la Grande Terre'. It's about four hundred kilometres long and the widest part is only fifty kilometres wide. The island's the shape of a cigar. From here you can see the sea, the reef, and the channel that gives access to the port of Kunéo. Look how dry and arid the ground is, with its sparse vegetation. It's typical of the west coast. If you turn around now and look at the east coast, you'll see that it's green from here to the sea in the distance. Isn't it both extraordinary and surprising?"

"It's splendid! The difference between one coast and the other is incredible," exclaimed Minh in awe and astonishment.

"The prevailing winds," continued Phúc, "come from the southeast and blow the clouds over towards the mountains which stop them there. So, the heavy rains on the east side make it lush and more beautiful."

"You're a real geography teacher," exclaimed Minh, smiling.

"We have to go now, it looks like our companions are getting impatient. Some of them have already started to move down towards the village," said Phúc, who had joined the young women by this time. "The village is just below us, on the eastern slope. We'll be able to see it as soon as we get to the first bend on our left."

Note

1 *Chân Đăng* was the name used by the Tonkinese at the time to mean that they were contracted workers.

The Camp

"Let's get going," said Lan. "We'd better not linger, otherwise we might have problems right from the very first day. That would be a pity!"

Even so, they were amongst the last to get underway. Once they got to the bend that Phúc had mentioned, they could see the workshops, the hangars, the control room for the overhead transporter with its bins filled with ore leaving, while empty bins came back up. A little lower down, the village spread over the side of the mountain.

"The beautiful houses on your right with their well-kept gardens are for the bosses and foremen. On the left is our village. The big corrugated iron buildings you see are our sleeping quarters."

When they finally reached the village, a few children covered in red dust came to stare with big curious eyes at the new arrivals, as if they came from another planet.

"Isn't there anyone in this village?" asked Lan.

"No, they're all at work, both men and women. Except for a few who are too sick and have stayed in bed," Phúc explained.

Pointing to a small group who had come to meet them he said, "They're from the personnel department and will register you. To make things easier," he added, "I can tell you now that they're also going to give each of you a blanket and a pair of shoes, then they'll show you to your respective dormitories. The men will join those already here and the young girls will have a separate room." I'll leave you now," he added, "and meet you this evening in the canteen."

"Phúc is so considerate," said Lan appreciatively.

"He's very thoughtful," Minh agreed. That evening, the whole community came together in the huge canteen building. There was joy on all their faces and they chatted happily; the richest, those who had been working there for several years, offered tea and sweet treats in honour of the newcomers to the village.

"I think there are more than three hundred of us in the village. I mean 'our village,'" said Minh.

"To distinguish it from the European village, we call it 'our camp,'" Phúc corrected him. "At the moment there are a lot of us, about three hundred and fifty with your arrival today. There are also some Javanese, but not many, at the mine. They live at the other end of the camp in the same conditions as us; they're very quiet and there are never any problems with them."

"All the women here seem to be married," remarked Minh.

"Yes, all, without exception," said Phúc. "They've found the man of their life. Even the ugliest had the privilege of choosing; they even played hard to get. We really are living in another world," Phúc shook his head unhappily.

Liên had met a young couple; the husband was from her native town, and, even though they had never met before they immediately felt like close relatives. This encounter made Liên's face light up and she joined eagerly in the conversations, replying as clearly as possible to the many questions that both men and women asked her, knowing that each piece of news or detail was precious and important for these people who were far from home, on this isolated mountain.

Lan kept herself a little apart, not because of her injured foot or because this noisy, joyful company bothered her; on the contrary she was happy to now belong to this far-flung community. It was, rather, that she felt an indefinable anxiety; was it because she had not found or met a single person from her village? Or was it because she was afraid to find herself alone amongst all these men?

She knew she was young and beautiful. She was also certain that she would have no trouble finding a companion amongst this large male population. But she needed a man for life, for the rest of her days, so she would have to think about it and choose well, because she could not afford to make a mistake. Only time and patience would allow her to avoid making the wrong choice. But would these young men give her the time? Lan was afraid of her own thoughts.

"Why torture myself with these ideas?" she asked herself suddenly. "Didn't I come here just to work, in the hope of earning enough money at the end of the contract to buy a plot of land and build a small house? Not a castle—far from it—just a small house."

Lan began to dream. "The roof will be made of red tiles and the walls will be whitewashed, yes, that's it! Those colours will be perfect. Mother, father, and my two little brothers will come and stay, and we'll all live happily together just like before!"

Lan was shaking. "Will that ever be possible?" she fretted, knowing that between dream and reality there are inevitably huge gaps which are often difficult to close.

The girl from the country who had never known anything other than a dilapidated straw-hut deep in the rice fields, began to shiver, for suddenly she could see the faces of her father, her mother and her two little brothers, still squatting in their miserable shack where the wind got in through the cracks in the walls and the rain seeped insidiously through the holes in the thatched roof. There were tears in her eyes as she remembered their last days together. She had had to use all imaginable arguments she could come up with to wrest her father's permission from him. It was with a heavy heart that her parents had finally given in and allowed her to leave for a place so far away on the other side of the world. Lan was satisfied all the same. To have managed to persuade them and obtain their trust was quite a feat. She had sworn to them that she would return as soon as her contract ended.

Her poor mother had cried night and day, heartbroken to see her daughter, so young and frail, leaving. She began silently imploring the gods, at least those she knew about, to protect her daughter so that she could return home as quickly as possible.

In her mind, Lan could again see her father on the day of her departure, looking at her, as pale and lifeless as wax, incapable of making even the slightest movement or uttering a single word. His emotions were so strong that he seemed to have turned to stone, paralysed. Her little brothers, one aged fourteen and the younger one barely nine, clung to her as hard as they could, crying until they were gasping for breath.

"Stay with us, big sister, stay with us, don't abandon us!"

Lan could hardly contain her tears. Her mother threw her arms around her neck, pressing her face, dry and wrinkled from a lifetime of deprivation and hard work, against that of her daughter who, brave and resolute, was prepared to go so far away to save her family from poverty.

"My daughter, my daughter," sobbed the devastated mother, tears running down her hollow cheeks and drenching her tattered blouse. "Give up your plans, my daughter. We're happy as we are, we don't need money—please don't leave!" she begged.

Lan was also crying, unable to hold the tears back any longer.

"Poor Mama, her grief is so deep that she doesn't know what she's saying. Poor Papa, so sick and tired, without a cent to buy medicine."

In an uncharacteristic gesture, Lan gave each member of her family a long kiss. Through her tears she gazed at her loved ones, then she pulled away, first from her brothers, then her mother. She looked at them all one last time.

"I'll be back," she repeated, sobbing, "I'll be back." Then she left without turning around once.

Lan lingered over her memories. She could see the ship sailing away from the shores of her native land, then Minh and Toán helping her disembark onto Nou Island. Suddenly, everything went blurry, as if covered by a thick fog. Then a distinct image appeared, followed by a smile. She shivered, recognising Minh's face. Lan opened her eyes and came back to reality. She wiped away the tears which had misted over her eyes and saw Minh sitting at the back of the room. He was with about ten people, listening distractedly to their conversation. She observed him again, as if she wanted to read his thoughts, but the image of his smiling face kept coming back to her. At that moment it seemed as if these two images, one of them real, the other intangible, were superimposed on one another for a moment, and then blended together into one and finished up swirling around dizzyingly in her mind. It was very disturbing.

"What's happening? What's happening to me?" she wondered, wiping her left hand over her hot, clammy forehead.

Minh had noticed this gesture and he looked at her in turn. For a moment their eyes met. Lan, embarrassed, lowered her eyes, then started thinking, "Minh's a quiet, sensible young man. Whenever I or Liên need him, he's there. We can rely on his help and that's turned out to be necessary here. But," she continued, frowning, "he's distant and reserved. Unlike the other boys, he never says or does anything inappropriate. Still, he is a bit mysterious!"

Lan felt a presence in front of her; she looked up and there was Minh.

"You look exhausted," he said. "You should go and have a rest."

"You're right," said Lan docilely. "It was a tough day today, and we don't know what to expect tomorrow!" she added weakly.

"Don't worry about it. Go and have a rest. Let's take each day as it comes. Have a good sleep, we'll need all our strength and determination to get through the difficult times ahead."

Lan got up. "Good night, Minh."

"Good night, Lan! By the way, how's your foot?"

"Much better," replied Lan with a smile of thanks. "This afternoon, one of the young women heated some water for me and put a pinch of salt in it. I soaked my injured foot in this bath for a good quarter of an hour. It's a great remedy, look at the result!" She walked a few steps.

"See? I hardly limp anymore!"

Minh made one last suggestion before they separated, "Wrap up well, Lan. Phúc told me it gets very cold on this mountain! Good night, Lan."

Minh was the first of the men to get back to the dormitory. The solitude, although temporary, was very welcome. He unrolled his mat on the floor, put his things against the wall, turned off the light and stretched out. His hands under his neck and his eyes wide open in the dark, he sighed, "So from today, I'll be nothing more than number 3141! From now on, the bosses will only call us by our registration numbers. That's what they told us this afternoon at the recruitment office. We've all lost our names and our personalities. What do we have left?" He thought about his young women friends.

"Lan must be number 3142. I remember well because she registered just after me. It's strange, I don't remember Liên's number!"

He sat up on his mat, pensive, then with his chin on his bent knees, he wondered, "What have I got myself into? I had everything at home, there was no shortage of work in my parents' shop. If I wanted to, I could even have continued my studies. Why did I abandon everything? Everything, without a word, without saying anything. I'm an only child. What have I done? Oh, what have I done?"

Minh remembered his last carefree days in Hà-Nội. He could see himself strolling beside the small lake in the city and thought regretfully, "If not for that girl and my father's promise of marriage, I wouldn't be in this situation. Father wanted me to marry and to look after his business afterwards."

Minh also knew that, without ever saying it, his parents adored him; he was their pride and joy, their reason for living. It was to make him happy that they had chosen this girl for him. For Xuyến was a decent, hardworking girl, healthy and very obedient. They were sure their son would be satisfied, content with such a wife. Minh remembered a conversation he had had with his father about it.

"Yes, father, I'll get married . . . in a year or two, but only to a girl I love. I don't want to marry someone I have no feelings for!" he insisted.

"Who do you want to marry then?" his father asked with irritation.

"I don't know, father, I don't intend to marry yet."

For the first time in his life, his father got angry with him, refusing to compromise.

"You're too young to realise that you're wrong. I can see what's good for you. You young people with your modern ideas, you only dream of girls who are supposedly witty or educated. And skinny and delicate, to boot! Incapable of looking after a house, or working properly. No, Minh! There's no way you'll have a wife like that. You need a solid, obedient wife, not a doll!"

Thinking for a few seconds, he added furiously, "What's more, you have to respect our traditions! A promise is a promise! So you will marry this girl we've chosen for you; it's for your own good!" Then he walked off. His dear mother, to reconcile the two men, had tried to smooth things over, get them to calm down, but it was a waste of time—neither would budge.

During the New Year's festivities, his father solemnly insisted once more, "Minh you're twenty, you have to think about producing offspring for our family as soon as possible. I want you to marry this year. Your mother and I intend celebrating the engagement in a few weeks and you'll get married in the second part of the year at the latest."

To his parents' great surprise Minh did not fight them this time, but he did not accept it either. His father interpreted this attitude as acceptance, the natural obedience that a child owes his parents. He did not suspect that Minh, having learned by chance a few days earlier that some young people were going to try their luck in a new country, far, far away from Tonkin, was preparing to follow them, disguised as a peasant. He made enquiries, then made his decision. Nervously he signed up for five long years.

When Minh went home that night, he couldn't swallow a single mouthful, absorbed as he was in thinking of his parents' great sorrow. He stared at their faces and engraved their features deep in his memory.

"You haven't eaten anything, son," observed his father.

Minh lowered his head to avoid his eyes, then forced himself to swallow a little white rice, but his dry throat was so tight he couldn't get any food down. He had to quickly drink a glass of cold water to avoid choking. But he had made his decision: when the day came, he would leave, he would make his escape, like a thief, like an unworthy son. What did he care about what others said? He wanted to be free, live his own life and when he thought of the voyage, as the day of departure got nearer, this adventure to the ends of the Earth became more enticing. If he left, he would never again have to see this unfeminine girl that his father wanted him to make his wife. Minh lay down again and closed his eyes, the better to think things over,

"If I didn't leave Xuyến would become my wife whether I like it or not and I'd suffer all my life. Father can't understand me; we don't have the same idea of love and happiness."

He could remember clearly all the details of the plan he had thought up in case he couldn't leave, if, for some reason, his application was refused:

"In the end I'd consent to marry to save face, since my parents made this pledge. But from the first night we'd sleep in separate beds. I'd refuse any contact or intimacy with this girl who, I'll have to admit, has never done anything against me. But I really couldn't love her. There are too many differences between us, and we would've been unhappy after the wedding. Just poor pawns in the hands of ancestral customs. But I wouldn't stay long in such an unhappy situation," growled Minh as if he was experiencing it intensely. "Having fulfilled my duty, I'd go. Anywhere! And in all this, poor abandoned Xuyến would be the one to suffer the most. She'd suffer far more than me and she'd have no hope of remarrying."

Minh got up and, becoming more agitated, began to pace up and down the big room, his hands behind his back.

"Yes, I did the right thing. It was better to leave, it was the only way to avoid all this intrigue and drama! Too bad for tradition," he said gruffly, as if shrugging off something annoying which wouldn't go away. The night was cold, so he went back to bed; after a while the blanket warmed his freezing body. He remembered the recommendation he had made to Lan, "Rug up well, Lan. It's very cold on this mountain."

He could see the girl's smiling face in his mind, "She's pretty," he murmured and fell asleep with this sweet thought.

***

In the middle of the night, shouting and calls for help disturbed the sleeping village. Minh woke up with a start and rushed out of the room. He could hear wailing and thought he recognised first Liên's voice and then Lan's. When he got to their dormitory, about fifty metres from his, the young women ran to meet him.

"Liên, Lan, what's happening?"

"We've had visitors," said Lan frantically.

In the pale light of the moon Minh could make out the fear in her eyes. Without realising it, he took her hand and squeezed it in his own.

"Tell me what happened!" he said.

"Some strangers came into our dormitory," said Liên. "It was dark and we'd put out the oil lamp. No doubt our roommates didn't bolt the door properly. The men managed to get inside and the girls who were lying near this door were checked out . . . examined . . . by their wandering hands! They woke up, yelling, and fought against the men! Can you believe it? They wanted to force the girls to leave with them," said Lan.

"We defended them as best we could," said Liên.

"We scratched them!" Lan added, showing her nails, "and our cries also scared them off!"

"It was to be expected," murmured Minh. "We'll have to bolt all the doors and windows from now on, even reinforce them if necessary."

He took the young girls back to their dormitory. A small crowd had already gathered in front of the building. Inside, some of the girls were crying.

"They're afraid. They don't feel safe anymore," whispered Lan.

"Where's Thế?" cried Liên. "There are only nine of us here!"

"Thế was nearest the door!" said Lan, looking worried.

As soon as they had been alerted, a group of about ten men decided to set out to look for the missing girl. Minh and Phúc joined the group straight away. Holding a lamp in front of himself to light the way, Phúc was leading the operation, scouring the small streets one after another. They advanced in silence, without making a sound, so that they might hear any crying or wailing. If they managed to locate the abductor's refuge, Phúc would put out the lamp and they would catch him by surprise.

But as time passed by, they looked at each other in confusion, as nothing led to the slightest clue. Minh was getting more and more anxious, his expression was haggard. After a while they passed in front of a woman who was sitting on the ground in front of her doorway.

"Don't waste your time, boys," she said scornfully, "This sort of thing always happens here and will happen again, as long as there are girls to marry. It happened to me, in the same way. And he got me, the rogue! He's now my husband. Go on, go back to bed," she insisted again," with all your comings and goings I can't sleep."

"Maybe they're somewhere in the forest around us. We can't do anything more in the dark," said Phúc.

"Who says the young girl really needs us to come and rescue her? Have you heard any cries, or any sound at all?" asked another man. "This woman must be right, maybe they're fine up there, or somewhere in the camp."

"They could be right! Anyway, as I don't know the area, I can't do anything until dawn. If between now and then Thế is still not back, I'll ask some of the young newcomers to join me and we'll form search parties," muttered Minh, his face serious. "He'd better watch out," he added.

Lan had not slept well. Having men get into their room and take Thế had undermined her confidence. She was starting to worry about the future.

"I was right to be afraid of all these men, to wonder if they'd leave us alone. Now I fear they'll end up getting us all, by force. But I won't let them touch me," she muttered, her jaw clenched. "As of tomorrow, I'll try and get a knife. Even if it takes all my savings, I will defend myself!"

The first light of dawn was filtering in through the gaps in the windows when Minh knocked at the door. Recognising his voice, Lan opened it without hesitation.

"Good morning Lan. Did you sleep well?"

"Quite well, thank you Minh."

"Is Thế back?"

"Alas, no, I fear the worst."

"I'm going to organise a search party," decided Minh.

But he heard a thin, high-pitched voice coming from the street corner. "Don't bother, Minh. Here I am."

Minh and Lan looked in the direction of the voice. They were astonished and dismayed to see Thế coming towards them, happy and smiling. A young man of about thirty was walking next to her.

"Thế, do you realise how worried we were?" said Minh, a surprised look on his face.

"Oh, I'm so sorry. I didn't expect to cause so much trouble." Looking at the young man, she said, "This is Hiếu. I've come to get my things," she added abruptly. "We're getting married!"

"When?" spluttered Lan, not really knowing what she was saying, she was so astonished.

"We'll announce our marriage at the evening meal," replied Hiếu, his face radiant.

Confused, Lan remained pensive, then at last she said, as if waking from a dream, "So last night . . . the unlocked door . . . it was you?"

Thế lowered her eyes, then nodded, "Yes, it was me," she admitted, embarrassed.

"Well, that's reassuring, as I couldn't understand how the men could have opened a lock like that from the outside."

"I met Hiếu last night at the canteen," confessed Thế. "We agreed to meet again later, you see! I was ashamed to rush into things on our first evening here. I preferred to see Hiếu again that night. It was more discreet. But two of his friends knew about his rendezvous and wanted to try their luck. Unfortunately, things went badly for them, and the whole village found out about it."

"Well, as your escapade has ended in the best possible way, it remains for me to wish you lots of happiness and lots of children!" said Minh, smiling. Then, taking Lan's arm, he said, "Let's go to the canteen to recover."

A bell rang out as they entered the big building. Phúc was already seated at a table.

"What time is it, please?" asked Lan.

"It's five in the morning. That's the wake-up bell you've just heard. You'll hear it every morning at the same time. We start work in exactly sixty minutes. Come and sit down beside me." He continued, "We get a bowl of rice and some hot tea. But I don't see Liên. Where is she?"

"She's coming. Liên woke up just before the bell rang," said Lan.

The news spread fast and, in a few minutes, the whole camp was informed of the happy event to come.

The Mine

The new recruits were all assembled in front of the supervisors' office for their first day of work at the mine. Just like a tour guide, Phúc had taken them there. They were surprised to see Mainote in the office, giving orders to the foremen.

"He's the big boss, just under the directors," explained Phúc.

"You seem to know him," replied Lan.

"Yes, I work for him from time to time. As I understand French, sometimes he uses me as an interpreter when there are new arrivals, like today."

"Minh also speaks French very well," said Lan with pride in her voice.

"Yes, I heard him the other day when he was talking to Mainote in Kunéo. I don't think my services will be required today."

Phúc was about to leave when Mainote appeared in front of the door. "All men must report to the mine entrance. Half of you will do a big cleanup and the other half will follow the orders of Watard here who will accompany you."

Recognising Phúc he said, "Good timing! Dubord's sick, so you'll replace him for a few days. You're in charge of the women. Get them to clean the site of the future dock, near the power station."

Lan could see the look of satisfaction on Phúc's face. Hearing these orders was like sweet music to his ears. The two groups separated, Minh heading for the mine while Lan and Liên went in the opposite direction. Curious, Lan asked Phúc, "Do you often get to be in charge?"

"It's already happened several times, but I feel uncomfortable giving orders to my friends and compatriots. In this situation, you see, I'm torn between two things: friendship and performance. And during working hours I'm not allowed to talk with you unless it's to give you orders. Indeed, I have to inform you right now that the rules prohibit any discussion during work, so I'll ask you to obey this order graciously for both our sakes."

Once they had arrived at a shelter not far from the power station, Phúc said, opening the door, "Here you are. Inside there are pickaxes, axes, machetes. Take what suits you best, and then take a look at the bushland near the power station. All of this area has to be cleared and cleaned up as they'll be building a warehouse here shortly."

Then he added, addressing Lan and her friend in particular, "It's time to begin. So that no one is treated unfairly I prefer to move away from you during working hours. But I'll still be observing you," he said with a slight smile on his lips. "I ask for your understanding."

Phúc moved away from the two girls and began to behave like a true boss.

They set to work. Lan and Thế both had a long knife, Liên had an axe and others chose pickaxes to pull out the roots. They started cutting back bushes and then cut down branches from the trees before attacking the trunks. By ten o'clock their blouses were already soaked in sweat, but they had to keep working the whole morning in the burning sun. Liên had been thinking a lot over the last few days. She was now resigned to her fate and followed her companions and her friend like a lost soul, getting quieter and quieter and gradually withdrawing into herself. Lan was very worried to see her friend change as the days progressed. Liên worked like a maniac, as if she were angry with this innocent, lush, beautiful piece of nature which was going to disappear inexorably to make way for a slab of concrete, followed by a hideous corrugated iron construction. The resentment she felt increased her strength tenfold, but her mind was elsewhere, far away from this place where she would remain a prisoner for several years. She thought about Thắng, unable to forget him.

"Can one ever forget a man one loves?" she wondered, "No. It's impossible. I'll never be able to forget him! He's part of my life, despite the separation and the distance between us."

She asked herself other questions: "Will I ever see him again? What hope is there?"

At these moments she would lose courage. But her sense of duty made her pull herself together; wasn't she here to help her poor miserable parents? Hadn't she promised to send them a money order as soon as she received her first pay so that they could afford the medicine they needed for their ailing health? Otherwise, old and sick, they would never have the physical strength to wait for her to come home. So Liên had to accept, reluctantly, to follow her destiny. From this moment on, she was prepared to endure whatever she had to—to work as only those who suffer, and who are driven by the steadfast resolve of a sacred duty to perform, know how—so that her deep suffering and her sacrifice would not be in vain.

Lan, much frailer, was sweating profusely. Her cheeks had a rosy hue which made her even more beautiful, despite the beads of sweat and the clammy hair sticking to her face. Liên was neither pretty nor ugly, but she had a lot of charm. And her determination had changed her. From time to time, Phúc couldn't stop himself coming over to help her pull out the stubborn roots. The heat and the smell of the upturned soil made it difficult to breathe.

Finally, at noon, they were allowed a half-hour rest. Delighted, they all took refuge under the shade of those trees that had not yet been marked for destruction. They had lunch, a small piece of bread that they had been given that morning just before they left the canteen. Then they lay on some brushwood they had spread on the ground, to rest their aching bodies. Their inflamed hands were covered in painful blisters. They stayed like this, silent, their eyes blank, too exhausted to utter a single word.

Phúc came to sit beside Liên. He observed her for a while and then said, "You should slow down; you'll never be able to keep this up. If you carry on like this, you'll soon give in. It's too hot here to work at that pace." After a moment's reflection, Phúc added, "Normally, I shouldn't give you advice. My role, even though it's only temporary is, on the contrary, to force you to push yourselves to the maximum. But, believe me, Liên this is advice from a friend."

Liên was visibly irritated and agitated.

"Which region are you from?" asked Phúc, without taking his eyes off her.

"I'm from Hải-Phòng," replied Liên, staring at the bare ground.

"It's pretty strange for a daughter of the sea to find herself on the top of a mountain," joked Phúc, continuing, "I've been in this country for six years. I've just renewed my contract. Another four years and I'll be free."

"So will I in five years!" replied Liên dryly, more and more tense.

"You'll see, five years will pass quickly. It's actually quite hard for me to realise that I've already spent so many years at this mine! It seems as if it was . . . yesterday!"

"It's easy when you spend your time watching others work," retorted Liên bitterly.

Lan sensed that it was time to intervene. She put her hand gently on her friend's shoulder as if to say, "Keep calm, Liên, calm down, my friend."

Phúc without the slightest sign of impatience carried on, "Actually, Liên, I've also suffered a great deal. And I continue to be subjected to the same harsh conditions as everyone else. But, through patience and perseverance I've managed to overcome many obstacles. Obviously I'd like to have days like today all year round. Alas, I regret that they're rare. When Dubord is well, I'll return to the mine, or to the port at Kunéo, like everybody else. It's even more regrettable as I won't be able to look at you all day," he added with a mischievous smile.

Liên was furious. Glaring at him, she said, "I don't need you or anyone else. I just want to be left alone."

Phúc got up and said to Lan, "Your friend's very edgy today. We'll carry on this conversation later, when she's calmer." Then he walked away.

"You shouldn't have spoken to him in that tone of voice, Liên. He's polite and friendly. Let's try to have friends rather than enemies in this village."

"I don't know why . . . but the presence of a man near me depresses and repels me. I lose all sense of restraint and I say whatever comes to mind."

They started work again a few minutes later, when the sun's rays beating against the mountain were harshest. They felt that they had no strength left and their heavy eyelids started to close in an attempt to claim a few minutes of sleep. The burning ground scorched their fragile feet, as, from the start, they had had to get rid of the shoes they were not yet accustomed to wearing. But they carried on working relentlessly brave and stoic.

Towards the middle of the day a part of the land had been cleared. They had formed large piles of freshly cut branches and grasses which, in a few days' time they would burn to cinders. But the area that still had to be cleared was huge.

A man's loud voice boomed out. They recognised Mainote, the fat giant, who was holding something unexpected in his hand: a whip! He addressed Phúc who immediately translated his instructions. Turning to Lan he said, "Lan, the head foreman wants you to go to his house tomorrow to do a few hours of housework."

Lan agreed, thinking, "I don't have a choice. He's the one who decides. Anyhow, it won't be as tough working inside, in the shade, as it is on the hot ground outside. I'll be able to see the inside of a nice house. I've never had the chance until now."

Their first day of work seemed very long to them. They were exhausted. Their movements became less sure, minutes seemed to last hours and hours an eternity. But everything comes to an end. With patience. Their day finished at about six. They went back to the village dulled by fatigue, their hands on fire, their eyes glazed.

Minh too was in a sorry state, lying in his dormitory, near his companions who, like him, had just finished their first day at the mine. Their faces were blackened by chrome dust, their clothes soaked with sweat, they were like human wrecks coming from who knows where.

"It was hell," muttered Minh, mulling over his exhausting day. He shook his head slowly as if he could not believe it, as if he had just lived through an awful nightmare. He remembered all the details; he would never forget them.

On Watard's orders, Minh had been sent to the mine platform. He looked apprehensively at the gaping black hole, which seemed to be swallowing everyone up into its intestines. Watard chose about twenty of the strongest men.

"You see those beams stored about fifty metres from here. You're going to carry them over to the entrance of the tunnel and deposit them there. Be careful not to block the way for the wagons that come and go depending on how quickly the ore is extracted."

Seeing the huge, heavy logs Minh nodded to two of his companions to come and help him. They were about to lift the first log when Watard intervened.

"No, no way! Two! Just two men to carry a log!"

Without a word, Minh dropped down on one knee. He lifted one end of the beam, placed it as gently as possible on his shoulder and waited for his companion behind him to do the same. When they felt the wood lift from the ground, they stood up together. Then, their backs bent and their shoulders slightly unbalanced by the weight, they advanced slowly and carefully in case they fell. Their feet trembled, unsure on the wet mountain path.

"Faster!" cried Watard.

But the men continued at a cautious, regular pace.

When Minh and his companion got to the entrance, they threw down their heavy load, jumping aside quickly to avoid the wooden beam hitting their legs. Then they returned to the starting point to begin once again. Each time, they tried to ease the load by changing the beam over to the other shoulder.

"Faster! Faster, for God's sake!" shouted Watard, more and more irritated by these new workers who, as far as he was concerned, were completely useless. But Minh and Đào remained deaf to his orders and simply adjusted their pace to that of the other teams. Suddenly, a thunderous sound boomed out above their heads, followed by the dreadful words, "Hurry up, you good-for-nothing bunch of slackers! Or else you'd better watch out!"

Minh, as he was moving forward, glanced rapidly to the side and realised that Watard had a whip.

"These foremen all have whips. But they'd better watch out if they dare to use it on me," he muttered.

Watard had become threatening and was moving around all over the place, gesturing chaotically, his eyes angry. The men, without exchanging a word, quickened their pace, but very soon they were covered in sweat.

Minh was out of breath and Đào behind him was trying desperately to keep up the same pace. The beams seemed to be getting heavier and heavier. The men were going through agony, their shoulders lacerated from the heavy wooden beams biting into their flesh. And the heat wasn't helping! They felt as if they would melt like ice in the sun. Their strength was sapping dangerously.

"Our legs will eventually give in," growled Minh, furious at the way they were being treated. He had barely finished his sentence when one of the men in the team ahead of them tripped on a stone and lost his balance. The beam lurched and then fell heavily to the ground. The men managed to dodge the dangerous weight just in time. Watard was beside himself with rage; his whip cracked again above the heads of the young men.

"I can't believe it! You should've finished this work a long time ago. What pathetic sissies you are! I'll show you what work is!"

The men took up their hellish pace again. A large stack of beams towered in front of the opening to the tunnel. But still they continued, relentlessly. Đào, drenched in sweat, was exhausted. His sight weakened by his extreme effort, he suddenly staggered forward as if drunk.

"Watch out!" cried Minh to Watard who was in their way.

But his cry was a waste of effort; staggering along, Đào had bumped into the foreman who, stunned by the impact, went reeling. However, moving his legs quickly, he managed to regain his balance. His helmet had fallen to the ground and he bent to pick it up. Then he followed Đào who, preceded by Minh, was heading towards the tunnel. When they had offloaded the heavy beam, the foreman delivered a violent lash of the whip to the young man's shoulder. Petrified by the pain, Đào, his face convulsed in agony, didn't understand what had happened to him. He turned around abruptly as if alerted by some mysterious intuition. He faced Watard threateningly, ready to jump on his tormentor. The latter was getting ready to lash his whip in Đào's direction for the second time. Minh was terrified but, even so, had the presence of mind to rush towards his companion; he grabbed him by the arm and pushed him to the ground before the whip could reach them. Holding him firmly he said, "Don't lose your head, Đào! I know it's terrible to be treated like this, but he's stronger than us. For heaven's sake, control yourself! We can do nothing against them!"

Minh was furious; clenching his teeth he made a huge effort to keep his temper. Pale and silent, he stared at the man with the whip. His eyes expressed a dull and terrible anger.

***

When the beams began to pile up and block the way, they had to start loading them onto the empty wagons going back inside the mine.

A sense of foreboding gripped Minh; paradoxical as it may seem, he was drawn towards the black hole ahead of him, which fascinated him, while the instinct of preservation held him back. Đào and his companions also hesitated.

"Well, we have no choice! We have to accompany the load; we're responsible for it," thought Minh. Turning to Đào and the small group waiting he said, "Let's get going, men."

They entered the tunnel, walking near the wagons. The noise of the metal wheels on the steel rails resonated oddly in the darkness. Minh recalled the difficult days in the port of Kunéo where he had spent his time pushing the exact same wagons heavily laden with ore. This time, other miners were pushing them and Minh was just following them to unload the beams at the end of the tunnel. Was it fear or his vivid imagination that made him tremble like this? Advancing cautiously, his dilated eyes could see the rock face covered in enormous beams as long as the ones he had had to transport all morning.

Water seeped out from all over the place, dripping to the ground with crystal-clear sounds. The carbide lamps on the wagons cast startling oversized shadows on the vaults and rock face. Minh was pensive and in awe at the same time. "Man is pretty brave and inventive to venture like this into the heart of the mountain to rip out the riches buried there!" he thought. The idea of a catastrophe, always possible, made him shiver. To keep his dangerously overactive mind busy, he tried to measure the distance they had covered by counting his steps. But it was no use. The tunnel was not straight; it had been dug deep into the mountain, following the whimsical traces of the veins of chromium. Thus, the men moved sometimes to the right and sometimes to the left. When they got to the end of the railway line, Minh felt disoriented. They laid the beams against the rock walls and went out into the fresh air to begin all over again.

By midday, all of the beams had been taken to the end of the tunnel, and they were able to go outside in the sun for lunch in the fresh air.

"The piece of bread they gave us this morning is not enough. Really not enough for all the hard work they made us do!" they complained. As there was nothing else to eat and they still had almost half an hour's rest left, most of the men stretched out on the ground to try to recover their strength. Some fell asleep in the sun on the sharp black gravel, too tired to look for a shady spot. About five minutes before work was to resume, they heard a loud voice bellow out, "Get up! Hurry up!"

Minh hadn't been able to sleep, and he got up, recognising Mainote who, a nasty look on his face, was obviously looking for a pretext to let his foul temper loose.

"This man's behaviour is not normal. He acts like a drunkard or a madman" thought Minh.

His companions, exhausted by fatigue and the heat, got up one after the other, making a huge effort to get back to work. But one of the young men was still asleep, despite the repeated calls of his friend. His loud, regular snoring exasperated Mainote even more. He took out his pocket watch and chain and waited with real impatience for the second hand to get to one o'clock exactly. He put the watch back in his jacket straight away. Then, bending down, he grabbed the sleeping man by his shirt front, pulled him up and struck him brutally several times.

"You lazy bastard!" he yelled, dropping the poor man to the ground, completely dazed. Mainote turned around towards the group of dismayed men.

"May that be a lesson to you all!" he shouted.

But the young men, stirred by anger and indignation, muttered under their breath, "You'll pay for this! You'll pay, you bastard!"

"Enough time wasted! Get to work!" roared Mainote again. The men obeyed listlessly.

Minh was shocked and worried. "These people have complete control. Will I have the courage and patience to take all this abuse lying down?" he wondered.

"The team transporting wood will continue down to the bottom tunnels. There are men waiting for you there. They'll show you what you have to do," said Watard.

Minh and his companions went back inside the mine where a few men were waiting for them.

"You have to put these beams in the metal cage, in the lift you see over there. Then we'll take them down to the tunnel at the bottom," said one of the men.

"How many metres to this tunnel?" Minh ventured.

"About sixty!"

Minh's fears increased. He tried to light up the vertical shaft with his lamp, but the feeble light did not reach the end. Minh could only make out the steel rails, which disappeared into the black gaping void. He began to imagine the cracked rock faces collapsing. "Everyone around would be crushed or buried for ever," he thought.

"Come on, Minh!" said Đào. "The beams've all been taken down. They want us to go down too."

The apprentice miners took the rudimentary lift, looking dazed. The lamps drew strange enigmatic shadows on the wet rock face, which seemed to be moving upwards very quickly.

"I've definitely got a lot to learn," muttered Minh, his eyes open wide before this fascinating spectacle.

The teams came together on the lower platform. "It's like a termite hill," thought Minh. "Tunnels in all directions!"

The central tunnel was lit by the yellowish light of the lamps.

"So, all these beams are used to consolidate the ceiling and the walls and prevent them caving in," observed Minh silently. "They need a lot to protect all these tunnels. The beams we've just brought down will be for new tunnels."

A supervisor had just come out of the darkness. "Each new recruit will work with an experienced miner. That's how you'll learn the best way to work underground."

"This supervisor also has a whip!" Minh observed. "Is it really necessary at the bottom of a mine?"

"Come on!" said Minh's companion, a stocky little man with a mocking expression on his face. He already had one end of a beam on his shoulder and he got up suddenly before Minh was able to make the slightest movement.

"Hey, new boy! Are you coming or not?"

Minh crouched down and tried to lift the other end. But from this position the log seemed to weigh a ton. Đào saw Minh was in a difficult situation and came over to help him, and it was only with two of them and a great deal of difficulty that they were finally able to lift the log and put it on Minh's battered shoulder. Pale and seething with rage, Minh walked behind his new partner, grumbling, "I'm just like a slave. I have only one right: the right to obey. These men are bullies. They enjoy making us suffer. And that includes my own compatriots!"

Minh was also thinking about the miners who had gone back home. "The workers who return home boast of how much money they've been able to make. They never talk about the difficulty and suffering they've had to endure. It's wrong, as they lead us, unsuspecting, into the cruellest of situations."

The more Minh advanced, the more his anger grew, crushed as he was under the terrible weight of the wet log that was digging into his shoulder. Once he got to a small tunnel no more than two metres high, the miner in front slowed down. Holding a lamp in one hand, with the other he gripped the rock face. Advancing cautiously, he said, "You have to bend down now—the tunnel gets smaller and smaller."

Minh followed his companion, his back bent, hunched over. In this position his load seemed to weigh a ton. His hands gripped the rocks whose sharp edges cut into his flesh. But there was no way he could let go! Their eyes wide, the men knew that in this position the log would crush them if they lost their balance. They were very careful not to trip over the stones on the ground. Minh was drenched with perspiration. The sweat ran down his forehead and his cheeks, which were blackened by the dust. He was so tense that he forgot his fatigue and concentrated his efforts on the task. Like the others, he couldn't afford to make a single mistake. The water from the walls dripped onto his torn hands, ran along his arms and spread all over his body, soaking his clothes, which were filthy from the dust and the mud. Finally, they put their load down at the end of the narrow tunnel.

Four men who were even dirtier than Minh were busy working in this place in the stark light of the strongest lamps. Some were digging, others were using crowbars to break off enormous shiny wet black blocks. Minh, panting, looked at them, his mouth wide open as if to breathe in all the air from the small tunnel.

"This is what you can look forward to, what we do, every day," said one of the men. "Extract the ore, rip it out of the mountain to earn a crust. You'll have to get used to it, buddy!"

Then, grabbing Minh by the arm, he pulled him along. "Come, let's go and get the others. We need at least another four beams like this one!"

This man, covered in mud, was being friendly. Minh was astonished, "He's treating me like an equal!" Surprised, Minh followed him. When they got to the central tunnel they came face to face with a supervisor who, a whip in his hand, was watching over the men like an eagle ready to swoop down on its prey. This brought Minh back to the sad reality. . .

With his eyes half-closed, stretched out on his mat, dead with fatigue, he shook his head again as if he couldn't believe it. The image of his parents came back to him, but this time Minh felt more upset than usual because he thought he could see tears in their eyes. He sat up, emerging from his deep dream.

Minh looked at himself, alarmed to see his torn hands were black with dirt. His shoulders were aching terribly and the filth that stuck to his body and his clothes depressed him even more. He realised that he would never again be the young man who, not so long ago, used to stroll nonchalantly along the streets of Hà-Nội.

The Young Girls

That night the newcomers, both men and women, weary from the harrowing day they had endured, ate their dinner in silence in a corner of the refectory. Minh and Lan, sitting next to each other, their heads bent, stared at the table and their bowls of rice. They didn't even have the energy to utter a word to each other. Those who had been in the camp for some time, however, chatted and joked together noisily. They seemed to be in top form. Minh commented to Phúc, who had just arrived, that there were fewer men there than the day before.

"The men you see here are all single. Married couples prefer to get their food rations and do their own cooking in their quarters."

Phúc observed his companions for a moment and added with a smile, "The reason they're speaking so loudly is to attract the attention of the young girls."

He looked at Liên and continued, "It's a tactic as old as the world! They know that only the smartest and the boldest stand a chance, just a small chance, to start a family. They all want to be amongst the first to attack!"

Thế snuggled up to Hiếu. The day of hard labour had not dampened her spirits and her face was radiant. Hiếu seemed more solemn. He was worried, waiting for the moment when he would have to stand up and announce the happy event. His hands gripping the big wooden table he stood up, hesitating. His eyelids began to flicker, the words would not come out and, choking, he had to sit down again. Thế looked at him lovingly in encouragement. Then, smiling, she whispered,

"Speak, Hiếu. Speak, my dear. I'm here, at your side. From now on we're together. You'll never be alone again. Be brave!"

Hiếu, his emotions running high, got up and announced hoarsely, "My friends, my dear friends. . ."

The conversations stopped, the noise subsided, and everyone stared at the hesitant speaker. Thế got up in turn, her face radiant. She pressed against her future husband to encourage him.

"Dear friends," repeated Hiếu, whose voice had come back. "May I introduce my wife, Thế. As you know, or you will soon," he said, looking at the new recruits, "on this mine we can't marry legally since the authorities are all far away in Koumac. Since we can't take time off work, even for a day, I ask you all to be the witnesses of our union."

Immediately, there was cheering and shouts of congratulations. Minh observed this astonishing spectacle with great interest.

Lan whispered, "Just like that! They're now considered to be man and wife. How easy it is. Oh, if only it could always be so simple to give your word and keep it."

And she set to thinking of a marvellous world where there were no bad people, no egoists. She was brought back to reality by Liên's voice. "Come on Lan, let's go and congratulate the newlyweds."

Like a robot, Lan got up and followed her friend, "What's this? Here I am imagining things, dreaming like a child. Is it fatigue playing tricks on me?" she wondered.

With a heavy heart Liên congratulated Thế and Hiếu, chatting with them for a while, as if to avoid thinking about her own predicament.

Two young men that Minh knew well, taking advantage of the happy ambiance, together decided to approach the young girls and ask for their hand, before anyone else could get in before them. The girls appeared delighted and relieved as they knew these boys; they had been observing them since they had all left Hải-Phòng together. But they didn't want to appear too eager or show how happy they were, so they asked them for a night to think it over.

"I'll give you my answer tomorrow," said each of the girls with a smile full of promises.

Despite her hostile demeanour, Lan found herself surrounded. Minh chose to go to his dormitory as he had decided to write a letter to his parents to send them his news. Phúc remained alone, near Liên who had become taciturn and sullen again. Feeling a little disconcerted by her attitude, he said, "It's been a hard day for you Liên. With time I . . ."

"We're no longer at work as far as I know," said Liên scathingly. "If you have any advice, you can wait until tomorrow."

"Calm down, Liên. There's no use losing your temper."

"I'm not losing it. I'm just asking for one simple thing: peace. Do you understand? Peace!"

"Liên, stop attacking me, let's try and live together on good terms," said Phúc calmly.

Liên was surprised by his conciliatory tone. Remembering Lan's advice, she relaxed and opened up a bit. She continued, "We're living in a hostile environment. Let's try to understand each other so that we can respect each other."

"I'm sure you're different from what you are trying to make me think," said Phúc.

Liên looked puzzled.

"Yes, because I've been observing you and I've come to the conclusion that your attitude is like a mask you force yourself to put on your face. I don't know why . . . since the first day I met you—do you remember, we were together at Kunéo?—I've often told myself that this mask doesn't suit you. . ."

Embarrassed, not knowing how to respond, the young girl looked away.

"Have you suffered a lot?" Phúc asked.

Liên was troubled by Phúc's perceptiveness. It suddenly seemed that he could read inside her soul. She nodded gently, without a word.

Phúc got up and said, "Come, let's walk a little; it'll do you good."

Without knowing why, Liên gave in and followed him, leaving Lan and her companions behind. The fresh air brought her to her senses; she felt afraid and wanted to go back to the canteen, but Phúc held her firmly. "No, Liên, I promise you there's no need to be afraid. Why don't we walk for a moment?"

Liên resigned herself to the situation and walked along beside Phúc. They walked in silence in the dark through the narrow lanes of the camp. But the memory of Thắng suddenly came flooding back, as if drowning her. A smothered sob shook her whole body.

"Come, Liên. Let's go and have a hot tea. You're cold. I'll just ask one thing of you—trust me. I'll take you back to your quarters afterwards. I promise."

Liên obeyed without hesitation, with a serenity that surprised even herself. When they got to the long building, Phúc opened one of the doors and they went inside to a big tidy room. Near the door was a small wooden table with a bench on either side. Inside on the right was a large bed covered with a mat. On the other side of the room was a wooden cupboard. On their left, near the entrance, was a small door leading to a kitchenette. Liên was astonished to see that there was no open fireplace like the one she had had ever since she was a little girl. Phúc took a kettle, filled it with water and put it on a strange device that he had preheated using a small amount of kerosene. Then, using the pump on the tank, he turned on the stove and a flame ignited under the kettle. The water began to boil after a few minutes.

Phúc had noticed the girl's astonishment at the strange machine. "It's a kerosene stove," he said with pride. "With this instant fire, there's no need to chop wood, or have the cooking pots blackened with soot."

Wisps of white steam were now rising to the ceiling. Unable to take her eyes off the magic flame, Liên thought, "What an extraordinary invention." She imagined how easy it would be for the fortunate housewife who owned such a device.

Phúc served the tea, inviting the young girl to sit on one of the benches. Then he too sat down opposite his guest and observed her, but Liên looked sullen and gloomy again. Her head hung as she stared at the bare floor.

"Pull yourself together Liên. You have to keep fighting against everything, against yourself, otherwise you'll never have the strength to get to the end of your contract. You're here like me, like most of us, actually, because we need to work, for whatever reason. It's absolutely necessary and you . . . we can't allow ourselves to be beaten by adversity."

Liên began to cry uncontrollably.

Phúc remained silent, waited for a moment, and then continued, looking solemn, "I've also suffered a lot . . . I am a widower. My wife died over five years ago, just after we arrived at Pimboé. A terrible accident. A clumsy fall, one Sunday . . . we were out walking. A fracture . . . to her head." He mumbled, as if to himself, "I loved her a lot." But he regained his calm quickly and continued his story.

"I became hot-headed and angry. I even lashed out at my supervisors and was sent to prison several times. At that time, I was angry at the whole world. Then I came to my senses. I told myself that I didn't have the right to destroy myself, as no one is master of his own destiny. You have to accept it and live like a man, like a thinking responsible human being. There's no use in giving up, in letting yourself drown in distress. That can only lead to debauchery and vice."

He gazed at the young girl, adding, "You see, Liên, that's what saved me. I pulled myself together. From then on I worked with courage and perseverance without complaining. Until one day, my good conduct and knowledge of French cancelled out the bad behaviour of the past. They trusted me, and now I have a good position, an enviable one in our community. Let's just say I earn a bit more than the others here. But let's not talk about these base materialistic preoccupations. Tell me about yourself instead. It'll do you good, you'll see."

Liên hesitated, thinking, "Phúc seems sincere, but I still don't know him well enough to confide in him."

She took her head in her hands and began to think, "He has also suffered, so he can understand me and perhaps even guide me. I can't rely on anyone else here. Minh and Lan are as disoriented as I am."

Liên made up her mind and began to tell him of her misfortunes in great detail.

"You see," said Phúc once she had finished, "I was right, we have the same problems. The only difference is that Thắng's still alive. But what can we do against fate? You're here, and Thắng's somewhere else in this harsh, austere country."

Phúc observed the girl again and then said, "I'm sorry to distress you even more, but you have to face the facts, don't you think? In this colony, we're governed by laws and regulations and our own obligations. There's nothing you can do to find him until your contract comes to an end—that is, in five years!"

Phúc was quiet for a moment, then added timidly, "Do you think that Thắng, by that time, will. . ."

"Please," interrupted, Liên sharply, looking shattered. "Don't say another word! I don't know! I don't know anything anymore!"

She began to sob again, as if she were alone in the room. Phúc respected her need to grieve and she gradually calmed down. Knowing Liên needed a good night's sleep, Phúc said, "Come on, Liên, it's getting late. I'll take you back to your quarters. But, if you want, you can stay here to rest tonight. The locks are solid, and I can go and sleep with friends."

Liên declined the offer. She preferred to go back to her own mat in her dormitory, and her friend Lan.

As for Minh, he had just finished his letter, which was very brief, containing nothing but a white lie. He was keen to reassure his parents: "Everything is fine for me in this new country," he wrote. "My morale is good, and the people are welcoming. Don't worry about me at all."

Then he concluded by saying that he would be coming home in the not-too-distant future, omitting however to give them a precise date. Minh checked that he had written the address correctly, sealed the envelope and fell asleep immediately, overcome by exhaustion.

The Foreman

Liên saw Phúc again the next morning on the work site. He was with Mainote who seemed to be in a good mood. The young man gave a slight nod in her direction and Liên replied with a smile, but she wished immediately that she hadn't. However, even while she was working, she couldn't stop herself from looking at him from time to time. His serious, determined look commanded respect and his direct gaze seemed to reach right into her soul. Liên felt proud to have a friend like him.

"The foreman's waiting for you," said Phúc to Lan. "He'll take you to his house to show you the work you'll have to do."

So, Lan left her friends and followed Mainote, feeling very apprehensive. She didn't like doing housework, as she wasn't very good at it. She would actually have preferred, if she could, to carry on working on the site in the sun, pulling out bushes and grass.

Once she had arrived at the foreman's dwelling, a pretty house surrounded by a big garden, Lan didn't dare go inside. The floor, covered with shiny grey cement, reflected the daylight. Brightly coloured pictures hung on the walls, painted a bright yellow that she found relaxing. A big table and chairs made of solid wood had pride of place at the back of the room. Four armchairs made of a precious local wood covered with a shiny varnish were placed around a low table. An electric lightbulb, under a lampshade decorated with a flowery pattern, was hanging above this living area. Elegant antique ornaments brightened the big sideboard with their beauty. Lan was tempted for a fleeting moment to make a comparison between what she had and what she could see in front of her eyes, but she managed to control herself and thought of something else so that she would not be overcome with jealousy.

Mainote had to insist before she would allow herself to set foot on the shiny floor. He told her what work she had to do, but she couldn't understand a single syllable and wished that Minh had been there.

"Ah! If he could be here with me," she murmured. "He could've translated all these commands easily."

Unusually for him, Mainote was extremely patient that day. His miming was not very convincing, but Lan could still understand and Mainote was completely satisfied with his efforts. He managed a smile on his fat, round face. To

Lan it looked like a grimace and she was fearful, but Mainote left straight away, leaving her alone in his beautiful house, and she regained her calm.

Lan set about working, cleaning and washing the cement floor, then she dusted the furniture and wiped the armchairs, which shone even more in the bright daylight. Everything was done methodically and efficiently. As she had some time left, she went out into the garden and took out the weeds, pebbles and gravel which had got into the soil of the flowerbeds. After some time, she heard voices and footsteps coming nearer. Lifting her head, she recognised Phúc and Mainote. The foreman inspected his house for a moment and came back looking delighted. He asked Phúc to translate.

"The foreman's very happy with your work. You can rest now, it's almost mid-day. Did you bring your lunch, Lan?"

"Yes, I have it here with me. I put it in the corner of the veranda," Lan answered.

"Good," said Phúc, "have your lunch, then relax a bit. Mainote told me he'll give you more work after his siesta."

Phúc gave her a friendly smile and left quickly. A few minutes later he was back at his work site, where the young women, hard at work, were covered in perspiration. He made them stop working and walked towards Liên who was completely soaked, as the heat was even more extreme than the day before.

"Would you like to come and have lunch with me in the canteen? It's much cooler there."

Liên was sitting in the shade of a tree. "That's very kind of you," she said, "but I prefer to stay here. I'm waiting for Lan who'll certainly be back any minute."

"Lan won't be back for a while, she still has work to do for Mainote. Come on, Liên!" Phúc repeated.

"Please, I'm too tired to come with you and, to be honest, I prefer to stay here with my friends."

"Oh well, too bad for me," said Phúc, giving up. Confused by this strange girl, he disappeared. Liên wanted to be conciliatory, to say something nice to him before he left, but in the end, she decided not to. After she had eaten her piece of bread, she wanted to doze a moment on the thick grass, but the air was humid and the ground too hot, so she had to move from her spot.

A moment later, Phúc found her under a big tree on top of the hill. There was a slight breeze and Liên felt revived. As if to excuse herself she greeted her new friend with a wide smile, which disconcerted the young man even more. He stayed with Liên, not knowing what to talk about. He seemed both nervous and serious. Suddenly he looked at the young girl and said, "I thought a lot last night, Liên and I . . . I also thought about you!"

He hesitated for a moment, and then, lowering his head slightly, he added, "I know it's not the time or the place to broach the subject, but. . . well, I mean. . . Liên will you be my wife?"

Liên jumped up, furious, "How dare you ask me?" she cried.

"Calm down, calm down, Liên," said Phúc, putting his hands out in front of himself as if to contain the young girl's anger. "I understand your indignation, after everything we said to each other last night, but please spare me a few minutes. Listen to me, just like you did last night and then you're free to do what you think is right. You can even shoo me away if you want to."

Without giving her time to reply he continued, as if he were afraid that he would never be able to speak to her like this again.

"You see," he said, "as I've just told you, I thought things over last night. I had the same problems as you a few years ago, well, nearly the same, so I'm sure I can understand you better than anyone else. As for you, you're a young defenceless girl surrounded by all these men. They'll never leave you alone in peace! They'll end up getting you, I'm sorry to say. They'll try first by stealth and if that doesn't work, they'll take you by force. Have a look around you. In the camp, are there any single women apart from those who've just arrived? No! Because even the most unattractive have been able to choose their husband. Yes, I said 'choose'! There's no lack of men! Speaking from long experience, I can guarantee that in two weeks' time the girls will all be married. That is, married the way we do it. Your friend Lan included. No girl can escape this fate! And very soon, perhaps in the next few days, you yourself are going to have to choose a man who'll become your husband, even if you love someone else. Excuse my bluntness, but I've always preferred to state things just as they are. I can assure you, it's so that you understand that here, we're living in a strange world where the usual rules and customs don't apply. . . . As for me," continued Phúc, "I've loved you from the start, from the first day I saw you at the port at Kunéo."

Liên was stunned by these frank revelations, even though they confirmed her innermost fears. She was disconcerted, and all traces of anger had disappeared from her face. "He has his own particular way of revealing the facts," she said to herself, "he doesn't try to hide anything."

Phúc checked his watch and gave the order for work to begin again.

As for Lan, unable to check the time, she had gone back to work earlier than expected. She could hear the foreman's snoring, so loud it reached the rosebushes and, while she was waiting for him to wake up, she continued to pull up the weeds as quietly as possible.

Mainote appeared a moment later in front of the main door. With a wave he ordered her to come and join him. Lan hesitated as he was not wearing trousers. His long thin white legs seemed to have difficulty supporting his huge body. His round stomach stuck out, covered by a jumper that stretched obscenely over it.

Lan was shocked and and could feel an indefinable fear gradually overcoming her. She turned away from the man's eyes, which were swollen from sleep. He called a second time. Lan had to obey, but she did not move from the veranda. Mainote tried to make his ugly, greasy face look as reassuring as possible, but that only made the young girl more afraid and disgusted. But Mainote repeated more firmly that she should follow him. This time Lan refused to obey.

"Why doesn't he tell me what I have to do?" she wondered. "I'd do it if he came outside."

Mainote seemed to have lost patience and he rushed towards Lan, grabbed her suddenly with his strong arms and dragged her across the living room to his bedroom. He seemed to have lost all control of himself, as if driven by a bestial desire. He threw her on the bed and tried to embrace her. Lying across the mattress, her face both terrified and threatening, Lan seemed even more beautiful to him. Mainote wanted to cover her in kisses. Lan fought desperately but couldn't free herself as Mainote was too strong and heavy. Suddenly she had a horrendous idea; as quick as lightning, she lifted her hands up to the giant's face and, with all her strength she dug her nails into his flesh, then, with a sudden movement from top to bottom she made a deep gash in his face. Mainote screamed in pain. He threw the girl violently against the wall. With his right hand he touched his cheek and was aghast to see that his fingers were smeared with blood.

Lan was crouching in a corner of the room, paralysed by fear and by what she had done to one of the mine's top bosses. There would be serious consequences.

Mainote, furious, wanted to slap her, beat her, but his raised hand fell back and suddenly an eerie light glinted in his eyes. Grabbing the young girl, he dragged her brutally towards the backyard. When they got to the end of the garden, he took her to the wild bushland covered with vines and thorny bushes. He pointed to a wasp's nest which was hanging, like a bizarrely perforated bell, from one of the branches. Lan, her eyes wide open, could see the dangerous bright yellow insects. Some were flying into the many tiny holes of the nest while others were flying out, swirling above her head, the beating of their wings producing a menacing sound.

Mainote, like a furious bear, his eyes as red as his cheeks, ordered her to destroy the nest. Terrified, her pupils more and more dilated, Lan suddenly saw herself as an innocent young girl, when, for the first time she had wanted to catch a wasp, just like these ones. The wasp had settled on the back of a buffalo she took every day to graze at the edge of the woods. She could still remember the moment her little fingers finally managed to grab the insect. She had felt an excruciating pain as the wasp stung her. Her hand had swollen up very quickly and she could feel the sting for a long time after that. It seemed to her like yesterday!

The hellish circling of the wasps continued insistently just above her head. A thump to her back pushed her forward. Mainote had hit her with a long pole, as if to give her a warning. Trying not to lose her balance, Lan waved her hands wildly about in the air. By accident, one of her hands knocked the nest, which fell down at her feet. She jumped aside, out of the way of the dangerous yellow horde, which was flying in all directions. Just as she landed with all her weight on the ground, she felt a shooting pain, as if something hard and sharp had just pierced her bare feet. She looked down and discovered with horror that she had jumped with both feet together onto the branches of some dried rosebushes left there by a gardener. Lan pulled out the thorns, crying out in pain. She was just about to throw the branches away from her when she heard Mainote's commanding voice. Out of danger himself, he continued to threaten her, gesturing and shouting wildly. In a raging fury, he ordered her to put the branches back on the ground.

Lan suddenly realised that she was dealing with a madman. She was so afraid that she ended up obeying his orders, like a robot. However, the wasps, crazed by the sudden collapse of their nest, were flying all around her body, her face and above her head. Their buzzing became more and more unbearable. Then Lan watched in horror as a wasp suddenly landed on her forehead. She felt a sharp pain near her eyebrow, then another, even more intense, at the corner of her right eye. Distraught and blinded by these painful stings, Lan almost fell over. Balancing precariously on one foot, she managed, with jerky movements of her arms, to keep upright. But when she put her foot down again on the thorns that she herself had spread on the ground, she let out a loud cry. Her head began to wobble and then to spin dizzyingly. Nothing could hold her up as she collapsed with all her weight on the sharp thorns. She was dazzled by lights flashing before her eyes, like electric shocks.

Her disentanglement from this hell was slow and difficult. She came to later, slumped on the ground, inert and disfigured. Her eyes had almost disappeared under the swellings from the wasp stings. Mainote looked at her with hatred. His bloodied face still showed the deep grooves that her sharp nails had made. But his shining eyes seemed to relish the abject state the young girl was in.

When Liên got back from work she found her friend stretched out on her mat, shivering and feverish. Her face was buried in one of her blouses, hidden from the eyes of the others in her dormitory. Liên sat down next to the ailing Lan, put her hand on her burning forehead and pushed the blouse away a little. She frowned, intrigued by the unusual shape she could feel under her fingers. Delicately she lifted the blouse and discovered the hideous sight.

"No!" cried Liên. "No! What happened to you? What happened, my sister?"

"Yellow wasps. . ." Lan replied weakly.

Distressed, with tears in her eyes, Liên ran outside without a word. She picked up a handful of fine black earth and put it in the hollow of her hand, poured a little water onto the powder with the other hand, then mixed it to make a sticky paste. She went back to Lan and applied the mud to the swollen areas of her face. Soon Lan's deformed face was covered in strange black spots.

"You'll see," said Liên affectionately, "as the mud dries out it'll draw out any stings that may still be in there and the venom will come out. In a few hours there won't be any trace left of these bites."

By nightfall, Lan's face had become presentable again, just as Liên had predicted. She had taken the thorns out of Lan's feet with a needle.

"Without my remedy you would've had your clown face as well as the pain for at least another twenty-four hours," she joked.

Lan was quiet, absent, as if she had heard nothing. The horrific scenes from the afternoon kept coming back to haunt her.

"You're hiding something from me, I'm sure of it. What exactly happened, Lan? You can confide in me!" Liên insisted.

Lan decided to tell her the truth. When she had finished, Liên was livid.

"We have to find a way," she said, her jaw clenched in anger. "We have to take revenge against this dangerous animal. We can't accept being treated like this for ever!"

"We shouldn't try to provoke anything, Liên. That won't help us. They're stronger and we need money. He punished me, but, actually his male pride is also wounded. I can't call him 'a man', he doesn't deserve it, just a male. I also left him some painful souvenirs! We're even!"

Lan tried to console herself in this way, without too much conviction. Could she forget all of this so easily? She lifted her face anxiously up to Liên and said, "I'll just ask you one thing; please don't say anything about this to the others. . . to Minh in particular. I wouldn't want him to worry or have problems because of me. Promise me, Liên!"

Liên accepted reluctantly. She thought about the conversation she had had with Phúc, but decided not to say anything, at least for the moment.

"Lan's too upset today for me to trouble her with my own problems," she thought.

After the meal Phúc came to find her. He invited her once again to go for a walk with him that night. Liên had been completely wrapped up in Lan's problems until then, but she accepted. She had a question to ask him. "Why don't the men and women on this mine band together to fight against these people who are blinded by power and dominate and exploit us so shamelessly?" Liên blurted out, once they were outside.

Surprised by this direct but obvious question, Phúc replied with his usual calm, "Because, you see, Liên, we're like birds in a cage. Far away from our country, isolated on top of this mountain, on this island in the middle of the ocean. If one of our employers, for whatever reason, decided one day to take away the smallest thing, our food, for example, we'd be like caged birds deprived of their grains. We depend on them for everything: work, our survival, and even to be able to go home one day. Remember that the boats don't belong to us!"

"Nothing belongs to us here! Not even our own existence!" protested Liên, weary all of a sudden.

"And if we lose our calm," continued, Phúc, "I mean, if we rebel they'd have all the pretexts they need to put us in prison! Don't forget we're prisoners and they have the right to dock several months of our pay! I don't think anyone on this mine would be prepared to lose the money they've worked so hard for. We're trapped and we can't afford any mistakes," Phúc continued, "Our fate is hard and cruel, but what can we do? On one side are the rich and powerful, who give orders; on the other, the underlings, who carry them out. We're in the second category."

"So, we're doomed, unable to defend ourselves," observed Liên sadly.

"Alas," replied Phúc bleakly, "we all need to work and each one of us hopes to make a bit of money before going home, don't we?"

He added sadly, as if regretting it, "I don't know many who don't need money. You, even more than me, since your whole family's counting on you!"

Phúc walked in silence for a moment. The lights from the buildings lit up the small lane faintly. "Think about it, Liên," he said finally. "Would we be happier or freer at the moment in our own country? Under the present regime? For most of us here, I'd say 'no'! If everything were perfect at home, would we have had to leave like this? Remember those we met in Tonkin who'd returned from this island. You met some before you left, didn't you?" he asked.

Liên nodded.

"Did they tell you about their suffering or the bad treatment? No! Never! Because human beings can adapt to any situation, especially if it involves money. You'll see, Liên, in a few months, you'll get used to these tough conditions just like us!" Phúc continued, "Did you know that our employers keep part of our wages, which are put aside and given back to us at the end of our contract, when we leave this colony permanently? After five years, it should be quite a bit of money. On that day you'll be as happy as those who left before you."

"Even so, do we still have to accept everything?" replied Liên.

"Maybe you're alluding to what happened to Lan this afternoon?"

"How did you know?" she answered sharply. "And you said nothing, did nothing for her? You're just as bad as the foremen!" cried Liên furiously.

"I understand why you're so indignant; your reaction's completely natural, but I must tell you, if you promise to stay calm, that these things have happened before and will happen again, as long as there are single young girls here. Obviously Mainote has crossed the line! I met one of his colleagues who told me what happened. But they're not all like that. The management was alerted by witnesses, Europeans, who saw this appalling incident. Mainote has received a strict warning. I don't think he'll do that sort of thing again for a while."

"Well, I will never trust this man . . . this monster!"

"What he did is terrible, it's true, but he's a lonely man, and Lan is so young and attractive that he lost control."

"You defend him well!" grumbled Liên. "But he'll always be, for me, for Lan, and no doubt for most of us, the devil incarnate. We'll always distrust him and he should watch out for us too! Because the day will come when things change, I'm sure of it."

Then she was silent. Her intense emotion was betrayed only by her breathlessness. Their conversation had taken them far from the village. Without a word they turned at the same time and headed back. In the sky dotted with stars, the mischievous moon at last came out from behind a black cloud, spreading its faint yellow light over the mountains and over the two young people. Phúc observed Liên who had suddenly fallen silent.

"You said that similar events had already occurred in the past?" she said in a low voice.

"Yes Liên. There have been kidnappings, gang rapes. I mean, several men locked a poor girl in their dormitory and took advantage of her. Well, remember your first night in the camp with Thế! Fortunately, there were no problems as she was consenting, but often girls are assaulted and molested by our own countrymen."

Liên looked at him, perplexed. "And these men still manage to get the girls to marry them?"

"It happens," said Phúc, "as the girls here are alone, friendless and often very ignorant. Most of the time, they don't know anything about men, and so when they find love, they cling to it. They fall in love with their jailers or their benefactors, call them what you will!"

Liên followed Phúc, and then, when he invited her into his quarters, she went inside for the second time without any misgivings, as if she were used to coming to this place. Sitting on one of the seats, as she had the night before, she remained pensive, her eyes half-closed as she drifted into a deep daydream. Phúc gave her some hot tea. He could now observe her at his ease,

"How beautiful you are, Liên!"

When she came back to reality, he had taken her hand in his. Almost unconsciously Liên did not withdraw it. At this simple contact Phúc's heart beat furiously. No longer able to stop himself he mustered all his courage and said, his voice full of emotion, "Stay with me, Liên! I love you, let's get married. You won't regret it, I promise you!"

Liên lowered her head. She was no longer the rebellious determined young girl. She felt confused. "I don't know, I don't know any more, Phúc. Give me a bit more time," she begged.

As she walked back to the dormitory with Phúc, Liên's conscience was plagued by many conflicting thoughts. Before going back inside, she tormented herself with questions.

"What should I do? Where is my Thắng at present? Do I have the right to betray him, to forget him after only a few days? Oh, certainly not. I'll never forget him. But what can I do in this situation, which is so dangerous for a woman alone? For I feel that Phúc is right and that anything could happen in this place, where hundreds of men live crowded together!"

They reached the door and then separated, wishing each other good night.

"What should I do?" she asked herself again as she went inside. "If I have to choose a man, why not him? Yes, why not Phúc?"

"Oh, I don't know," she said, lying down on her mat. Then she closed her eyes, promising herself to ask Lan's advice when she got back later.

***

Lan was one of the first to go to the evening meal and the canteen was still almost empty. She hoped she would be served quickly so that she could go back to her dormitory. Then Minh would not see her in this state.

She was surprised to see some young, almost elegant, people appear as if by magic. Some were even wearing clean white pith helmets. They were cheerful and relaxed, obviously a lot better off than Minh and his friends who arrived a few minutes later. The latter were much less eloquent, and they looked tired and demoralised. Minh sat down, as usual, next to Lan.

"Good evening Lan," he said and then added, "I don't know why, but I was very worried about you today."

Lan stared at the wooden chopsticks and the bowls on the table, not daring to look at him.

"I hope your day wasn't too difficult, Lan?" asked Minh.

Unwittingly Minh had just touched the most sensitive point, the deep wound in her soul. Lan had a strong urge to cry, to tell him everything, but she managed to contain herself.

"What's the matter, Lan? Why are you like this?"

Then, intrigued, with his right hand Minh lifted the girl's chin and saw her slightly swollen face. Lan said quickly, "Yellow wasps. I was stung by yellow wasps on the work site."

Tears ran down her cheeks; she couldn't stop them.

"Poor little Lan," said Minh in sympathy. He squeezed her hand in his as if to lessen the pain.

At the end of the meal, the two young women who had been proposed to the night before joined their future husbands and, by mutual consent, without any further formalities, the two couples announced their union to those present.

"That makes three of us who are married," thought Lan.

After the new brides had left, the remaining single women were surrounded by males. Proposals rained down from all sides and Lan was one of the most sought after. Phúc had taken advantage of the moment to invite Liên to go for a walk with him. Minh was pushed aside callously. "What can I do?" he said to himself, "Lan's a friend, she has a right to make her own home."

But instead of calming him down, these thoughts just irritated him more! He couldn't bear seeing all these men hanging around Lan, disturbing her peace. He wanted to get up and go home to bed. He was exhausted. The second day had been as gruelling as the first. But he couldn't take his eyes off Lan. She seemed distraught, at a loss amongst all these agitated men.

"What's happening to me?" he thought, "Why am I so annoyed? Could I be jealous, by any chance?" Without answering these questions, he got up and made his way determinedly towards Lan. He grabbed her right hand and took her outside, under the furious eyes of the elegant young men.

They walked side by side to the end of the village and stayed together a long while in the dark night. Minh was overcome with confusion. He had suddenly forgotten his fatigue and realised at that moment that his anger had disappeared and he was happy.

"Lan seems to have a lot of power over me," he realised. "Here she is by my side and without saying a single word, she's made me feel at peace and relaxed!"

This thought troubled him. He had fled his parents and a young girl back home to be free, to live his life as he wanted and now, suddenly, he no longer felt in charge of his actions or his feelings. He shuddered. He was afraid of losing his freedom.

"But does freedom really exist here on this land, tainted as it is with power and hatred?" he wondered.

Back in front of Lan's quarters, they sat down at the top of the wooden steps in front of the door. Lan was delighted to have Minh by her side. They stayed like this without a word, wrapped up in the silence of the night. From time to time a loud burst of laughter rang out from the canteen in the cool evening air.

"Minh's so strange," Lan thought. "Sometimes he's withdrawn and distant and at others gentle and considerate. I can never really understand how he thinks. But at least he's by my side now and everything seems to be easier. I've even managed to forget my terrible ordeal today; I don't even remember Mainote. It all seems a long way away, lost in distant memories." She now felt only a deep sense of well-being and joy to be so near Minh, whose presence made her drunk with happiness. Nothing else existed around her. Then, she began to worry again.

"How long will this happiness last? One small moment? A few more minutes? Then Minh will go away, perhaps without even wishing me good night?"

On the verge of tears, Lan looked at Minh; she needed him so much. Couldn't he understand that? What was he thinking about at this moment? All these questions, if only she could ask him to share them. Life would be so much more beautiful! But she was determined to accept his decisions; she would remain silent and obedient. She had loved him too much since the very first day—she was sure of that now—to impose anything on him. A long moment passed. In the peace and quiet of the night they both felt deeply troubled. Before they separated, Minh said softly to Lan, "Don't make any hasty decisions, Lan."

"What decision, Minh?"

"I mean, don't reply straight away to any marriage proposals from other men. Be patient, I need to think things over. Because I'm not someone who can do things lightly. That's the way I am," he said, then, hesitating, "because I think. . . yes, I think I love you, Lan!"

The young girl wanted to fling her arms around his neck, kiss him, yell out with joy, but she controlled herself. However, she did take Minh's hand and kept it for a long time in hers, before letting him leave. It was her way of showing him her joy and expressing her love for him.

The next morning was long; the hours seemed to take pleasure in stretching out interminably. When it was finally time for a break, the young girls dropped their heavy tools with relief. Most of the land had been cleared of its roots and cleaned up. In spite of their big hats, in the oppressive sun their skin had tanned a little and they seemed even more beautiful, these marriageable young girls! Lan and Liên were bewildered to learn that five of them had made their choice and would leave with their husbands that evening.

"So, we're the only ones left!" cried Lan. She shivered, she was afraid, for she knew that her friend would leave with Phúc. They had talked about it after Minh had left the night before. "What's going to become of me?" she thought anxiously, "Minh will have to decide quickly. I'm afraid of all these men! I'm afraid of being alone at night in this huge dormitory. I know they're capable of anything. What a frightening place I'm in," she moaned.

Liên was also deeply disturbed and, shaking her head, she said to her friend, "No matter how I try, Lan, I can't forget Thắng, it's beyond me. He's still present in my memory. I love him so much and I don't think I'll ever be able to forget him." But she added, resigning herself to the situation, "I do know that we have... I have no hope of seeing him again, not for five years in any case... if I manage to last that long," she added, giving a tired, sad sigh. She continued, "In this village the men are going crazy and are ready to pounce on any poor woman they see. I know we can't escape marriage, alas. What a strange marriage! More like finding a protector or a defender than a husband. Well, that's what it is for me."

Lan agreed, "Yes, here we're doomed to accept a man without having enough time to think things over." Then she added, with conviction, "You have an incredible opportunity with Phúc. He's level-headed and sincere, which are great qualities. And he can help you in many ways. I'm sure you'll have a better job than the one we have now. You won't have money problems. With his seniority and his pay he'll be able to support you and with the money you earn you'll be able to help your parents a lot more."

Lan was elated. She really wanted her friend to find peace and happiness. She added, somewhat embarrassed, "Excuse me for speaking to you like this. You must think I put money and convenience before anything else. But sometimes you have to be realistic to avoid making mistakes. For it seems to me that each mistake has a huge price on this mine."

Lan wanted to add something, but she stopped herself. Phúc had come to join them. She had guessed what her friend was thinking. Looking at her with a complicit smile, she nodded her head slightly as if to say, "Yes, Liên, take him as your husband. He's a good man, and I'm sure you won't regret it."

Life in the Camp

Minh and Lan dined together that evening like real lovebirds. Everything seemed good to them; they were discovering life with new eyes. Minh now felt sure about his feelings—he could no longer live without Lan. He was about to tell her that when they were disturbed by the sudden arrival of Mainote who barged into the canteen without a word or a glance in anyone's direction and began a meticulous search, inspecting the premises thoroughly. He lifted the curtains of the shelves, opened the boxes and tins containing food rations, and checked the kitchen from top to bottom. Then, not finding what he was looking for, he left looking sheepish and annoyed. As he passed in front of Lan, he glared at her, then disappeared as he had come.

"What a bastard," cried the kitchen hand, lifting his hands to the sky. "He's turned everything upside down."

"Why did he come? What did he want?" asked Lan.

Minh didn't know the answer. He was asking himself the same question.

"It's one of their inspections," replied the furious cook. "To find out if we have any alcohol! They refuse to allow us any, in case it affects our performance."

Without really knowing why, Minh was outraged by the attitude of this Mainote. He was also very nervous to see that many men were leering at Lan. He got up, inviting the young girl to follow him, and they left the refectory. They were immediately surrounded by darkness. Minh took Lan's hand as he liked to do. It had become a habit, a contact, a necessary bond between them.

"Lan, I've decided, I've thought about it and I need you! I love you. Will you be my wife?"

A gentle glow lit up their faces. Lan was radiant, ecstatic. "Minh! Oh Minh! I'm so happy! I can say it now! I love you too. Since the first time we met, yes, I think I was already in love with you. Since for ever maybe!" She laid her head on his shoulder, both moved and happy.

"Let's go and announce the good news to the community so that everyone knows that you're my wife. Then they'll leave you in peace!"

"No, Minh, not this evening," said Lan a little awkwardly, "Can we wait a day or two?"

"I don't understand," said Minh, surprised at her reaction.

"No! There's nothing wrong, Minh, don't worry! I love you too much and can't live without you!"

"Well, let's get married then as soon as possible," interrupted Minh with slight irritation in his voice.

"I can't leave Liên alone in the dormitory. It's too dangerous. She has a serious decision to make; Phúc proposed to her. Do you understand? We both know her situation, and I realise it's not easy for Liên to make a complete break with her past, so I'm asking you to give me two more days. If Liên is still undecided after that, I'll leave her alone and I'll be your wife!"

"Yes, all right, I accept," said Minh, "two days, but no more! Agreed?"

"Oh Minh! My dear Minh! And if Liên accepts to marry Phúc, the four of us could all get married together. That would be wonderful!" exclaimed Lan.

Although Minh was a little disappointed, he thought it over, then said, "You're right. Let's wait a few days. That'll give us time to find a room somewhere, even if, like some couples, we have to sublet. It'll give us time to build our own shelter."

After some thought Lan answered jubilantly, "I've got the solution, Minh! That is, if Liên gets married. If she does, she'll go and live with Phúc, won't she? Well we could ask permission to stay in my dormitory for a little while!"

"You're right. I hadn't thought of that!" Then pointing his finger at the young girl's forehead, Minh said, laughing, "Very clever, that little brain!"

Lan was jumping with joy, "We'll have the huge dormitory all to ourselves. That's wonderful, isn't it?"

"Yes, we'll be fine there!"

***

A deep silence settled over the sleeping village interrupted from time to time by the barking of a dog on the distant mountaintop, like a guard making its presence and necessity known to its masters. A black shadow advancing with great care, seeming to slide along the small, deserted laneway, was making its way with quiet footsteps towards the girls' dormitory. A slight creaking could be heard as the wooden stairs complained under the weight. Then the shadow knocked on the door. Once, twice, but that did not wake the girls, so he waited an instant and then knocked again.

"Open the door, open the door quickly!" said the man at last.

Lan was sleeping peacefully She had been lulled to sleep by the image of her beloved Minh, her handsome, special Minh.

"Lan, open up!" the voice said again.

This time she heard it and she even thought she recognised Minh's voice. Dulled by fatigue and sleep, without really knowing what she was doing, Lan got up, went to the door and unlocked it. The door opened violently and a tall man appeared. With one hand he quickly grabbed Lan, putting the other hand firmly over her mouth to prevent her from crying out.

"Calm down! Don't be afraid!" panted the man, "I won't hurt you!"

Suddenly awake, Lan understood what was happening to her and let out a scream, which was immediately stifled by the stranger's hand. But Lan was not about to accept defeat. With all her might she sank her teeth into his hand. The man cried out in pain but dragged her furiously out into the night. Liên was woken by the din and, with her eyes half-closed, she stumbled towards the door. The cool night wind whipped her face, clearing her head. A quick glance around the room told her that Lan had disappeared. She could hear stifled cries, despite her fatigue. Liên suddenly realised how serious the situation was. Gathering up her strength she ran towards Minh's room and, knocking as hard as she could on the door, she yelled, "Minh! Come quickly! Lan's disappeared!"

The stranger had already taken his prisoner to the edge of the village. Lan had freed her face and was yelling with all her might, waking everyone in the camp as she passed. When they got to his dwelling, the man stopped and put out a shaking hand to open the door.

Lan tried desperately to free herself but couldn't extricate herself from the kidnapper's grip. Before he could drag her into the room, she suddenly had an idea. With her free hand, she grabbed the man's genitals and pulled as hard as she could. Surprised and crippled with pain, he almost let go of his prey. But with a supreme effort he managed to free himself, then, furious, he pushed the young girl inside roughly. Lan collapsed to the floor. The man scrambled into the room and locked the door behind him. He walked towards the girl, picked her up and delivered two loud slaps which shattered her. Calming down a little, the man suddenly said, "Listen to me, young lady. You have to marry me. You won't regret it! Forget this poor guy who won't bring you anything apart from worries! He doesn't have a cent to his name. As for me, take a look!"

He pointed proudly around the room, lit by a kerosene lamp on the table and began to speak excitedly. "Look at everything I have. A big bed with a mattress! Very few people here possess a mattress," he pointed out. "Look at my iron. It's heated with coal. And my white shoes over there on the shelf, for my days off. You'll have new shoes too. This is my second contract. I've got money, I'm rich. Rich! Rich!"

His face started to look threatening. His dilated eyes were looking at Lan strangely. Suddenly, there was the sound of loud knocking at the door.

"Open up, Ngạch! I'm ordering you to open the door!"

Lan recognised Phúc's voice, but the man seemed to have gone crazy. He dragged Lan over to the back of the room. Terrorised, she fought him off with all her might. Phúc's voice was menacing and commanding.

"Ngạch, open or we'll knock the door down!"

The commotion of the crowd outside got louder and Lan recognised Minh's voice. With panic in his eyes, Ngạch pushed her firmly towards his bed. He wanted to tear off the girl's blouse . . . there was the sound of violent blows, then the door gave way.

Minh rushed inside. Feeling trapped, Ngạch became enraged. Dropping Lan he grabbed an empty bottle from the shelf and threw it with all his strength at Minh who tried to dodge the projectile, but his foot tripped over a mat on the floor and he reeled slightly. The bottle shattered against his bare forehead. Minh saw a myriad of stars and then he collapsed, his face bloodied. . .

When he came to, his head felt heavy, like that of a boxer who had been knocked out.

***

Dawn flooded the room with gentle light. Minh recognised Lan's dormitory. She was beside him and Phúc and Liên were with her.

"You're very lucky," said Phúc. "Your wound's superficial!"

"What about Lan?" asked Minh, worried.

"I'm fine," she said beaming, "since you're here beside me!" Then she hastened to tell him what had happened.

"When he saw you on the ground with your face covered in blood, Ngạch took fright. He suddenly came to his senses, and he let go of me. Then he went towards Phúc in a daze, as if he'd just woken up from a terrible nightmare. He gave himself up without any resistance. We brought you back here to my dormitory straight away to look after you."

"Now you must make a decision about Ngạch," said Phúc.

Minh frowned, then grimaced as his forehead hurt. "I don't understand!"

"I'll explain, Minh! Ngạch has committed a serious offence, and if we inform management, he'll go to prison, that's for sure. I'll let you be the judge of what's best."

Phúc was silent as he waited for Minh's answer. Minh was thinking aloud, "Ngạch lost his mind, I'm sure of it. If I report him, he'll go to prison. But I've been told that prison here is like torture. I don't think he deserves such punishment. In the end, Lan was not molested!"

He put his hand on his bandaged forehead, saying "Obviously I'm left with a painful little souvenir."

Turning to Phúc he said, "I consider the matter to be closed! All right Lan?"

Phúc approved of this decision. Relieved, he said, "Lan agrees with you. You're both good people. And I think you're right to forgive him, because these men are so lonely that sometimes they lose their minds. They haven't had the good fortune to have a companion and sometimes they'll take their chances and go for the jackpot. They're poor unfortunates!"

Then, putting his right arm on Liên's shoulder, he announced solemnly, "Minh and Lan, my dear friends, allow me to introduce my wife." With a smile he added, "We'll celebrate our marriage this evening. You'll be our witnesses."

Minh sat up, his head was spinning a little, and he closed his eyes for a moment to regain his balance. Then, taking Lan's hand, he said, smiling with emotion, "Let me introduce my wife!"

Lan was elated. Her radiant face was as bright as the first rays of sunshine which were appearing in the distance in the east like promises of a new life. The gentle light made her eyes shine, then tears ran down her face—tears of happiness.

A Little House

The sky seemed brighter and life less monotonous. Lan continued to toil in the harsh sun, while Minh, black with sludge, languished in the underground tunnels. However, it seemed easier to face these difficulties now. Of course, they were exhausted at the end of a hard day's work, but they did not feel the same lassitude that used to overwhelm them before. After work Minh and Lan couldn't wait to get back to their room, eager to see each other and be together all evening and all night, before being separated again with the dawning of a new day.

"How wonderful it is when you're in love," murmured Lan. "Everything seems different, everything's bearable. You become gentle and tolerant, ready to forgive and even forget everything."

Minh and Lan didn't want to think about the past; the present was what mattered the most. When they met again at the end of the day, covered in dust, they looked at each other, happy and smiling. Stretched out next to each other on their mats, they told each other about their day. They always had something to say as they were apart for twelve, or sometimes fourteen interminable hours. Oh! If only they could work together in the same place—they would look at each other all day without tiring of it, they were sure.

The second week of their life together the young couple stopped going straight back to the dormitory after work. Instead they met on a plot of land near the forest. At Minh's request the mine management had made it available to them, and they had decided to build their own house there.

Bravely the couple would get straight back to work. Minh pulled out the trees, flattened the mounds in the ground and moved the heavy stones away. Lan cleared the land of bushes, then levelled out the ground with a spade. Often Liên and Phúc would come to help them. Liên now had her own comfortable home. She had become "Madame" Phúc, the little lady of the camp. Her affable character had made things a lot easier for her. However, in the beginning she was sad and distant, hardly speaking and daydreaming as soon as she had a moment's freedom. But Phúc was so understanding and considerate that she soon had to change her futile, negative attitude.

"I don't have the right to disappoint Phúc. He loves me, he adores me. I have to recognise that. This is my destiny and I shouldn't live in the past," she whispered sadly, resigned to her fate.

From that moment Liên was normal again, like the other women in the village. She had decided once and for all that she would keep her sorrow buried at the bottom of her heart. She would no longer show it to anyone.

Minh and Lan continued to work on their own land every day until nightfall. Sometimes they stopped for a moment for a break and also to look at each other lovingly, with a smile at the corner of their lips.

"This is how I'd like to work!" Minh cried out happily one day. "This is what work should be like!"

"We wouldn't be very productive!" said Lan with a playful sideways glance. They burst out laughing, loud, clear, heartfelt laughter.

The sun set slowly every evening and the mountain spread its black shadow over the whole village. That was when it was time to bring in the tools and return to their temporary lodgings.

"We've finished levelling the land!" said Minh one afternoon, looking with satisfaction at the platform they had made. "Very soon we'll be able to build our house!"

The next day, after work, they went up the mountain to a wooded area where the trees were tall and straight, exactly as they dreamed. A fresh spring, contained by a dam made of big stones placed on top of each other, supplied the village with water through a black pipe which snaked along the mountainside. The gentle murmur of the water and the cool of the forest invited the young couple to relax and they suddenly regretted that they were there to destroy these trees for their own selfish reasons. Minh and Lan had the same faults as all human beings: devouring plants and animals in order to live, destroying nature to have a more comfortable life. But they needed poles and beams for the frame of their house, so they got to work. Lan lopped off the branches and Minh cut the trunks into lengths of three to four metres. Then they took them down the mountain, taking great care not to slip on the wet leaves that lay on the ground all along the way. When they had enough wood they were keen to get started. Lan was impatient to be in her own little house, built with her own hands.

Thế and her husband, who were also building on an adjoining plot, were eager to participate, along with Phúc and Liên, in building the frame. This was of great comfort to Minh and Lan and they promised to help their neighbours when they needed it. The young couple didn't take any time off to rest at all. On Sundays they began very early in the morning and finished late, at the end of the day when, exhausted, they could hardly see a thing, not even a few metres in front of them.

The grass grew tall at the bottom of the mountain. They cut it, making big bunches of straw that they carried back up to the camp along paths so rough and difficult they often had to grab onto branches along the way to avoid falling. They finally managed to cover the roof, which was now looking good.

At the same time as they were doing this arduous work, the young couple had, for several weeks, been coming back from work with their arms laden with all sorts of objects that they stored in their dormitory: wooden planks and empty jerrycans they had taken from the work sites. In the evenings, Minh cut these containers into small, rectangular pieces that he stored with care in a corner of the building.

Towards the end of May, about a month after their arrival in Pimboé, the little house was almost finished. It was as strange and bizarre as all the different kinds of materials used to build its walls: planks and pieces of scrap metal!

Lan went inside her house and looked around at the single room with its small kitchen area.

"Oh! You can see through the planks!" she cried in dismay.

"I've given that some thought" said Minh confidently. He opened a small box and took out some old newspapers he had had the foresight to save, and they began lining the inside of the house with the printed pages. The flimsy walls now looked quite impressive.

The following afternoons were devoted to making furniture. First of all, Minh made a bed, a big bed raised on legs, as if to drive from their minds the memory of all those nights spent lying on the bare ground. Minh soon put the final nail into the boards that made up the bed base.

"We'll put our mat on it and we'll be more comfortable!" said Lan happily.

Minh was very satisfied with his work. With their first pay, Lan bought some kitchen utensils: a frying pan and a strainer made of fine slats of plaited bamboo made by skilful hands in the evenings after work.

When the table and benches were ready, they moved in, and received their own food rations. Lan was happy to be able to do her own cooking. They had made a home for themselves and now that they were partly independent, they felt freer. Of course, they knew that they did not have the comfort and elegance that Liên had! But it was their house, built with their own hands and they were proud of it.

***

As soon as Lan was settled in her new house, she was quick to send the rest of her pay to her parents.

As for Liên, she had been able to send her entire salary. It was a great joy to her, the happiest she had felt for a long time! At last she felt useful and realised that she had finally been rewarded for her physical and emotional suffering. She wished it was already the end of June so that she could send her second pay home.

Liên was radiant. She no longer regretted leaving home and abandoning her parents, since, with the money she sent at the end of every month, they would now be able to clothe and feed themselves and break out of the dire poverty in which they had always lived.

***

Minh and Lan kept working long hours together in the late afternoon. Minh had lost weight and was thin now.

"It's about time we finished working on our house," he said, "because at this pace, I won't be able to keep going another month. They're getting more demanding at the mine and we have to increase our productivity. Apparently, ore sales are rising at the moment!"

For several days Minh had been feeling pain in his shoulder from the hard work on the mine, but as he didn't want to worry his wife, he blamed the humidity and rheumatism.

Every evening Lan rubbed Minh's muscles and joints and discovered she was a good masseuse as, after about ten minutes Minh would doze off on the big bed, dreaming of the wonderful carefree days on Nou Island. They had dinner at sunset, as they had nothing else to do. Then they went to sleep very early to recover the strength they would need the next day. It was also a way of saving on the kerosene they bought at the shop in the European village, a well-stocked little shop where you could find everything, from basic necessities to beauty products. However, they bought very little, only the strict minimum, as everything was too expensive for them.

***

For some time, Lan had been worried. Her husband was getting more and more irritable, exacerbated by the behaviour of the foremen. One evening he said, "Do you know why Mainote and his gang are paid so generously, Lan? Well, I'll tell you why. They're employed solely to make our lives a misery, to whip us as soon as they have a chance and to send us to prison if we make the slightest move to defend ourselves. It's unbearable, unacceptable! We work like convicts and all we get is a pittance. It has to change!"

Lan had paled at these last words. She was afraid that Minh might finish up rebelling one day and that could only lead to violence. For she knew from experience that a man's gentle, sensible temperament could easily change into a violent rage if he lets anger get the better of him. So she tried to change the subject to calm him down. Suddenly she had an idea.

"Poor Toán! Our poor friend. Where is he now?" she whispered.

Lan had succeeded. Hearing Toán's name, her husband pulled himself together and returned to reality. "Dear Toán," he said, "I hope he's got himself out of trouble. Do you remember, Lan? He'd lost everything that day and we didn't even have the smallest amount of money to give him."

They were silent, thinking fondly of their friend. Lan, like Minh, had of course thought about Toán, but, absorbed and busy as they had been since they left Nouméa, they had never talked about him at all.

"I'd like to get in contact with Toán again. Find out what's become of him," said Minh.

"And tell him we're married!" exclaimed Lan. "I'm sure he'll be pleased to hear it!"

"Phúc should be able to tell us how to go about looking for him," thought Minh.

"Please be discreet, Minh. Don't talk about all this in front of Liên, I beg of you. It could bring back painful memories for her . . . Thắng, you understand? The wound hasn't healed yet; let's not hurt her again."

That evening, they visited their friends. Phúc, stretched out on his bed, was looking at his wife tenderly. His head lay on a wooden pillow, the varnish shining in the faint light of the kerosene lamp. Minh looked at the headrest with curiosity and envy.

"It's guaiac, a very hard wood," explained Phúc. "I made it myself."

Minh took the heavy object in his hand, examining it for a long time, and promised himself that later, when he had the time and the energy, he would go to the mountain to look for this precious wood. For the moment, he would settle for a more ordinary wood.

Liên was seated next to her husband on the bed, mending some work clothes; she put aside her task when the young couple arrived and went off to prepare a hot drink.

"How do you get into contact with the other centres on the island?" Minh asked once the two young women had disappeared into the kitchen. Phúc looked inquiringly at Minh.

"I want to find a friend," said Minh.

"Thắng?" asked Phúc in a worried tone.

"No, Toán. We love him very much."

"I think the best way to go about it," said Phúc, reassured, "is to contact Quyết. He corresponds a lot with several of his relatives. One of them is currently in Nouméa, where he works at the nickel-processing plant. The other works in Voh, I think. Yes, in Voh."

Minh was getting impatient. "Where can I find this man?"

"He's away from the mine at the moment," replied Phúc. Then he added, "Quyết is in Koumac at the moment. It's the administrative centre, quite a long way from here. He's in prison."

"So, he committed a serious offence?"

"He struck a foreman!"

"Oh, I didn't hear about that," said Minh, astonished.

"There was no way you could know since it happened just a few days after you arrived. We didn't want to tell you about it to avoid scaring you."

"Why did he hit the foreman?"

"Quyết was tired and sick. But Binet the foreman was allergic to sickness—other people's sickness. Instead of giving Quyết a few days off, he made him work harder than ever. Quyết was genuinely exhausted and couldn't keep up the pace. So Binet gave him a few kicks . . . you know where. Quyết was so angry, he lost control. He lifted a big rock and threw it with all the strength he had left. The rock hit Binet in the pelvis and he had to stay in bed for a few days. The result: forty-five days in prison and I don't know how many months of wages docked."

"They've found an effective way to make sure we remain passive," growled Minh indignantly.

"Quyết will be back in about two weeks."

"Is there anyone else in the village who has friends or correspondents on the island?"

"Not to my knowledge, no one here really likes writing. And a lot of our people are illiterate. At the end of every month I have to become a public letter-writer and make myself available to everyone, for free, to write letters to their families."

"I remember," Minh said. "When I first arrived, I also had to write several letters for people sharing my dormitory who were illiterate. That's the way it is, Phúc. These young people have never been to school. From a very early age the only companion they've had is a buffalo on a leash that they sometimes rode to the fields near the rice paddies to graze. At the end of the day they'd earned only a few cents which they had to give to their parents. . ."

Minh's passionate words were interrupted by Liên bringing hot tea. Lan had stayed in the kitchen to admire the small kerosene stove. Without mentioning it to anyone, not even her husband, Lan secretly hoped that one day she would have one of these revolutionary inventions.

Friendship

Of all the workdays, Saturday was the toughest, the longest. Was it because of the burden of the arduous days of the past week? Or was it just that they couldn't wait to see each other, spend time together, and make the most of the last evening of the workweek?

"Will you promise me, Minh, that you won't do any work tomorrow?" Lan asked at the end of each week.

And invariably he replied, "Of course, Lan. I promise! At least not before eight or nine in the morning. We'll sleep in until then."

"No, Minh. I'd like you to have a proper rest, all day. You need to relax."

"Oh no! Please, Lan, let me relax in my garden. I feel good when I'm near my plants."

Indeed Minh had created a beautiful vegetable garden on their plot. There were Chinese cabbages, magnificent tomatoes and tasty lettuces. To mark the boundaries of their land all around the backyard, Minh had planted banana palms which had grown at an astonishing rate. He was surprised and thrilled with his success.

The next day when the sun was still asleep in the cosmos, far away, Minh and Lan were already awake. The young woman was deeply disappointed.

"Why is it that when we want to sleep in, we get up at dawn?" she asked her husband, "when on weekdays we struggle to wake up? I can't understand why. Can you?"

Minh was saved from answering by a knock on the door.

"Who's come to disturb us at this early hour?" he grumbled as he got up. A little annoyed, he went to open the door. "It's not even five o'clock, it's only just half past four."

But when he opened the door, he let out a shout of joy. "You! Is it possible? Lan, come and see who's here!"

Lan jumped out of bed and rushed to the door. In the opening, at first, she could only make out a familiar shape, lit from the back by the faint light of the dawning day. Then, moving nearer, she was sure. But she still wanted to touch him, hold his hand to be certain that she was not dreaming. Then she cried, "Toán! Toán! My big brother! How did you manage it? Tell me I'm not dreaming, Toán!"

"No, you're not dreaming, Lan. It's me. I'm so happy to see you again."

They looked at each other, smiling with emotion, then Lan pulled herself together.

"Come in Toán. Come in and sit down!"

"Well, who would have believed it!" murmured Minh.

"I'll go and make some tea," said Lan. Then she corrected herself, "No, not tea today, we're going to treat ourselves to some coffee. A good coffee and a little rice to recover from all this excitement."

Toán was visibly tired. His eyes were red and, from the black rings around them, it was obvious that he hadn't slept all night. The hot coffee revived him. Minh and Lan could hardly believe that their friend was actually there in front of them.

"We were just talking about you a few days ago and you've turned up out of nowhere."

"You know, when you speak of the devil. . ." said Toán, laughing.

"We wanted to start searching for you," said Lan.

"Well I'm here to save you all that trouble," he joked.

"You seem to be in good spirits."

"Well I'm euphoric because I'm so happy I found you," Toán declared.

Lan was burning with impatience. Unable to wait any longer she fired off several questions without taking a breath. "Where were you? Where do you work? How did you get to Pimboé?"

"Give our friend a few more minutes! Let him recover," said Minh, serving the bowl of hot rice Lan had just put on the table.

Toán ate hungrily and, with the chopsticks, from time to time took a piece of the meat Lan had cooked for him.

"I'm starving!" said Toán swallowing the food. "I walked almost the whole night to get here."

Lan, tense with curiosity, waited impatiently to hear the rest.

"I work at Tenep mine, a chrome mine about twenty kilometres from yours. Twenty kilometres as the crow flies, obviously. When I left you on Nou Island. . . or, more correctly, when I was forcibly taken away from you, and I want to make it clear that they *did* use force, because before I got to the wharf I fought like a maniac, I didn't want to follow the bosses; they even had to get help from two gendarmes who happened to be there on the pontoon. They dragged me onto an ore ship. An hour later the ship left Nouméa with fifty of us on board and headed for the north of the island. As you know, I didn't have a cent to my name. I'd lost everything the day before. Do you remember, Minh?"

Minh nodded, then said knowingly, "Oh yes! I remember."

"So that evening, to forget my sorrows and stop thinking constantly about the three of you, Minh, Lan and Liên . . . by the way, while I think of it, what's become of Liên and Thắng now?"

"Liên's here with us. Thắng was sent away somewhere else. We haven't had any news of him. To be honest, we've all lost contact with each other since we left Nouméa."

"Except for you, Toán, as you're here now," said Lan, adding, "We'll visit Liên later on this morning. It's Sunday today, let her rest a little."

Toán nodded and then, preoccupied with his tale, he continued, "As I was saying, to drown my sorrows I organised a card game on board. What else was there to do?" he said, laughing, as if to excuse himself, "We played until dawn, a terrific atmosphere! Nobody felt seasick and I played like a champion. From nothing, by the early hours of the morning I'd made a nice sum of money. And I must have scared them off, as nobody wanted to keep playing with me. That night I was either too lucky or too good for them!" exclaimed Toán, his laughing eyes showing his great satisfaction. "The losers complained, got angry, while others gloated, singing. . . . At the end of the day we disembarked at a little port near Koumac."

"That name sounds familiar," interrupted Minh.

"It's the administrative centre for our two mining villages," explained Toán. "They took us to Tenep camp, about ten kilometres from there. We travelled by truck, sitting in the back with our possessions. It was quite pleasant, we could feel a cool wind on our skin, and I felt more cheerful after winning so much at gambling."

"You had a lot more luck than us," said Lan. "I'll remember our first days here and in Kunéo for a long time!"

"What happened next?" asked Minh with interest.

"The village of Tenep, nestled in a valley is divided in half by a small stream. When the rain falls on the nearby mountains the little stream becomes a tumultuous torrent and the red water overflows, cutting the village in half for hours, and at times for several days, during the rainy season. Our camp is in the eastern part. The western part belongs to the 'pointed noses', the Europeans. Some of the women are sent to do housework; the rest work in a new ore-crushing factory. The men are employed in the underground tunnels to extract chrome ore. The first time I was terribly afraid. I'd always lived between the sky and the water. I was in my element on the sampans and I've never wanted to be on dry land. And yet I had to go right into the heart of the mountain to blast out blocks of black rock with dynamite, under the watchful guard of aggressive, sinister foremen. I don't think there's anything harder or more depressing."

Toán stopped for a moment, his face grave, and then continued, shaking his head slowly.

"What could we do? What else can we do today, on this little island? Impossible to escape. And we're so far away from our country. There's only one thing left to do and that's work and obey to avoid the foremen's whips and the violence of the gendarmes. Until this day I've stayed strong and avoided any kind of provocation. They know in Tenep that I'm small, but stubborn and tough." Toán continued, looking serious, "But I'm afraid of the future. For the day a whip lashes the flesh of my body," his expression was tough and menacing, "I don't know what I might do, or how I'll react!"

He was silent. Slowly Lan moved her head back so that she was a little behind her husband where she could see him out of the corner of her eye. She was anxious, but Minh remained calm and silent. Lan felt reassured. For a moment she feared that Toán's remarks, which unwittingly concurred with Minh's opinions, would end up provoking strong reactions in her husband. Fortunately, that was not the case. Minh simply said, a little fatalistically, "We've already thrown ourselves to the wolves. But I don't regret it," he added. Taking his wife's hand, he said, "I've discovered a pearl!"

Toán went even further, saying, "Lan's more than a pearl. She's a big diamond!"

"Thank you both for your kind words; I'm very moved," said Lan whose cheeks had suddenly gone red.

"But you still haven't explained how you managed to find us," said Minh, more and more intrigued.

"Đạt, one of my roommates—yes I live in a building for single men, there are about ten of us in a room! I don't mind at all. As I'm married and have children, it suits me to live with others and it means I can also easily play cards. I don't have to run around looking for partners, they're all around me. Obviously, I chose the room with the most gamblers. So, my roommate, Đạt, came back from Koumac last Sunday. He'd been in prison for pretending to be sick, I think, and he met someone called Quyết, who works with you on the Pimboé mine. Often in the evening after work I used to talk about you to Đạt. I don't know why. No doubt I needed to confide in someone. In any case I don't regret it because Đạt, with this basic information and without having ever seen you, was able to describe you to his cellmate. So, Quyết confirmed that among those who'd recently arrived there was indeed a young man and woman fitting Đạt's description. Quyết even said that you were still together, he didn't know your names but that wasn't important for me. Because, from that moment, I was sure that I'd find you here.

"The whole of last week I tried to find out about your village, where it was and how to get here. Some men who've been here for years told me about a path they used to use sometimes when there was a day off, to come and see friends who were living at this mine. One of them even decided to come with me, as it would give him the chance to spend a day with a cousin he hadn't seen since the last Têt holiday. So, we left together last night.

"The weather was fine and the moon lit the way. We climbed many hills and mountains. Luckily, I hadn't ventured out alone, as I would've got lost, especially in the middle of the night. My companion used the stars and the mountain peaks to guide us. We stopped for a rest at about two o'clock, not far from here. But I didn't sleep a wink I was so worried. I was afraid I might've made a mistake and that I'd come all this way for nothing. Afraid I might not find you here. When we got to the cousin's house about an hour ago, I was filled with joy! In answer to my urgent questioning he gave me good news. I immediately forgot about my fatigue and rushed over here to your place."

Then Minh and Lan began to explain what had happened to them, telling first their story, and then Liên's, Thắng's and Phúc's as well.

"Poor Liên. They loved each other so much, it was a pleasure to see them together," murmured Toán. "But what can we do, except hope that they'll find peace of mind and maybe, one day, happiness." Then, shrugging his shoulders as if to free himself of this bothersome thought which might spoil his delight at finding his friends, he came back to reality.

"In the end, our stories are all similar," he said. "Whether we're here or elsewhere, the methods they use are identical. We all have the same problems."

They chatted together cheerfully, reminiscing about life on the ship and the wonderful days together on Nou Island.

Lan, who had gone to inform Liên, came back a moment later with her friend and Phúc, whom she introduced to Toán. They decided to spend the day together but let Toán have a much-needed siesta, as he had to leave at the end of the day to go back to his village in one of the valleys in the north of New Caledonia.

It was an enjoyable day, as they took comfort and solace in one another's company. They had found their friend and they were sure to see him again, Toán had promised. He would always be welcome at their house, just as parents welcome visits from their eldest son.

This reunion encouraged them and inspired them to persevere in the right direction, that of peace and understanding. In this way they would manage to triumph over the malice and greed of men. At least they hoped so.

The hours flitted by so quickly that they hardly noticed the time passing and it was soon the end of the afternoon when they had to part ways. Their faces were grave. With tears in their eyes and a heavy heart, the women forced themselves to smile, wanting to encourage their friend and wish him a safe trip back. They urged him to take great care, knowing that he had hardly slept since the night before, and that it would still take a lot of effort throughout the night for him to get to work the next day by dawn.

Toán met up with his travelling companion and they set out together. The young couples accompanied them in strained silence a small part of the way. At the edge of the village they stopped. After a last sad goodbye, the two men disappeared into the tropical forest, which swallowed them up in its lush vegetation.

They walked at a steady pace, knowing that it would be a long and difficult journey. Despite their day of rest, they were tired. The countryside blurred into a sort of dark mist which, as the sun disappeared, gradually enveloped the whole mountain. Night fell quickly, more quickly than Toán could ever have imagined. In the dangerous spots, to stop themselves falling or tripping up, with both hands they grabbed the branches to their right and left as if they were grasping a safety barrier, an unusual bushy green barrier.

The moon was still hidden by the black clouds, which blocked out a part of the sky, and they moved forward in the darkness, taking great care. Some tracks were slippery, either because the thick layer of dead leaves covering the ground trapped all the moisture, making it seem like a skating rink, or because of the tiny round pebbles which slid out beneath their feet. As time passed, the path seemed never-ending to the two men. They reached the bottom of a valley, crossed over another ridge, only to go down again and then have to climb again—up the side of a mountain which was blocking their way.

Toán's eyelids had become heavy. He needed to sleep. He could even have fallen asleep on his feet he was so tired. He made a huge effort to keep awake as he knew it was absolutely essential to avoid falling.

When by chance they heard the murmur of water gurgling from a spring or rushing down the mountain, they deviated from their path towards this beneficent source. They doused their hair and faces so that the cool of the water would keep them awake as long as possible. Then they set off again, getting gradually nearer to their destination.

Toán almost fell several times. He tried valiantly to stay in control, using any willpower he still had to overcome his fatigue and stop himself falling asleep.

They had no fear as they advanced; they knew that there were no dangerous or venomous animals in the dark vegetation surrounding them.

"No tigers or snakes like in our forests in Tonkin," Đạt had told him, adding, "The only wild beasts to fear here are men!"

The silence of the mountain had, like the night before, intimidated Toán at first, but he soon regained his calm and concentrated solely on walking. The sound of crickets and cicadas cheered them up as they walked. At one point, as they were walking through the bottom of a valley, they also heard the sound of a herd of deer galloping as they fled, frightened away by this unusual human presence. The moon appeared at that moment above their heads like a gigantic lamp. Its gentle light was welcomed warmly by the nocturnal travellers. It was late in the night.

"We've covered three quarters of the way," said Cung, Toán's companion who, as he walked, was looking at the mountain peak he was using as a landmark. Suddenly, his head swung forward as his feet stubbed against a fallen trunk lying across the path. Cung's hands waved desperately around in the air, and then, by chance, he managed to grab hold of the end of a branch, clinging to it and dragging it down with him, as, inevitably, he fell. Unable to get up, he had to let go of the branch. Like a spring, it bounced backwards. Toán saw the dangerous mass coming towards him at high speed. Not knowing what to do, almost instinctively he closed his eyes. He wanted to drop down quickly to the ground, but, before he could make the slightest move, the black branch hit him hard, right in his face.

Toán let out a plaintive cry and then dropped to the ground, stunned. He stayed there, stretched out on the ground in silence for a moment. When he came to his senses, he lifted his right hand to his wounded face, then moved it gently upwards as if he was afraid of discovering some terrible truth. His fingers stopped at a large bump which was forming on his forehead.

"There's no blood, nothing broken," he mumbled, relieved.

As he was getting up, he felt a slight dizziness, but did not think it serious.

"Cung, my friend. Where is he? I completely forgot about him."

Toán looked around in panic, then he began searching in the pitch darkness. But he couldn't see anything, felt no human presence nearby, as if Cung had suddenly vanished into thin air. Anxiously, Toán went slowly towards the treacherous branch. He peered again into the darkness and discovered a drop in the ground a few steps ahead of him. He leaned forward carefully and saw his companion standing on his two feet a few metres below, running his hands over his whole body, just like a cyclist checking out each limb and the state of his bicycle after a fall.

"Nothing broken, Cung?"

"No, I'm fine. What about you?"

"I'm all right. Shall we continue?"

"Yes, let's go!"

They set off again without a word, satisfied, despite everything, at escaping this ordeal without too much damage. But it was after this accident that fatigue really hit them. Toán had a terrible headache and Cung had bruises and scratches all over his body. However, they couldn't afford to take a minute's rest as it was imperative for them to be on time to start another week of work. Even though the night air was cool, they were hot, and their legs and feet were sore from trying to finish the arduous journey as quickly as possible. At last, from the top of a hill, they could see the corrugated iron roofs of the factory, covered with a fine layer of dew reflecting the moon's peaceful rays.

"We're nearly there," commented Cung.

"At last," sighed Toán.

"We just have a quarter of an hour's walk and then we'll be home."

Toán could already hear the barking of the village dogs at the bottom of the valley. Now that they had almost reached their destination, they were happy to slow down, but they were immediately overcome by fatigue and sleep. They moved like zombies; the slightest movement, the smallest step was agonising. Their bodies, crushed by so much effort, had given up.

"Let's rest for a moment," suggested Cung.

Toán's headache was getting worse and worse, and he wanted nothing more. He sat down listlessly on the side of the track as if drugged and looked for a big enough clearing to stretch out his exhausted body, then he lay down, curling up on the wet grass.

"Just for a moment," said Cung, lying down nearby. "It'll do us good. A few minutes and we'll be on our way again."

But when Cung woke up the sun was already high in the sky and he could hear the din of the engines coming from the factory, unleashed after their Sunday sleep. Terrified, Cung shook Toán roughly, waking him from his peaceful sleep. They hurtled down the slope, forgetting their fatigue and their physical pains. One single idea tormented them—they were late. And this realisation made them tremble with fear, as any unjustified absence could have very nasty consequences. Without taking the time to quench their thirst or rest at all, they went directly to the mine, two kilometres from the village.

"Where have you two been? Do you know what time it is?" yelled Costele, the foreman, a small highly strung man with a rough-looking face. "It's nine o'clock!" he grumbled again.

Although he had been on the island for a year and a half, Cung did not understand a single word of French and neither did Toán. They answered all of Costele's questions in the same way, deferentially, as if hoping to placate him, "Yes, yes, boss!"

It had the opposite effect. Costele was even more enraged and sent for an interpreter.

"The foreman wants an explanation for why you were late," translated the interpreter.

"We went to Pimboé to visit friends, but we were so exhausted on the way back that we fell asleep," Toán confided, "but tell him whatever is best . . . for us."

"They say they played cards until late last night and didn't wake up."

Costele frowned, looking dissatisfied with the answer. Then his gaze fixed on their necks, "Ask them why they aren't wearing their number plates."

"The boss has noticed that you don't have your number around your neck," said the interpreter harshly, as if to show how impartial he was, "You know the rules: It's compulsory for all workers to wear their number plate during working hours!"

"With your names that all sound the same, how do you expect me to recognise you?" stormed Costele again, adding, "in any case they must report to my office this evening after work."

The day was tough for the two men, but now that he had had the experience, Toán was already making plans for the future. "Next time I'll leave earlier, and I'll organise with one of my colleagues here to work the afternoon shift so that I can rest all Monday morning after I get back."

These thoughts gave him courage and hope, as, despite all the suffering he had endured during the expedition, he was ready to do it again. He needed to see his new family again from time to time.

In Prison

Costele was in his office when they reported there at the end of the day. Sinh, the interpreter, was waiting for them outside. Toán and Cung were wearing a copper number plate which hung like a pendant from a string around their necks. Costele wrote their numbers in a register and then declared, "You'll both lose two days' pay and you'll have to chop wood for an indefinite period."

When Toán heard these words translated by Sinh, his face turned purple.

"Bastards, tyrants. A punishment and two days' pay docked for a couple of hours' absence!"

As they had no way of getting out of it, they turned up the next morning to the mine entrance. Costele, cold and vindictive, was waiting for them in person. Sinh was beside him.

"This is what you have to do: with that cart over there," said Sinh, "you'll go and get the wood from the hangar about two hundred metres away, down there. We can see the roof from here."

"I can tell you that you're going to be very busy, because this old steam engine they've just got working again swallows a huge amount of wood," whispered Sinh a little later.

"Why did they get it going again?" asked Toán, intrigued. "Surely they didn't do it especially for us?"

"Of course not. The diesel engine broke down a few days ago, and it'll take months to get the necessary spare parts. Fetching the wood is hard work, so Costele likes to force the troublemakers to do it."

Toán glanced around quickly and then asked, "So where are the oxen?"

"What oxen?" asked Sinh, his turn to be surprised.

Toán pointed to the cart. "The oxen to pull that!"

Sinh lowered his eyes and said uneasily, "*You'll* be pulling the cart." Then he moved away saying, "Costello seems to have something against you, I don't know why. I'd advise you to get to work straight away."

The two men, feeling irritated and humiliated, began to pull the cart. They headed for the warehouse, filled the archaic vehicle with heavy logs and then, pulling with all their strength, they climbed the winding slope full of holes and ditches hollowed out by successive rains. With their heads and torsos leaning forward they looked like buffalos pulling ploughs in the black mud of rice fields or, rather, like rickshaw-pullers weighed down with their load.

Toán and Cung were distressed at how hard it was to satisfy the steel monster spitting out its hot fumes into the sky; it seemed to be devouring both their strength and their will. Costele came back to see them towards midday. Toán, using precise, expressive gestures, asked for an extra worker to help them in their difficult task. But the foreman, more aggressive by the minute, simply gave Toán a violent kick in the groin in reply.

His face distorted with pain, Toán glared at Costele, then suddenly, raging like a tiger he pounced, grabbing a nearby spade. He lifted it high in the air and then spun it around and brought it down hard towards Costele's face. His eyes wide in surprise and fear, Costele only had time to move slightly out of the way, but fortunately for him, a strong gust of wind pushed the spade aside, deflecting it from its path. However, the sharp edge of the spade did hit the man's scalp, behind his left ear. Furious, Toán wanted to strike him again, but his compatriots who were tending to the boiler, had seen his act of madness and, rushing over to the crazed man, managed, after a struggle, to restrain him.

Costele, slumped on the ground, his head red with blood, was yelling at the top of his voice, calling his colleagues for help. Three foremen appeared suddenly from nowhere. Two of them took hold of Toán straight away with their strong arms. The third and strongest hammered him in the stomach, punching him like a boxer at training beating a sandbag. Toán grimaced in pain without uttering a cry, but under the barrage of blows, his face quickly turned pale and deathly, and he lost consciousness.

The three men left him on the ground and went to Costele's aid. He was a terrible sight; a piece of skin hung miserably in some hair that had been torn out, exposing part of his bare bloody skull. Costele had lost all signs of arrogance. He was quivering in fear for his life. "Is it . . . is it serious?" he asked hesitantly, looking anxious.

"No, I don't think so. The spade touched the side of your head and ripped out part of your scalp," answered the boxer foreman looking at the wound with a grimace.

"We're going to take you to the infirmary, Monsieur Costele," said the second.

Then, turning towards Toán, who was crouching to the ground, the man tore off his shirt and pulled his hands behind his back. Using the torn shirt as an improvised rope he tied Toán's hands tightly together, thus preventing him from making any aggressive moves. Toán was locked up in a small room, guarded by two men armed with truncheons made of tough beef sinew.

A few hours later, in the middle of the afternoon, the sound of hooves could be heard outside. A heated conversation then took place under the veranda on the other side of the door. Toán couldn't understand a word. However, he knew that the men were discussing what to do with him. He was certain that this time there would be no interpreter to help him. They would make themselves understood with the most brutal of methods. But he didn't regret his actions for a moment and was ready to suffer the consequences.

The door opened, and a black gendarme appeared. His face confirmed Toán's fears; he was blind in one eye. His left eye was turned inside out, exposing the white part veined with red. He was observing Toán at length with the other eye, an ironic, arrogant smile on his thick lips. On the orders of his chief who had remained on the veranda with the mine bosses, he walked deliberately towards Toán. But the latter, exasperated by the provocative attitude of the native, and, without thinking about what he was doing, suddenly pounced, head first, onto his future jailer. The two twitchy guards were waiting for the opportunity and gave him two terrible blows with their truncheons, one of them striking him with a thud on his chest and the other on his back.

Toán was so angry that he didn't seem to feel anything. The one-eyed gendarme used the opportunity to grab him and punch him as hard as he could. After so many blows, Toán was shattered and they took him outside without much resistance on his part. The gendarmes freed his hands from behind his back and tied them again to a long rope, which they attached to the saddle of a horse.

"Come on, John!" ordered one of them once they were in the saddle.

Toán was dragged along, forced to follow at a frantic pace, helpless and miserable, a human wreck left to his merciless fate. When they got to the village, Toán's village, the gendarmes made the horses slow down, the better to show the prisoner to those rare inhabitants who happened to be in the camp at this time, as a grave warning to any future rebels. Then they crossed the bridge to the European village. There, the people on both sides of the street, in their gardens full of flowers, enjoyed the moment, just as they would a circus parade, pointing cheerfully at Toán and showing him to their children. With his head down, Toán followed the horses, immune and indifferent to everything that was happening around him.

When they left the village, Toán felt his arms being violently tugged forward by the rope. The gendarmes had accelerated their pace and he had to run. The rapid pace made him breathless and, with his mouth wide open, he took great gulps of air. His face was red from the heat of his body and sweat from his forehead dripped into his exhausted eyes, forcing him to blink several times to get rid of it. Toán was afraid of falling, as, if he fell, he would be dragged along the ground like a grotesque bundle, like a vulgar contorted dummy.

When the horses were completely saturated with sweat, the pace became more bearable. Toán could at last close his eyes from time to time to try to recover his strength or recite a prayer.

In the evening they reached the prison of Koumac on the edge of a swamp a short distance from the sea. The gendarmes untied the prisoner who fell onto the grass like a heavy stone. His eyes closed and his mouth wide open, Toán was breathing erratically, his heart pounding. John, the one-eyed gendarme, pushed him inside a cell. A short time later, the jailer brought him some water, which Toán drank greedily. Then he lay on the bare ground, dazed, drunk with fatigue. He did not even have the force or the courage to pull himself up onto the wooden boards attached to the wall, which he could have used as a bed. Time passed quickly, and he felt at ease lying bare-chested like this on the concrete floor with his eyes closed. All he wanted at that moment was peace. To be left in peace! To do nothing, think of nothing. To sleep, yes, sleep, sleep, and then he would see.

"Hey! Wake up. It's time to get up!" Toán heard, but he didn't budge.

"He must be deaf! Hey! Get up, you in there."

Toán muttered something incomprehensible and then carried on snoring.

"Get up, my friend! Before they come and wake you up . . . with their boots!" insisted the man leaning over Toán. The small, stocky, moon-faced stranger had a jovial, friendly air about him.

"Who are you? Where are we?" asked Toán in a daze.

"Hey, man, if you ask me all these questions at once, I'll never be able to answer. I've got a bad memory, you know!"

"What day is it?" asked Toán, as he got up.

"It's Wednesday morning . . . yes, Wednesday. And it'll soon be five o'clock according to the sun," he added, looking at the sky through the bars.

Toán rubbed his eyes, yawned several times and then said, "Now I remember, the horse, the road, the prison . . . fifteen kilometres behind their horses . . . can you imagine it?"

Then looking at the man, frowning, he said, "But you weren't here yesterday, in this cell!"

"I was working on a site and came back very late. When I came back to the cell, I saw you stretched out on the ground, but you were sleeping so soundly that I didn't want to wake you. Sleep's very important, you know!"

"That's true. I was sleeping so soundly I didn't hear a thing."

"But," said the man, intrigued, "I think I heard you repeating certain names! If I'm not mistaken, I think it was . . . Minh and . . . Lan. If they're the same people I know, they're well known, those two!"

Toán jumped up, "You must be Quyết from Pimboé!"

"How did you know?" cried the man in surprise.

The noise of a lock was heard as the door opened, and the ghastly face of the one-eyed guard appeared. The two men couldn't help looking at his blind eye.

"Number 3140, the boss wants to see you in his office!"

Toán followed him. The gendarme, sitting at a large wooden table piled high with files, was waiting for them.

"Number 3140!" he said gravely, "You are sentenced to two months' prison and three months' suspension of your wages! And you'd better behave yourself! Or else. . ."

Then the gendarme looked at John, the native, with an ironic smile, full of innuendo. Obviously Toán hadn't understood a word. John, an excellent mime, took pleasure in explaining, using the subtle language of gestures, the punishments that the boss had just announced.

One of the prison workers was put in charge of guarding the prisoners. He gave them some tools and then led them to an uneven piece of land, not far from the swamp and ordered, "Even out this land! And it's forbidden to speak to each other at work!"

Toán dug, and Quyết cleared the soil away with a shovel, while, from the shade of a tree, the guard watched them closely. He was no doubt hoping for some small slackening on their part so that he could satisfy his primitive instincts, the pleasure of striking and brutalising people.

The sun was harsh that morning. Toán was still bare-chested, and it was only because he was sweating so much from his labour that he had been able, so far, to escape the sun's dangerous rays. He worked even harder than before, like a maniac, relentlessly. But his body now needed water after sweating so much. His throat, his tongue, his mouth were all dry. He signalled to the guard that he needed to drink, but the answer was categorical; no drinking during work time. Dismayed by this peremptory response, Toán had to wait for the break to get a small cup of water. "What can I do with so little water?" he said anxiously. "My body needs much more to replace what I've lost," he muttered, disoriented.

The guard brought them some white rice. Toán saw his companion grimace as he ate it, and after he had taken the first mouthful, he spat it out immediately, complaining, "It's salty! The rice isn't even cooked, it's just sludge!"

"You should still eat it, so you can keep going," said Quyết. "They cooked it in seawater."

Toán followed his companion's advice. He forced himself to swallow a small amount and then left the rest. Quyết, who had lost a little of his cheerfulness, whispered, "Their rules forbid us to eat or drink during working hours. They only give us water during the break and the rice is this revolting porridge cooked in salty water they get from the swamp."

Toán gritted his teeth silently, then murmured as if to comfort himself, "I'm going to have to put up with this food. Quyết seems to manage on it. I was so angry I completely lost control and struck Costele. I don't think he'll try the same harsh methods on me for a while, but I'll have to learn to control myself from now on and not make any more mistakes. Three months without pay means three months with no money for my wife and children. That's the worst punishment for me!"

Then, as it was not the right time to dwell on the subject, to avoid torturing himself with thoughts of his family back home, he lifted his head suddenly and tried to calm down by contemplating the foam on the crests of the waves out at sea.

They went back to work a moment later. The sun was getting more and more unbearable; Toán could feel an intense heat all over his back, and his shoulders were burning.

"I'm thirsty, too thirsty!" he muttered.

At about three in the afternoon he felt dizzy, his mind numbed by an unbearable headache. By the end of the day, the top half of his body was completely red. He felt the beginning of a fever as the burning got more and more painful. That evening, Toán felt that his body was abandoning him and no longer obeying his will. Once again Quyết had to force him to eat. Toán went back to his cell a moment later, his head heavy, his body weak and limp. When he tried to stretch out on his wooden bed he screamed in pain; his back was too sore to take his weight. He had to lie down on his stomach.

He remained in this position, lying still in the dark, unable to sleep a wink. In his weakened state, fever took over his body. His lungs were also affected by the intensity of the sun's dangerous rays, and for a moment he couldn't catch his breath. He wanted to cry out to free himself of this choking feeling, but this simple effort made him dizzy. His body jolted with violent convulsions, he let out a few moans and his eyes convulsed as if he was going to breathe his last.

Quyết was beside himself with worry. He took off his shirt hastily and folded it into a big handkerchief, then fanned the air with it in front of Toán's face. Toán remained in this critical state for some time. Then, no doubt because of his strong constitution, gradually he managed to recover. His breathing went back to normal and, at the first light of dawn, the fever dropped and he was finally able to doze off.

Quyết let him sleep for as long as possible. Only at the last minute, when he heard the guard turn a key in the lock, did he wake his companion. With wild gestures, Quyết pleaded with the guard to allow the sick man to stay out of the sun, but his plea fell on deaf ears. Quyết rushed to the back of the cell, opened his bundle of possessions nervously and came back with a shirt that he held out to Toán.

"Wear this to protect yourself," he said. "Otherwise you'll be completely burned by the end of the day!"

Toán tried to put the shirt on, but his face contorted with grimaces as the shirt touched his inflamed back. He took it off as quickly as he could, "No, it's impossible," he said, "I can't bear it, my back hurts too much!"

"But you must protect yourself," insisted Quyết. "Wait a minute, I've got an idea!"

Quyết put the shirt lightly on Toán's back, then he tied the two sleeves together around his neck. Then the two men followed their jailer despondently to the work site they had left behind the day before. Toán's head spun dangerously and he had to lean on his new friend from time to time to avoid losing his balance. Even though he was feeling so weak, Toán couldn't hold back the question he had been dying to ask. Turning slowly to Quyết he said,

"That man . . . the guard . . . is he a native? . . . A native of this country?"

"That's right, yes, you see before you a native of New Caledonia."

"Are they all as cruel as this one? Where do they live?" asked Toán, his face tense, but without taking his eyes off the dark-skinned guard who was walking a few steps in front of them, holding in his right hand the long whip which he never let go of.

"Fortunately, the natives are not all like this . . . this torturer. They live in their tribes near the sea or in the mountains, cut off from the world we've become part of, which is driven by greed and the pursuit of money. According to what I've heard, the natives are pretty peaceful. Obviously, there are always exceptions, like this one who abandoned his people to come and work here as a prison guard."

Fever, the sun, his sore back! The sun, his sore, blistered back, fever! Toán's face was pale and he felt a terrible giddiness when he had to bend over to work. Each movement of his arms made his burns stretch over his muscles, increasing the pain in his back and shoulders, and causing abrasive rubbing between his inflamed skin and the shirt placed lightly on top of it. Toán was in agony. The heat of his own body which was again ravaged by fever and the heat from the bright blue cloudless sky came together fiercely as if they both wanted to destroy him.

"This rice, this salt. It's really revolting," he cried out at lunchtime. Closing his eyes, grimacing in disgust, he forced himself to eat a small amount, refusing to let himself be defeated by fate. He clung desperately to his goal: to get out of this hell for the sake of his children and his family, who were depending on him alone to help lift them out of their life of poverty. But no matter how determined he was, it still didn't ease his physical pain. It felt as if the skin on his back was now stretched to the limit and was going to be ripped apart by the pressure of his cooked flesh, ravaged by the sun's rays.

Toán spent a second difficult night, lying in pain on his stomach. In the cool of the night his skin lost some of its heat and soreness, and, by the morning of the third day, his fever had gone. Carefully he took off the shirt which was still tied by the sleeves around his neck. He lifted his head and glanced sideways over his shoulder at the part of his body which had caused so much pain. With horror he saw that the thin skin on his shoulders was coming off in patches. For fear of making it worse and infecting his bare skin, he did not pull the skin off; he did not really want to imagine what his back looked like.

In the afternoon however, something seemed wrong; his skin was getting abnormally heavy and his shirt was wet in some places, as if a thick sticky liquid had escaped from his flesh. Toán couldn't do or see anything. The one-eyed guard was on duty that day and wouldn't be making any concessions and, in any case, he didn't want to ask anything or owe anything to these men who followed the harsh rules so blindly.

In the evening he asked Quyết to look at his damaged skin. Horrified, the latter exclaimed, "The skin on your back's covered with blisters filled with a yellowish liquid and some of them have broken, leaving pieces of skin hanging off the flesh."

"Is it serious?" stammered Toán anxiously.

"I don't think so. Well, I hope not," said Quyết, grimacing, "You mustn't touch it or try to pull all the loose skin off."

From that morning onwards, Toán was surprised to feel his strength coming back. His back still bothered him, but he didn't have the same severe pain. From time to time he still touched the wound anxiously as if to feel it, inspecting its progress. In some spots he could feel something hard which burst under the light pressure of his fingers.

"The dry skin is a good sign," he murmured in satisfaction.

That night however the two men were puzzled by a strange smell. Rather anxiously they wondered where it could be coming from. They both inspected their side of the cell to try to find the source of this nasty smell.

"Nothing, no dead rat or other animal," said Quyết when they found themselves in the middle of the cell.

"Oh, it's you. . . . The smell's coming from your back!" cried Quyết suddenly. His face was just above Toán's back.

They waited impatiently for dawn, and then for the day to start. They were afraid for Toán, that there might be a serious infection or gangrene, or any other sickness their overactive imaginations could conjure up during the night.

"Well, I've really been punished now," said Toán sadly. "I'm still alive but I can already smell the stench of my own body as bits come off."

But with the light of a new day came hope and better spirits. Toán assessed the situation.

"The fever's gone and I'm not tired anymore. So maybe this smell's normal, the skin coming off my body is dying because it no longer gets any nutrition and decomposes a little before drying. The only thing I have to worry about is infection!"

Toán trembled at the thought, but there was nothing to worry about; his dead skin came away easily without any complications. And the following Monday he was in good health again. Sickness had gone, just like Quyết, who, after an emotional farewell, had left to join his colleagues up in the mountains. He had just completed his prison time.

"He's a fine young man," muttered Toán, alone in the cell. Watching Quyết as he went off into the distance, he repeated, "A fine young man."

Thắng

After Thắng was forced to leave his friends from Nou Island, he was transported by sea, like the others, to the mine at Karembea, on the east coast in the south of Grande Terre.

It was a peaceful seaside village. Every day the water was an intense blue and, in the mornings, at sunrise, Thắng had to squint because of the dazzling light reflected on the water which almost blinded him. Small, gentle waves broke gently on the fine sand. A mischievous fish jumped out of the waves from time to time as if to see what was going on in the outside world, then it dropped back into its element, making concentric ripples which got bigger and bigger until they were absorbed into the cool calm water of the morning. From his room Thắng couldn't spend too long contemplating this tranquil scene even though it made him feel good and eased his broken heart.

Liên was still present in his mind at every moment of his life. At night when he finally fell asleep, after hours of battling insomnia, it seemed that Liên was there next to him, they were together, impossible to separate two beings who love each other so much! They held hands, moving confidently towards the future. Who could dare to destroy such happiness? A whole life of hope and love?

Sometimes he stretched out his hand as if to take her, hug her in his arms and kiss her. Wasn't she his wife? She had promised it more than once. But in the chilly darkness of the dormitory, his shivering arms did not find Liên; they wrapped instead around his own naked chest, finding nothing else there. At these times he felt a vast emptiness, an unbridgeable abyss. He would start crying as he fell asleep. A desperate wail, like a dog howling in the night, would sometimes escape from his chest. Thắng would wake up, sitting on his mat, his eyes vacant, and look from right to left, thinking his cry had been so loud that he might have disturbed his neighbours. But he realised that no sound had actually escaped from his throat. He hadn't cried out. It was just the desperate moans of his lonely heart!

Alone in the dark, his head on his bent knees, he meditated in silence, "My life's ruined, I have no reason to live! I was alone back home, an abandoned child with no father, no mother, no ties. I wanted to try my luck with this adventure to the other side of the world. Along the way I met the only person who has ever loved me. Where is she now? Far away, somewhere in this unfamiliar land. My life has no meaning now." He repeated, "There's nothing left for me, and I have nothing left to lose either."

The cheerful sound of a rooster greeting the new day snapped him out of his daydreaming. "It's daytime already. Another day," he sighed sadly, as if blaming nature.

The sun was rising slowly on the horizon, projecting its bright light, which turned from pale to bright yellow, like a multitude of golden rays giving the illusion of infinite richness spreading over the sky and the smooth shiny surface of the ocean. But as the day dawned fully, the intense light blocked out the warm colours of the rising sun. Thắng loved to watch this peaceful magical scene in the morning.

"Come on Thắng, we have to go now," said Yến, the young man Minh had saved from the sea.

"No, I won't go!" growled Thắng, brought back to reality by this friendly presence. "I'm staying here."

"Are you mad Thắng? Don't make a fuss, please. There's nothing we can do. . ."

Thắng was silent.

"Don't provoke these people, because if you ever stand up to them, we'll all suffer the consequences. They're not exactly lenient."

Thắng thought for a moment and then sighed listlessly, "Okay, I'll come . . . Just to please you."

"Let's go!"

Joining the group of new workers who were waiting for them a little farther on, they climbed up the mountain on a path cut into the steep mountainside. After an hour's walk, they reached the top which was red and bare after years of picks, shovels and the sweat of men. It was always an impressive sight for the two young men. Most of the men from the village were already at work on the huge site, removing the brown earth from the mountain—this earth, the great wealth of New Caledonia.

The new workers, as they did every morning, stopped a moment to observe the miners who were handling their shovels and picks skilfully. But the experienced workers, in spite of the strict rules of the foremen who spied on them all, took pleasure in provoking the "rookies," the inexperienced, clumsy apprentices.

That day Thắng, as usual, was sullen and taciturn. Yến felt uneasy as, nearby, Trần, one of the best miners, was doing his best to ridicule the young men.

"Come on! Get on with it!" he said sarcastically as he lifted a huge block of stone. "You're working like sissies! Work like me, like men! Come on—get on with it, boys!"

These absurd and unnecessary taunts sounded to Thắng's ears like a lot of provocative insults.

"Hey, you over there, the gloomy one," he said, addressing Thắng, "you're even more pathetic than your mates!"

Yến was getting more and more worried as he watched Thắng out of the corner of his eye. Thắng looked pale as he clenched his teeth and continued to dig.

"I bet," continued Trần as he passed by with another big rock in his arms, "you can't even . . . that you're useless with your hands." He burst out laughing, dumped his load a bit farther away then came back, still laughing.

Thắng could not bear any more. Dropping his pick, he suddenly grabbed Trần by the arms and pulled him roughly towards him. Without a word he began to punch him in the face, in the stomach, and again in the face. Surprised by this brutal reaction, Trần tried to escape, but an even stronger punch made blood spurt from his nostrils. Thắng continued to attack the unfortunate Trần when the lash of a whip, delivered by Missard, the foreman, hit his back with a sinister crack. A sudden pain shot through the young man's body. Without waiting a second longer, as if driven by a rebellious instinct that had been contained for too long, Thắng turned to face his new enemy. He was beside himself, his face contorted with anger and hatred. He was a horrific sight, like a hunted animal, terrifying and ready to pounce. For him, the man with the whip opposite him, was the representative of this supposedly superior race, responsible for all his misfortune.

Missard took fright at the behaviour of the crazed man. Slowly and imperceptibly he took a few steps back, hoping to get enough room to crack his whip again. But Thắng, like a wild beast, did not leave him the time. He pounced on Missard with his hands wide open, ready to grab his enemy. Missard raised his arm quickly to strike again, but Thắng was quicker, and, using the weight of his body, threw Missard to the ground with all his strength. With the handle of the whip he struck the foreman hard in the face and on his body. Missard managed to bend over and curl up in one final attempt to shield himself from the blows.

Yến and his fellow workers, horrified by the sudden violence, struggled to control Thắng who continued to yell, as if he wanted to destroy this brutal, inhuman being lying on the pile of ore, his face swollen and bloody.

Thắng was tied up in chains and led under heavy guard to the village down below near the bay. The brutality he was subjected to on the way, along with the heat and the sun, eventually got the better of him. He returned to his normal self, dazed and haggard, as if he had just woken up from a nightmare. As he came to his senses, Thắng realised the seriousness of his actions and was frightened to see how easily he had been overcome by hatred and violence. He followed his masters docilely, chained up like a dog on a leash, wondering, "What have I done? What have I done now?"

He was locked up in the only prison cell. Then, at the end of the afternoon he was taken to the village centre. He was surprised to see how many people were gathered there. He recognised Yến, then realised that all his fellow workers were there. He was taken to the centre of a circle of about three metres in diameter. The interpreter brought in by management announced:

"Phan Văn Thắng, number 3056, by his criminal act perpetrated on the person of the foreman, Monsieur Missard, deserves to be punished as an example. He will receive twenty lashes of the whip! He is forbidden to leave the circle which has been traced out in white chalk on the ground. Any time he goes over the edge of the circle he will get five extra lashes! The management wishes you to witness this punishment so that it may be an example to you all!"

A native man came forward, tall, strong and black as ebony. He stopped at the edge of the circle, then raised his arm, adjusting his whip. There was a heavy silence. The blow tore through the air and the leather straps stung Thắng's flesh. He clenched his jaw as tightly as he could; the second blow came as an excruciating burning feeling on his shoulder, then the blows rained down implacably, shattering his body and his mind. Thắng fought desperately, fiercely, against the pain, trying not to give in and fall outside of the circle. There was an atrocious ringing in his head and he felt as if it was going to split into a thousand pieces with every new blow that felt as if it were striking his very soul. The blows continued to rain down: Fourteen! Fifteen! Sixteen!

Thắng was on the verge of fainting; he couldn't take any more. With his eyes closed and his teeth clenched, he said to himself, determined not to give in, "No! I must not let myself go! I must not faint . . . I must not fall. . . !"

He staggered like a drunk each time the whip bit into his flesh; his body was horribly bruised, swollen and torn by the leather straps. The bosses and foremen all had an expression of satisfaction on their faces while Thắng's friends looked tense, pained and resigned, knowing that there was nothing they could do. The women wept silently. Crouched on the ground, Thắng received the final blows. He could not stand up any longer. He had still managed to keep inside the circle, but with the final lash of the whip, he collapsed unconscious, his head sinking into the dusty ground.

Yến spent most of the night watching over his friend who was lying on his mat, his body inert. The slightest movement was torture for him. Yến could see him grimacing in pain often, even though he didn't complain. Several women from the camp had come in the evening to bring healing potions for the sick man and Yến had brought his own mat. He remained vigilant and silent next to Thắng who was lying on his stomach, unable to keep from groaning plaintively.

The pain spread through his body during the night. He was cold and had to be covered with blankets kindly lent to him by his roommates. A few minutes later he was hot and Yến had to take everything off him again. This continued several times during the night until it turned into an intense fever. Thắng was delirious and often mumbled Liên's name with great affection.

In the early hours of the morning Yến, who had hardly slept at all, brought him a bowl of cool water, some food and a strange mixture saying, "You're in no state to go to work, but they won't let you stay here, they'll force you to work. I've been warned about it, as this isn't the first time a man has been beaten like this, even though it's never been as bad as this before. I've been advised to get you to apply this tobacco juice to your eyes right away. When they notice you're not on the site they'll come to get you. By the time they come the liquid will have had time to act and your eyes will be blood red and your eyelids puffy. You'll hardly be able to see anything."

"?"

"Don't worry. . . . As soon as they leave, you'll wash your eyes and they'll go back to normal during the day. It's a method they've already had to use on several occasions when someone is too sick to work."

"! . . ."

"Yes, because here, even if you're sick and feverish," said Yến wearily, "you don't have the right to a single day of rest. And in your current state it's better to do this," he pointed to the bowl of juice, "than to try to go to work. That would be suicide."

Thắng took the bowl docilely, opening his eyes wide. He threw his head back and, grimacing with fear, steadfastly poured the drops into his pupils. He remained in this position for a while without moving.

"Okay, now that you've done that I can leave in peace," said Yến, picking the bowl up. As he went towards the door he gave a last piece of advice.

"Don't forget to rinse your eyes as soon as they leave. Have a good rest, Thắng and, I beg of you, stay calm, don't lose your temper when they come to see you!"

Then he left to join the small group waiting for him outside, and, as they did every morning, they climbed up the mountainside.

When they got back from work at the end of the day, the men and women went to see their new friend. Thắng, unwittingly, had become the hero of the Tonkinese colony—the man who had dared to strike one of the bosses. It had never been done before! The women came back in the evening to treat his wounds with an ointment they made from rare herbs and leaves that the men had brought back from the mountain.

The next morning Thắng was even weaker. On the advice of Yến and the villagers, who had met hastily, he had to carry out the same dangerous treatment on his eyes, so that he could stay one more day in the village.

Thắng was astonished at how easily he had consented to this treatment again, without really thinking of the consequences it could have on his sight in the future.

"Anyway," he said to himself, "I don't care about anything anymore. The future consequences have absolutely no importance to me."

He had nothing more to lose and would have preferred not to go back to work, to leave, to go back home and leave behind this inhospitable colonial island for ever. He couldn't bear to be ordered around and treated like a workhorse. The presence of these bosses, who in the end were no different from him, outraged him.

"They have two feet, two hands, a head, just like me," he thought, "the only difference is the colour of our skin. What makes colour so important that they think they can treat us like this?"

Overcome by deep anger, he was astonished to realise how easily violence could take over. But this didn't frighten him anymore; he was determined to get back at his tormentors, those slave-masters, even if it meant sacrificing his life! If, by giving his life, he could make things easier for his fellow workers his sacrifice would not be in vain. So that other young passionate couples would never be arbitrarily separated, when a minimum of understanding and human kindness could have solved everything. But to do that, they would have to be able to discuss things as equals. At the moment he knew that this was only a crazy dream. Still, he was sure that one day they could make it happen. He would no longer be alive to benefit from it, but even so the idea warmed his heart.

Thắng was torn suddenly from these dark thoughts by the sound of footsteps approaching. Although he didn't really expect much, he began to chew on some red peppers that Yến had brought him at the same time as the tobacco, giving him the following advice:

"Chew the peppers for a long time before you swallow them! That way your body will be burning and if they want to check your temperature, make sure you put the thermometer in your mouth! You may be a couple of degrees hotter. I don't know if it really works," Yến added sceptically, "but someone gave me this advice for you. Do it just in case, as to have one more day's rest you should do whatever you can!"

Thắng masticated the burning red peppers conscientiously and his body turned into a ball of fire. His masters and enemies came into the room, accompanied by a nurse. His eyes were completely swollen. They examined him and then went away, bemused.

Yến

Young Yến adored Sundays, the only day of rest after a week spent slaving away under the watchful eye of the foremen, who had become more and more on edge after the accident the month before which had made of Thắng a hero, albeit an involuntary one.

Yến felt cold in the morning on this wind-swept mountain near the ocean. It was a cool wet June wind, which froze him to the bone. He remembered with revulsion when he had had to work like mad, his hands filthy and sticky, and his feet wading through the viscous slippery mud, on rainy days when the wind would whip their drenched numbed bodies.

A slight breeze caressed his young face from time to time. And yet his direct, determined expression showed a maturity that forced his friends to respect him. Everyone now knew that Yến had come to this country by falsifying his birth date as he was too young to be legally accepted. To get the official papers he had used all his savings, as well as those of his mother who was still back home with his two little sisters. His father had died when Yến was barely five years old. Yến had sent his first money order home as soon as he was paid at the beginning of June. On that day he was happy, perhaps the happiest of men!

But what also made him happy was the sea, the vast ocean. The sea was still his friend, despite the bad memory he had of the stingray on Nou Island. Since then he had an indelible black spot on his foot, left by the sharp sting which had penetrated his flesh. But that was now a distant memory.

The sun was getting fiercer and fiercer, burning his skin which was brown from working in the open-cut mines. Yến left the village with a small package under his arm and headed for the beach, alone, relaxed and happy. As he walked, he could already feel the pleasure of dipping his bare feet in the morning waves.

When he got to the fine sand, a swarm of young blonde girls and boys were thrashing around in the cool water. Yến moved away and headed towards the end of the bay. When he got to a deserted spot, he took off his clothes and then walked slowly into the sea. Yến delighted in the water which, gently, very gently, as he advanced, enveloped his feet, his hips, and then the whole of his naked body. He forgot everything, not wanting to think of anything apart from the present moment of feeling at one with nature. He enjoyed the stillness for some time and then thrashed around, frolicking like a carefree child in the water. All this exercise and the sea breeze had given him an appetite. He got out of the waves and went towards the water's edge where black rocks appeared or disappeared depending on the tides. Succulent oysters clung to the rocks in bunches. Yến opened them with a knife, then swallowed them nonchalantly. It was delicious, a real treat, but he would need a lot more than that to satisfy his hunger.

"What a pity Thắng doesn't like the sea," he thought. "Actually, he doesn't like anything anymore," he added, shrugging his shoulders. Yến chased this idea quickly from his mind. Looking at his body he burst out laughing; he was as naked as a worm. Yến made his way up the beach and then stretched out for a moment on the sand to dry off. He got dressed again and opened his package, taking out a reel of thread made with the bark of a beach hibiscus he had plaited himself in the evenings over several weeks. At the end of this primitive line was a hook made with a safety pin. Yến turned over a stone just under the surface of the water, grabbed a shellfish, crushed it and used the animal which was still alive as bait. There were a lot of fish, but he only managed to catch a few. He lost most of them, as they fell very easily off the primitive hook.

"I'll have to find something else," he said to himself, "I'll have to find something else."

He lit a fire and grilled the fish—salmon trout with delicate-flavoured flesh.

Yến only got back to the camp late that afternoon. He didn't like gambling or women. "I've got plenty of time for that," he said to himself. "Later, yes, later."

He found Thắng stretched out on his mat, as if lost deep in thought. Thắng had gone back to work after the two days of rest he had managed to get thanks to the tricks he had learnt from the "veterans" in the camp. But Yến had noticed, with some apprehension, that Thắng seemed weaker and made no effort to lift his spirits and get better.

Without a word to his friend, Yến went to consult the older men who recommended someone he could talk to. The man was about forty and this was his third contract. A record! Apparently, he was gifted with healing powers. Following Yến's explanations, the man made up some medicine for Thắng.

Yến went to see Thắng one evening with a brownish potion. "Drink this medicine, it'll do you good. It'll calm you down and you'll get better again."

"?"

"I can assure you that you'll feel a lot better afterwards."

"I'm not sick," grumbled Thắng, lowering his head to avoid looking at Yến. "I don't need any cures."

"Be sensible," insisted Yến. "I went to a lot of trouble to get this potion."

"?"

"Drink it, Thắng, for my sake."

"Why do you want to force me to drink this concoction? I told you. . ."

Seeing the disappointed look on Yến's boyish face, he said, "All right, okay. Give me the bowl. It's for your sake, to please you that I accept. But next time," he said seriously, "let me know if you're going to contact a healer!"

Yến was so pleased that he nodded, then held out the liquid to Thắng who brought the bowl to his lips but put it down again straight away.

"It's got a strange smell, your medicine," he complained.

"It's a fantastic remedy. You'll see!"

Thắng lifted the bowl once more to his face. Grimacing in disgust he closed his eyes and emptied it all at once.

"You're great Yến, thank you. You're looking after me like a real mother. But, please, I beg of you, no more remedies like that," begged Thắng, adding, "It's really disgusting! Yuck!"

From that moment on, Yến spent most of his free time observing his patient. He watched Thắng's reactions and made a note of them, but to his disappointment Thắng had not reacted in the way he hoped.

"Well at least his condition's stable," he said, as if to reassure himself.

A week passed and the miracle had still not occurred. Thắng had not changed at all and became extremely agitated and threatening in the presence of a foreman.

"These men have really become his enemies," observed Yến, in fear.

In fact, Thắng didn't understand what was going on, either.

"The bosses aren't the ones who separated me from my dear Liên. They aren't responsible for my unhappiness, I shouldn't begrudge them," he said to himself, in his lucid moments, when he was alone, meditating in the quiet of his dormitory. However, these sensible thoughts became meaningless as soon as he found himself face to face with a "long nose," as he liked to call them.

Yến was getting very concerned and he went back to the maker of the miracle elixir.

"Your remedy hasn't had the expected results on my friend," he said reproachfully.

"!"

"And yet you promised me that at the end of the third day he'd be healthy again, both physically and mentally!"

"?"

The man looked at Yến silently, without blinking.

Yến was getting impatient. "Give me an answer, say something!" he cried.

"I don't understand," said the healer. "It's not the first time I've used this remedy, and it's always worked before!"

"Tell me what's in your concoction!" shouted Yến suspiciously.

"!"

"You have to answer me, I have a right to know. I paid you a lot for this."

"It's . . . it's a secret," muttered the healer.

Yến became threatening.

"Well, if you insist, here it is . . . seven leaves of the Kanak apple, they can only be found on this island, soaked for two nights and a whole day in . . . poultry droppings. With some spring water. . ."

"!"

"But be careful, not any old poultry, only selected young chickens. This medicine contains many substances that help the regeneration of the heart and of . . . love."

Yến was so shocked he didn't know what to say or do.

"I'm telling you it's not the first time I've used this. I repeat, I always get excellent results."

Reluctantly Yến had to admit that he had heard nothing but warm praise for this man with his strange remedies.

"Maybe Thắng isn't physically ill," said Yến to himself, "and that's why there's been no miracle."

He now felt remorse for having made his friend swallow droppings, even if it was only poultry droppings! Never would he dare to admit this terrible truth to him, at least not for the moment. He was torn from his troubling thoughts by the nasal voice of the peculiar doctor.

"Perhaps I could suggest another . . . cure. It will be harder to stomach, but it could give positive results."

"Tell me what it is first," said Yến, now disillusioned and suspicious.

"No special preparation," he said calmly as if to reassure the young man.

"?"

"Obviously the sick man needs to be willing to do it." he added.

Yến was more and more intrigued by the man's equivocal attitude.

"Tell me quickly, what is it?"

"Well, if I dig a little at the sea's edge preferably in a muddy spot, I could easily find you some earthworms."

"Earthworms?"

"Yes, to be more precise, only earthworms living in the mud near the sea."

Yến was horrified. Opening his eyes wide he repeated, "A mixture made of worms. . . !"

"No, no mixture, nothing to drink, no water," replied the healer proudly.

"To eat, then?" asked Yến, ready for anything now.

"No, you will take your friend three round worms, the fattest and thickest. He will swallow them alive, one after the other, without chewing. I repeat one after the other and not all. . ."

"Enough!" shouted Yến, beside himself, grabbing the man by his shirt collar.

"Enough or I'll fetch them myself and make you swallow them all in front of me right now, you charlatan. You deserve to be strangled!"

Fishing

The following Saturday, when he came home from work, Yến didn't have his shower straight away, as was his custom. He went to see Thắng who had also just got back. Yến seemed unusually agitated.

"What's going on Yến?" inquired Thắng.

"I . . . it's hard to explain . . . I . . . " stuttered Yến.

"Do you have problems Yến?"

"Oh no, no problems. Well, I can trust you . . . can't I?"

"?"

"Of course, I'm so stupid, I'm sorry Thắng."

"What's the matter, Yến? You've got me worried," said Thắng, frowning slightly.

"Well, I want you to keep this package for me."

He took a small package wrapped in newspaper from his bag.

"I don't dare keep it in my dormitory. And as you rarely leave your room, I think it'll be better here with you."

"What is it? Why so much secrecy?" asked Thắng, intrigued.

"It's dynamite. I took it from the mine. Tomorrow I'm going fishing with it. I've heard about this kind of fishing! You do understand, don't you? There're a lot of fish around here."

"You shouldn't have. You shouldn't. Be very careful."

"Don't worry, Thắng," said Yến confidently, "I've given it a lot of thought, and I've calculated everything over the last week. I'll be a long way away and the water will deaden the sound, no problem."

"I don't want anything to happen to you," said Thắng nervously, "I'm fond of you, you know. Do it once, and once only, since it gives you pleasure. But, I repeat, be very careful!"

Yến nodded hastily and then ran off to his dormitory, feeling calmer.

Very early the next morning, Yến came to get his dangerous package, then left the camp and headed for the sea. He walked for a long time, a very long time, until the village looked tiny, at the very end of the bay.

Yến put a short wick on the detonator, prepared the stick of dynamite, then waited. After a while there was a slight swirling in the water about twenty metres from the beach. He opened his eyes wide in order to make out the shapes under the bubbling surface of the water.

"Fish, lots of fish!" he shouted happily. "A whole lot!"

Yến looked frantically for the box of matches he had hidden at the bottom of his bag. Trembling, he lit the short wick, his heart pounding. He was beginning to have misgivings about what he was doing. He was so afraid! But he hadn't dared to ask anyone at the camp for fear of revealing his secret. He regretted it a little now—he should have. . .

Yến had no more time for regrets. It was too late! Thick smoke was coming from the wick and he could hear a distinctive whistling sound. He knew his wick was very, very short, yet he shouldn't throw the stick of dynamite immediately. He had planned everything meticulously; if the wick reached the water too early it could go out, so he would have to hold it as long as possible in his fingers. But just long enough. Not too long, that would be the end—at least the end of him. The dynamite would go off in his hand and he would be torn to bits, or, if he was lucky, if you could call it luck, he would only lose a hand and maybe an eye. Yến had heard this kind of story one evening in the camp.

His body shivered at the idea. The wick was still spitting out its thick grey smoke which rose instantly to the sky. His face tense, Yến had his eyes fixed on the end of the wick, wanting to choose the right moment. Then suddenly, like an athlete, he threw the projectile with all his strength into the sea to the exact spot he had pinpointed earlier.

The dynamite landed in the sea causing the water to swell immediately with a dull noise. Yến waited, his heart pounding, his eyes wide. The water was murky around the area of the explosion. Gradually Yến could make out shiny white shapes, floating on the surface.

"Fish!" he shouted at the top of his voice, "Fish!"

Yến undressed hurriedly, then jumped into the sea, swimming as quickly as his arms and legs would allow. He returned a moment later to the beach, his hands laden with fish.

After about twenty minutes Yến was exhausted from this continual to-ing and fro-ing. More and more white shapes appeared on the surface of the water. And on the beach the happy fisherman had already managed to deposit dozens of fish, each weighing one to two kilos. There were all species of fish: long mullet, surgeonfish with dangerous dorsal fins, sea bass as shiny as metal, gold and red mullet. . .

Yến ignored the small fry floating on the surface and concentrated on grabbing the big fish only. "I'll never be able to take them all," he thought as he swam along. "There should have been at least two of us for all these fish."

He dived to retrieve the fish floating under the water. Suddenly he saw a disturbing shadowy black mass moving around swiftly at the bottom of the water a few metres away from him. As he didn't have goggles, he couldn't identify what type of fish it was, but he could not afford to take any risks. He took fright, dropped his catch, and went back up to the surface to get his breath back, and, as fast as his limbs would allow, swam towards the beach using all his strength.

"Sharks, sharks," he gasped, swimming even more quickly, for fear of leaving a leg or some other part of his body in the belly of the voracious man-eating monsters. When, exhausted, he at last got to dry land, he turned around, panting. Wide-eyed and terrified, he could see black fins twirling around where he had left the dead fish. The shiny spots disappeared from the surface little by little, then the sharks swam away from the shore once they had eaten them all.

"Another close shave with these terrible creatures," murmured Yến, wiping his brow nervously. "I'll have to be more careful next time."

He took his spectacular catch back to camp. It turned out to be a good idea—even selling the fish at a very cheap price, he made quite a lot of money.

"Two or three more times like today and I'll be able to buy what I need to make a net," he thought happily, adding, "I'll have to stop this dangerous game as soon as possible."

***

A week had passed, and Yến had another go, but without saying anything to Thắng this time. He remembered only too well the promise he had made to his friend. The evening before, Yến had hidden the dynamite he had stolen from the mine in a hole that he had dug near a tree quite some distance from the beach. To be safe, he had wrapped it in oiled paper.

"There won't be a problem with moisture or rain with this waterproof paper," he said to himself with obvious satisfaction.

Yến left very early in the morning. Once he got to the spot where he had had such an adventure the week before, he unpacked his gear. This time, to be safer, he was accompanied by one of his workmates, as, for the whole of the last week, he had not been able to forget the terrifying sight of the shark swimming in the water just in front of him. Together they prepared the explosive. Yến modified his technique slightly; he had wrapped the dynamite stick and part of the wick carefully in the oiled paper.

"This way there'll be less risk," he said. "Last time I had to keep the lit dynamite too long in my hand and I only threw it at the very last second. It's too dangerous. This way," he explained to his companion, "I protect the charge and the wick with the oiled paper, taking care of course, to tie it all tightly so that it's perfectly waterproof! Then I can throw the dynamite a bit earlier as it won't get wet. There's no danger with my new system," he concluded proudly. When he saw a school of fish whirling around in the water at some distance from them, he calmly lit the wick and threw it as hard as he could in their direction. Yến was very skilful and the projectile fell exactly where he wanted it to. Then they waited, very pleased with themselves. Suddenly Yến jumped up as if he had seen the devil in person.

He hastily picked up his things which were spread all over the sand, grabbed his friend by the hand and pulled him away. They disappeared into the wild bushland. He ran as fast as he could; his companion followed with difficulty, not knowing what was happening. In a flash Yến had understood his mistake; the waterproof paper stopped the dynamite sinking into the water and it was floating on the water, burning like a piece of dry wood skimming over the waves.

A loud explosion shook the whole bay, like a cannon blast coming from the sea. The mountains sent back the echo in all directions. Yến turned as pale as death and ran as quickly as he could, afraid of getting caught. His companion had at last understood the gravity of the situation and was running even more quickly than Yến.

They got to the village completely exhausted and out of breath, incapable of uttering a single word. Thắng and the people in the village had heard the detonation and when they saw Yến and his companion arrive in such a state they understood immediately. Thắng looked at his young friend, his eyes heavy with reproach.

Yến lowered his head without a word like a naughty child. A few minutes later, they could hear the sound of galloping horses coming from the bay. The hammering of their hooves on the hard red earth got louder and then reverberated through the narrow village lane, stopping in the centre of the camp. Thắng suddenly felt worried, sure that this unusual presence was directly linked to the explosion. He came out of Yến's dormitory, pushing the young man back inside, saying, "Don't move from here. You've seen and done nothing, right?"

Yến stammered something incomprehensible. His eyes were darting around, a sign of how anxious he was.

A crowd had formed around two foremen perched on their horses.

"Where's number 7542?" one of them asked.

"Here I am, boss," answered the interpreter who had just arrived, out of breath. "I rushed here as soon as I saw you coming," he panted.

"Tell them this!" The interpreter listened. After a moment, he spoke up.

"The head boss, Mr. Santoni, says that he was out hunting not far from where the explosion went off. He was with Mr. Horace, the second boss, who you see here. When they heard the loud blast," continued the interpreter, "they rode as fast as they could to the beach, and they had just enough time to see thin smoke rising in the sky about ten metres from the beach. There were dead fish floating on the surface of the water. Mr Santoni and Mr Horace understood immediately what had happened. Someone had used dynamite! They combed the surrounding bush looking for the culprit but didn't find anyone. Whoever used this dynamite, which they stole from their company, says the chief Santoni, was very quick, quicker than their horses. So, he has come here to get him himself. He orders the culprit to give himself up!"

A heavy silence bore down on the crowd. Most of the people present knew without any doubt that the main culprit was Yến, the awkward young apprentice fisherman. But no one spoke up. They remained immobile, glassy-eyed, not wanting to denounce a fellow worker and countryman. This made Santoni furious. "I want the person who stole and clandestinely used equipment belonging to the company," he yelled.

Calmly Thắng moved the people in the front rows aside and stood in front of the foremen.

"It's me, I'm the culprit," he said.

Santoni and Horace knew Thắng as they had been there when he had been punished in public a few weeks earlier. The two men frowned, surprised and clearly uneasy at Thắng's impassive attitude.

"Number 7542!" said Santoni. "Take note of his number and tell him to be sure he cooperates with management!"

He nodded to his colleague and they rode away quickly, spurring on their horses.

Yến had hidden at the back of the room. Looking like a hunted child, he stared insistently at Thắng, in silent interrogation, when the latter came back to the dormitory.

"I heard everything," said Yến at last.

"Everything's been sorted out, you have nothing more to fear," said Thắng comfortingly.

"Have they gone?"

"Yes, they've gone," murmured Thắng. Then he sat down cross-legged opposite his young friend. "Promise me you won't do it again."

Yến looked down and nodded, "Yes, yes, I promise, Thắng. I swear I won't."

"Yến, never forget that you are here on a mission, for yourself first, but also for your mother and your two little sisters who are counting on you," insisted Thắng, his expression serious. "You're their only hope. Never forget it, Yến!"

Yến nodded again, silently, his eyes shining with tears.

"This must never happen again. You don't have the right to take any more useless risks. Do you understand Yến?" Then he said as if to a brother, "Forgive me for insisting like this, but I really want you listen to what I say and always keep it in mind," adding, after a moment's reflection, "Always remember my advice, even if one day . . . I'm no longer around."

"Are you going away?" asked Yến, looking bemused.

"No, of course not. I can't leave just like that. How I wish I could." He whispered this last sentence as if speaking to himself.

"I'm lucky to have you here with me in the middle of nowhere," exclaimed Yến suddenly. "You could have been . . . I mean, you're like a big brother to me!" he added looking at Thắng, his eyes full of admiration.

Return to Nou Island

Everyone went back to work the next day without making the slightest reference to the incident of the day before. From time to time, the foremen glanced furtively at Thắng as he worked. Thắng noticed this but didn't worry too much about it. He also noticed a strange heavy silence in his presence, but that didn't bother him at all. Instead, he felt a kind of satisfaction, a feeling of well-being all over his body which brought comfort to his aching heart. Thắng felt as if he had achieved a small personal revenge against his masters, even if it was only temporary and ephemeral. They had not dared, at least for the moment, to punish him a second time. Nevertheless, he remained vigilant. "We never know what these people are plotting, what they have in mind for us. However, I'm ready for anything," he added, so that Yến wouldn't worry.

The following week Thắng was assigned to work at the small port, loading nickel ore onto barges which were lined up neatly, their gaping bellies being filled up with red-brown earth which the workers were then to transport to the ship anchored not far from the shore.

Under Santoni's orders, Thắng worked long, difficult days. Once the holds were full, Santoni ordered, "Go back to your room, get your things and come back here to the port immediately."

Although he was surprised, Thắng followed the orders without trying to understand them. He was ready to endure anything to save his friend. He picked up his clothes and the few possessions he had, put them in the middle of his mat, rolled it up carefully, then went back down to the port.

He took a final look at the camp, now empty of its inhabitants for the day, like someone observing his village before leaving on a long trip. For Thắng sensed that this time something significant was going to happen to him.

When Thắng got to the waterfront, he saw the foreman surrounded by gendarmes. They made him get into a motorboat, then got in themselves and sat on the seat at the back, waved to the sailor to cast off and headed for the big ship waiting for them.

"They must be taking me to prison in Nouméa," Thắng said to himself. He had been expecting a harsh punishment, but nothing like this. "At least I have the satisfaction of knowing that Yến isn't a suspect now," he murmured. "He'll be able to continue working without fear and help his family. That's good." He sighed, "What a pity I couldn't say goodbye. . ."

He was jolted from his thoughts by the loud voice of the gendarme, "Come on, get up now! We've arrived," he said, pointing to the gangway.

Thắng picked up his things and climbed the ladder. One of the gendarmes followed closely, while the second went back to Karembea with the sailor. Thắng gave one last glance at the barge as it pulled away.

"Farewell, my companions," he murmured. "Farewell or see you again?"

After half an hour, when the ship had left the bay and was heading for the high seas in the south, the gendarme, who had noticed there were several Tonkinese sailors on board, asked one of them to translate for Thắng. "Tell him that I have to take him to the prison in Nouméa. If he promises to behave properly, and doesn't cause any problems for anyone on this boat, I'll let him move around on the bridge, and even speak with you!"

Thắng eagerly accepted this unexpected proposal which meant he could meet his fellow countrymen. The three men had already been working for three years on the ship.

"The conditions here on board are much better than on land, and I earn a good living," confided Thơm, one of the sailors. "It's my second contract in Caledonia," he added.

"We also suffered a lot," said Cam the second sailor, "but now things are good for us on the boat, no more beatings, like what we had to endure at the nickel-processing plant. Now our work is to take the ore from the mines to the plant. I'm so happy on the boat, away from the blows and bad treatment that, for the moment, I hardly even think about marriage."

"I want to earn a lot of money so that I can go back home and get married at the end of my contract," said the third.

"I'm married and have four children," said Thơm, continuing with a subject that was particularly difficult for Thắng. "My wife's in Tonkin and she's waiting for me. She often writes, and she'll wait for me as long as she has to. I regularly send her money and she's already bought some land with our savings. I'm staying a second time so that we can build a house when I get back."

"As for me," said Cam, laughing. "I wouldn't mind marrying a pretty girl, but there's no chance of that since I'm never on dry land when a new contingent arrives!"

"I don't think there's been a new ship from Indochina for some time now," Thơm pointed out.

"That's true, not since the one which brought me here in April," said Thắng.

"It doesn't matter to me," said Cam again. "Whether there's a boat or not changes absolutely nothing for me. Because you see," he continued, laughing, "if, by some miracle, and it would be a miracle, I find myself one day with a ring on my finger, well, without a shadow of doubt, I'd be one of the biggest cuckolds on the planet. The men on the land would never leave my poor wife alone to wait for me!"

Thắng's face tensed up slightly when he heard this last remark. "My dear Liên," he murmured gloomily. "Where is she? What's she doing now?"

He would have preferred to talk about something else to avoid thinking about these things. For he was sure that Liên could not be living alone in this country where, in the presence of women, men behaved like a pack of hungry dogs around a bone.

"Hey you, the new one. Why don't you say anything?" Cam said suddenly. "Are you married?"

"Yes," Thắng nodded, looking away.

"Where does she live? Here in Caledonia?" asked Thơm.

"No," replied Thắng, shaking his head, "She's . . . dead."

Thắng was astounded by his own reply. "Why did I say that?" he asked himself, feeling guilty at his impulsiveness. "I shouldn't have."

The boat docked at the port of Nouméa, where more gendarmes were waiting for him. Without wasting any time, they took Thắng to Nou Island where a few months earlier, he had spent those unforgettable days. They didn't take the path leading to the accommodation centre that Thắng knew so well. Instead, they went in the opposite direction, and then, a bit later, entered a group of buildings surrounded by high walls on top of which there were sharp, broken bottles of all colours. It was the main prison of the colony.

News from Home

Liên was now employed as a cleaner for the director of the mine. The work was much less arduous and easier than anything she had done before. She had just received a letter from Tonkin. It was a small thing, but this piece of paper with its sweet tender words was a huge consolation to her. In this letter her parents let her know that her second money order had arrived as quickly as the first.

As soon as work was over, she ran to tell her friend the news. Unusually for her, Lan met her in front of her door and said, "I'm very happy for you Liên. I've also just received a letter from my parents who say that they got all the money I've sent without any problems. This way we give some meaning to our lives," she added her face radiant. "It's a beautiful thing, you know."

Then, lowering her voice, she continued discreetly, "Please, I beg of you, don't say anything about this to Minh. Not tonight. He too got a letter, from his Mum. But now he's withdrawn into himself, wrapped up in his thoughts, and I'm very worried."

Indeed, Minh was lying still on his bed, staring into space. The letter lying on his chest had been carefully folded. From time to time he opened it again, read a few lines and then put it down again listlessly in the same place.

"Poor father, my poor dear father," he kept mumbling.

Lan was pained to see her husband in this state. She had difficulty holding back but made an effort to be as discreet as possible. She understood that in these moments it was wiser to leave Minh alone for a while with his thoughts rather than disturb him or overwhelm him with indiscreet questions or sad words.

A long, moment passed by. The silence became heavier and night had already spread its dark veil over the whole mountain. Lan lit the wick of the oil lamp and put the glass back around the light so that the wind would not blow it out. Then she put the lamp on the table and came over to sit on the bench near the bed, as silent as a nurse watching over her patient.

In the gentle light Lan was relieved to see that Minh's face was more relaxed. She put her hand gently on her husband's head and he looked back at her tenderly as if to thank her for her thoughtfulness. He kissed her fondly on her forehead and invited her to come and sit next to him on the bed. Then he showed her the letter, saying, "Mama has written to me. She's very unhappy and Papa even more so. When they got the letter I'd posted from Hải-Phòng, they couldn't believe it. They'd thought that I'd just run away for a while and would be coming home soon. They were so unhappy. I'm their only son, you know, they rely on me to help them and look after them as they grow older. Papa stopped eating, waiting for me night and day. He believed he saw me in every customer who came to his shop. When my second letter arrived, they were devastated to see the envelope had stamps from a foreign country. At that moment they understood that I was really a long way away. Papa trembled as he read my letter. His tears prevented him from finishing it. Mama had to read the rest. Poor father, he was so proud of his son. In her letter Mama tells me that he's been sick since then and he does nothing to try to get better. She asks me to return home as soon as possible. My poor parents! If they knew what situation I've got myself into," sighed Minh staring at the ground. He continued, "All of this is his fault. . . . Poor father! No, it's not his fault completely, after all. He's a prisoner of his principles and traditions, that's all. That's the tragedy here!"

For a moment Minh didn't say a word. Lan said nothing either, staring sadly at a section of the wall which was covered in newspaper. Minh continued, muttering as if he were alone, "If father had understood me and hadn't imposed that girl on me. If only he had left me free to live my life. After all, I was almost of age. I'd still be with them now. But they gave me no choice, that's their mistake."

"Now," he muttered, "I'll never be able to write to them again and tell them the sad truth. I'll always have to lie and tell them in my letters that I'll soon be home. Each time I'll ask them . . . just a little more patience! I could only ever give them false hope. It's shameful! I'm completely at a loss, Lan, I don't know what to do. I love my parents so much," he sighed.

Then Minh pulled himself together and, looking at Lan, he took her hand sadly, saying, "I'm sorry, my dear Lan, that's the way I am. I like to express my feelings freely, say what I think and what my heart feels, to those I love. Forgive me if I hurt you, because I love you, too. I love you more than anything now. And I don't regret coming here, despite everything. You're my life now, my happiness and I thank heaven for bringing me to you."

Lan was shaken and moved by this sudden declaration. "Minh, my darling, my dear husband. I love you too, I love you more than myself. And I'm so sad to see you suffer so much."

Then she continued more calmly, "I understand how broken-hearted your parents must be. You're so far away and the way you left was, well, unusual. But what can we do about it now?"

Lan thought things over for a while, then she said, frowning, "I think the only solution that can give them any comfort and bring joy to their lives again is if you write to them often, so that they can feel closer to you."

Minh nodded, saying, "You're so sensible, Lan, you're an astonishing girl!"

He kissed her again tenderly as if to thank her and at the same time show her his admiration. She had given him back his courage, helping him clear his mind which had been clouded by sorrow. Minh regained his confidence and was smiling again. Then, with the help of his wife, he began to write a very long letter.

Madame Lucas

Their young healthy bodies were not prey to restlessness or insomnia, and so, after a good night's rest, Minh got up early, when the roosters were crowing at the tops of their voices to announce the dawning of the new day.

He went to the kitchen and took a handful of twigs and dry grasses from a corner of the room, then put them on top of the ash which was still warm from their meal the night before. On top of this small pile Minh added some logs which would soon be turned into a fine powdery black ash by the heat of the fire. What a terrible fate for things that are necessary for man's survival, he thought.

Minh lit a match and put it down in the middle of the twigs which caught fire immediately and, after a few minutes, the tiny room was filled with a sweet warmth. A curl of grey smoke rose from the fire and entered Minh's nostrils. He exhaled it noisily through his nose, but his eyes, still recovering from the night's sleep, were then filled with smoke. He had to blink several times to get rid of it, his eyes watering involuntarily. Minh poured cool water into the small iron cooking pot, which was blackened from so much use; they used it to cook everything, from rice, to meat, to vegetables. They also used it as a frying-pan and a kettle first thing in the morning. Minh put the pot on the fire which was now blazing, red and gold.

When the water started singing and the bubbles danced on its surface, he woke his wife and served the tea. Breakfast did not take much time and they went off into the cool of the morning, hoping that the day would not be too long; they couldn't wait to be together again. They separated at the edge of the village, he to climb up to the gaping holes on the side of the mountain and she to continue on to the European village.

Lan had been sent to do gardening and housework for one of the bosses of the power plant. It was difficult right from the first moment. Lan didn't understand a thing her new boss, Madame Lucas, said to her, not a thing. She was a very stout woman, with short dishevelled hair and a round face with multiple chins. When she spoke in her loud deep voice, her protruding bottom lip showed teeth ravaged by nicotine.

"She smokes like a chimney," thought Lan, a little apprehensive.

Minh had to reassure her and after the evening meal, he taught her the rudiments of the French language.

At work Lan carried out the most difficult tasks meticulously. Once a week she cut the grass by hand; she had become expert at using the sickle and the machete. Often she sawed logs from thick tree trunks. That was the hardest task, too hard for a woman.

However, it was bathing the dog, a huge Alsatian, that bothered Lan the most. Not that she didn't like animals, but simply that washing an animal with soap was intolerable for the frugal young woman. Each time, she felt guilty at this incredibly useless waste. She herself had never in her life had the luxury of bathing her young body in perfumed soap.

Lan always worked extremely hard at these difficult and unpleasant tasks, thinking her pleasure would be even greater at the end of the month when, once again, she could send another money order home. That was why she worked so hard, avoiding problems and bearing the brunt of her boss' bad moods. She was a diligent worker and gave the best of herself without ever complaining.

So she was very disappointed when she realised that Madame Lucas did not appreciate her efforts at all. She seemed instead to be looking out for the slightest mistake or shortcoming, like a bird waiting to jump on its prey to tear it apart. Indeed, Madame Lucas was eternally dissatisfied. Her spiky, messy hair made her look like a huge menacing cat showing its claws, ready to attack. Lan was like a little mouse caught in a trap, a toy between the fangs of the tigress.

Madame Lucas spied on Lan as she did the ironing. No doubt she was hoping that the young woman would burn herself when filling the iron with white-hot coal, or drop a few pieces of coal on the floor. But Lan was on her guard; she took care with every move, not wanting to make any mistakes. Madame Lucas was disappointed. Vindictive as she was, always gesticulating, that day she would have loved to strike Lan. Indeed, she had already hit her more than once and at those times her voice had become sharp and cutting and her round eyes, wide with anger, terrified the young woman.

However, Lan would not allow herself to get discouraged. She took it all, never complaining, like the reed in the fable, bending under the furious onslaught of the wind.

"Are they all like this, these men and women they call 'long noses'?" she asked one evening.

"Some are good and some are bad, like everywhere else in the world," replied Minh.

"The ones here don't seem to have heard of the word 'kindness'," retorted Lan.

"It's completely normal." said Minh.

"Oh! And what do you find normal in all of this?"

"Well Lan, here we are in a colony that is protected, and even encouraged by the powerful metropolis to exploit as much wealth as possible, by whatever means necessary. Our employers, whether they're factory-owners, shopkeepers or settlers have the law and the authorities behind them. It's inevitable that they think they're our masters!"

"What are we then? Animals? Slaves?" cried Lan, bitterly.

Minh looked glum. "That's colonial privilege. They think we owe them obedience and respect."

"I hope all this will change one day!" Lan exclaimed.

"They're the ones in power, Lan. They have no idea of our plight."

"That's not surprising, as they have never once, not even for a moment, put themselves in our place to try to understand us."

"Why would a rich man put himself in the place of a poor man? Anyway, that's life: there are the poor and the rich. We're poor," sighed Minh melancholically.

"So, we'll always be poor and live in these conditions?" cried Lan in horror.

"Things'll get better for us, it's inevitable that attitudes will change, I'm sure of it!" Minh said. He continued, pensive, "Maybe not for us, at least I don't think so, but I'm sure things will improve for the future generation, for our children."

"Do you think our children will stay here?" asked Lan anxiously, her eyes wide open.

"Oh no, our children will go back home with us, of course! We'll all leave together! But I meant that science progresses so quickly that the children will benefit from all these changes, here and elsewhere, and in the home country."

Lan laughed loudly. "We speak about 'our children' as if we already had them, as if we're an old couple talking about our future plans."

"We'll have children soon, I promise," said Minh, laughing in turn. He got up, took his wife's hand and leaned over the oil lamp to blow it out. The light flickered for a moment, and then darkness flooded into the house.

***

It was towards the end of the year—about November—the cool season had been over for several months, but Lan still remembered some nights when the temperature was quite low. Sometimes the thermometer in Madame Lucas' house showed ten degrees in the early morning and once or twice it had even gone down to six degrees. A slight shiver went through her body when she recalled those icy nights with the wind blowing continuously through their house, through the gaps in the planks and the metal sheets. The newspapers which lined the inside were useless against the cold. She could see herself curled up all night next to her husband. The blanket she had been given when she arrived was so thin that she couldn't warm her freezing body. And the humidity that she had to breathe in all night spread through her whole body, often giving her a headache when she woke up in the morning.

Today Madame Lucas had ordered Lan to wash the whole house, from floor to ceiling. She was on the veranda. The hot morning sun fell on the smooth skin of her face and warmed her bare arms. Her feet were wading in tepid water, her black trousers rolled up to her thighs, exposing the white skin of two fine supple legs which the sun caressed gently. At that moment Lan felt an indefinable well-being. Using a long-handled broom, she pushed the stagnant water from the floor towards the outside. The water made a curious gurgling sound before disappearing into the soil in the garden. She was alone; Madame Lucas was still in bed at the other end of the house.

From time to time Lan closed her eyes, lifting her head slightly towards the sun, the better to store these sensual moments of pleasure that nature offered which would revive her for the rest of the day. She had already experienced this in the past and so she made the most of these fleeting moments, without any ulterior motive or guilt. Because, in the end, it was also good for her mistress, indirectly, since these pleasurable instants allowed her to work even more efficiently afterwards.

Lan had started cleaning again. She leant over towards a bucket of water on the floor to rinse the cloth when suddenly she felt a strange unfamiliar discomfort. Her whole body felt numb, her mind was paralysed for a moment, followed by dizziness, like someone very sick who has been lying in bed for months who suddenly tries to get up. As she leant over the bucket Lan almost fell forward, but she managed to put out her arms to stop herself falling. A strong desire to throw up everything she had in her stomach gave her a nasty, unpleasant feeling in her whole body. She stayed for a moment in this ridiculous position.

"A good thing the boss is still in bed," she thought as she stood up straight. "She might've thought I was putting on an act."

Lan got back to work and, to her surprise, there were no more episodes during the rest of the morning or during the afternoon. She didn't even speak to her husband about it in the evening. "It must've just been a moment of fatigue," she reassured herself.

Lan prepared the dinner. The rice was ready in a metal bowl on the little kitchen table. It was white and hot, and curls of white steam twirled up to the thatched roof, making them hungry. Next, Lan wanted to make a dish of meat and Chinese cabbage, one of Minh's favourites. She waited for the fat to melt from the heat of the wood fire and turn into an oily liquid at the bottom of the pot. Then she fried some white onions. Lan loved the smell of fried onions, but this time she had to leave the room quickly, holding her nose. Outside she took a deep breath of fresh air to get over the terrible desire she had to bring up everything she had in her stomach again.

"What's the matter?" asked Minh who was working in the main room. For the last few weeks he had been making things out of wood. He made clogs that he sold to his colleagues in the village. With this, he saved a bit of money so that they could buy white onions, pepper and other small things which improved everyday life for them.

"I don't know, I feel unwell," complained Lan.

"What is it, darling? Please tell me," said Minh, worried. He was already by her side.

"I feel dizzy and . . . nauseous. . ."

"Dizzy?"

He racked his brains, frowning as he tried to think what might be making her feel sick. He seemed to remember, a long time ago, something similar which had happened. Was it his father? His mother? No, his aunt. Yes, that was it! Suddenly he remembered it well. Minh was still, his mouth open, his eyes wide and his face radiant, as if he hardly dared believe it. Then, taking his wife, he hugged her in his arms, against his beating chest. He cried out, "Lan, my wife, it's wonderful."

Lan stopped his emotional outburst. "Tell me what's going on!" she said. She guessed what her husband's great joy meant, but she wanted to hear it from him. "Tell me what's going on," she insisted, "I also have the right to know."

"If I'm not wrong, you . . . these are the early signs of pregnancy. You'll soon be a mother! Do you realise? You'll soon be a mother!" cried Minh happily.

"Don't forget that in that case, you'll also be a father!" replied Lan, hugging her husband even harder.

The smell of grilled onions coming from the kitchen forced them to separate.

***

The days flew by. Lan had certain cravings; for example, she wanted to bite into fruit and eat things that couldn't be found on the mountain, simple food that she used to be able to get easily back home. In Madame Lucas' garden there was a mango tree that had magnificent, delicious fruit. Lan knew this as, with the aid of a pole, she had picked several for Madame Lucas, who greedily devoured the juicy mangoes. It was torture for Lan. Her mouth watered.

One day, before Christmas, there had been a strong wind and dozens of ripe mangoes fell from the trees. Lan picked them up and put them in a huge fruit bowl which had pride of place on the large dining-room table. When she was leaving at the end of the day, there were several strong gusts of wind and Lan saw a mango fall outside the garden in the middle of the dusty track. She picked it up, wanting to take it home with her.

"It's not quite ripe, it'll be delicious. I like mangoes when they're still green, they're more bitter," thought Lan, staring at the fruit which had fallen from the sky.

A loud commanding voice rang out. "Number 3142! What are you doing there? What have you got in your hand?"

"!"

"Come here immediately!" the voice roared.

Shocked, Lan opened the gate and went back to her boss.

"She must have been spying on me, from her window," she thought. Lan managed to communicate to Madame Lucas that there was nothing wrong with what she had done, since she had picked the fruit up from the path outside. In any case, hadn't she put all the other mangoes on the table? All, without exception, without ever daring to touch a single one.

"How dare you steal from me?" yelled the woman, her hair awry. "Take that for your efforts! Ouf! Ouf!"

Lan received several hard slaps which made her cry. Not because of the pain, although her top lip was bruised, but from rage—the rage at realising how impotent she was in the face of injustice. Madame Lucas took the mango and threw it to the ground, crying, "And what's more, it's green. What a bitch!"

Lan ran as fast as she could, her tears blinding her at times. She wanted to get home . . . be beside her husband as quickly as possible. Only the presence of Minh could ease her pain.

Terrible News

Some sad news reached them like a cold shower, causing consternation in the Tonkinese community. Phúc gathered his countrymen on the small village square. "The management has asked me to announce some terrible news: the Japanese have invaded Indochina. War has been declared! All communication we have with our country is suspended."

Dismay could be seen on all of their faces.

"It's impossible!" cried Lan, in tears.

Liên's face was haggard and her eyes red from too many tears, as Hiếu had told her the news first. She was standing, dazed, the picture of desolation.

The men didn't say anything. They were silent, their heads lowered, so great was their disappointment.

"My letters . . . I won't be able to write to my parents anymore," lamented Minh. "I won't get their news. It's not possible. They need comfort, now more than ever!"

To try to reassure the community, Phúc said, "I'm sure this war won't last. In a few months everything will return to normal and we'll be able to correspond once again with our families. The only thing we can do now is save our money and, once the post is working again, our relatives will receive a bigger money order than usual," he concluded, smiling.

It was an odd, forced smile, which betrayed his real sentiments of deep sorrow. Anyway, no one was listening to him anymore; they were all absorbed by their own miserable thoughts.

"Do you think the war will last for a long time?" asked Lan, naively, when they were at home with Phúc and Liên.

"I'm afraid it might. I've never heard of a war lasting less than a few months, and sometimes they last years," sighed Phúc wryly.

"My poor parents," murmured Liên.

"Will we ever see them again after all these upheavals? Will they still be at the same address?" wondered Minh, devastated, shaking his head in a gesture of helplessness. The image of his mother came to him clear and insistent, while that of his father was blurred, as if hidden by a thick fog.

"Has father recovered his health? Is he still sick? Is it really my fault?" he sighed dejectedly.

"Did I do the right thing to leave them? Was I right to venture so far away?" wondered Lan. "If I can't help my family anymore, all this is useless!"

Her gaze met Minh's; he was staring at her intensely, upset to see her in this state. Lan pulled herself together, smiling slightly.

"No, I didn't come for nothing, since I found love here," she said to herself.

With the back of her hand, she wiped her tears away. They stayed like this together, all four of them, silent but solitary, united in the good times and the bad. Only their shadows projected onto the walls by the flickering light animated the room a little. For they remained still, inert, lost in deep contemplation in the night.

New Hebrides

Thắng was sailing again.

"I'm like a cork floating on the ocean," he thought. "I don't even know where I'm going or what they're going to do with me."

He peered at the sailors' faces, but he had to face facts; there were no Tonkinese amongst the crew. Thắng was disappointed.

"What if they're taking me to another mine?" he said to himself. "I've heard that's happened before . . . What if, by some miracle, I found Liên?" His face lit up and he began to have some hope again. But it was, alas, as short-lived as the light of a falling star. "No, it's impossible, there's no chance anymore. It's all over now," he sighed, shaking his head.

Thắng contemplated the wake left by the ship on the rough sea. When he lifted his head a moment later, he realised that the boat was heading straight for the ocean. The big island was gradually disappearing in a thick white mist far away on the horizon. He looked questioningly at the sailors on the bridge in the hope of getting some information about where he was going. But nobody took any notice of his dismay. In any case, he couldn't understand these people who spoke in another language!

"Why don't we all speak the same language?" Thắng wondered. He thought about creating the basics of a universal language, but had to abandon this fantasy and bring his mind back to the sad reality of the present.

"Where are they taking me? Am I going back home to Tonkin?" He kept asking himself all these questions which, alas, remained unanswered.

The boat anchored a few days later in a tranquil bay under grey sky and heavy rain.

In the plantation he had been sent to, Thắng was agreeably surprised to find others from the home country. There were more than fifty of them living in basic huts which had been built under the thick foliage of gigantic trees. A little farther along, on the edge of the forest were some other simple dwellings.

"Married couples live in those houses," his roommate explained. He was a strong, solid young man, like all the men and women living there, something Thắng had noticed as soon as he arrived. But what intrigued him the most was the grave, austere expression on their faces.

Sheltered under the huge branches, Thắng gazed at the giant trees, whose trunks soared dizzyingly towards the sky, as if they wanted to reach the dark clouds of dusk. In the gentle light on a grassy hill, he could make out a large colonial-style house surrounded by a magnificent, perfectly maintained garden. The young man pointed to the hill and said, "That's where the owner of the place, Monsieur Chauvedin, lives. He's a hard intractable man. He doesn't know the meaning of the word 'mercy', or at least he chooses not to know."

Thắng had not yet met his new boss and listened attentively to the young man without a word.

"My name's Bích," the young man told him.

"My name's Thắng, and I've come from New Caledonia," he introduced himself.

"From Nouméa? That's extraordinary!" Bích exclaimed.

"Haven't you been to Caledonia?" asked Thắng.

"No, we came straight from Hải-Phòng to this island of Spiritu Santo, in the same boat as those going to Nouméa. Actually, I have many friends who are there now. But we've lost contact since they separated us."

"Hasn't anyone come back here from Nouméa yet?" asked Thắng.

"No, to my knowledge, you're the first."

Thắng thought for a while. "I don't understand it," he said at last. "Why did they bring me to this island?"

He couldn't think of a satisfactory answer to his question. Then, at Bích's request, he began to tell the story of his adventures. When he had finished, it was Bích's turn to reflect at length, after which he tried to give some sort of plausible explanation for the mystery, "Here in the New Hebrides, when a boss sacks a worker for whatever reason, the local authorities send him straight away to another landlord—if there's already been a request for more labour, of course. At the moment they need workers, as they all want to increase their production. Indeed, Chauvedin has asked for more labour. But so far, he hasn't been able to get any because of the international situation. Apparently, it's extremely difficult, if not impossible, to get another contingent of workers from our country."

"Yes," said Thắng, "I was with the last convoy. There hasn't been another one since. But that still doesn't explain why I'm here."

"Yes, it does!" said Bích. "They wanted to get rid of a worker who was difficult, you could even say . . . aggressive. Sorry to be so blunt, Thắng, but it's so as you understand. Knowing that here on this island we need workers, they could get rid of a troublemaker like you by putting you on a ship for Santo. Even if you've come on your own, it still means two extra arms, you know!"

"You're probably right," admitted Thắng. Then he continued, more relaxed, "This country's beautiful, despite the rain this afternoon."

"Don't delude yourself, my friend. As of tomorrow morning, you won't have any time to admire the beauty of the scenery," said Bích bitterly. "It's better I warn you straight away," he continued. "It's strictly forbidden to speak while at work, and to rest, even for a single minute. It's forbidden to smoke as well. The guards are constantly there watching you, watching us."

Thắng was expressionless, but he nodded as if to say, "I know all about that sort of thing."

Nevertheless, he asked, "What kind of abuse does the boss mete out?"

Bích listed them, counting on his fingers. "There's whipping, kicking, rationing the food, which is completely inadequate as it is." Bích continued, "If he felt like it, he could even make us work a whole month, sometimes longer, without a single day of rest. If he decides to, he can dock our pay for several weeks, depending on how serious the misconduct is," specified Bích. "And that last punishment is the one that really scares us."

"So why did you choose to come to this country?" asked Thắng, curious.

"When our ship stopped here, it was the first port of call on the way to Nouméa. I noticed that those who got off here were given a mosquito net as a bonus. So I volunteered to work on this island. You have to understand that I'd never had a mosquito net in my life, and for me it meant a step up."

"Didn't you have any trouble getting hired?" Thắng asked.

"Not at all, they wanted young men and women with a robust constitution. That's what I have, and they took me on without any problems."

Then, changing the subject, he said, "I advise you to set up your mosquito net if you want to sleep, Thắng. It's not a luxury, as I thought, but a necessity. You have to protect yourself against the mosquitoes, which carry a disease that is common here, malaria. You must take the quinine tablets they give you from time to time. Don't throw them away," insisted Bích. "Even the water you drink will have to be boiled. Everything's very dangerous for our health here if we're not careful!"

That night, Thắng couldn't get to sleep. Strange, confused thoughts spun around, collided, and then whirled around in his head. And the buzzing of the dense swarms of mosquitoes outside, around his "protective cage" made him restless and irritable. Sometimes, one of these insects, no doubt more vicious than the others, would cling to the mosquito net, just near his ears and start making a continual whining sound that was even more exasperating. The night was hot and humid and Thắng had difficulty breathing. Sweat made his skin unpleasantly slimy and sticky and it was only at about one in the morning that, exhausted from the voyage, he finally slipped into a deep sleep.

The light of the early morning was still quite faint when they set off for the plantation. Several young women were carrying their babies, holding them affectionately; some were newborns, others a few months old. They got to a huge, well-maintained piece of land covered with regular rows of coconut palms that stretched as far as the eye could see.

"This is the coconut plantation," Bích whispered to Thắng. "Do as we do, just copy us and everything'll be all right. Good luck."

After that, Bích moved away, just in case, so that they couldn't be caught talking at work.

The foremen, on horseback, were already there. The weather looked menacing; grey clouds were gradually covering the whole sky and the weak rays of the morning sun disappeared again, like at the end of a very short day.

Thắng worked all morning under the black sky, along with men and women who were pouring with perspiration. And yet he felt as if he were alone on the land, as no one dared to straighten up or even look at anyone else. Some were squatting, hunched over as they concentrated on pulling out roots or weeds that grew in abundance under the coconut palms, which were the wealth of the plantation. Others tended the cocoa trees on the adjoining plot of land.

The aggressive-looking foremen moved from one end of the vast domain to the other, with extreme vigilance. They seemed to be defending the boss' interests with disconcerting zeal. The workers were persecuted from the first moment by swarms of flies which landed on any uncovered part of their bodies. The flies seemed to be attracted in particular to the eyes, nostrils and lips and, as they worked, the labourers had to constantly shake the flies from their heads with sudden movements, but the flies came back quickly with a vengeance.

An awkward movement had caused Thắng to graze his right arm. Blood came to the surface of his skin and, with horror he saw a mass of insects swarm to his wound, covering it totally, and forming a repulsive dense black spot on his skin. "It's a real paradise for flies here," muttered Thắng, furious, "there are at least fifty on my sore!" He swatted them away in case they infected it. "I have nothing to treat the wound or protect it." Other flies were already trying to settle on Thắng's arm. His eyes lit up as he had a sudden idea. He was working under the huge cocoa trees just at the edge of the forest. He moved imperceptibly towards the dense vegetation, grabbed a soft, broad leaf, pulled it off the tree and then tore out a small vine and used it as a natural rope to attach the leaf to his wound.

Halfway through the morning heavy rain fell on this part of the island. They were drenched from head to foot. The children, who were on their own in a corner of the plot, were crying and shouting as the cold shower soaked their fragile bodies. The young mothers, with heavy hearts, anxiously glanced over at them, without slowing down and wondered, "Is that my baby I can hear crying so loudly?" But they couldn't afford to stop working to go and see them, even for a brief moment. The only thing that mattered was productivity, and the guards were driven solely by the idea of keeping their jobs through blind obedience.

But, for the labourers, Chauvedin was the one responsible for all of their hardship.

At midday, during their short lunch break, the mothers rushed over to the children, who were drenched and exhausted from crying too much. Then, swallowing their meagre food they breastfed their babies. During the break Bích approached Thắng.

"I'm still hungry. What about you?" he said.

"The ration of rice is really not enough," said Thắng.

"That's what everyone thinks here. For us men, it's bearable, but look at those poor women. They have the same amount of food as us and with that they have to feed their children," Bích grumbled indignantly.

"Why don't you ask for more food, if not for us, at least for the women?"

"We have . . . I mean, their husbands have asked several times, without any luck. All they got as an answer was a kick in the guts," said Bích caustically. "But anger is mounting, and we'll end up going on strike or fighting back if nothing changes soon."

A strident whistle called them back to work. For the second part of the day Thắng was put into the team collecting the dried coconuts strewn over the ground. There were coconuts by the hundreds, scattered over the plantation, enormous brown fruit which had fallen from the sky, decorating the green grass. The men all had a big bag in their hands. Thắng copied his fellow workers: he picked up the coconuts, filled his bag and then took it to a cart, which moved along the central path at the same pace as the pickers.

The men worked like this for most of the afternoon. The ox-drawn cart had, in the meanwhile, unloaded the coconuts in a clearing, where they formed a huge pile. They stopped collecting and went over to the pile of fruit, and, with a sharp blow of the axe, some of the men began cutting the coconuts in half. Thắng was among them, but he was a pitiful novice, bewildered by the rapidity and precision of his colleagues. Other men were expertly wielding a tool which looked like a big spoon. With a single deft movement, they removed the kernel from the coconut. They slaved away at this task in silence until the evening. When Thắng saw Bích in the dormitory he asked, "What do they use the coconut kernel for?"

Bích couldn't believe his ears. He burst out laughing. "Don't you know, Thắng?! It's the famous copra! That's what makes the wealth of this land. It'll be dried and exported to many countries to make coconut oil, butter, soap and other things!"

"I didn't know anything about the commercial use of coconuts. But I'm thinking about it," said Thắng. "In Tonkin, the kernel's very popular."

"Yes, it's sought after as it's so nutritious."

"Considering we don't get enough to eat, why can't they increase our rations with coconut kernels? There's so much of it here!" exclaimed Thắng.

"I know, we all know. Alas!" said Bích, sorrowfully. "Woe to the man who dares to take a coconut for himself!" Then, with his eyes wide open and his arms raised to the sky, he added, as if Thắng had committed a serious offense, "Make sure you never do that, Thắng. You don't know what they are capable of!"

As Thắng didn't understand, Bích explained, "You're new here, you don't know how we've had to suffer. So listen to what I'm about to tell you. Our boss, our master, is an unscrupulous man, a tyrant, a madman. He's done us too much harm. For even the most futile things, such as taking a coconut, for example, he'd be capable of . . . torture."

Bích confided, "I and my fellow workers have reached the end of our tether. We're on the verge of revolt. It wouldn't take much to drive us to action. If that happened, it'd be too bad for him, or . . . too bad for us," said Bích, his face serious and determined.

Surprised, Thắng stammered, "You'd be capable of. . . ?"

He didn't dare finish his sentence. Bích looked hard and severe, and nodded his head.

"Yes, we will do it!"

As he lay down on his mat, Thắng mused, "I'm here in this country because I struck one of the bosses, and now I'm again faced with another even more serious problem, a plot for an imminent revolt. What will become of me after all this?" He wasn't scared, but he could see that he had been dragged inexorably onto this path of hatred and vengeance.

"Is this my destiny?" Thắng wondered. He recalled his childhood of deprivation and poverty, but he had always been against violence and he didn't remember ever being brutal or nasty. Now he was afraid for himself, and of how evil was infiltrating his mind and his whole being.

"Is this a normal reaction? Is it the resentment of a broken heart?" he asked himself again. But Thắng was incapable of finding an answer to his questions.

The next day he continued collecting coconuts. Above their heads, the sky was blue and the sun had reappeared, its rays reflecting in the dew still on the coconut leaves from the night before, making them shine in some spots like precious stones. Thắng couldn't resist raising his head and contemplating this extraordinary spectacle for a few seconds. At that very moment a man arrived, muttering incomprehensible curses. His fat, round face could not contain his anger.

"I don't pay you to admire the clouds!" he yelled at Thắng. At the same time his thick hand came down brutally on the young man's face. Thắng staggered but did not flinch. "So this is the master of the place," Thắng said to himself as he bent down to pick up the coconuts as if nothing had happened.

Chauvedin turned to his foreman. "Is this is how you watch the men? Good for nothing! You spend your time daydreaming, sleeping. It's unbelievable! Next time you'll be out, do you understand?" His prominent paunch before him, he continued his morning inspection, gesticulating, striking and yelling.

"So, this is the ferocious beast, the incarnation of evil Bích told me about," murmured Thắng.

At the end of the gruelling day, sitting on the grass in front of his dormitory and looking up at the tall trees, Thắng observed the flocks of birds of all sizes flying around with a loud beating of their wings. It seemed as though they were looking for a refuge for the night. Their calls merged together, becoming louder, spreading over the whole plain like a joyous melody. Thắng saw other dark-coloured creatures flying from the high branches. To him they looked like miniature dogs flying around in compact groups, spreading their huge, delicate black wings. He had already seen these strange creatures of the night and remembered what Bích had told him when they were going to the canteen the night before.

"They're flying foxes, a kind of giant bat. They only come out at night to feed on the fruit. During the day they hang upside down on the branches. Their flesh is much appreciated." He added, "Our bosses love it. They cook it in wine, I think." Thắng grimaced in disgust at hearing this, for these animals reminded him of vampires. But the flying mammals did not scare him. He envied them—he too would like to have wings, to fly away into the sky, free. Free! Free of all constraints!

"Come on, Thắng. It's dinnertime. Let's hurry, there's a meeting later on this evening."

Thắng got up and followed Bích docilely without answering. He had difficulty coming back to reality. After the frugal meal, the couples came to join the single men in the canteen. The women had their newborns with them, happy to finally be able to cuddle them after so many hours of separation.

Pháp, one of the married men, got to his feet, his face solemn. He began speaking after Thắng, the newcomer, had been welcomed. He spoke about their terrible work conditions, before broaching the subject which had been concerning them more than anything else over many months.

"As you all know, my dear friends," he said, "our bosses only give us the minimum amount of food but demand huge efforts from us!" Pháp turned to Thắng. "This may come as a surprise to you, but if you follow my reasoning carefully you'll understand." Then, turning back to the group, he said, "If we're not careful, in the near future we risk serious consequences from this inadequate nutrition, in a country overrun with malaria. Each one of us certainly remembers what great physical shape we were in when we came here. Take a hard look at us now. What do you see? I'll answer that very easily; we've all aged and lost weight. Many of us still carry the sickness in us, and others are right now in the throes of constant onslaughts of this terrible illness. To survive both the terrible living conditions and the punishing climate, we need adequate food. It's an absolute necessity for our health and that of our children!"

He stopped for a moment, wiped his forehead which was inundated with sweat, then continued gravely,

"Our attempts to speak with Chauvedin have led to nothing at all, so some of us here have contacted our countrymen working on other plantations on the island. What we found out is that we are all, without exception, mistreated and undernourished. We've all agreed to send a letter of protest to the authorities to make our demands heard and ensure they're met as quickly as possible! If we get a negative response from them, we'll go out on strike. I stress that I'm talking about all of us on the island! We must expect some kind of repression, or perhaps some kind of retaliation. But, even so, we have to act. It's time to act, we have no choice anymore!"

Pháp observed his audience. "Those in favour, raise your hand!"

Everyone accepted, without exception, including the women.

"Are you ready to bear the consequences of our actions?" he asked.

"Yes," they replied, as one.

"This is the letter our compatriots and friends from the other plantations have signed. Let's put our signatures to it now. Those who can't write should put their fingerprint on the paper. Here's the ink."

The conspirators carried out the instructions calmly, one by one.

"Everything's in order now. The letter will be handed over tomorrow to the administration by those comrades nearest the town. I'll take it to them myself tonight. And if, in a weeks' time, we haven't received what we're demanding, we'll go on strike for an indefinite period. Remember that we all have to stand together. It's crucial if we want things to move quickly!"

Pháp stopped and when he spoke again his expression was serious.

"Dear friends! You've all voted for us to take this action, so it's too late to back out of it. I'll warn you again that those who, through cowardice or self-interest, want to abandon the struggle after the operation has begun will be severely judged and punished by the whole community. Do you all still agree?" Pháp asked again.

No one replied, but all together without consulting one another, they spontaneously raised their hands in approval.

Thắng was one of the first to sign the petition. For he felt it was necessary for him to participate, along with his fellow workers, in the fight for a more decent and humane life. A few days later, he was pleased to hear that the petition had had the effect of a bombshell all over the island.

After long and difficult negotiations, the employers had to give in to pressure from the administrators, and they reluctantly accepted an increase in food rations and the principle of more social justice for the workers. From this memorable day onwards, Pháp and all of his friends received not only more, but healthier food.

"It's a great victory!" cried Bích happily.

But Thắng remained sceptical.

"You don't really seem satisfied," remarked Pháp.

"I'm pessimistic," said Thắng. "In my opinion we've obtained better food, that's all. I know our boss, and I doubt whether he'll improve our conditions."

Pháp thumped him on the back, then laughed, saying, "Forget all that. Don't be so defeatist! But I must admit you're clever. Let's forget all this, come and relax with us. We'll have a chat, okay?"

Thắng was happy. From this moment he felt he had been accepted by everyone in the camp.

Red Ants

The days passed by, long and difficult. They had more food, but the blows and punishments increased in the same proportions.

Since the day he had had to give in to the decisions of the immigration authorities, Chauvedin had become extremely agitated. As if his defeat in the face of these peasants, these beggars, had diminished him and wounded his pride. As a result, he became even more vindictive and merciless.

"I wasn't wrong," muttered Thắng.

The master came more and more often to the plantation, watching not only his employees but the foremen as well, demanding that they be even harsher.

"Will we have to put up with this barbaric treatment for ever, without ever retaliating?" cried Bích one evening.

He was completely exhausted from a gruelling day of work.

"We're working a lot more than before and the hours've been extended arbitrarily," said Thắng soberly.

Pháp was listening to their conversation and added, "You were right to distrust this man, Thắng. He's the only one who isn't meeting his commitments. The other employers on the island have all improved working conditions substantially for our compatriots, all except Chauvedin!"

"He's smart," admitted Thắng. "He knows it's difficult for us to prove to the administration that we're mistreated. Our word's nothing against his. It has no weight."

"We have just one solution left," said Pháp, "to wait, wait patiently. Until the day he commits a serious mistake, and only then that will we be able to act without danger."

"!"

"Tomorrow it's Christmas Eve," said Bích suddenly. "Let's not speak about all of this, let's forget hate and revenge." Feeling calmer, he continued, his eyes half-closed, "Let's prepare to welcome Our Lord baby Jesus." Bích was Catholic. He was not practising, but he celebrated Easter and Christmas.

Thắng relaxed a little upon hearing these words uttered so fervently.

The next morning, they returned to the coconut plantation. With the help of his wife, Pháp put his son under a tree with the other children. The parents were careful to leave them, as they did every day, in a spot well away from the coconut palms, in case a ripe coconut dropped suddenly from the top of the tree. The trees were tall, fifteen metres high, some even twenty-five metres tall, and a coconut falling from this height could injure or even kill a child. Pháp left his son, thinking, "He looks like the baby Jesus Bích was telling me about yesterday."

Pháp and his wife joined their respective teams as quickly as possible, as they knew they could arrive early but lateness would be punished: either they would have to make it up on Sunday, or else they would lose some of their meagre salary at the end of the month. But Pháp was preoccupied that morning; he was thinking about the baby Jesus that he had heard so much about but didn't know.

"Maybe one day I too will discover Jesus," he said to himself. His thoughts kept coming back to his son whom they had left with the other children under the tree away from the coconut palms. Often cries and shouts reached their ears and all the parents wondered at that moment if it was their own baby crying.

At midmorning, as work had progressed quickly, the men and women had already reached the edge of the coconut plantation. Despite their distance from the children, they could still hear the insistent, uncharacteristic cries of one of the babies. The parents immediately became nervous, but the watchful foremen remained menacingly near Chauvedin, who, certain he had tamed these "nhà quê," these peasants who had dared to defy him, had been revelling for some time in his revenge.

The crying got louder and louder, piercing through the plantation. Unable to contain himself any longer, Pháp, with a terrible sense of dread, got up and walked towards Chauvedin. He wanted to get special permission from his boss to go and check on the children, even if it cost him a whole Sunday of rest. But the foremen stopped him. Grabbing him roughly by the arm they sent him back to his place. However, the poor father would not admit defeat so easily. He turned around sharply and then looked anxiously at Chauvedin. Pháp wanted to speak to him again, but Chauvedin and his men rushed at him and beat him savagely.

"Get back to work immediately!" shouted Chauvedin when Pháp was stretched out on the ground. "Otherwise you'll be taken before the tribunal and severely punished for rebellion!"

Thắng was holding back his anger and indignation with great difficulty. Without realising it, he was squeezing the handle of his machete so hard that it almost broke. The tension was about to boil over. The foremen could sense it and had their whips at the ready in case they needed them. Chauvedin remained calm. He had a smile of satisfaction on his thick lips and with his right hand he held the butt of the rifle that had been slung over his shoulder for the last few months.

"Don't lose your temper, Pháp, I beg of you! Don't let your anger get the better of you, my darling!" cried Tý, in tears as, like her compatriots, she watched, powerless.

Distraught, Pháp had to go back to work, with a heavy heart. Then everyone calmed down as the child's screams had stopped. Nevertheless Pháp was still worried; a dreadful premonition gnawed at him, squeezing his chest. When at last it was midday, all of the parents rushed over to the children. Pháp was the quickest. He looked for his child and found him alone at some distance from the tree and the other children. He walked nearer, but suddenly froze, as if petrified, his arms spread out wide. Tý arrived at this moment, looked at the flesh of her flesh, her eyes bulging, horrified, not wanting to believe what she saw. Then she began to scream in anguish, the screams of a desperate mother.

Once the moment of extreme shock had passed, Pháp ran towards the baby and tried with his shaking hands to wipe away the enormous red ants which swarmed over his now inert body, covering his face, and entering his nostrils and his mouth.

"My son!" yelled Pháp. Then, his stricken face ravaged with despair, he put his ear to the little chest. He thought he could still hear a faint heartbeat. Drawn by the parents' cries, Thắng arrived at that moment. Once he understood the awful drama taking place before his eyes, he quickly took off the baby's clothes. Then he began to get rid of the ants which had lodged in the skin. Thắng could see that the baby's whole body, as well as the face was horribly swollen from the bites.

"My poor baby, my poor little baby," wept the poor mother miserably. She couldn't accept such a tragedy. She refused to believe it was all over.

"Fetch a healer!" She cried, "Can't any of you do anything for my child?"

Nobody dared answer.

"What can we do to ease their pain?" Thắng wondered.

He was jolted into action by the distressed father who was shouting, "Do something! Don't just sit there!"

Thắng went up to the child and put his ear to the small bare chest. He took the tiny hand in his to test the pulse, but then lowered his head, visibly dejected. Gathering all his courage he looked at Pháp who was waiting, his pupils dilated, as if hoping for a miracle. Thắng looked down again at the ground and shook his head.

"There's nothing we can do for him," he murmured softly. Pháp was still holding his son in his arms. He grimaced in pain. Then he kneeled down and placed the body of the innocent little baby on the thick grass of the plantation. He wept, desperately, at length.

When he had no tears left, his expression hardened. He stared into the distance towards the hill as if looking for something. Then his eyes fixed on Chauvedin who had remained a short distance away on the path which led to his house. He was chatting with his foremen calmly, as if the tragedy of Pháp and his wife did not concern him. The men and women, those who were mothers hugging their babies nervously, were scandalised by his indifference.

"He knows a painful tragedy is taking place at this very moment on his land and yet he walks past without deigning to stop, even for a moment," they said.

"The child's dead because of him," shouted others. "It's his fault!"

Calmly and coldly, Pháp glared at his enemy, like someone who has just made an irreversible decision.

Thắng helped Tý, the tearful mother, get up. She had been lying with her face to the ground. "My son! My darling child. Leave me alone, I want to die with my child!" she wept.

Still kneeling, Pháp, his face buried in his work-worn hands, murmured weakly in a desperate voice, "Today, tonight, is the celebration of the birth of baby Jesus. Why, oh why did mine have to die? Why?"

Disappearance

The end-of-year festivities came and went very quickly. Chauvedin, who had witnessed the dreadful scene on Christmas Eve, felt nervous, despite his apparently serene behaviour. But, to his astonishment, everything continued in total calm. His employees had not reacted, let alone protested. They actually seemed to be more conscientious and submissive.

"You see! They're a bunch of cowards and sissies!" he enjoyed telling his foremen. The fat landowner gradually regained confidence and, needless to say, increased his demands on the workers. But, even then, he was astounded to see that his "nhà quê" obeyed docilely, without grumbling.

For the celebration of Tết, the Indochinese New Year, the community made a gesture of goodwill; they invited their employer to participate in their meal to celebrate the new lunar year.

Chauvedin accepted and turned up on the day at the agreed time. Even so, he adopted his usual superior attitude, as if to warn them that he was still their master. He noticed that the women and children were absent, but that didn't bother him in the least. The Asian cuisine was delicious and Chauvedin was glad he had come.

The next morning very early, the whole community went back to work diligently. However, the foremen were extremely agitated. They seemed unsettled and anxious. At about eight in the morning the gendarmes arrived, accompanied by an interpreter. The workers had to stop work and assemble immediately in front of their huts. The gendarmes set about interrogating them separately, well away from prying ears. It was Thắng's turn.

"Where were you yesterday?" they demanded.

"I was in the camp with my compatriots." Thắng replied.

"What were you doing all that time?"

"Preparing the special feast."

"And then?"

"We all chatted together until the evening. The boss had given us a day off for the celebrations."

"What time did Monsieur Chauvedin leave you?" the gendarmes continued.

"At about one or two in the afternoon I think, in any case it was just after the meal."

"Did he go straight back home?"

"No. He took his horse and went to the forest at the end of the coconut plantation."

"Okay. You can go!"

After the last man had been questioned, the gendarmes conferred.

"All the statements match. They all saw Monsieur Chauvedin leave for the forest after the meal," said the first.

"Well, that's where we should start looking, then," said the second.

"Could he have had an accident? Maybe he fell from his horse," they speculated. They then disappeared straight into the forest but returned a few hours later with nothing; Chauvedin was nowhere to be found. In the meantime, his horse had come back on its own.

The search was on again the next day, and the following days, but nothing was found.

All the Europeans on the island, including the police, and Chauvedin's employees, accompanied by their foremen, formed a huge search party. They scoured the whole area, including the maritime zone. But they had to face facts; the ruthless landowner had disappeared.

The gendarmes had not come up with any evidence which could throw light on the situation, so they were starting to suspect Pháp and Thắng: Phap because he had lost his son, leading the foremen to consider the possibility of revenge. As for Thắng, the gendarmes mistrusted him simply because he had already fought and seriously injured one of the mine bosses in New Caledonia. However, they had no proof, and had to release the two men.

Nevertheless, they did not give up the search. On the contrary, with the help of police dogs, they took up the investigation again, searching methodically all over the huge property and even outside of it. Every nook and cranny was inspected meticulously, but again nothing was found.

The weeks passed by and the mystery remained unsolved. The gendarmes were not prepared to give up and wanted to start the investigation all over again. One evening, as they were coming back from a search nearby, the gendarmes turned up with their dogs to the workers' camp, to try to get more information out of them as they were the last people to have seen Chauvedin alive. When they got to the canteen, the dogs were particularly agitated, and their masters had difficulty holding them back. For, at that moment, a cat was standing in front of the door, its fangs and claws bared. One of the dogs suddenly slipped away from the guards and dashed towards the cat. Without a moment's hesitation, it chased the cat into the common room. It was dinnertime and the people inside the canteen were surprised by the unusual menacing presence. They tried to shoo the dog away, but it growled as it came farther into the room. It stopped suddenly, after hesitating a little, next to the big wood fire which was still crackling under the cooking pots.

The gendarmes, both intrigued and suspicious, entered the room and the two dogs began barking in unison, sniffing the ground nervously in the spot near the fire. Meanwhile the cat had disappeared into the dark of the night.

***

A few months passed by. The Tonkinese community was now under the orders of a new landowner. From this time on, the plantation became a model of its kind and the workers seemed to be completely satisfied with their conditions. However, Pháp and Bích were still very sad.

"Poor Thắng, I still don't understand why he did it," sighed Bích. "He's such a good man."

"I think he wanted to sacrifice himself to save us, even though we were responsible for the crime," Pháp said.

"Thắng was innocent!" protested Bích. "He played no part in the assassination of Chauvedin."

"He knew very well, my friend, that we older workers, most of us married men, were the ones who stabbed Chauvedin to death. Thắng and you, I remember clearly, only helped us bury the body."

"I think," Bích said, "that it was at that moment, while we weren't looking, that he threw his own knife into the grave, if you could call it a grave, at the same time as Chauvedin's body."

"Where could he have got the knife?" Pháp asked, intrigued.

"He often had it on him, at least in the last few weeks before the incident."

"Thắng was smarter than the rest of us, the knife is proof of that. And he could see that, despite all our precautions and the scenarios we'd thought of, they would find Chauvedin buried under the wood fire."

"We hadn't thought of the dogs," sighed Bích with regret, "otherwise we could've. . ."

"Through his act," interrupted Pháp, who was trying to find a logical explanation for Thắng's courageous gesture, "he managed to direct all suspicion onto himself."

"Thắng was so brave," murmured Bích, "to have sacrificed himself like that so that we can carry on living."

"Yes, but do we deserve it," Pháp wondered, "as we now have a death on our conscience?"

"In the end I don't think we should have any regrets, or blame ourselves for this, but I'll have a lot to answer for on the day of the last judgement," thought Bích to himself.

But to persuade Pháp he continued, "Chauvedin was not a man, he was a tyrant, the devil in person. If he were still alive, there'd certainly be more deaths on the plantation. Mainly children. And more than anyone, Pháp, you bear none of the blame!"

"Do you know where Thắng is now?" asked Pháp, comforted by his companion's reasoning.

"I admire Thắng and I've been following what's happening to him. I've just found out that he's been sentenced to twenty years," sighed Bích. "They can't keep him prisoner for so long here, and our home country is now at war with Japan, so they decided to send him to the main prison in Nouméa. That's where he must be now."

"He's so brave, it's admirable," Pháp said to himself, staring sadly into the night.

"Even more admirable," Bích pointed out, "is the fact that that he's always been willing to sacrifice his freedom, and even his life, if necessary, to combat injustice and the feudal methods we endure in this part of the world."

The Midwife

Lan's pregnancy was going well and her stomach had grown bigger. Minh was the most considerate of husbands. He took over all the household duties despite his wife's many protestations.

"You're doing too much," she said. "I'm not sick and I can easily do the cooking."

"No, no! I want you to rest," said Minh categorically. "Your work for Madame Lucas is hard. Even though you've never wanted to complain to me, I know, all the same. . . And you're exhausted from carrying my son," he added looking at Lan's stomach.

"How do you know it's a boy?" she asked, laughing.

"I know," said Minh, with conviction. Then he put his hand on her belly, adding, "Because he's moving so vigorously in there. It'll be a boy, I'm sure of it!"

He thought for a moment, then he cried out happily, "It's April now, that means he'll be born in August. Do you realise, Lan? It's not so long to go now."

Lan suddenly looked worried. "It's April," she said preoccupied, "and it's already the last week of the month, that means it's a bit more than a year that we've been here."

"You're right . . . time passes so quickly," said Minh, astonished.

"And communication with our country still isn't possible," sighed Lan sadly.

"I'm sure it soon will be, it's just a question of months, a few months at most. You'll see," said Minh without really believing it. But he wanted to reassure his wife, as he knew that in her state, she shouldn't have anything extra to worry about.

However, it was Thế who surprised them. Towards the end of June, she gave birth to a magnificent baby, an adorable little girl!

Hiếu was urgently called home and arrived after the birth. He was disappointed at missing the birth of his child. But his disappointment did not last long; he was the happiest of men. With his pupils dilated, he stared in wonder at his baby, "My daughter!" he cried. "My dear little daughter!"

Hiếu wanted to help Madame Sửu clean the room, but he was so excited that he couldn't. His movements were so uncoordinated that he almost looked as though he were dancing. He went from one end to the other of the room, looking lovingly at his wife and smiling blissfully at his daughter.

"She's already the spitting image of her father," he said, waving his hands around.

Madame Sửu made him leave. "You mustn't disturb the baby," she said sternly.

Madame Sửu was employed by the mine and had arrived in the colony two years earlier. Like many other women she was sent to work in the gardens. But expectant mothers always asked for her help when there was a birth in the Tonkinese community, and the managers allowed it.

"Why don't you go and inform the management about the birth of your daughter," she said, "instead of running around in circles like you're doing now."

"I'm going, I'm going," said Hiếu.

"Don't forget to ask for an interpreter," the midwife advised,

"For such a simple declaration I don't need one," said Hiếu confidently. "I get by quite well in French now," he added.

"Don't be silly Hiếu, ask for an interpreter, it's easier and, what's more, it's free."

But Hiếu was already on his way, running along as happy as a child who has just received a special treat. When he got to the manager's office, Hiếu lost all restraint and entered without even knocking. The manager was holding a meeting with his supervisors; he got to his feet suddenly, his face tense and his eyes hard.

"What are you doing here? Didn't you see the sign on the door outside?" he yelled. "'Don't disturb, meeting', don't you know what that means?"

Coming sharply back to reality, Hiếu, stunned, looked sheepish.

The man shouted again, "What do you want? What are you doing here?"

Gradually realising what was happening, Hiếu gathered his courage then searched his memory which was now failing him, for the words he needed to justify his presence in this place. He hesitated a moment, thinking, then made up his mind. He took his right arm behind him, made a fist on his lower back, then stammered, gesturing, "Woman of me make poo little one!"

The manager was beside himself with rage. He hadn't understood a word of this mumbo jumbo and, interpreting Hiếu's gesture as obscene, he slapped the poor man hard and continued to hit him several more times before sending him unceremoniously away.

There was a small trickle of blood at the corner of Hiếu's mouth. Hurt and humiliated in his joy at being a father, creator of a new life, he could not contain his bitterness. He screamed with all his strength at his boss.

"You white man, black heart!"

Then he walked away calmly and with dignity, without turning around.

***

It was the cool season again. It was very cold on the mountain, buffeted by winds from the Pacific. Lan was getting tireder and she shivered in her thin clothes when, early in the morning, she had to go to work for Madame Lucas. Ever since the second fortnight of July, she had had a lot of difficulty moving around. And she felt a slight dizziness, as well as numbness in her limbs, when she tried to bend over to clean the floor. One afternoon, as she was going down a small staircase leading into the garden in the backyard, holding a basin of water she suddenly lost her balance. She panicked as she realised how serious the situation was and tried desperately to regain her balance. But it was a wasted effort; her enormous heavy stomach made her fall over and she found herself lying on the ground.

"My child. My child!" she cried, terrified.

Lan was still dizzy as she got up and looked at her limbs, her body, her belly. "My baby!" she moaned again. "I hope it wasn't bumped and that there won't be any serious consequences for its life, or for the coming birth!"

She worried, thinking she could feel a pain in her belly, but she couldn't say where exactly. Lan was afraid, which only gave her a headache.

"What are you doing, number 3142?" she heard Madame Lucas shouting.

"Nothing, Madame. I'm coming, Madame!" said Lan, going up to Madame Lucas, who had just appeared in the doorway. Relations between the two were not as tense, since Lan was now able to express herself in French and understand what her boss was saying.

Lan continued working until the contractions came on, in the first days of August. She suffered for two days, but, stoically, she went to work for Madame Lucas without a word of complaint. But from time to time, then more and more often, towards the end of the second day, her face turned pale and haggard, stricken by pain.

That evening, lying beside Minh on her bed she uttered a few groans and then, unable to take it any longer she burst into tears. Minh was in a real state; distraught and tormented, he seemed to feel the pain as much as his dear wife did. He had already called Madame Sửu twice.

"It's not yet time," she said after each check. "Later, tonight or tomorrow morning," she continued confidently. Then she added, "I'll come back at about midnight."

Minh would have preferred her to stay beside his wife. He didn't dare ask, but his eyes spoke volumes.

"Don't worry. I'll be back very soon," said Madame Sửu with a smile to reassure him.

At about one in the morning the contractions had become more frequent and stronger and Lan realised that the moment they had been waiting for had at last come.

"Come on! Push!" Madame Sửu encouraged her.

Minh was standing nearby. His eyes dilated from the intense nervous tension, he also urged her on, "Come on, Lan! Come on, push, push!"

However, the capricious baby only came into the world at about four o'clock.

"It's a boy!" the midwife announced.

But at that moment Minh was leaning against the wall on the other side of the room. Without realising it, he had automatically recoiled at the sight of the baby gradually leaving its mother's insides. Naturally he had never witnessed such an event and was rather disconcerted by the sight of a contorted, sticky baby, his baby, as it came into the world.

However, on hearing Madame Sửu's last words he rushed forward.

"A boy? A son? . . . My son!" he stammered.

Minh moved towards the newborn the midwife was holding, looking at it but not daring to touch it. Then at last he went to Lan, his face lit up. "You see, I wasn't wrong! I was right, it's a son! Our son! Can you imagine, I'm a father now?"

He was dazed, pensive, "I'm a father . . . ," he repeated once more.

"Don't forget that I'm a mother too!" smiled Lan.

Suddenly Minh began to inspect the baby anxiously from head to toe. "Everything's all right, there's nothing abnormal," he said at last with relief. Looking carefully at his son again he remarked, "His head's very big!"

"It's a good sign," said the midwife, "it's a sign of intelligence."

"!"

"It's the beginning of August so, according to the French horoscope," continued Madame Sửu, "your son was born under the sign of Leo, the lion."

"The what?" asked Minh.

"The lion."

"He'll also be a dragon, as according to our lunar calendar, it's the year of the dragon!" said Lan, feeling happy and fulfilled despite her fatigue.

"A dragon! That's a sign of determination and strength!" cried the happy father.

"We'll call him Hồng!" said Lan. "Won't we, Minh?"

"Yes, yes, let's call him Hồng. I like the name!"

They were both overjoyed.

While the young mother was on maternity leave, she took special care of Hồng. Liên often came to see them after work.

"Thế has a daughter and you a magnificent boy. I'm so happy for you both!" said Liên one evening. Then, hesitating for a moment, she added, "Phúc hopes to have a son like yours soon, but I'm really worried. We've been married for over a year now, and I'm still not pregnant."

"Don't worry, don't fret about it, Liên," said Lan kindly. "You're strong and sturdy and in a few years' time you'll have at least ten children!"

But Liên was still silent and melancholy.

"I think the moment just isn't right for you to be a mother yet," continued her friend, "but it won't be long. You'll see, don't worry, it's just a question of time and patience!"

"You're a good friend, Lan. I'll wait. Your reassuring words do me a lot of good," said Liên with a grateful smile.

Lan had to go back to work a few weeks later. Hồng was still very weak, and, as it was absolutely necessary for him to be near his mother, Madame Lucas allowed him to lie on his little mat in a corner of the veranda while his mother went about her daily work.

When the child was bigger and could move and crawl around on his hands and knees, Minh and Lan had to resign themselves, reluctantly, to leaving him alone at home.

Minh had made a playpen with carefully selected wood from the forest. So Hồng was left to himself, away from his mother. Lan would go home at lunchtime as quickly as her legs would allow and, in the evening, she was in even more of a hurry.

The child was growing without causing his parents any problems. He moved around, slept, and played in the limited space of his pen, king of his little domain. But what Lan dreaded the most when she went home was to see her son smiling, his face smeared and his mouth full of the nauseating yellowish secretion from his own body. Lan would never forget this image. At other times, Hồng put his little hand through the bars keeping him prisoner and grabbed a handful of earth which he put in his mouth and started eating conscientiously, pulling his face at the taste. Whenever Lan saw her son in this state, she would invariably repeat the same sentence, "The proverb says: The child who eats soil will live a long time! The child who eats soil will live a long time. . ."

A year had gone by since the birth of baby Hồng. Minh and Lan would often think about their parents, but they had not been able to get a single letter or any news from their families. They were desperately worried and wondered with a twinge of sorrow whether they would ever see them again after the inevitable upheavals of war.

Fortunately, Hồng's presence soothed their minds and lessened the apprehension brought on by fear and uncertainty. The happy, carefree child had become the centre of their universe and the purpose of a new life. From time to time he stood up and tried to take a few steps, but he was clumsy and uncoordinated and would fall down on his bottom, roaring with laughter, communicating his joy to his whole family. Very often he would look at his father, saying, "Papa! Papa!" When Minh, a few months earlier, heard these simple words for the first time he exclaimed, "Do you hear, Lan? Did you hear? He called me Papa!" Then Minh lifted his son and holding him at arm's length, looked at him in wonder. At that moment his face expressed immense pride. "He calls me Papa," he repeated. "He recognises his father, the cheeky boy. It's wonderful!"

Lan was happy and every time she witnessed these tender scenes she felt at peace with the world once again.

Collective Punishment

One evening, when she got home, Lan found Minh completely distraught; she was not accustomed to seeing him in this state, "Is something wrong, Minh?" she asked.

"Yes," murmured her husband, looking down at the ground.

"At work?"

"Yes," he replied again.

Minh was silent for a moment, then he decided to talk. "We've been summoned by management," he said.

"Who has?"

"All of the men on this morning's shift, forty-two of us!"

"What have you done? What have they done to you?" asked Lan anxiously, eager to find out the truth.

"We were all underground, in the mine. I was in a small tunnel, preparing holes for the dynamite when the bell rang for end of the shift. So, we put away our things and came up to the surface as usual. The first thing we noticed, which really surprised us, was that there was no team ready to take over from us. The head of our shift was really surprised, too, but let us go anyway before he went to the office to let management know."

Minh looked first at his wife and then at his son and continued gravely, "An hour later, that is, in the middle of the afternoon, an order reached us in the camp, summoning the forty-two workers from the morning shift to the office immediately. When we got there, there were several foremen there with the manager in person and the mine engineers. They all looked grim. Mainote the head foreman asked us, 'Who touched the clock in the mine?' But no one responded. You see, Lan, someone put the mine clock forward an hour. That's why the head of our shift gave us the order to go back up and why there was no team to replace us when we got there. We'd left work early! So, the mine was abandoned for an hour without any special preparation. There could have been serious consequences," concluded Minh.

"Did you find out who did it?" asked Lan worriedly.

"No, alas," said Minh, irritated, "no one wanted to own up to it. Nobody admits to it."

"So, what are they going to do?"

"They're going to call the gendarmes, they said. Which means it's serious. Anything could happen now!"

"And don't you suspect anyone?" insisted Lan, feeling even more nervous.

"No, it's impossible! Could one of us really have committed this offence? We can't assume anything."

"!"

"Nobody wants to admit to having done such a thing at the moment," he continued, "even if he did it to gain an hour's work. He didn't think it through, couldn't know that it would go this far," said Minh dejectedly. He added, "I think the management considers this to be an act of sabotage."

Lan said nothing, lost in her glum thoughts. The three of them had a peaceful evening together, but this type of calm made Lan fear the coming storm.

The warrant officer from the gendarmerie and two auxiliaries, amongst them the one-eyed John, had to travel for most of the night to get to the small mining village by early morning.

The forty-two men were interrogated for over an hour, but the gendarmes did not get the confession they were expecting. There followed a meeting between the management and the gendarme, from which the latter emerged to give the following orders to his men:

"Take these men away. They're under arrest!"

The manager handed a coil of rope to the auxiliary. "Here's the cord you asked for," he said.

"Thank you," replied the gendarme, "that'll do, instead of handcuffs."

"It's very strong! You won't have any problems with it!" the head of the mine said quickly.

Turning to his aides, the warrant officer said, "This is what you must do. Tie these men together in pairs with this rope. Attach the right thumb of one to the left thumb of the other, leaving a space of twenty centimetres at the most between them. Tie the knots well so that they can't undo them along the way!"

When the prisoners had been put into twenty-one pairs, the gendarme got back on his horse and gave further orders to his men. "I'm going back to Koumac via Kunéo, along the coastal track. You and the prisoners will take the mountain tracks. You'll go past the mine at Tenep. That way, not only will these men be punished, but it'll also be a warning to their compatriots on that mine."

Sitting high on their horses, the auxiliaries became the masters of this human herd. They went from one end of the village of Pimboé to the other before disappearing into the green forest. The one-eyed man shouted, yelled and took pleasure in waving his whip above their heads, cracking it with a sharp movement of his hand like a stockman driving his cattle. At the head of the convoy his colleague pushed his horse on, as it struggled along the steep dangerous slopes.

The track was also very slippery in some places, and the prisoners had to make a huge effort to stop their legs slipping; they knew that if they stumbled and fell, they would bring down their companion with them.

Minh had difficulty walking, as Nguyễn, his companion in misfortune, was complaining of pain in his stomach. Beads of sweat had formed on his pale, sick forehead.

"Come on, quicker! Hurry up!" shouted the one-eyed auxiliary. But he wasn't using his whip anymore, as he himself was having trouble keeping his balance on his horse.

The men were in agony, as the rope pulling at their arms cut into their skin.

The sun was already high in the sky.

"There's still a long way to go," thought Minh. He remembered the stories his friend Toán had told him about what had happened on these tracks in the middle of this mountainous wilderness.

The heat was making the auxiliaries irritable. They did not appreciate having to venture out like this into the wilds with more than forty men in their care.

Nguyễn was getting weaker and weaker. Minh, despite the rope which was in the way, had to support him, and dragged him along so that they did not fall behind and get beaten by the auxiliary who seemed to be waiting for the first opportunity to use his whip again.

When they got to Tenep in the early afternoon, they had to march past the ore-crushing and sorting factory. The Tonkinese factory workers had been invited to attend the spectacle.

"They must've received a phone call," thought Minh. "They seem to be aware we'd be coming through."

Through the sweat covering his face, Minh tried to see if he could recognise his friend Toán amongst the men.

"No, Toán's not here, what a pity," he murmured. "Well no, actually, it's better. If he saw me tied up like this, he'd be so furious he'd probably do something stupid!"

The terrain had flattened out, and as the horses were no longer at risk of falling, the auxiliaries quickened the pace. The men were exhausted, but still had to keep up with the horses. Minh did everything he could, using all his determination and strength to help his sick companion. The journey seemed interminable and they hadn't eaten since the morning. Only once did they have the right to drink water from a mountain spring. Nguyễn's eyes were listless and his complexion cadaverous. He struggled to move, pulled along by Minh's great efforts.

The men's thumbs were mangled and painful from the fine rope biting cruelly into their skin. They looked like a herd of slaves that were being taken by their unscrupulous masters to be sold after they had been snatched from their families. Despite his exhaustion, Minh ran when he had to, walked when he was told to, dragging at his side the heaviest burden he had ever had to bear. He murmured, "I'm going through the same ordeal as Toán, along the same path! My friend, what did we do? What did I do to deserve this torture?"

Once again, he was overcome with rage. "I'll get my revenge one day. I'll get even," he said. Then he thought of Lan, his wife. He had seen her as they were leaving. She was standing still in Madame Lucas' garden. Hot tears were flowing down her cheeks, but she watched him pass by with his companions, without a word, for fear of making things worse for her husband.

As he was running Minh also thought of Hồng, his child, his son. "I wonder what he's doing at this moment. Perhaps he's calling for me?" The image of little Hồng smiling with his cheeky eyes calmed him down somewhat, and gave him some peace of mind, helping him carry on, dragging the sick man along with him.

They got to the police station late in the afternoon. The men dropped heavily to the ground. But without wasting a minute, the prison wardens cut their ropes, then packed them all into two narrow prison cells.

"Twenty-one per room," Minh noticed with trepidation.

The weary men did not have enough room to move and only the most exhausted could lie down on the concrete floor. The others had to stand on their shaky legs.

Rice and water were handed out a little later at sunset. But the space was so small that the jailers had to let the prisoners out into the courtyard to eat. Sitting on the soft thick grass they tried to swallow the food they had been given, making horrible faces.

"The rice is salty!" grumbled Minh who knew nothing of the culinary speciality of his "hosts." Nguyễn had regained some of his strength by now. "They've cooked it in saltwater, the murky swamp water you see over there," he said. "I know these rogues," he added, "I spent time here last year, for . . . disobedience!"

Nguyễn couldn't continue his story, as suddenly he began to grimace in pain. "Here we go again, the stomachache has come back." He put his hands on his stomach crouching down as if to contain his pain. His head was almost touching the green, perfectly mown grass.

Minh did not eat much. The rest of his time outside in the fresh air he spent in deep, gloomy meditation as he gazed at the sea, a little way off to his right. The sun was being absorbed by the horizon, gradually disappearing as it spread its last rays over the sea and projected them into the sky. Its red and gold light shone over the beaches with their fine sand and the huge coconut palms, the whole scene an enchanting image of the South Seas. But he had to leave this haven of peace, so close, just on the other side of the barbed wire fence.

Minh helped Nguyễn back into the narrow cell. He was in excruciating pain and totally exhausted and hadn't been able to swallow anything. His companions offered him the bed and he lay curled up on the cold, hard plank, moaning. Minh and the other men in his cell got ready for the night. Some were leaning against the thick solid walls, others were sitting, as there was not enough room for them to lie down. Several of them who had been in good health the night before were now sick and feverish, because of the harsh treatment they had endured that day.

In the middle of the night Nguyễn murmured between two groans, "Please forgive me . . . but . . . I can't hold on any longer . . . Forgive me!"

The men were dozing off in the dark and didn't understand what he meant at first. Minh wondered if Nguyễn was having a dream, or rather, a nightmare, uttering meaningless words in his agitated sleep. Alas, he soon realised that Nguyễn was not dreaming when an unbearable smell pervaded the crowded cell. Alarmed, Minh put his hand to his face to try to filter the air he was breathing, but it was a waste of time as, just like the other poor prisoners, he had to breathe in the nauseating stench.

"I did everything I could to spare you . . . but I just couldn't wait any longer," stammered Nguyễn feebly, to excuse himself once again. Then he was quiet, not daring to say another word. He was not groaning as much, as he had managed to rid himself of what was poisoning his guts. But now it was the other occupants of the tiny room who had to put up with the smell. However, nobody blamed him. But some, more sensitive because of their fatigue and insomnia, felt sick and started vomiting on the ground and onto the limbs of those nearest them.

"It's exactly like in the ship's hold," thought Minh, his face contorted with disgust, "like in the ship's hold."

They waited impatiently for the sun to rise. Then, as soon as the door was unlocked, without waiting for John's permission, they rushed outside. A disgusting stench clung to their clothes and their skin.

Then the column marched off, led by the jailers. Nguyễn, although he was still weak, was not allowed to stay in the cell. He had to wash the room from top to bottom before joining his companions. The men were put to work repairing and rebuilding the road along the edge of the swamp a little way away from the police station. They worked all day in the blazing sun. Their guards watched them carefully, especially one-eyed John who had a special gift for making prisoners suffer. There was no mercy for the sick and the weak. To them he gave the hardest and most thankless tasks, using his hands and his feet to get them to carry out his orders.

During the midday break, a short meeting took place between the occupants of the two cells. "We're all being punished, that's clear enough," said Minh, "But I'd still like to know who the sorry individual was, who tampered with the mine's alarm!"

"Yes! We'd really like to know who it was," replied a dozen workers together, looking serious.

"We'll get him," added another, furiously.

Nobody answered. Minh repeated his question, but it was a waste of time.

"We'll never know the truth," he thought. Frowning, he asked himself, "Was it really one of us? If so, the culprit will never dare own up to it, as everyone here who's been unjustly punished because of him, would make his life hell!"

"Could it be one of the foremen wanting to play a dirty trick on us?" he wondered for an instant, all the while knowing he would never discover the truth.

"I think the best course of action for us is to follow orders," said Minh aloud. "We won't achieve anything through disobedience or thoughtless actions. Instead, it could do us more harm, as these men are paid to force us to obey their orders and their laws."

Minh thought for a few seconds, then continued, "Let's show them that we only want peace and tranquillity, that we're human beings too, and that we're intelligent and capable of reason, not savages as they seem to think, since that's how they treat us!"

"You're right, Minh. We're with you!" the men agreed.

"However, I'll point out again to whoever made this serious mistake that the reason we're here, abused and mistreated in this prison is because of their thoughtless act. If they ever repeat such an act, they'll be punished one day either by men or . . . by the heavens!" He concluded by saying, "Despite everything, as far as I'm concerned, I forgive whoever it was who brought me here."

John, the guard, approached the group, curious. The men dispersed, unable to bear the presence of this evil man, the very incarnation of blind brutality.

"You're too forgiving, Minh," Nguyễn protested when they were alone a little later.

"I'm doing everything I can to avoid resentment and violence. I can't help it, Nguyễn, that's who I am."

"He should follow your example!" grumbled, Nguyễn staring at the one-eyed guard.

"He's just doing his job, "said Minh, "a loathsome job, it's true."

"I'm sorry, but I can't agree with you. This nasty character is a sadist, a dangerous beast," said Nguyễn. "He raped several of the young women who were held in this prison. These women are our compatriots, Minh!"

"When did it happen?"

"About four years ago or maybe a bit longer," replied Nguyễn, beside himself with rage. He frowned as he tried to remember, then said confidently, "Yes, four years! I remember now. It happened just after I was sent to Pimboé."

Minh thought for a moment and then said, "How long has John only had one eye?"

"Let me think," said Nguyễn. "Let's see, I know it was an accident. It caused a big stir, and many of the Tonkinese in the region were really pleased to hear about it. Yes, that's right," he continued, "John fell off his horse a few months after his despicable actions."

"You see," said Minh. "The sadist was punished! All crimes and all serious abuse will be punished one day, I'm sure of it," he added.

That evening, they were once more packed into the tiny cell.

"It's Thursday today, so that makes two days that we've been here. Lan's with the baby at the moment and they're alone in the house," thought Minh sadly, and he too felt alone in this human beehive. His mind wandered freely, unfettered by chains, far away from the prison cell.

A voice suddenly called out of the pitch dark of night, "I hope we'll be able to breathe tonight, without too much difficulty! Isn't that right, Nguyễn?"

There was stifled laughter, then silence fell on the men who were getting ready to spend, as best they could, their second night in the cell.

Heavy rain fell over the region the whole of the next morning. The work site had become a huge, muddy plot and the men were chilled to the bone as they toiled in the sticky, slippery mud. The downpour had made the soil wet and heavy and they had to work harder to move it by the shovelful.

Minh was tired and sullen. He had hardly slept, and his mood was so dark that he couldn't be bothered keeping up good relations with everyone. He worked without raising his head, without deigning to look at anyone. It was his way of showing his anger. Was it against whoever had sent him there? Was it against his torturers, who were constantly present, more aggressive than ever in the cold rain that got deep into the bones? Was it against the inhuman company that exploited them blindly using the most barbaric methods to get rich?

He didn't know the answer, and he got even more moody at lunchtime when they brought the disgusting pot of rice. Minh would have liked to force the prison guards to swallow the whole lot themselves. He didn't want to swallow another single grain of this revolting food and would have liked to throw his ration onto the soggy ground.

He didn't though, as the instinct of preservation or, rather, the fear of making things worse, took precedence over his bad mood. And, of course, his wife and his son needed him and were waiting for him. He didn't have the right to forget the sound principles which had guided him so far. Wincing with disgust, he forced himself to eat his bowl of rice.

Sitting on the wet grass, the forty-two men tried to keep warm in the continual rain by huddling together.

After the meal which had given them no joy, they were even colder, as a storm suddenly descended on them, darkening the sky and forming a thick, dense fog all around them.

When they went back to work, the one-eyed guard started yelling, "There's a prisoner missing!" His good eye seemed to panic. With the help of his colleagues, he got the prisoners to line up in pairs and he began to count them. It was true—one of the men had disappeared!

"There are only forty-one here!" he cried.

"Heavens! Nguyễn isn't here!" Minh said to himself softly. The auxiliaries were furious. They took their prisoners back to the cells hastily and locked them up without wasting a minute.

The rain outside was still torrential. Minh didn't mind being in the shelter of the cell, and the heat generated by all the bodies warmed the room. However, he was extremely concerned.

"Are we doomed to being stuck here, packed into this overcrowded cell, unable to make the slightest move?"

The idea frightened him, as he was certain they would not be allowed to leave the prison before morning.

"There are over twenty of us and we'll all have cramps and be stiff if we have to stay in this room for sixteen or eighteen hours," he said to himself.

So, the men discussed what they could do, and it was agreed that they would try to occupy the least space possible so that they could take turns lying down in a spot in the middle of the cell. Minh forgot his own worries and thought about Nguyễn. He was afraid for his companion. The guards, in their haste, had not closed the door and, through the doorway, which was protected by solid bars, Minh could see the daylight gradually disappearing and his fear grew.

The rain ceased, interrupting the hammering of thousands of drops on the corrugated iron roof. Then night fell rapidly. One of the men could hear faint sounds coming from far away. They listened carefully, holding their breath. A heavy silence filled the room, and they all tried to hear any noise outside. But only the slight whistle of the wind disturbed the calm and tranquillity of the night.

A few minutes later, they could hear dogs barking. Then the sound of hooves echoed loudly in the dark night. Harsh raucous voices rang out in the night air and could be heard in the prison cell. Then the lock of the cell clicked, and the heavy door creaked as it swung on its hinges. The anxious men watched attentively as Nguyễn, disfigured, his clothes in rags and his flesh bruised, was pushed brutally into the cell, landing heavily on those inside. He was motionless for a long time, weak and dazed, as if drunk. Minh cleared a way for himself in the dark, through all the bodies huddled on the ground and approached Nguyễn.

"What happened?" he asked once he was near him.

"I wanted to escape," said Nguyễn listlessly.

"You've been here a while, Nguyễn, you know perfectly well it's impossible to escape from this island! Wherever you go, they'll find you!" said Minh in astonishment.

"Yes, I know," sighed Nguyễn, "but it happened so fast! And actually, I still don't understand what was going on in my mind at that moment! I just had to get out . . . leave . . . go anywhere . . . flee this slavery! I took advantage of a moment when the guards weren't looking, and I rushed into the bush in the rain. I couldn't see twenty metres in front of me."

Despite his exhaustion, Nguyễn continued his story, as if he wanted to pour it all out, and justify his actions.

"When I got a fair distance, I gradually came back to my senses and I took fright. My first reaction was to think of you all here. 'They must think I'm the guilty one now,' I said to myself. 'Guilty of changing the time in the mine!' I strongly regretted having left, but it was too late to turn back. 'In any case, the gendarmes are certainly looking for you at the moment!' I said to myself again. 'And they've already alerted all their colleagues from the surrounding villages.' This thought made me leave the coast and turn back towards the mountains. But I was too weak from a combination of sickness, bad food and hard labour and I couldn't walk very quickly. I had to trudge through some difficult places in the rain."

Nguyễn stopped talking. His companions waited for the rest without a word. The silence was heavy. Nguyễn continued his account, "The gendarmes didn't take long to find me. I didn't think it'd be so quick! Maybe it was because of my footprints in the muddy ground. Or was it because of their dogs? Perhaps a villager spotted me as I ran across the clearing at the end of the village. In any case I didn't have time to ask myself any more questions. They were already quite near, so I hid in a dense thicket. But, alas, I couldn't escape the dogs! As soon as they discovered my hiding place, the dogs jumped on me, tearing my trousers and shirt with their claws and fangs and mauling me, as you can see."

Nguyễn stopped for a moment, gasping for breath as if he were reliving the dreadful ordeal. He continued his story wearily, "I gave myself up without resistance, I couldn't do anything else, in any case. Their dogs are well trained, and I was both terrified and too exhausted to get away from them!" Angrily, Nguyễn added, "That didn't stop my jailers from punching me in the face and all over my body. I found myself lying unconscious on the ground. When I finally came to, I was tied to the end of a long rope and then they dragged me here through the bush."

After a moment's hesitation, he stammered, "I hope there are no consequences for you because of all this. As for me," he added, "I'm beyond caring."

Discouragement

After Minh left, Thế and her husband Hiếu often visited baby Hồng and his mother. They always brought their adorable little girl along with them.

Liên and Phúc also they did their best to console and support Lan who was getting more and anxious.

"It's already Saturday evening, that makes four days now since Minh left," she sighed sadly.

"They'll be back soon, I'm sure," said Phúc. "The mine managers can't afford to lose over forty men just like that for several weeks. There are a lot of problems at the moment because of their absence," he added. "All the men have been mobilised to replace them, and it's pretty difficult!"

"Their departure caused a lot of dismay in our community," said Liên.

"Phúc, you're in a position to know what's going on," said Lan suddenly. "Haven't you heard anything?"

"Alas, I'm really sorry I couldn't find out anything, Lan. I get the impression that they don't know themselves!"

Suddenly they heard a little voice crying, "Papa! Papa!" It was baby Hồng, who had just made his presence felt.

"Oh! We'd forgotten about him," said Lan. "For the last few days, he's been asking for his father a lot more often."

"Papa! Papa!" the child called again.

Lan took him in her arms and hugged him close to her heart, telling him tenderly, as if he could understand, or as if she already wanted to hide the painful truth from him, "Your Papa's gone away . . . he's on holiday, my child!"

"Papa! Papa!" insisted Hồng, starting to cry.

***

As for Minh, he had a lot of trouble containing his impatience and discouragement.

"Four days already," he sighed, "four days of forced labour, a packed cell and rotten food. It's too much to bear! It's really too much for an innocent man!"

He would often strike up a conversation with Nguyễn to keep his mind occupied. He recalled a conversation he had had with him the night before.

"I noticed," he said, "that on your right foot, the toe is mutilated. Was it an accident at work?"

"Yes," replied Nguyễn, a little embarrassed. "That is . . . No! . . . Well, not exactly! It was an accident which was, well . . . deliberate!"

"Deliberate?" asked Minh, astonished.

"It was about four years ago," began Nguyễn. "I'd just arrived here, and the work conditions were too harsh for me. I got bronchitis straight away, bronchitis with complications."

His face grave, Nguyễn stared at Minh and then explained, "It was very serious. It was getting painful to breathe and I was constantly out of breath. The beginnings of asthma, I was told. And, as I still had to work, I couldn't prevent the sickness developing. Some folk from the village up in the mountain gave me plants to cure it. Very effective, apparently, but only if you rest for one or two weeks. As the sickness persisted," continued Nguyễn, "my friends asked me to do the impossible —give myself an injury, cut the palm of my hand with a sharp object, such as a piece of glass. I tried to do it several times, but each time, at the last moment, I didn't have the courage to go through with it! Yet I really needed the rest, it had become absolutely necessary. If I waited any longer, it'd be too late. And there was really no point asking the bosses for a few days off!"

Nguyễn was getting agitated. "One day I made the decision. We were in the mine. I took off one of my shoes and stayed back in the dark in the tunnel. Focusing all my determination on what I had to do, I put my toe on the railway. At the contact of the cold hard steel I shivered, I was very afraid. But my fear just brought on an intense bout of asthma and that forced me to make a decision.

"When my workmates came out of the tunnel pushing a heavily laden wagon, they couldn't see me. I closed my eyes. My heart was beating wildly and, trembling, the sweat pouring down me, I waited for what seemed an interminable length of time for the metal wheel to roll over the end of my toe. I let out a piercing scream as the wheel crushed my flesh. I was even more horrified when I realised that a good part of my toe had been squashed. It had to be amputated. But, thanks to this 'accident' I was able to stay in the camp for over two weeks, which allowed my body to combat the terrible disease. The plants helped too, of course."

Nguyễn added philosophically, "I don't regret it at all. The sacrifice was necessary. I got my health back and I think that's the most precious thing."

Minh was shocked by the story. "I hope we won't have to endure this much longer," he murmured. "Otherwise we'll all lose our minds. We've been very patient so far, but will we still be so patient in a year or two?"

Then he murmured sadly, "We'll have to be, we'll have to be." He added with a sigh, "And to think we live in the middle of an ocean with such a tranquil, reassuring name, the 'Pacific Ocean'. How ironic!"

By sunrise the next morning, Minh had already been moping for hours. He observed the gentle light of dawn as it came through the gaps in the door. The cocks in the area were crowing loudly.

"It's Sunday today, but we can expect the worst," he said to himself wryly.

A bell rang continuously in the distance, then stopped. It rang again, insistent, echoing strangely in the morning air.

"It must be the telephone," Minh said to himself, intrigued. Snippets of voices engaged in an animated conversation reached the cell.

"They have a lot to say," said one of the men.

"What could they be talking about at this time of the morning?" asked Minh.

"They're organising to go fishing or hunting. That's how the 'long noses' enjoy themselves on their day off," said another man caustically.

"Well, it's normal for them to want to get some exercise on Sundays since the rest of the week they're paid just to beat us up," added a third bitterly.

But they had to stop their contemptuous remarks as they could hear footsteps outside. The door opened wide and daylight immediately flooded into the room.

"Get up in there!" It was the chief warrant officer himself who had come.

"I wasn't wrong, there's no Sunday in prison," murmured Minh through clenched teeth, his face ravaged by fatigue and disappointment.

"Line up in the courtyard for inspection!" ordered the chief. The men from the two cells obeyed in silence, as slowly as they could. The man in charge stared at them one by one sternly. "Forty, forty-one, forty-two. They're all here," he said at last, satisfied.

"I've just had a telephone conversation with your boss," he announced. "You're free. You can go back home!"

Pointing to Nguyễn he said, "You, you're not leaving with the others!"

Then, turning towards the men who were still in line, he said, "You can leave now."

The men received the news without a word or reaction, not wanting to show their joy to the wardens. Only their eyes, suddenly still, betrayed their deep astonishment. They soon set off on their way, filled with joy at finally being able to leave this inhospitable place.

"This place would truly be an earthly paradise without these men and their prison," thought Minh. He took one last look at the sea in the distance, then at Nguyễn, who was being led by the one-eyed prison guard back to the cell, which was too big for him alone.

Minh joined the men who formed a long straggly line stretching out along the path.

"Don't spread out all over the place!" he shouted. "We're already tired from sleepless nights and bad food. We should conserve what little strength we have left and walk at a regular pace. Otherwise, we'll never be able to make it along this long road in our present state. Don't forget that we still have to climb up the mountain!"

The men followed Minh's wise advice docilely. They walked forward in a compact group, the strongest coming to the aid of the weakest. Taking the path along the coast, they arrived at the port of Kunéo at about ten in the morning.

"Here we are again at our first port of call, Kunéo," thought Minh. He remembered very distinctly the arduous days, when they had had to load up the boat anchored in the bay. Without resting, they had climbed the steep slopes of the mountain in the blazing midday sun.

When the men got to the camp in the early evening, Lan and Hồng were in front of their door. "You're back again! My husband! My dear Minh!" cried Lan, happily.

She gazed at him as he embraced his son. "You've lost a lot of weight," she said.

Minh looked at her tenderly, then took her into the house. "I'm finally back here with you both," he murmured, lying down on the bed where he remained, motionless, his eyes half-closed, without saying a word. He was exhausted. The little boy snuggled up to his body.

"I'll get you something to eat," said Lan rushing to the kitchen. She came back a moment later with some warm rice and a dish of meat and raw vegetables. Minh wolfed down the food and then, to his wife's astonishment, asked for some bread.

"He doesn't usually like bread," she murmured.

Minh had guessed what she was thinking. "Bread is delicious and good for you! I'll explain," he said, laughing, "I'll explain!"

He was smiling again. He had never in his life enjoyed a meal as much as this one.

Dramas in the Camp

Toán was now the personal cook of the Tenep mine director. It was a promotion for him. He had claimed that the art of cooking was his great speciality back home, but he accepted the position, which was greatly sought after, with a certain degree of apprehension; he had to rack his brains to remember the recipes of the many exquisite dishes the cook used to make with astonishing ease on the junk he had sailed on just before coming to this place.

But, although he applied himself and took great care with his dishes, Toán was often unsuccessful. Fortunately, thanks to the many hot sauces and spicy condiments at his disposal, he managed to satisfy the delicate palates of his masters, who were unfamiliar with exotic cuisine. With time and patience Toán became an expert in "Indochinese gastronomy," and from then on, he had more freedom.

Alas, however, all his free time was devoted to gambling. He won money, but unfortunately, whatever he won disappeared as fast as the fleeting glimpse of a shooting star in the sky. He went through a difficult period, without even a centime to his name. Toán had already borrowed money—some thought too much money—from his friends. He counted it one day, and he was appalled to see that his debts amounted to all of his next salary and even the following month's. He could not, in all decency, get into further debt.

Luck turned up in the person of his boss's wife.

"Toán, I'd like a nice dish of sautéed rabbit, just like you know how to cook it!"

"?"

"Here's some money. Go and buy a nice rabbit at the village shop and cook it for us for dinner."

Toán jumped at the chance, took the money and put it in his pocket with unusual eagerness.

"Yes, Madame. Madame will be happy. Madame will have rabbit for this evening!"

Then he hurried to the Tonkinese village and managed to find a few gamblers who weren't working at that moment. With the money that didn't belong to him, he anxiously tried to win back some of his losses.

But the incorrigible gambler had a stroke of bad luck. Of the money that his mistress had given him, nothing was left, not even enough to buy a box of matches! Even so, Toán was not demoralised; he had seen worse. He went back to the European village in the afternoon, with, at the bottom of his bag, a skinned rabbit, already prepared for cooking.

That evening after the meal his boss congratulated him.

"I've never eaten such a delicious rabbit as that one. It was a real treat," he said with a smile. "Very good Toán!"

Toán had been particularly anxious and nervous all evening, but was cheerful and lively once more. "That was a close shave," he sighed, flopping down on a chair when at last he was alone in the kitchen. For Toán was anxious despite the great care he had taken with the dish. The rabbit was in fact a cat which he had stolen from one of his neighbours. Toán had cut it up very patiently into suitable pieces, leaving the head, skin and paws in the forest nearby.

That night, stretched out on his hard new bed, Toán pondered his fate. "I have a great weakness, I admit it; gambling is a reprehensible act. However, if I compare the consequences of my vice and the severe consequences that my countrymen have had to endure for some time now, I prefer my plight to theirs."

In the silence of his dormitory he recalled the events of the last few months in great detail. He could see poor Thức again, a tall strong young man coming out of the mine after eight gruelling hours in the tunnels, when a jealous husband stabbed him in the stomach with a long, sharp knife. Screaming and crying, terrified by the image of death which was already enveloping him, the injured man had tried desperately with his two filthy, blackened hands, to hold in his guts which were falling out of the gaping wound.

The husband ran back to the village after this criminal act and forced his adulterous wife to undress and, threatening her with the bloodstained knife, made her parade completely naked through all the lanes of the camp.

"That's your punishment this time!" he yelled in rage. Then he glared at her, and showing her the dangerous knife added, "Next time, it'll be with this!"

"All these dramas," said Toán to himself, his eyes wide open in the warm, dark night, "all these dramas are the result of the war. Many of these men and women completed their contract months ago and they should have been repatriated! They can't wait to get back to their families. The married men are in a hurry to get back to their wives and children. The single men hope to marry as soon as they get home. They deserve it after so many years without any physical contact with women. Some of the young men have never known a woman's body."

Toán thought for a while. "The damned war affects us too, stuck as we are on this island at the end of the Earth!" he muttered. He remained lost for a moment in his troublesome thoughts, then added, "Apparently it's a world war. Let's hope it finishes quickly! Otherwise there'll be more dramas and more crimes of passion at this mine!"

Toán was sure of it, as another memory just as terrible as the last, came back to him. He knew the culprit well. She was a beautiful, brave young woman. She was willing to work and, until then, had been reliable. She loved her husband, but, overwhelmed by an avalanche of sweet talk from innumerable suitors, she ended up giving in to one who was bolder than the others. She wanted to break it off immediately afterwards, but this illicit love affair was so exciting that she lost all sense of reason. So she continued with the affair without her husband's knowledge.

Her husband only found out much later. Jealous and desperate, he confided in one of his workmates. When the latter heard about the poor husband's problems, he answered, "My poor Năm, I feel so sorry for you! But please be forgiving. Don't provoke another drama like what happened recently." After a moment's silence he added as if indifferent, but embarrassed, "Alas, we'll all be the victims of cheating some day. Pardon my frankness, but it's my turn to confide in you and I can tell you that I myself have been cheated on."

"You. . ."

"Yes, it was very painful, I'll admit, but I had to get over my heartache and jealousy to keep my wife. Because I love her in spite of everything."

His eyes wide, Năm couldn't understand the man's logic.

"Otherwise, she would've left with my rival, or with someone else. There's no lack of choice for the women in this bloody camp!"

"That's true," said Năm, "at home there are too many women, and here it's the opposite! But I'm too jealous to share!" he added sadly, staring vacantly in front of him. "How can you accept it?"

"This is what I tell myself to convince myself: as long as your wife stays at home, all is not lost, you don't need to worry," said the man, remaining surprisingly calm.

"Funny way to convince yourself! Odd attitude too!" cried Năm outraged. He walked away quickly from this strange character. However, Năm did nothing which could arouse the suspicions of the two lovers. He was preparing his plan meticulously. He was courteous to his rival as if nothing had happened. He even invited him to come and have lunch at his house. Persuaded that the husband didn't suspect anything, the man became bolder and more familiar.

He often came to visit the couple when Năm was there and visited his wife when he was not. One day Năm decided that the day had come to get his revenge. He sacrificed a part of his savings and bought a magnificent pig that he slaughtered the following Sunday. He prepared some delicious dishes with the help of his friends who knew nothing of his murderous plan. Amongst all these appetising dishes, the most popular was the famous dish of fresh blood, coagulated with offal and finely chopped herbs. Needless to say, Năm invited his rival, insisting on giving him the bowl of congealed blood himself.

The lunch continued in general merriment. The two lovers had lost all self-restraint and were exchanging passionate glances. But nothing escaped the jealous husband who had an eerie smile on his face during the whole meal. After the guests left, Năm lured his wife's lover into a corner of the room. Then, with an ominous voice and cruel eyes, he said slowly, one word at a time, as if to engrave them on his enemy's mind:

"In the dish of blood that I just prepared for you, just for you, you bastard, I mixed with the offal and the herbs, especially for you, a tuft of my finely chopped hair. Look at my head if you don't believe me! You are going to die suffering the most atrocious pain. My hair will kill you slowly, very slowly. The chopped hairs will gradually puncture your intestines! You'll die, and no one will be able to do anything to save you, you lowlife!"

"He was right, this Năm," thought Toán, wiping his sweaty brow, "as the man died a few months later with terrible pains. Was it really the hairs from Năm's head that killed him? Or did he die simply from fear of . . . dying? Perhaps he poisoned himself with dangerous, dodgy remedies?"

Toán was tired and refused to search for an answer to these questions.

He relaxed and soon sonorous snoring sounds escaped from his mouth, rising into the night and mingling with those of his companions.

Accident at the Mine

1944

Due to his hard work and conscientiousness, Minh was assigned to the electric power station. After a week of training on the site, he was put in charge of the diesel engines. These huge machines were connected to alternators to produce the electricity needed for the lighting and effective operation of the mine facilities.

The first time he found himself in front of a control desk covered with dials and levers, Minh was completely overwhelmed. His main task was to keep the network tension as stable as possible, despite the overloading caused when the winches were activated in the mine.

Once every fifteen minutes Minh also had to perch on a metal ladder to oil the moving parts whose delicate mechanism required constant maintenance. The machines were very old and through an enormous and complicated system of pipes, they bellowed thick smoke and deafening blasts into the atmosphere.

Minh liked "his" factory as the work was interesting and much less taxing than anything he had had to do until then. However, the rules were very strict—no negligence or mistake was permitted and Minh knew it. The incessant rounds made by the foremen, and sometimes by the managers, didn't worry him at all as his mind was at ease, knowing he had done nothing wrong.

One afternoon when Minh was on duty at the control panel, glancing from time to time at the dials, he was interrupted by one of his former foremen from the mine. It was Watard. The blood had drained from his haggard face. Between two gasps, he ordered, "Sound the alarm!"

Minh had sensed a catastrophe as soon as he saw the panic-stricken man and immediately pulled the emergency lever as hard as he could. A strident screech tore through the air, spreading over the whole mountain in mournful echoes.

In the village and on the work sites, everyone shuddered when they heard the sinister siren.

"There's been an accident!" they shouted in horror.

Immediately, all the available men, including those who were off duty, came running from everywhere and converged on the power plant.

"One of the lower tunnels of the mine has caved in! Fifteen men are stuck inside!" Watard, now more composed, informed them.

"I need men to help me get them out!" said the manager, visibly shaken by the accident. All of the men present volunteered for the rescue operation. They organised themselves into small groups so that they could go down the mine at different intervals, in case there was another collapse. When they got to the site of the accident they got to work immediately. Hiếu, Thế's husband, was one of the first volunteers.

The men were horrified by the scale of the damage: the huge solid beams had been broken and dislodged by the incredibly strong pressure of the mountain. The tunnel was completely blocked by tons of rock.

"The tunnel's cut in half," murmured Hiếu anxiously.

"We'll try to make an opening in these boulders, but we need to be careful," said the manager.

Hiếu worked like a maniac, knowing that most of the men walled in on the other side were his compatriots. He was greatly encouraged to keep going by the fact that all the men, without exception, including the bosses and the principal manager, had joined the rescue party and had got to work vigorously. Even though the bosses weren't as effective as the mine workers, their physical strength and determination was of great assistance.

After working relentlessly for three hours they managed to make a hole big enough for a body to pass through. Rather dazed, eleven men and two foremen came through the hole one by one, to join their rescuers, and life itself.

"There're still two men in there, stuck under the fallen rocks. We couldn't get them out," said one of the foremen. "Numbers 3127 and 10 683."

"It's Bảy and Ngọc," thought Hiếu anxiously.

The thirteen survivors were immediately evacuated, while the rescuers squeezed inside the collapsed tunnel. They set to work again. After several agonising hours struggling against the mountain, against fear and against any further rockslides, they finally managed to free Ngọc. Hiếu leaned over the wounded man, listened to his heart and said, "He's still breathing! Very weakly, but he's alive."

Ngọc was carried with great care up to the surface, where the medical workers were waiting for him.

"There's still one more; it's number 3127," said the director.

Hiếu and the other volunteers in the tunnel continued their dangerous rescue work. Bảy was lying completely still under an enormous beam. With great patience they tried to move him carefully to avoid causing another landslide which might bury them too.

When the beam could finally be lifted without too much risk and Bảy was removed, the men's faces darkened. "We've lost him—he's dead!" they conceded.

Indeed, the beam had crushed the chest of the unfortunate Bảy under its own weight and the pressure of the mountain. Hiếu wept; he knew Bảy well. "He was a good man!" he murmured, his throat tight with emotion and pain. The whole of the Indochinese community agreed; Bảy was one of the youngest workers, single and always ready to help. They liked to call him affectionately "the kid." None of them had ever heard of a single reprehensible act on his part. He was hardworking and in good health and had never been punished for any professional misdemeanour. However, he had been to prison once. He was part of the group of forty-two who were imprisoned, with Minh, when the mine clock had been mysteriously put forward. The clock of the mine which in the end had crushed him and taken him from his friends.

Funeral Ceremonies

The whole community, gathered together before Bảy's mortal remains, decided to offer a funeral in his memory. The dormitory where his body lay was transformed into a funeral home. As a special gesture, he was allowed incense sticks which, as they burned, gave off a thick whitish smoke with a pungent odour. The wailing of the young women mourners, who had spontaneously joined the wake, caused intense emotion, even in the most hardened hearts. In the dark, sad night, both the women and the men, overcome by emotion, felt as if they were back home somewhere in their dear, distant country.

Little Hồng, now almost four years old, watched this strange spectacle with astonished eyes, not really understanding the difference between sleep and death.

"Is the man sleeping? Why's he sleeping there?" he whispered to his mother.

"The man's resting," Lan said softly. Then, leaning towards the toddler she said, "He's resting . . . for ever. You can't understand it yet, my boy! Be good and go home to bed! Mama will be with you soon."

Hồng obeyed, but he was sorry to leave this scene which seemed so mystifying to his young eyes.

"Really? You'll come home quickly, won't you, Mama? You know I don't like to sleep alone at night!"

"Don't be afraid. I'm coming back with you," said Minh. And the little boy left quietly with his father.

The next afternoon those men and women who had been able to get a few hours off work joined the small group watching over Bảy's body. A constant drizzle of rain had been falling on the mountain since dawn. The low grey sky, spreading a dark, dull light seemed to be participating in the grief that was felt throughout the camp.

The procession moved off with a bugle at its head played by one of the men who, inseparable from his instrument, became a funeral musician for the occasion. Next came the coffin which six men carried on their shoulders. The mourning women wept and wailed with heartbreaking sincerity. The other participants in this final ceremony in honour of a body returning to the earth were sombre. Lan followed the cortege slightly behind the others, holding the hand of her son who had refused to let his mother go on her own.

By the time they got to the tiny Tonkinese cemetery at some distance from the village they were soaked to the skin and freezing. They burnt the funeral money drawn and decorated by a skilful hand, according to tradition, on pieces of paper the size of a bank note, so that the dead man would not be too impoverished when he arrived in the next world.

Clinging to his mother's legs, young Hồng was cold, his little legs shivered, and he began to cough. Once the ceremony was over, Lan hurried her son home to change him and put him to bed.

As for the men, as soon as they got back to the village, they made sure the dead man's things were shared amongst them. Minh preferred to go straight home. But he hardly had time to get changed before one of Bảy's friends turned up at his door. "This is for you," said the man, handing an item of clothing to Minh.

"But . . . I don't understand!" said Minh in astonishment.

"It's a shirt! A beautiful brand new shirt! It belonged to my friend Bảy."

"I don't have any right to it. It belongs to you, this shirt!"

"Accept it, Minh. Keep it as a souvenir of the boy, as, even if you didn't realise it, he admired you a lot! He often spoke to us about you and when you were together in prison in Koumac!"

Minh was touched and surprised by Phung's words, but he protested, "You're the one who should keep this shirt! You deserve it more than me. You were his friend!"

"No! We've decided, my friends and I, that you should have it."

Phung put the shirt in Minh's hand, adding, "You should accept it! Bảy himself wouldn't be satisfied if you refused one of his last souvenirs on Earth." So, to please Bảy and his friends, Minh inherited the shirt.

That evening, young Hồng had a fever and was coughing more and more, a great cause for concern for his parents.

Outside the rain continued to drop its millions of cold liquid arrows onto the earth.

"Poor Bảy, it's finished for him. He'll never be able to see the home country again," murmured Lan sadly.

"What about us? Will we be able to see our native land some day soon?" asked Minh, staring at a corner of the wall to avoid showing Lan his dismay. They remained wordless for a long moment beside the child, who was whimpering, his forehead blazing with fever.

"Can you hear those noises?" asked Lan suddenly, straining her ears.

Jolted suddenly from his drowsiness, Minh replied, "No, I can't hear anything."

"Yes, listen!" insisted Lan, looking anxiously at the roof. "Listen, it's a mournful sound, like . . . sobbing," she added.

This time Minh could hear it distinctly. Strange creaking sounds in the metal walls and mysterious noises up on the thatched roof, like light footsteps.

"Listen Minh. It's coming from outside!" Lan whispered, her eyes wide with fright.

"The moaning's started again. It sounds like weeping. Someone's walking on the roof!" she said again fearfully. "It's him! He's come back to see us! No doubt he wants something!"

"Who?" asked Minh.

"The dead boy, obviously!"

"?"

"It's Bảy! It's his spirit letting us know he's there outside," she explained. "Listen, he's moving, he's walking around up there on the roof!" Minh remained sceptical. He didn't share the supernatural beliefs that so imbued Lan. His own logical reasoning prevented him from believing in this dogma which he thought should belong to the past.

However, the moaning was getting louder in the rainy night.

"Even if you don't believe me," Lan said furiously, "let me do things my way!"

Taking the shirt, she said with conviction. "It's a brand new shirt, no doubt his favourite! He's come back to get it! Don't you understand?"

She opened the door wide, put her head outside, then said in a loud voice, addressing the dead boy's spirit, "I know you've come to get what belongs to you, Bảy! But don't worry, you'll have it in a moment!"

Minh sitting still on the seat like a spectator, watched this strange scene passively. But he was curious all the same. Lan went into her kitchen, lit the wood fire, waited a moment, then threw the shirt into the fire. It burned quickly. She opened the door again and cried out in a loud voice, "It's done, Bảy! You can take back what's yours! Go away now!"

To Minh's astonishment, the strange, alarming noises which had disturbed their peace and quiet stopped suddenly.

"Don't be sorry about the shirt," Lan reassured her husband. "It's now in Bảy's possession, in his new realm!"

Her face calm, she added, "He must be wearing it now! Maybe he was cold?"

The Recovery

Nothing disturbed the silence in the room, apart from Hồng's loud, regular snoring. He had dozed off, but, alas, he didn't sleep for long. After about twenty minutes, his eyes still closed, he complained, grimacing in pain.

"It hurts, Mama, it hurts!"

Lan was quick to ask, "Where does it hurt, my love?"

"I . . . don't know," he said shaking his head feebly. Then pointing to his little chest, he added, "It hurts all over . . . in there."

He began coughing violently, gasping for breath.

Minh and Lan were distressed but helpless in the face of the child's suffering.

"What should I do Minh?" asked Lan anxiously.

"I don't know," said Minh, with a desperate gesture.

The child was suffocating now.

"My son! My baby!" murmured Lan again and her eyes misted over.

"I'll go and see the midwife, Madame Sửu! She must know a remedy for this!" said Minh getting up. He disappeared into the persistent rain and the darkness.

Hồng moaned, convulsing with each new fit of coughing, which only exhausted him further. It was getting difficult for him to breathe, and there was a strange wheezing sound in the top part of his body. It was as if his lungs were shrinking, the tubes blocking up as the pain got worse.

"Mama! Mama!" he cried, choking, his eyes convulsed and his body stiff from the repeated efforts to get his breath back. Lan felt as if she were suffering the same pain. She couldn't get enough air and she felt slightly dizzy, almost fainting with worry.

Minh came back a moment later, soaked through and blue from the cold. When she saw him come back alone, Lan felt desperate, her dilated eyes glowed strangely; it was the glow of fear.

"No, don't worry," said Minh. "Madame Sửu will be here in a moment, she just had to change."

Lan calmed down, feeling hopeful again. "Go and get changed Minh. You mustn't get sick too!"

A black umbrella appeared in the doorway, followed by the face of Madame Sửu. The midwife looked tired and her red eyes seemed to be in need of a good night's sleep. Nevertheless, she smiled her gracious smile.

"I'm really sorry, Madame Sửu, to trouble you at this time of the night," said Lan. "I know you've been up all night watching over poor Bảy," she continued," but I am . . . my son . . . well, he's really sick and I don't know what to do to help him get rid of the sickness, Madame Sửu!"

The midwife, smiling as always, replied, "Don't torment yourself even more! I love children." Lowering her eyes, she murmured, "I would've loved so much to have one myself!"

She lifted her head resolutely as if to chase away her sudden melancholy, and then, a little guilty at her weakness, she said to herself, "You came here to look after the little boy, not to feel sorry for yourself."

Madame Sửu put her hand calmly on Hồng's forehead. Lan observed her reactions carefully, but, to her great disappointment, the midwife remained stony-faced. She leaned over Hồng's chest and, this time, she winced a little. Finally, she stood up, put her right hand inside her blouse and took out a parcel that she had hidden between her breasts.

"It's to protect it from the rain," she smiled. She opened her pouch and with her fingers took out a little grey powder and a pill. Then she prepared a brew.

"Give him this to drink and the fever will disappear. You must still keep him warm though; I fear he might have bronchitis or something similar," she added.

The child swallowed the unpleasant-tasting remedy, snivelling a little. After a while, his breathing was normal and the strange wheezing in his chest lessened. Lan felt relieved, as if she had been delivered from some terrible evil whose name she did not know. She walked Madame Sửu to the door, thanking her effusively.

"You should rest, get some sleep," Minh said to Lan affectionately, when they were alone again. "You have to go back to work very early tomorrow morning." To reassure her he said, "I'll look after the little one, as I'm on the afternoon shift tomorrow. I've got the whole morning to rest!"

Lan accepted reluctantly. "It's too distressing for a mother to sleep while her child is sick," she sighed. "But we don't have any choice," she added stoically. "Until the last day of our contract, that's the way it'll be; work comes first!"

"Fortunately, it'll be over in a few months," said Minh, who now felt more confident about the future. Then he added soberly, "Do you realise we've been here for almost five years. Five years, already!"

Lan woke up very early the next morning. Minh had dozed off nearby, stretched out on the bench. The young mother realised that she had slept right through the night without a thought for the boy. Hồng coughed from time to time, the wheezing noise interfering with his breathing.

"It's not serious," Lan said to herself. "The noise will go away when the fever disappears. He's still feverish."

At this juncture, Madame Sửu arrived. "I've come to see how the little one is, before I go to work. Today I have to clean up the manager's garden," she said. "I don't know . . . I don't understand why I get so anxious when I have to go and work for that man!" she said, her face tense.

She prepared a new potion. Hồng was awakened, at the same time as his father, by the sound of voices, but, remembering the revolting taste of the brew from the night before, he refused to swallow it. Minh had to force him to drink it and he gulped it down grimacing and crying, fighting like a little maniac, which exhausted and suffocated him even more.

The rasping in his chest became even more intense and his breathing was difficult. He started to cry out, "I'm suffocating! I can't breathe!"

Minh and Lan looked in panic at Madame Sửu.

"It's worrying," said the midwife, her expression suddenly anxious. "I fear he may have an asthma attack—he has all the symptoms of the illness!"

"Do you have a remedy for it?" asked Lan, frowning.

"No! As far as I know medicines can only ease the attack, but alas, there is no spectacular cure. However," she added, "Hồng's very young and what he has now may not be all that serious." She continued, "The herb extract I've just prepared is very effective. He'll feel better in a moment!"

"I've known asthmatics," said Minh, who was now also worried, "and they suffer terribly!" Looking pityingly at his son gasping for breath, he added, "I wouldn't want my son to go through the same thing. It really is a burden to go through life with this affliction!"

He stood up suddenly, his face animated. "I remember two remedies my uncle used," he said, clapping. "He was also asthmatic. Let's see . . . the first, and apparently the most effective . . . No! It's too disgusting, it's impossible for a child this age, he'll never be able to!"

"To what?" asked Lan, intrigued.

"Yes, that's it," said Minh, thinking. "You have to catch a young lizard, a baby one. Then you have to wrap it in healing plants or, if necessary, a lettuce leaf. The patient then has to swallow the whole thing alive, completely raw, as the animal must enter the stomach alive. Apparently, the gall or the bile is most effective this way!"

"No, I beg of you, not that!" cried Lan who was grimacing in disgust. "Not for our son! He's still much too young," she added as an excuse.

"What's the second remedy?" asked Madame Sửu.

"The other is much simpler and . . . more pleasant. But I'd like to think about it, to be certain, you understand. I have to go to work this evening, so I'll tell you about it tomorrow."

Lan saw that her little boy had fallen asleep, just as the midwife-gardener had predicted. So the two young women left, leaving the little patient in Minh's hands. As soon as they had disappeared to the end of the village, Minh started searching for something which was apparently so important that he had to move all the furniture and then look in every nook and cranny to find it.

"When you want them, you can't find them," he grumbled, "and when you don't want them, the filthy creatures come out from everywhere!"

Moving a small box, he cried out, "Ah! There's one, at least!"

Minh grabbed a shoe from the shelf and began looking around, hitting the ground nervously. After a half hour using both tricks and patience, he managed to catch six huge fat cockroaches. "One more and that'll make seven. That's the right number, I think!"

Minh continued his hunt. "Finally!" he cried, after another quarter of an hour's hunting. "The last is always the most difficult to find," he added, wiping his sweaty brow.

Minh put the seven cockroaches in a bowl. Using a knife handle he began to crush them carefully until they turned into a thick, sticky paste. He added half a glass of water and mixed it all together. Then, he picked up young Hồng, who was still having trouble breathing, and forced him to drink the disgusting beverage. Naturally Minh was particularly concerned at making his own son swallow the mixture when its effectiveness was so questionable. But the memories of his uncle who suffered, with every asthma attack, a horrible sort of exhausting choking for several days and nights, made the poor father determined to do something to try to free his son of this excruciating suffering.

When the two young women got back at the end of the afternoon, little Hồng was playing peacefully in the house. All the abnormal sounds in his chest had disappeared.

"My baby! He's cured! He's not gasping for breath anymore," cried Lan who could hardly believe it.

"He's still tired, but that will pass quickly," said Madame Sửu, delighted. "And to think I feared an asthma attack!" she added.

"And Minh wanted to make him swallow those dreadful mixtures!" added Lan, happy to know that her child would soon be strong and healthy again.

Minh came home very late, at about midnight, but his wife was waiting for him. She wanted to tell him the good news. Minh listened carefully to what she was saying and then glanced at his son with tenderness and satisfaction. But before falling asleep, he wondered nevertheless, "Did Hồng just have a bad cold? Or did my remedy really save him? Parents always overreact when their child is a little off-colour!"

These thoughts troubled him, but he didn't dare tell his wife the truth, at least not for the moment. He said to himself awkwardly, "There are some times in life when it's better not to say anything. Maybe some day, later on! Yes, later on, not now!"

The Revolt

The people of the camp were gathered in a large building, waiting. They were no longer the submissive, resigned workers of the past. Their determination could be seen on their grave faces. A small man got up and addressed the meeting.

"My fellow workers, we are gathered this Sunday in this place that we will call our community house from now on, a sort of home—for support, a meeting-place for us all. We have to show solidarity and that we form a single united and inseparable group. It's now 1945, which means that we've gone beyond the stipulated duration of our contracts. Those who were here before us have been here in the colony for over seven years. They haven't been able to go home because of the war!

"Those of us who are part of the 1939 contingent are now in the same worrying situation. We should already have been home for more than six months! Obviously, we can't accuse the mine management or the public services on the island for this delay. They're not responsible for the current situation, they didn't create the war. However, our employers have deliberately broken the promises they made. They have not respected their obligations towards us. Yet, they've forced us to respect ours and allowed no relaxing of the rules."

The man observed his audience, then continued.

"The bosses don't want to lose their privileges, or spend a single cent to improve our lives. To this very day our children have never received any kind of help since the day they were born! The women are treated with as much respect as pack animals. This can't continue— it's lasted long enough. Too long!

"The time of whips and kicks in the belly must be abolished for ever! We have to fight against these barbarous methods and defend ourselves. We have to demand higher wages, so that we can live a little better while we're waiting to be repatriated!"

In front of the men and women who were listening with interest, the orator raised his voice.

"Remember that we've never had a pay increase since we arrived on this island. No allowances, nothing, absolutely nothing! During this time, the bosses have got richer. Look how comfortably they live! Compare all their accumulated wealth with our dilapidated shacks and hovels.

"Look at the new facilities and modern machines that have been used recently on the mine. They were able to buy all this machinery thanks to our labour and our suffering. Although we tried several months ago to get management to have some consideration for our plight, to this day we've received nothing!"

The man stopped talking for a moment, asked for a glass of water, wiped his forehead, then continued his speech.

"According to the letters and news we've exchanged with our countrymen in other centres all over the island, it turns out that all of us, without exception, are in the same tragic situation! Just like the very first days in 1939 when we arrived here!

"We have therefore decided, by common accord, to prepare ourselves for a fierce struggle for our freedom and our rehabilitation. For our basic rights to be treated like men, not slaves!

"Some centres, thanks to contributions from everyone, have been able to buy a radio broadcast receiver, which allows them to get news from all over the world. The world is changing rapidly. The radios speak of the war, which is raging at the moment in Europe and even in the Pacific, all around us. But they are also speaking of independence and freedom for the peoples of the world."

A heavy silence reigned in the crowded room. The orator, sure of himself and his cause, continued.

"We can't remain on the sidelines of all these movements. From now on we have to let our former masters know, and I want to make it clear that they *are* our former masters, that we have changed. Our patience has come to an end. We'll let them know that we'll never accept to be enslaved again!"

With his hands leaning on the table and his face pushed forward he added, "Of course we can expect many reactions from our colonial bosses. They're tough, as you've all discovered; the marks on your flesh are proof of that. Let's expect the worst and organise our defence carefully. But I'll hand over to Minh now. He's going to tell you about our plans!"

That was Chín who, because of his energy and vision, had been elected by a large majority to lead the movement. Minh started to speak. "I agree completely with Chín!" he began. "The time for patience, hope and passiveness is over! It must belong to the past! Now we must fight for our future, for the right to freedom of movement."

Minh outlined his ideas. "We're brave, hardworking and reasonable. What we're asking for is, after all, perfectly legitimate. It's what any man living in supposedly modern times aspires to. But, for our demands to be successful, we have to fight! We'll organise demonstrations, petitions, whatever's necessary, to get what we want.

"We'll have to be particularly vigilant, we can't afford to get caught. The slightest error of judgement or wrong move would be the end of it. They'd never let us get away with it. We must wait for the instructions to start the movement and, at that moment, all the centres on the island will go on strike indefinitely until our demands are met."

Minh's face hardened. He spoke slowly so that his comrades could take in what he was saying more easily.

"As of this moment, we must start preparing for this operation!" he said. "Stock up on food, buy rice and milk for the children. But you need to be very careful: buy in small quantities so that they don't suspect anything. Surprise is our main strength. Hand over any medication you may have to Phúc. Even if he has a better position than we do, he's with us. He's in charge of the infirmary, with the help of Madame Sửu. All empty bottles that you find must be collected and brought here to our community house.The women and children can also participate in this. As for the men, they have to prepare weapons in case we need to defend ourselves. Only in case of any danger which may put our lives at risk!"

Minh's voice softened. "These orders coming from me may surprise you. But don't worry, I haven't changed. The principle of peace and nonviolence is still deeply ingrained in me. But that doesn't mean that we have to always bow down without a word. There are certain times in life when we have to defend ourselves and fight, if necessary, for a just cause. Personally, I hope we don't have to see it come to that!"

His face was strained. "But we'll fight them if they won't give up their blind domination over us! And that's what I fear, alas," he added, "as they will never consent to giving up their advantages for workers who have, until now, always been submissive. In my opinion, they won't hesitate to use whatever forces are at their disposal to crush us! So, I repeat, we have to be careful and ready for any situation! If we want a successful outcome, we have to make the administrators aware of our plight. And to do that we'll definitely have to provoke them to jolt them out of their complacency."

Minh concluded, saying, "As you can see, we still have a lot to do. But we must be ready on the agreed day. Get to work! Get to work! And thank you for your attention."

The next morning, the women started to stock up on food and medicines, to the astonishment of the shopkeepers. The shelves of the only shop in the centre were emptied quickly by people who, ordinarily, wouldn't buy so much at once.

"It's for our festival, big celebration. Soon!" the women said to avoid any suspicion.

The men, for their part, came back from the night shift, some with pickaxes, others with crowbars. Machetes disappeared unaccountably from the work sites, and empty bottles piled up quickly in the community house.

Minh cleaned his weapons meticulously. First of all, he acquired an axe, which he had to learn to use properly.

"You're much better at taking care of people than attacking them," Lan giggled.

However, Minh did not let himself get discouraged. He attached a long handle to the biggest kitchen knife in his possession. Once that was done, the weapon was about one-and-a-half metres long. "It's like a bayonet," he said proudly, posing like a soldier. Then he practised at home, far from any prying eyes, marching around with his weapon on his shoulder, under the amused watch of Lan and to the delight of little Hồng.

"Mama, what's Papa playing at?"

"Your Papa's pretending to be a soldier," replied Lan, unable to stop herself laughing out loud.

***

Very soon, the big day arrived. The signal was given. The men didn't go to work. They all assembled in the community house, apart from about ten of them who, with the permission of the action committee, went to maintain security in the mine.

A small delegation led by Chín and Minh then took the petition, with its many signatures, and placed it on the general manager's desk. Half an hour later the foremen—who had been made aware of the situation by the mine manager—tried to enter the camp, but they were unceremoniously refused entry. Their eyes showed astonishment at the impertinent attitude of the workers who, up until yesterday, they considered backward and primitive. The strikers were themselves surprised; some didn't believe their eyes.

"Did you see that? They're capitulating. They're going away . . . without even trying to beat us!"

The women and children were sheltering in a building at some distance from the headquarters. The men were busy—some were securing a long mast in front of the building; others, on the roof, were piling up boxes of empty bottles.

Phúc and Madame Sửu stayed at their post in the infirmary. But the day passed without any further incident. The men waited calmly for a response.

"Be patient!" said Minh. "They know we'll stay on strike indefinitely, until our demands are met."

That evening, the men kept careful watch, carrying all sorts of arms as they patrolled the camp.

"Keep calm! Avoid any provocation. We mustn't make any mistakes!" Minh said again.

"If the administrators refuse to listen to us, we've got a big surprise for them. The mast is ready," said Chín, his eyes shining with malice. The next morning it was the gendarmes and their auxiliaries who turned up in front of the strikers. A few of the foremen had insisted on coming too. However, they had to stop at the edge of the camp, which was guarded by men who were both threatening and determined. The tension was at a critical point.

"They represent the authorities, so let's provoke them!" cried Chín. "We've got an unpleasant surprise for them . . . it's the only way to get the authorities to take any concrete action in our favour."

Turning towards the men at the foot of the tall mast he said, "Come on! Let's go for it. Raise the flag!"

A banner appeared on top of the building in front of the astonished, then outraged, eyes of their opponents. It was the red flag with a yellow star with five points at its centre.

"It's the flag of the Indochinese guerrillas! They're led by someone called Ho Chi Minh," shouted a gendarme. "At this very moment they're fighting against the French army, our army in Tonkin and in the whole of Indochina!" he explained.

"We have to seize the flag!" cried the enraged warrant officer. "Charge!"

But the gendarmes were the only ones to attack—the foremen stayed back cautiously. The demonstrators allowed the gendarmes to approach without reacting. The attackers continued to advance, but when they got near the front of the building, they were suddenly on the receiving end of projectiles raining down from the roof. The empty bottles struck the gendarmes violently and, without any effective protection, they had to retreat.

Afterwards, Minh and Chín assembled the men. "Thank you for your self-discipline," said Chín. "You manoeuvred well and it was a good idea to raise the flag—it provoked the reaction we expected."

"Those who are injured should go to the infirmary!" said Minh. "From now on, we must be extra careful," he suggested, "as they will no doubt return to the attack. . . . But it has to be absolutely clear that we must avoid bloodshed. That would be counterproductive!"

"We just want to show them we reject their colonial policies. We're not at war!" insisted Chín. "Even so, we'll fly the flag as long as we need to. Until victory. It'll be the symbol of our freedom and determination to succeed."

"The men in charge of the mine's safety must be sure to relay each other. The rest should divide themselves into several groups, to take turns keeping watch night and day over the camp," ordered Minh.

Chín continued, "We've come too far now to be able to afford a single defection. We have to be more united than ever! The action committee will be located here in the community house permanently as, without any contact with the outside, we can only rely on ourselves. However, we know that our compatriots in other centres are reacting just like us at the moment!"

Chín was silent. To keep up the men's morale, Minh said, "Meanwhile, our opponents are shouting themselves hoarse on the telephone and fussing around the Morse equipment, sending telegrams to inform the colony's supreme authorities of the situation. It's a good sign, it's encouraging. We must persevere as victory is near!"

The second night was as peaceful as the first. Lan and Hồng had gone back home to sleep without Minh. From the first light of dawn the men anticipated a hectic and probably decisive day.

"I think," said Chín, "we're going to receive a visit, that's obvious. Because this calm is not normal! The management will no doubt try to negotiate to find a compromise to appease us. But this time they won't trick us!"

Chín was not wrong. At about ten in the morning a delegation led by Mainote himself, turned up at the entrance to the camp. Their barely contained rage was reflected on their faces. Nevertheless, the head foreman addressed the demonstrators politely, which greatly amused them.

"We want to talk to the leaders of the strike," he said.

Mainote and his men were led straight away to the headquarters, where Chín and Minh and the whole committee were waiting to receive them.

"The roles have been reversed," thought Minh, observing Mainote with boldly mocking eyes.

Mainote was making a tremendous effort to control himself. He said, "The manager asks you to come to his office to try to settle this dispute amicably. It can all be settled very quickly, very easily . . . as you know, all it takes is a little goodwill and we'll be able to come to an understanding!"

"Minh, you can speak the French language really well. I'm putting you in charge of negotiating with these people on behalf of all of us," said Chín. Minh nodded, then he addressed Mainote calmly.

"Thank you for your invitation, Monsieur. However, on behalf of all of my compatriots on this mine, I regret to inform you that we no longer wish to deal with you or your managers. To tell you the truth, we no longer believe your promises. So, it would be pointless for us to meet with your bosses, wouldn't it?"

Mainote insisted, so the demonstrators modified their position somewhat. Minh stated, "Before any meeting we demand that a representative of the colony be present. They're the ones who are responsible for our presence here."

The foreman turned bright red; he could hardly believe his ears. His hands which were so used to using the whip were shaking nervously. Flabbergasted by such arrogance, he left, escorted like a puppet out of the camp by his former coolies.

"Times have changed indeed," they gloated. "This is the best revenge!"

In the early afternoon Minh and Hiếu were chatting with Madame Sửu when two men came to find them.

"Several vehicles are heading up here. Scouts posted on the high ground have just let us know," said one of them.

"How many vehicles?" asked Minh.

"At least five! They're driving really fast on the new road."

"They'll be in the village in ten minutes!" replied the other one.

"It must be the backup they were waiting for to replace us at the mine," said Phúc.

"What kind of vehicles?" asked Minh anxiously.

"Trucks . . . We couldn't see who was inside with all the dust from the tyres on the new road."

"It doesn't matter," said Minh. "Let's wait and see what happens. We can be confident that we're within our rights, so there's no reason to fear anything or anyone."

Turning towards the two men he ordered, "Go back to the scouts and tell them what I've just told you."

Then, leaving Phúc and Madame Sửu to their potions, Minh joined Chín and the committee. A moment later, the military trucks came to a standstill above the mine. Armed soldiers immediately took up their positions around the camp. Chín and his friends were surprised; they had not expected the armed forces to come. Their barracks were at the other end of the island, more than four hundred kilometres away.

A meeting was held immediately as the situation was becoming critical.

"Guns wielded by well-trained soldiers against our knives. It's completely unequal," Chín had to admit.

"Should we abandon the struggle?" asked one of the men.

"They're too strong. Will we always be at their mercy in this country?" cried another, devastated by the change in situation.

"We've always asked you to remain hopeful and confident, whatever the difficulties," said Minh, his expression determined. "It's now or never that we must prove to our opponents and to ourselves that we know exactly what we want! Let me explain. If the mine management has called on the army for assistance, it means they're afraid of us. That's obvious, and it's also encouraging. So we must maintain our action without fail."

"The fact that the army's here in front of our centre," added Chín, "also means that the highest authorities in the colony, both military and civilian, have been alerted! And our demands are either being examined at this moment or have already been examined. It's only a question of patience now, we can't afford to capitulate. It's a decisive moment."

"We must remain firm and stick to our positions!" insisted Minh. Speaking more moderately he continued, "I don't think . . . I'm sure they wouldn't dare massacre us or fire at us for no reason, without the motive of legitimate defence! And we'll do everything we can to avoid giving them that pretext. I've always insisted on that and now it makes sense."

Chín added, "Things are getting tight now! If you know how to use them, words often have more force than arms. Let's wait for them with the same calm we've always shown."

Half an hour later, the mine manager himself came to the camp. He was accompanied by a stranger who was elegantly dressed in a beautiful white suit. The imposing pith helmet, perfectly adjusted on his head, protected his light-coloured eyes from the sun. The soldiers surrounded him to protect him.

Lan was there with several other women who were worried about the turn of events. Little Hồng clung to his mother in fear. He had never witnessed so many things in one day: first, he had seen the five trucks arrive like steel monsters, screeching and belching out clouds of dust, and then he saw these men all dressed identically and carrying the same equipment, their sullen eyes empty.

"I'm scared, Mama!" he cried suddenly. "Why are these men coming to see Papa? I'm scared, I don't like these men!"

"Don't worry, my son. Papa's very strong, and he's not afraid of anyone," said Lan to calm her son down, but there was fear in her eyes.

The stranger and the manager stopped in front of the strikers. Chín, Minh and another strike organiser were waiting for them.

"I'm a government official," said the man politely. "I've come to sort out the conflict between you and your employers."

Then, pointing his finger at the top of the community house, he said, "But before we can begin discussions, I insist you take down that flag! Don't you know that it's the emblem used in Indochina by the guerrillas against the French? I refuse to participate in talks with you in front of that flag!"

"It's your turn now Minh," murmured Chín.

"Monsieur, we welcome you if you're here to deliver impartial justice. But you have to admit that you've taken your time to come and visit us. We've been waiting for you for a very long time! And as we have so much to tell you, we will not take down this flag until you have listened to us and we have had the chance to present our demands! Let me assure you, Monsieur, that what we are demanding is in no way illegitimate. On the contrary, all we want is to live in peace as free men in this land while we are waiting to be repatriated to the country of our ancestors. Freedom to decide our fate! Freedom from all constraints and persecution! In a word, to be able to live like the other ethnic groups on this island!"

Minh caught his breath and then continued.

"Monsieur, you come from a country which proclaims to the whole world, 'Liberté, Egalité, Fraternité!' Our demands are for basic human rights. It's urgent for you to hear our plea, so that slavery be abolished for ever in this so-called modern world! Yes, Monsieur, I declare that we are the unfortunate victims of blind colonialism. We demand, with all our might, that you free us from our conditions as slaves!"

Minh stopped speaking. He stared at the official and saw he was listening carefully. Minh gave him the petition and said, "As you have listened to our grievances which I hereby hand over to you in written form, to please you I will have the flag taken down!"

He waved to the men perched on the roof and they lowered the flag with the golden star.

"I understand that your conditions are harsh," said the man, looking around with curiosity. "I will refer it to my superiors but ask you to be patient for two to three days for their response."

"Monsieur, we agree to wait, however we will maintain our strike until the final victory!"

Surprised by this reply, the man's face clouded over. "I have received strict orders that I hope I won't have to use! Go back to work," he insisted. "Don't worry, you have my word. We will examine your case with particular care. I repeat, it's only a question of days, a few days!"

Minh replied unequivocally, "We know about promises and what they are worth, Monsieur. We don't accept them anymore. We'll maintain our strike."

"In that case," said the man, visibly sorry, "I find myself obliged to arrest you. I am arresting you! It's your choice. You can still change your mind!"

Then pointing to the soldiers, he said, "My men are here to execute the order!"

Chín, Minh and their companion looked at each other questioningly. A slight nod was their unanimous response. Minh addressed the official firmly:

"We're your prisoners, Monsieur. We prefer prison to our present conditions!"

"We'll give you fifteen minutes to get organised. After that my men will take you away!"

The man thought for a moment. Then, after a quick talk with the mine manager who was now very agitated, he turned towards Minh and said, "If you accept on your honour that the security of the mine will be ensured by your men, we'll only take fifty of you!" He hastened to add, "It goes without saying that you and your organising committee will be amongst the fifty people arrested!"

Minh looked queryingly at his companions.

"Let's accept!" said Chín.

"Those who stay behind must not under any circumstances go back to work!" said one of the committee members.

"They'll continue the strike until we get back!" said Minh, adding, "If after four days we're not back, the men in charge of the mine security must stop work! They must stop all work on the mine! That's the only bargaining tool we have."

"Phúc won't be coming with us!" said Chín. Then turning to him he said, "You'll be in charge of the community while we're away!"

Phúc and the men nodded discreetly. Minh then addressed the government official, saying, "We've just discussed your proposal in our own language and we agree to it."

He hastened to specify, "However, I must warn you that those who are staying here in Pimboé will only go back to work when we return and our demands are satisfied!"

The man in the white suit accepted, then left with the distraught mine manager.

"I don't understand these people!" he complained. "They have everything they need and they protest, they want even more! Ah! What terrible times we live in, Monsieur! I've never seen anything like it!"

Minh went home, got some clothes, trousers and a shirt, kissed his wife, hugged his son close to his chest, covering him in kisses, then went to join his companions.

A few minutes later, escorted by the soldiers, the fifty prisoners were asked to get into the back of the trucks and they left without delay.

Lan watched the vehicles leave the mountains with slight apprehension and some pride. Her husband was going to prison, it's true, but it was to fight for the right to a decent life! She did not feel the same bitterness as when he had had to leave the first time, tied to his companion by a rope and guarded by unscrupulous gendarmes.

"This time he's left voluntarily for a noble cause, to combat backward laws and be able to walk with his head held high. Like a human being."

Lan had confidence in Minh and his companions. She was certain of victory, of their final victory! Indeed, she had noticed a deep change in the behaviour of the men who, yesterday, were still so aggressive, but today were treating them with some consideration and respect.

"If all these men, of different races and beliefs could get to know each other and understand each other, that would be their greatest common achievement," she dreamed. "If we could get along on an equal footing, in this land, this new land, while we await our return to our native country, it would be wonderful! We could do great things. We could contribute even more to the development of this country, forget the past and build a better future together!"

These secret hopes overwhelmed Lan. She went home with Hồng; it already seemed to her that she was a stranger there. She was rediscovering her life with new eyes, shining with hope. "I'm sure my dream will come true. I'm certain of it!"

The trucks descended the dusty road noisily. Minh was sitting between Chín and Nguyễn. He began to think, "What a coincidence! How extraordinary chance is! Here I am sitting beside my former cell mate again, heading for another stay in prison. But things have changed since then: progress, the cars, the trucks, this new road. It's astonishing!"

Minh saw himself again clearly, climbing the same mountain for the first time, his bare feet on the winding path. He had had to support Lan, the young girl who had cut her toe on a sharp stone.

"How things have changed since then," he thought. "But it must be said that this road exists because of our hard work!"

He looked at the soldiers sitting nearby, still and impassive and, thinking about the many Europeans who were in charge of them at the mine, he murmured, “These men could've become good friends, or at least good bosses. The atmosphere in the village and productivity would've been so much better. But, alas, we've inherited laws and regulations from the colonial era of the previous century, with all its privileges, where it's all about submitting to the despicable power of money!”

The deep blue sea suddenly appeared. “This panorama is unique,” thought Minh. “The silver fringe in the distance, parallel to the shore, is even more beautiful and luminous today. It could be a paradise, this island of New Caledonia! And these trucks hurtling so easily down this new road—it's astonishing. What a remarkable day—yes, remarkable!” He heard himself murmur.

Then, suddenly coming back to reality, he reproached himself, “I'm too sentimental, I shouldn't be. This is no time to indulge in this sort of contemplation. No! I should be thinking about the present struggle. I'll have enough time to dream later. Yes, later.”

The trucks reached the port of Kunéo in record time.

“Half an hour to do the trip instead of four to five hours on foot!” exclaimed Chín, in wonder.

The soldiers instructed them to go down into the hold of a barge that was moored against the small dock. It was one of the barges that transported the ore from the port to the ship anchored in the bay.

Minh remembered clearly how, as soon as he had disembarked from the old coaster, without being allowed a minute's rest, he had had to push the wagons loaded with chromium until he was gasping for breath in the blazing sun.

Under the surveillance of about ten armed soldiers, the barge left the port, pulled by a tugboat toward the ocean. The men wanted to know why they were taking this sea voyage and where exactly they were going. But it was a waste of energy. The soldiers, already on board well before they arrived, remained mute and unperturbed. The ship sailed inexorably away from Grande Terre and made its way towards the ocean.

After about an hour and a half, a tiny dot appeared on the horizon to the right.

“It's a small island. An island!” the men shouted.

Snake Island

Lying on her bed Lan stared dully into space. Her mind wandered, and strange and chaotic thoughts tormented her. She blamed it all on her irritation.

"They've already been gone for two hours," she murmured. As if to reassure herself she hastened to add, "But it'll all be settled quickly—this situation can't last!"

Another image distressed her, that of her parents. Lan's face clouded over even more.

"Will we ever see each other again in this world?" she wondered sadly. She frowned, staring up at the thatched roof.

"Why haven't I ever had any more news from them? Nor has Minh, he never got a single reply to the many letters we never stopped writing for almost a year. I don't understand it!" she said to herself. "Other people here, like Liên, have had letters quite regularly. Why haven't we? Has the war forced our dear parents from their houses? Are they still alive? It's terrible not to know what's happened to them." Then she murmured bitterly, "We came here with a simple goal, but we weren't able to help them for very long. Poor parents, poor dear parents!"

But Lan was awakened from her gloomy daydreaming by her son Hồng who burst suddenly into the room.

"I'm hungry, Mama!" he groaned putting his hands on his stomach.

"I'm so lucky you're here, my little boy," said Lan looking at him with tender eyes.

"Why Mama?" he asked astonished.

"No, it's nothing, my darling!"

She got up, saying, "I'm going to cook you a nice meal! Your favourite."

***

Slowly the tugboat approached the small island. Delightedly, the men on the barge contemplated the white sandy beach surrounding this tiny piece of land, only a hundred metres long, in the middle of the ocean.

The fifty prisoners felt reassured by the soldiers who, although strict and reserved, were not violent and treated them with courtesy. They were surprised and enchanted to be allowed to spend a few days in the sun. They were even more astonished when they landed on the shore.

"Oh, the island isn't deserted!" they cried out together. There were about sixty people already on the beach.

"Welcome to our island, Minh!" cried one of the men. Minh recognised his voice.

"You're already here, Toán! You beat us to it! I'm happy to see you again," he said, rushing towards his friend.

When the men had all disembarked, the tugboat left immediately with the soldiers on board, pulling the empty barge behind it.

"Are they abandoning us on this island?" asked Chín.

"Yes, they have nothing to fear. We can't swim to the mainland," said Toán. "In any case we have enough food and water to live for at least a week."

They walked towards the centre of the beach and Toán told them, "They unloaded it all this morning when we arrived."

"Tell us about the demonstrations in Tenep," said Chín, very interested.

They sat down on the fine sand, and Toán began. "We started the movement on Monday afternoon."

"I think you mean Tuesday morning," rectified Minh.

"No! Normally we should have respected the order for a general strike and only begun action on Tuesday morning as agreed, but Cầu, our chief, well, the one we designated to lead the movement, was in too much of a hurry. He wasn't able to follow the exact orders of our people in Nouméa who coordinated the operation!"

"It's a serious mistake on Cầu's part!" grumbled Chín severely. "He could have derailed our movement!"

"We made the wrong decision, but he was severely punished. He's now in hospital in Koumac, badly wounded," said Toán, continuing his story. "Cầu called the strike on Monday afternoon—today is Thursday. We'd installed two flags in front of our community house. There was one which was red with the yellow star and the other was red, but with the hammer and the sickle, also yellow . . . like the star! Apparently, it's the Soviet flag. It was Cầu's idea. We didn't have to wait long for the Europeans, or should I say the French, to react. They came immediately to demand that we take the flags down, saying it was a flagrant provocation on our part against their authority. But Cầu was overexcited. He'd bottled up his resentment for too long and got carried away. The two groups got so heated and the tension was so great that there was no avoiding a confrontation. The first attack was made by our adversaries. There were injured men on both sides, slight injuries, but we managed to push them back!"

Toán's face became animated and he spoke quickly in his excitement.

"Before they could launch a second offensive, Cầu and about ten other men climbed quickly onto the roof, near the barrels full of empty bottles and iron bars to defend the flags! The Europeans attacked again, as we had predicted.

We fought. But our assailants were stronger, and we couldn't push them back a second time. They wanted to tear down the flags. Our men on the roof began to throw all their empty bottles at them . . . but very few managed to hit their targets!

"At that instant, Cầu lost his temper completely. He grabbed a heavy crowbar and threw it at one of the foremen! The foreman saw the dangerous tool coming for him and managed to dodge it. Then, as quick as lightning, he grabbed it and with all his strength threw it back at Cầu. It hit Cầu right in the stomach. He collapsed on the roof, and, just in time, the men nearby grabbed him and stopped him from falling to the ground four to five metres below! The wound was very deep. He needed urgent medical care, possibly even a complicated operation! We had to cease our resistance, as he needed a doctor straight away. Only the hospital in Koumac could save him!

"The Europeans ransacked all the equipment in our centre, including the radio that kept us informed of the situation in the country. But we still continued the strike, without Cầu!"

"So, he's in hospital now?" asked Chín with irritation.

"Yes, but, as we're here we've had no more news of him!"

"What about the soldiers?" Minh asked intrigued.

"The soldiers only came to the village last night. All the men they considered suspect were kept in custody, then taken away on their trucks this morning at dawn. They drove us to the port at Kunéo before putting us and some food supplies on a barge heading for this island."

"You almost ruined the operation. Do you realise that?" growled Chín again. "If they'd got wind of our overall plan, everything would've been ruined. We would've been crushed by their strength, and the movement would've been nipped in the bud!"

"I don't think they could've broken us up so easily," said Minh. "Even with their army and their gendarmes, they can do nothing against our determination. Of course, that doesn't mean that we don't think Cầu did the wrong thing!" he added.

"His only excuse," said Toán, "is that he couldn't stand these slavelike conditions a moment longer."

"Let's change the subject!" suggested Chín, stretching out on the fine sand. "We won't be staying long on this island, so let's make the most of these few days of holiday before going back to our underground tunnels. Every day of strike represents a huge loss for their mining companies, and indirectly for the whole island."

"Watch out, Toán!" yelled one of the men suddenly. "Don't move! Don't move!"

Toán remained still, his questioning eyes wide open. The man seized a small dry branch on the sand. He rushed towards Toán's feet and with the stick he picked up what looked like a supple vine about a metre long and threw it away from him. The strange black-and-white-striped creature hovered over a short distance before falling back onto the white sand.

"It's a snake!" yelled the men.

The reptile remained still for a moment on the beach, then it wriggled quickly back into the sea. The sun set slowly on the horizon. The men forgot the events of the day and were amazed and fascinated by the spectacle, a giant red and gold painting. It seemed to them that the sun had made a path of light on the ocean with its rays, as if inviting them to come and join it. The clouds were motionless but their hues changed rapidly from dark blue to the brightest violet colour, no doubt because of the angle of the setting sun on the flat surface of the water.

Cool air blew over the island. Minh had his feet in the water; it seemed colder than in the afternoon. Some of the men climbed up towards the grove of trees in the middle of the island where they had left their food.

A frightening spectacle greeted them: snakes, dozens of snakes, the same size as the one they had seen that afternoon, were slithering around lazily in the scrub under the trees and around the boxes of food. Some had even taken refuge in the clothes left on the ground! The men inspected the area rapidly. They were appalled to discover that more snakes, too many to count, were coming up out of the sea, as if they were coming home after a day in the water.

"I know these snakes," said one of the men. "I've already seen several like this, when we were loading the boats in Kunéo. They aren't dangerous, if we are careful not to get bitten between the fingers or toes. Their mouth is so tiny that they can't bite us anywhere else! I even saw one of the foremen walking around with a snake around his neck," he added.

"The only spot they haven't taken over is this patch of beach where we are now," Toán remarked anxiously.

Most of the men who were usually so brave, working deep inside tunnels, turned into frightened children in the face of these repulsive animals.

Minh himself was no more reassured than the others—far from it! So to try to gather his wits, he sat down for a moment on a black rock on the edge of the beach. When he felt something brushing his right hand on the rock, he turned around suddenly and what he saw completely unnerved him: a snake's head on the back of his hand! The reptile hesitated as if it were looking for its way or wondering what this warm soft matter was; with its five short, light-coloured tentacles it looked a lot like some new species of small snake!

To avoid showing his fear to his companions and frightening the dangerous animal, Minh clenched his jaw tightly as he slowly extracted his nervous hand. Then he got up quickly when he was out of the creature's range. His brow was sweating despite the cold wind blowing over the whole island. Moving backwards, Minh stared closely at "his" snake, but behind it and between the gaps in the rock he could see other shapes, other striped bodies clinging to the hot stone.

The bewildered men cleared a path through the snakes, throwing them as far away as possible to left and right using dry branches. Then they managed to remove their food from under the trees. They sat down on the small beach, the only place which was free of the creatures.

"We'll sleep here," they decided. The bravest returned to the centre of the island to get dry branches and dead trunks which had fallen to the ground. They took them back to the sandy beach and made a huge campfire. They ate quickly; some of them had suddenly lost their appetite, even though they hadn't eaten anything all day.

"We'll sit around the wood fire," said one of the men, reassured by the heat of the blazing fire.

"Yes, but there are more than a hundred of us! The beach will be too small for all of us," said another.

A third stood up, his eyes wild, and said, "I'm too scared . . . Please let me sleep near the fire!"

"Okay Hải," said Chín, "as you're the youngest, you can have your spot near the fire."

Night fell rapidly. About twenty men had taken refuge on branches in the trees, preferring to spend the night perched in this uncomfortable position above the knot of snakes crawling aimlessly about in the thick grass. The others, including Minh, went to sleep on the sand a few metres from the sea.

As agreed, young Hải was lying next to the fire, when suddenly, around midnight, near the still warm ashes, emerged a tiny black head, then the whole wriggling body of a striped snake. The creature approached the young man slowly and then came to take refuge against his abdomen. Hải couldn't sleep and he felt something strange and soft against his body straight away. He got up suddenly and, in the reddish light of the still-crackling wood fire, he recognised the repulsive animal. Terrified, he threw himself backwards with force, tripping and falling onto the bodies of his nearest neighbours. His cries woke everyone, and others realised that they too had served as a refuge for the reptiles.

"They're attracted to the heat of our bodies," said Minh, "and aren't afraid of hot ash."

"It's terrifying. There could've been an accident!" said Toán. "They're probably venomous."

"The water's so cold at night. No doubt that's why they come on to dry land," thought Minh, although he was not really sure.

The small community got themselves organised. To take up as little space as possible, some of the men slept curled up or seated on the sand. They formed teams, taking turns for the rest of the night to drive the undesirable invaders away. But in the dark the fight was unequal between man and the tiny black creature. Some of them managed to slip past the men who were standing high up on their legs. They got into the camp, climbing up tired limbs, and taking refuge next to soft warm bellies.

At the first light of dawn, all the prisoners were already up. Those who came down from the branches were stiff from spending most of the night on their uncomfortable perch, trying to keep their precarious balance.

"With daylight and the sun," said Chín, "the snakes will certainly go back to the sea."

"Alas, I don't think there'll be any sun today. Look at the grey sky," said Toán miserably. "It looks stormy."

Toán was right. There was a fine persistent drizzle for the next twenty-four hours. Keeping a constant watch out for the snakes and without anywhere to take shelter, they were soaked, freezing and exhausted. They felt as if they had already spent weeks, if not months, on this piece of land in the Pacific.

"Now I understand why they left us here. It's both punishment and revenge for our rebellious actions," said Chín, his face blue with cold.

"They abandoned us to the snakes' paradise, or rather, to man's 'hell'. Depends how you look at it," said Minh bitterly.

"These repulsive reptiles are everywhere! On the ground, on the sand, hidden in the gaps in the rocks, under the grass and in the water," muttered Toán, who appeared thin after so many harrowing hours. He was so upset that he did not even have the time or the inclination to suggest a game of cards.

By dawn on the third day they were all completely worn out. Their morale and determination were gradually fading. Their eyes were getting tired of looking out for snakes and peering at the sea. They couldn't wait to get back to the main island.

Some were so demoralised that they would have preferred prison, the whip, or kicks in the backside, to having to stay one more night in this godforsaken place. This tiny island would remain for ever in their memory as "the abominable snake island!"

Towards midday, their dull eyes, reddened from lack of sleep, made out the tugboat of deliverance. The barge reached the beach which was swarming with people. But the men remained motionless on the beach, seemingly indifferent, as if they didn't want to leave.

The government official, astonished, appeared on the bridge. He cupped his two hands in front of his mouth to make a kind of rudimentary megaphone, then shouted, "We've come to get you! We've had a response from the capital. You are free men. Do you hear! You are free!"

Chín turned towards the men his face shining. "Now you can give free rein to your joy, the joy of being fully-fledged men! And of being able to leave this inhospitable place!"

A general hurrah rose up from the island. These disciplined men had been dying to show their delight as soon as they saw the boat, but for tactical reasons and, to preserve their pride just in case the response was negative, they wanted to give the impression to the authorities that the sea snakes had not bothered them. They boarded the barge with obvious satisfaction.

"Now that victory is total, it's pointless to keep up this stupid game," thought Minh.

And turning towards the government official he said, "Monsieur, it was about time you came to fetch us."

"Monsieur, it's also about time that I take you back, your bosses want you back immediately," replied the man with a sincere smile.

The Last Incident

As their wages had increased, Minh and Lan were now able to live a little more comfortably and feed their growing child better.

The foremen were rather unnerved, as they now had to learn to treat their men with more consideration and couldn't raise their voices in the abusive way they were accustomed to. Their whips were a thing of the past, now banished for ever.

Amongst these men, Mainote was the most disappointed. Having lost most of the authority he had had until now, which had suited his belligerent nature, he moped around in his role as head foreman. For him the loss in status was a serious blow to his person and authority.

Minh and his compatriots often saw him in the throes of violent outbursts of anger which in earlier times he would have vented on the backs of his men or on the frail face of a woman. But with the new regulations, all he could do was gesture agitatedly as if strangling an invisible enemy. With his eyes twitching he stared at the sky, crying, "Oh, what terrible times we live in!" Both his memories of the past and his repressed violent urges troubled him deeply. Finally, unable to control himself any longer, he decided to ignore the rules. At the first opportunity, the smallest pretext, like a ferocious wild beast he would unleash his fury.

One evening Mainote was at the mine entrance, when the night shift team was finishing after eight hours of uninterrupted work inside the mountain. One of the men forgot to return his carbide lamp as he came out of the tunnel. Mainote, who had been watching for the perfect opportunity, immediately accused the forgetful man of stealing. Then, he walked over to the man threateningly and with his thick hand slapped the miner's face several times with uncalled-for force.

The poor worker reeled, his head ringing like a church bell at Easter. He didn't understand what had happened to him. However, his workmates had witnessed the scene and approached Mainote, forming a circle around him that got progressively smaller and more threatening. Mainote understood the danger and felt sure that the men who were staring at him in silence had decided to punish him. He suddenly realised that he had failed to move with the times, and he almost regretted his actions. Gripped by fear, he found the strength to push several workers roughly aside and rush quickly through a gap in the circle, running so fast he seemed to have shed his excess weight. But he had to turn back, as the path leading to the factory, then the village, then freedom, was blocked by men who were faster than him. Disoriented, no longer knowing what he was doing, he disappeared into the bushes.

"He likes to hit others so much, yet he's so afraid to get hit himself!" cried one of the men, hot on his heels.

Mainote was out of breath but thought he had found a way out when he spied a tall tree a few steps ahead of him. Without hesitating, as nimble as a cat, he climbed it and took refuge on one of the highest branches which could support his weight.

Close behind him, his pursuers remained on the ground and began throwing stones, aiming carefully. The projectiles hit Mainote's body with a dull sound, muffled by the excess fat. Despite the blows, Mainote clung to the branches as tightly as he could, all the while hoping his assailants would give up the chase. But they had finished work for the day and, relishing their revenge, waited patiently for their prey to come down. Even though he was tired, Mainote forced himself to keep his balance between Heaven and Earth. It was the first time in his life that he found himself perched at the top of a tree. Stones began to bombard his body viciously again. Some missed their targets and continued their trajectory, whistling loudly as they passed above his head. Suddenly one of them hit his forehead. The violent impact rattled him and clouded his vision; he saw stars dancing before his eyes and almost let go of the branch. Blood trickled down his left cheek, got in between his thick lips, then dripped down, staining his shirt red.

The workers considered that this corporal punishment was sufficient for the vile, cowardly head foreman and they stopped their barrage of stones. However, they stayed under the tree, determined to keep up their siege as long as necessary or at least until Mainote could take it no longer and would have to leave his perch. The men wanted to humiliate him and inflict the supreme insult—a kick in the backside!

"Look at this pathetic man, this torturer, this master of the whip and savage beatings!" cried one of the miners suddenly. "He hasn't suffered one hundredth of what he put us through and he's already terrified!"

Mainote was indeed trembling; his wild eyes were looking desperately for a way out, some providential help to free him from the dangerous horde. He said a prayer, surprising himself, and his prayer was answered. The manager, who was going up to the mine for his daily inspection noticed an unusual gathering outside the work site. Curiosity drove him to go and see what was happening, but he was shocked to discover the tricky situation his foreman was in. He had to use all his talents of diplomacy and persuasion to free the huge man from his unfortunate predicament.

When he was back on the ground, Mainote, bloody and pathetic, received several kicks in the backside. However, he seemed unaware of the affront; he was too happy to be back on solid ground. Then, embarrassed and awkward in front of his manager, he offered him profuse apologies and explanations. Forgetting all his problems and the punishment he had just received, he hastened to thank his saviour with gusto, covering him in high praise.

That was the last noteworthy incident for the men at Pimboé mine.

Free Men

The new regulations allowed former workers to move around the whole colony as they wished and to change employers if they wanted to. Some families came to live in Pimboé, while others wanted to put a good distance between themselves and those who had caused them so much suffering.

Phúc and Liên wanted to try their luck in the capital, as Phúc wanted to start working in a restaurant.

Minh and Lan hesitated, wondering if such an upheaval was really necessary. Wasn't it more sensible to stay here in the camp while waiting for the day to return home which couldn't be far off?

Rumours circulated in the village announcing that the terrible world war had at last come to an end. This news could only be true as young Hồng no longer saw the American planes flying high in the sky as they returned from their war missions above the Coral Sea. Hồng used to be in awe of them, unable to comprehend that men could be inside these tiny flying machines, high above the clouds. Several times, the child had climbed a hill and tried to catch them with a long stick!

***

At the beginning of 1946 Toán visited Minh's family. Afterwards he wrote to them several times asking them to come and live in Tenep. The village was nestled in a valley and it would be much nicer for Hồng, he claimed, to be able to run around in a bigger space without worrying about falling down dangerous mountain slopes, which could happen in Pimboé.

But what really incited Minh and Lan to leave was when Toán told them that his employers were prepared to hire him at the electricity plant at a higher rate of pay.

So they left "their" mine with some nostalgia as they had spent more than six years of their lives at the top of the mountain. Hồng was not at all perturbed at leaving the village of his birth as he was still too young to understand; he was enthralled at the idea of riding in a car.

"I'm going to ride in a car!" he said proudly to anyone prepared to listen.

Once they were in Tenep, Minh bought his wife enough cooking utensils to lighten her workload and equip their new house. Then he bought a secondhand bicycle for himself. Every day after work he put Hồng on the pillion seat and took him for a ride. The child spent some exhilarating moments with his father.

When Minh was at work in the afternoon Toán would look after Hồng and they would ride together along the winding road. The sun disappeared behind the tall mountains and the cool evening wind caressed their faces. They were truly happy.

Lan didn't work outside the house anymore. She had learnt to knit from one of her new neighbours and had set herself up making all sorts of pullovers, which helped bring more money into the little family.

Hồng adored his parents and appreciated the company of Uncle Toán, as he called him. But after so much use the bicycle tyres eventually wore down. In these postwar times it was impossible to find any in the only shop in the village, so they had to leave the bicycle in a corner of the house, to everyone's disappointment.

Minh, fortunately, found a solution to this difficult problem. From the company he bought a length of strong black rubber hosepipe which was reinforced inside with several layers of canvas. As the external diameter of the pipe was the same as the original tyres, nothing could stop Minh's inventive mind. So he cut two sections, fitted them carefully onto the bare rims and then tied the ends of each tube with a thick wire. When it was finished, Minh observed his work, not without a little pride. He said to Lan, "It's so simple and yet no one thought of doing it before me!" Then, putting the modified wheels back on the bicycle, he added, "And this way you don't need inner tubes!"

Minh got on his bike to prove how "resistant" his tyres were. Clearly satisfied, he got his son to join him on the first test ride. The bike went along normally. Upon leaving the village, Minh took a steep path that he knew well, but it was strewn with small black stones, as round as tiny beads. Minh suddenly realised that his smooth tyres would not be able to grip the slippery ground. He lost control of his bike, which, with the weight of its passengers, skidded over a few metres before ending up in a deep ditch. Father and son ended up lying one on top of the other on the red dirt, which was also covered with sharp stones. After some amazing aerial acrobatics, the bike landed on top of their bruised bodies.

From this memorable date on, Minh didn't want to hear another word about his invention and young Hồng had contracted a mortal fear of all the bicycles in the world.

***

In his new life at the new mine, Minh felt completely at ease. As he had never known the foremen or the bosses from the terrible times of contract work, he now worked with them without any feelings of bitterness or frustration.

During his time off, he made his famous wooden clogs which were popular as they were solid and finely crafted. But he was not content with this success alone, and set about with just as much gusto making, first, frying pans, then antimosquito pumps which were a rudimentary sort of insecticide spray. As a result, soldering and cutting metal sheets held no secrets for him.

The community was extraordinarily well organised. Some set themselves up weaving mats, while others patiently made large conical hats as good as any you could buy in Tonkin. Baskets with finely woven bamboo strips, very practical for the Indochinese housewife, appeared in large quantities.

But the hope of returning home any time soon gradually faded as news reached the mine that the Indochinese war was becoming more and more violent and bloody.

During this time, the children grew as quickly as the passing of the seasons. Hồng was almost seven. The community had to organise lessons in the Annamite language, which had become a pressing need for the children's education. One of the men chosen amongst the most "literate," or rather amongst those who knew how to read and write fluently, was put in charge of their education.

But Lan didn't want her son to go to class the first day. She wanted to consult the local wise man, who would make the decision about the best date for his first lesson. She had her beliefs and principles, and nothing would convince her to let her little Hồng venture out into the world without all the guarantees for success.

The wise man was very young, forty at the most. He had a crew cut and his eyes were hidden behind a pair of round glasses pressed to his angular face, which gave him a mysterious impenetrable air. Khuy, that was his name, asked a lot of questions about the young boy, then consulted a large book written in ancient characters. After some serious thought he said, "According to what is written in my book, Hồng must go to school next Tuesday. That's the best day. He'll have luck on his side that day!"

Lan followed Khuy's advice closely, to her son's great disappointment, as he just wanted to be the same as all of his friends. It was only a week after the beginning of class that the excited young boy was allowed to go to school at last. However, at the first break he wanted to go home. "I've finished my lesson, sir!" he said to the teacher, "I want to go home now!" The teacher had to use all his powers of persuasion and a great deal of patience to keep him there. It was a problem the wise man had not foreseen.

Hồng gradually got used to school and enjoyed the company of his school friends; he finally grew to love school and made quick progress, to the satisfaction of his parents and his teacher. However, the teacher had a unique approach: the children had one hour in the afternoon to learn their daily lesson by heart. It was always the best part of the day for them as they could recite their lesson aloud, at the tops of their voices, or, even better, they could shout as loudly as they liked for an hour. Which they did very willingly. Hồng's school was undoubtedly the noisiest in the world!

It was also at this time that Hồng discovered the good things in life. Uncle Toán had promised to take him the following Sunday to the horse races in Koumac. All week Hồng spoke about it excitedly to his schoolmates, and so the whole village knew about his upcoming excursion.

The big day finally arrived. The boy was quivering with impatience. He would have liked to be in the car already, on the gravelly road, kicking up clouds of dust. He had an indelible memory of his first trip in a truck when they had moved from Pimboé to come and live in Tenep. Since then, the car was for him one of the most wonderful things in existence!

The time came to get ready. His mother had made him a blue shirt and fresh white shorts. And to top it all off, she had bought him a beautiful pair of black shoes, so shiny that they reflected the light of day. Hồng looked at each shoe happily, then hugged them to his chest, stroking them as if they were two good little kittens. He admired them so much that he didn't dare wear them, for fear of spoiling them or dirtying them. It was certainly the best present he had ever received.

Uncle Toán said to him, "Hurry up. Put your shoes on!" He urged him on, saying "Look at me! I'm ready and I'm waiting for you."

The boy had to resign himself to putting the shoes on his feet. A few minutes later, while Toán was chatting calmly with his parents, Hồng stood up and shouted, "I'm ready too, Uncle Toán!"

But suddenly the sweet smile on his face disappeared, giving way to bewilderment and dismay. His whole body was pulled to the ground.

"Your new clothes!" cried Lan in distress, picking Hồng up quickly. "What's the matter?" she asked him anxiously.

"I don't know! I can't stand in the shoes," he complained, his eyes filled with disappointment.

"It doesn't matter," said Minh looking at the shoes. Then he added, "Hồng has put the shoes on back to front and, as he's not used to wearing them, he fell over like a small tree that's been uprooted."

Indeed, the young boy had never worn a single pair of shoes before; he was used to running around barefoot by day, and by night he wore only the clogs his father made for him.

But the incident was soon forgotten and Uncle Toán and Hồng left for Koumac a moment later. What with the brand new clothes, the shoes and now the taxi, it really was a wonderful day for the little boy. The panting horses that he saw at the races seemed to his overawed eyes like the most handsome thoroughbreds in the world.

Mysticism

"Oh, your lemonade is delicious, Mama! And so fresh! But what's this transparent thing you've put in my glass? It's funny, it burns my tongue and hurts my teeth," said Hồng, grimacing.

"Don't worry, my boy, it's ice. It's just frozen water, that's all," Lan smiled.

Toán appeared at that moment. He was holding a letter and his face was deathly pale.

"My brother," he cried, "what a bastard! I don't know what's stopping me going to beat him up."

"Calm down, Toán, don't get too worked up," said Lan, adding, "have a glass of this lemonade I've just made. It'll calm you down. And then you can tell me what's happened."

While she was speaking, she had filled a glass. She held it out to Toán, who accepted the timely drink eagerly, as his throat was dry from his furious anger.

"Oh, you spare yourselves nothing in this house!" he exclaimed after the first mouthful, "Ice, if you please!"

"It's excellent to cool down," Lan said.

"Where did you find it? The ice, I mean," asked Toán curiously. "Did you buy a machine to make it?"

"Oh no," said Lan, "You know we could never afford such a luxury. The truth's much simpler."

"There's not a lot around," continued Toán.

"Yes, there is! Well, as you want to know everything, I'll tell you, but don't be shocked if I tell you the honest truth."

Lan hastened to add, "In any case, as ice melts, it cleans itself, and gets rid of any dust which might stick to it!"

"?"

"Ten minutes ago, I was coming back from the shop where I'd gone to buy food. I was walking past the canteen for single Europeans when I saw a block of ice melting in the sun on the pavement, quite far from the gutter," confessed Lan, a little embarrassed. "The cook had probably thrown out the surplus from his ice box."

Hesitating a few seconds, Lan continued, "I wanted to let Hồng taste it. So I picked it up, and I don't regret it, as it meant I could also enjoy a nice glass of iced water."

She suddenly remembered Pimboé and said, "When I worked for Madame Lucas, I often used to make ice for her, but I never had the chance to have any . . . Now I have," she added with a smile.

"Thank you for the lemonade, Lan. It was very refreshing. It calmed me down!" said Toán. Then without waiting any longer, he launched into an animated explanation, "You see, Lan, I've just received a letter from home."

"Another letter!" interrupted Lan, astonished, "You're really lucky! Minh and I have been trying for months to contact our parents. But alas, without success. It's hopeless."

"I'd prefer to be in your shoes, and not receive the sort of news I've just had," Toán said grimly.

"!"

"Can you imagine, Lan! He dared to do this to me!"

"Who?"

"My brother! I mean this idiot called Thuý who used to be my brother!"

"Is he. . . ?"

"Oh no! He's not dead, the bastard, he's just as alive as you and I!"

Toán was silent for a moment, thinking, and then continued, "Do you remember all the letters I received from him? Each time, he told me that my wife and children were in good health and that if she'd never written to me it was simply because she was very busy with work and the children!"

Toán stopped again, then continued his story gruffly. "Thuý told me that because of the war, and because she hadn't received any news from me for years, my wife had to work hard from morning to evening. So, she'd asked him, the oldest in the family, to keep up the correspondence with me! That seemed logical to me, especially as my wife doesn't know how to write very well. Writing has always been torture for her, and the oldest brother is always the head of the clan. What could be more natural?"

Toán was getting more worked up. "So I was quick to send them money, which I did through Thuý. It was money I'd saved from working, and also from gambling. A fortune! Thuý wrote to tell me that my wife didn't have to work anymore and that all this money had allowed her to buy some land and that he, Thuý, was in charge of overseeing the building of our house. A big house with a red-tiled roof. While they were waiting for me to return. Recently, in reply to one of my letters, he told me the house was almost finished. He just needed a little more money for the fittings. But he especially wanted to tell me some good news: my oldest son had just passed his first exam. A primary school certificate, I think. I was overjoyed!"

He looked upset as he said, "Do you understand Lan? My son had just turned fifteen and from that moment on I just had one wish and that was to be able to go home as quickly as possible. Not to waste any more time and the rest of my youth here. I'm well into my forties. It's time for me to go back to my children before they all leave home."

He gazed at Lan and then said, "I've never spoken about all this before, to you or to Minh, because, despite all your efforts you never managed to get into contact with your parents. So I would've felt a little guilty if each time I received a letter I spoke about all my news from home. Especially as the news was always so good. That's why I always just said that all was well without going into any details. I don't regret it," he said hoarsely. Toán couldn't continue. He looked for a bench and sat down, his face dark. He was completely dejected.

"What happened? Have you had bad news Toán?" asked Lan, sitting down on the other bench opposite Toán.

"Yes, very sad news," murmured Toán, staring at the ground. "My wife and children have been dead for a long time, for a few years. During the great famine there were thousands of deaths. My whole family was carried off by a terrible disease that was raging because of this catastrophe, cholera! I'm told that there were so many victims that the living didn't even have the strength to bury the dead!"

"Who told you?" asked Lan, in shock.

"My aunt. She'd asked Thuý for my address several times, but of course, he never wanted to give it to her. My aunt told me in this letter that I'm holding that she was scandalised by Thuý's despicable attitude and behaviour! Thanks to her cunning and her patience she was finally able to find out my address. She wrote to me straight away. There you have it!" said Toán, completely devastated.

Lan too was stunned by this dreadful revelation. She remained silent, not knowing what to say.

Toán was still, his head lowered, and his back was stooped like an old sick man who had difficulty bearing the weight of his years. From this moment on, his life changed completely. However, Lan and Minh remained his most faithful friends and he continued to be the best of uncles for young Hồng. But cards were banished for ever. His free time was devoted to prayer and meditation. The priest came once a month to say Mass in the little chapel in the village. Toán waited for this moment impatiently as prayer and Mass were what now nourished his life!

The French School

Minh and Lan were sitting next to each other on the big wooden square bed at the end of the room. It was their living area where Minh liked to receive his friends and chat, sitting with his legs crossed on the polished wooden surface.

"Finally, we can breathe," sighed Lan looking tenderly at her husband. "That nauseating odour has finally disappeared! It lingered all day."

"It's Chung again with his barrels of pickled fish that cause these foul emanations stinking out the whole valley," protested Minh. "I wonder if it's just fish inside—it's really vile!"

"What are you insinuating?" asked Lan smiling.

"I'm not insinuating anything, I wonder if his product is really made according to the rules, even though he dares to call it Nước Mắm!"

"It's really good though," said Lan, her mouth watering.

"He keeps his secret well and everyone in the village is asking questions!" continued Minh.

"Be happy, my dear, that there are at least one or two people who take on this task for the pleasure of our table. I must admit we do need this sauce! However, you have to have an iron stomach just to lift the cover of the barrels for the final preparation," added Lan grimacing.

"That mustn't worry Chung overly!" continued Minh. "To fertilise his garden he doesn't baulk at using human excrement!"

"I remember the days, not so long ago, when he walked past our house carrying a jerrycan filled with foul-smelling matter he collected from people's houses," said Lan adding, "fortunately the health service now prohibits the use of this waste."

"That doesn't stop him pouring urine into barrels on the sly, which he then dilutes to water his vegetables," retorted Minh.

"I think we should change the subject, otherwise we might turn into real gossips," said Lan smiling.

"You're right, Lan, I let myself get carried away, drawn into pointless concerns. No doubt the smell of Nước Mắm has something to do with it!"

They laughed as they looked at each other.

"In that case, from now on we'll buy our Nước Mắm from Kính. He lives a little farther away at the other end of the village, but he's ingenious too. He's bound to succeed in life!"

"I agree. Luckily, Hồng is with his uncle Toán," remarked Lan. "Otherwise what would he have thought of our conversation!"

Minh's face suddenly looked serious. "I've been thinking about our son," he said, frowning. "We have to find a solution for him. Hồng's eleven now, I spoke to his teacher this morning and he told me that Hồng won't be able to progress any further at his school!"

"!"

"He knows a lot now . . . as much as his teacher," he said. "He'd be wasting his time if we leave him there."

"The teacher's conscientious, but he doesn't have enough training or a high enough level of education," agreed Lan, nodding.

"We can't blame him. Like us, he came here to work, and we nominated him to be the teacher even though he didn't have the qualifications . . . it's nobody's fault," sighed Minh. "It's just the circumstances of life."

"Maybe we could put Hồng in the French school in the village centre," said Lan her face lighting up at this new idea.

"Yes, you're right!" cried Minh. "Let's put him with the French! That way he'll learn several languages. That's a good thing!"

"Yes, but there's a serious problem," said Lan pensively. "Hồng's already eleven, and he can only speak our language. That'll be a big handicap for him."

"We don't have the choice. He can't stay here rehashing what he already knows!"

Then, nodding his head resolutely, he said, "Tomorrow I'll go to see the mine director to get a place in the school for Hồng."

"We should think about it . . . not rush into it. . ." ventured Lan.

"It's decided," said Minh, with authority. "He'll go to the French school!"

He added, smiling, "Actually, you're the one who had this idea, Lan. And it's an excellent one!"

So, a few days later, Hồng found himself in a comfortable classroom with a nice, friendly teacher, which reassured him straight away. But he soon had a problem when he started chatting in Tonkinese with his new classmates. He was automatically placed in the first-year level until he could learn the rudiments he needed to understand the new language. The first day when he went home, he rushed up to his father saying, "Papa, I have a nickname."

"?"

"They gave me a name!" repeated Hồng, with pride.

"So what do they call you?"

"They don't call me Hồng, maybe it's too complicated for them," he said pensively. "They call me. . . . Let me remember—yes, that's it! They call me Chink. Is that good Papa?"

Minh almost fell over backwards. "No. Tell them your name is Hồng, that's all! Don't answer ever again when they use the other name!"

"!"

"I'll explain later. . . . Okay?"

"Yes, Papa, I'll do what you say."

Several weeks had passed. Hồng made commendable progress, but not as rapidly as Madame Rolland seemed to think. Indeed, for the school's big annual fête the teacher selected some of her students to act in a sketch. Hồng was chosen to play the role of a gendarme and Bernard, his classmate, the second gendarme.

The rehearsal began. The accused, a little girl with short red hair, was brought before the two young policemen, and a boy, his face serious, imitating a judge perfectly, stood in front of the group. At a given moment, on the order of the young judge, Hồng and his friend had to grab the thief and take her to prison. The scene played out normally. Hồng remained impassive and vacant as one would expect from a policeman in the circumstances, when the judge called out, "Gendarmes, take this woman back to prison!"

Bernard grabbed the young girl and dragged her to the other end of the classroom. As for Hồng, who had actually not understood a thing in this play of words and fine phrases, seeing Bernard leave with the prisoner, he pounced on the judge and led him off in the same direction! There was a boisterous commotion in the classroom, then loud laughter from all sides. The teacher, shaking her head in desperation, had to ask Hồng to return to his seat.

Madame Rolland was amazed that, after several months of lessons, the boy could already understand and express himself with astonishing ease. "Children have an extraordinary ability to remember things," the teacher sometimes said to herself in wonder.

Hồng obtained his Certificate of Primary Studies after three years at the school. He had just turned fourteen. After this, Minh and Lan thought about leaving the mine for good to go and live in the capital. Hồng was very upset at the thought of leaving all his friends. His favourites were Bernard and Robert, two little French boys, Zowi, a native child, and Vinh and Nghĩa, his young compatriots. He loved them so much! Social barriers and racial problems didn't exist between these children who were happy to live on the prosperous island which had now become a French territory in the Pacific. The former term "colony" was banished for ever; it no longer had its place in the modern world.

After the fall of Điện-Biên-Phủ and the departure of the French from the former Indochina, Minh and Lan, like all their compatriots, were considered to be fully-fledged Vietnamese. The names "Tonkinese" and "Indochinese" were now relegated to a bygone age. These "new" Vietnamese voluntarily chose not to tell their children about the events of a past that was both difficult and miserable. Never would they speak about these harsh times and the days of suffering, to avoid sowing hatred and resentment in the innocent hearts of their children.

From this time on, under the bright skies of Grande Terre, also known as "The Isle of Light," people of all religions, races and backgrounds, came together from all parts of the world to build a better future for themselves.

In the same way that the sun is radiant again after dark stormy days, New Caledonia turned resolutely toward the path of progress and brotherhood.

Prosperity

Minh and Hồng had just reinforced the shutters and barricaded the gaps in the doors and windows of their shop, but this did not stop the wind forcing water through the cracks.

It was almost midnight. Minh could do nothing but wait and hope that the building would resist the raging elements and that the corrugated iron roof would not fly off with the next gusts of wind.

"That'd be a catastrophe!" he thought, sitting in silence on a chair in the dining room while Lan was mopping the floor.

Hồng had withdrawn into his bedroom which had been transformed into a workshop where he studied as well as slept. He had turned into a tall strong young man. In his free time, he helped his parents in the shop and the rest of his time he devoted to his passion: radios. With the help of lessons and books he entered the mysterious world of electronics. He loved tinkering with the bizarre circuits that Minh and Lan found far too complicated when they came to see his experiments.

On this stormy night Hồng was sitting at his workbench, but his mind wandered as he recalled his two years studying at the technical college in the capital. Although he recognised that the level of education was high, none of the subjects on offer had appealed to his deepest aspirations. So, with the permission of his parents, he enrolled in an electronics school by correspondence. He was working that evening on a particularly difficult problem. Outside, the moon, the stars and the mild sky had disappeared, and gloomy black clouds were unleashing torrential rain over the town. The wind was now blowing twice as hard. However, Hồng smiled as he remembered a conversation between Hược, his classmate and a cantankerous teacher.

"What nationality are you?" the teacher had asked Hược out of the blue.

"Umm. I'm Caledonian!" replied Hược, surprised.

"Why are you Caledonian?" asked the man mockingly.

"Well, because I was born in New Caledonia, sir."

"So, if you'd been born in an aeroplane, you'd be an aviator?"

The terrifying wind was howling, tearing off branches, uprooting trees and damaging the roofs of the houses. Panic-stricken, Minh and Lan contemplated their fortune, contained in all the merchandise on the shelves.

"This must be the most frightening cyclone we've ever experienced!" murmured Lan.

"It's normal that this one seems bigger than all the others as we didn't have much to lose before. It's different now," sighed Minh. Frowning, he looked around the shop. "Four years of hard work without a single day's rest."

Then Minh cocked his ear. He thought he could hear the roar of the ocean. The sea, normally so calm, had turned furious and threatening. Its huge waves broke, with an alarming rumbling, on the port some hundred metres away. The small boats were torn from their moorings and thrown onto the shore like wisps of straw.

In the pitch-black sky, the electric wires swayed and banged furiously together causing blinding sparks. One of the cables, still live, had been torn from the pylon and was lying dangerously close to Minh's house.

From time to time, Minh went to the window and through the gaps in the blinds he glanced anxiously outside. In dismay he looked at his car. It was a comfortable Citroën 11 CV that he had bought second-hand over two years before, but as there was no garage, he had had to leave it on the side of the road.

Despite the fear she felt at the possible catastrophe about to take place, Lan remained stoic to avoid upsetting her husband even more.

Hồng was unable to concentrate on his work on such a night and had joined his parents. At about three in the morning the wind and rain suddenly ceased. An eerie calm settled over the town.

"We're in the heart of the cyclone," said Minh. "Now we can expect the worst."

"I hope Liên and Phúc haven't had any damage either," murmured Lan anxiously.

"I'll go and see them," said Hồng.

"No, Hồng, it's still too dangerous to go outside. The wind could come back at any moment," said Minh, then added, "Anyway, their house is much more solid than ours."

Minh was not wrong. Suddenly the wind changed direction and blasted fiercely over their part of the island. The radio antennae were torn from their bases. With his eyes glued to the window Hồng witnessed the terrifying spectacle of neighbouring roofs flying up into the air. One of them even landed on a terrace fifty metres away.

"It's horrific!" said Lan looking tensely up at the ceiling. "The wooden frame is taking a beating. I can hear it cracking at all the joints."

"But I think we're out of danger," said Minh who was feeling a little more confident. "The wind's now coming from the west and we're protected by the building opposite us which is blocking it."

"The car's completely unprotected!" said Hồng who was watching helplessly, petrified by the spectacle in front of his eyes.

The branches of the hundred-year-old trees swayed in all directions before breaking off the trunks with a sinister crackling sound. Some of the coconut palms, formerly so tall and proud, collapsed and tumbled to the ground with a terrible crash.

"The car!" cried Hồng suddenly.

As quick as a flash Minh ran to the shutters, just in time to see an enormous branch fall from nowhere on to the ground a few centimetres from the car. Minh wiped his brow. "With the next branch we may not have a car anymore," he growled, disheartened.

But things calmed down soon afterwards, and by dawn the cyclone had disappeared out to sea leaving behind it a scene of desolation.

Minh and Hồng were finally able to go outside to inspect the house.

"We can consider ourselves lucky," said Hồng looking at the dismal scene around them.

"Even so, we still need to make the roof stronger," murmured Minh. "I'll ask the landlord as soon as possible."

While Lan and Hồng were sponging up the water from the flooded floor, Phúc appeared at the door. "Nothing serious, my friends? Nothing broken?"

"No, we've survived the horrific night," said Minh visibly relieved. Then he asked, "What about you? Any damage?"

"No. Everything held up well! The house is solid! The landlord had it fixed just two months ago."

Phúc had put on weight and his hair was going grey, but he was livelier than ever. The success of his restaurant with its picturesque sign *Café Thé La Soupe* attracted even more clients. Liên spent most of her day in front of the enormous cooking pots where delicious dishes simmered, each more enticing than the last.

Suddenly Toán burst into the shop. His lips were reciting a silent prayer, while his mournful lifeless eyes seemed to be lost in intense internal contemplation.

"I see all's well," he said finally. "I'm happy for you and also for you Phúc. . . I've just met Liên in front of the restaurant."

Then he added, "I went to morning Mass and now I've come to visit you. What a night it was!"

The desire to go to church every day, and also to see his friends and Hồng again, had finally forced Toán to abandon his mining village. He had been living in Nouméa for a year and he already had one of the best vegetable gardens in the town.

"My dear friends, although I'd love to stay, duty calls," said Phúc, standing up after drinking a big bowl of hot tea. Then, turning towards Minh he said, "Don't forget the meeting this evening Minh!"

"Oh no, don't worry Phúc, it's much too important to forget!"

The Call of the Native Land

Assembled at the back of the shop were about ten men, each representing a different locality. Lan had come to observe the proceedings and was standing to one side. For the sake of courtesy she went up to Madame Bát, the owner, who, busy cooking, was not very talkative. With her eternal black velvet scarf on her head, she was working, even though it was ten o'clock in the evening. Madame Bát, as usual, simply gave an unintelligible answer, or a quick nod, to any question, which rapidly became a tedious and disheartening monologue. No exception was made for Lan.

"This woman's a real machine, working from dawn until late at night," she said to herself. She felt sorry for Madame Bát. "Is she capable of any independent thought or interesting conversation? Or is she just a work animal, good only for labour and obeying her husband's orders?"

Lan thought about it for a moment and then observed her closely.

"This is exactly the sort of wife Minh's father would have wanted for his son. A woman with no soul or character."

Lan began to imagine how Minh had fled Hà-Nội, abandoning his family and his country to escape from that fate. She suddenly remembered that her father-in-law, whom she had never met, had been desperately ill after his son left. She glanced over at Minh, who was sitting at a corner of the table chatting like a brother with Monsieur Bát. Monsieur Bát suddenly stood up and started speaking.

"Dear friends. I'll ask for few more minutes of patience. Phúc has let me know that he has many customers this evening, but he's doing everything possible to get here as soon as he can. There's hot tea in the tea pot, help yourselves while we're waiting," he added.

"Even so, I don't think Minh regrets leaving like that," pursued Lan. "As for me, despite the difficult times over the years, I don't regret coming here. Minh is the best of men and we still love each other like on those very first days."

Phúc and Liên appeared in the room at that moment.

"Please excuse me, my friends," said Phúc, glancing around. Liên had joined the two women in the kitchen. She had put on weight; it suited her as did her peaceful life. Liên, who had never been very pretty, had now become a very attractive woman.

After a polite banal conversation with Madame Bát who continued all the while to scrape her pots vigorously, the two friends joined the men assembled there. Their faces were grave as they started to debate a problem which was particularly close to their hearts.

"I came because I heard you were here," Lan whispered into her friend's ear.

"My dear friends," began Bát, who was sitting at the end of the table near the kitchen door.

Lan was leaning against the wall opposite him. From this position she could see Madame Bát now busy furiously scrubbing the side of a huge pot.

"We're gathered together this evening for the second time. I can tell you that, in the meantime, we've been able to contact our comrades in the other centres on the island. Their replies, which we received this week, show us that they're with us. They're impatient for us to prepare the petitions, which they'll sign immediately!

"It's already 1958, that is, more than nineteen years since we left our country and our families. Those who came before us have now been here for over twenty-five years!

"We're getting older, alas! We're now all over forty, apart from a few exceptions of course—those who managed to falsify their birth date to get hired! During this time, our children have grown up. Some are already eighteen, some even older. So, it's now time to think about going home. And this time, they can't find a pretext to keep us here any longer, as the Second World War and the Indochinese War have been over for some years now.

"Obviously, our country is now divided in half. It's regrettable, but what can we do about it? We come from North Vietnam, and that's where we'll demand to be sent. We all know that life there will be very different from the way it was before. We're well aware of that, but I don't think that the change will affect our determination to return home at all! This is how we can demonstrate our willingness to participate as soon as possible in the reconstruction of our beloved country."

Then Bát continued, "We all have the right to free repatriation. This country owes us the return trip, that's undeniable! Our country has gained independence, so we must demand our rights and insist that we be repatriated as soon as possible."

Bát sat down. Phúc then addressed the meeting:

"After so many years away we all want to see our native land again, and live there the rest of our days so that when our final hour comes, our bodies can come to rest in the land of our ancestors!"

Phúc was silent, overwhelmed by his own declaration. When he had calmed down, he continued, "We want to go back to the land where we were born and be reunited with our parents and our families. What could be more natural?"

Phúc stopped again. He looked around at the men who were silent, their eyelids half-closed, staring into space.

"Through hard work and perseverance, we've succeeded in many domains: commerce, building and trades . . . some of us are tailors, some hairdressers. As for our vegetable gardens, they're admired by all the market gardeners. Our young people have become mechanics and electricians and are valued employees. Even though we've been successful here, we want to go home; in our hearts the call of the native country is as strong as ever."

Quát, a tall slim man, then took his turn addressing the assembly:

"I'm the father of a big family," he began. "I approve this action totally and I'd like to explain my own story. I arrived on this island well before most of you. I now have grown-up children; my oldest son is already the father of a young girl and my fourteen-year-old daughter is also married. My two other boys are aged seventeen and eighteen and, well . . . can you believe it? These rascals still refuse to get married! Despite threats from me and my wife, despite our constant lecturing and insisting that the child should obey and respect his parents, it's no use!"

The man's face darkened. He continued disconsolately, "All they have to do is say, 'Yes, father, I want to get married'. We'll organise everything. We'll find a hardworking, healthy young girl from a suitable family. My sons won't even need to look for their future wife! I really don't understand young people today. If my parents had ever given me such an opportunity I would have answered a thousand times 'Yes, father, yes, mother, I want to get married!' But these two imbeciles say they're still too young, and that they have plenty of time to think about having a family!" said the poor father, getting a little worked up.

He remained pensive for a moment and then asked, "Is it their Western education which leads them astray?" He added, "Alas, I'm afraid that's it. Everything we've taught them, all our customs will soon be called into question! I feel very strongly about this."

Lan followed what Quát was saying with particular attention."Until now, we've managed, more or less, to hold on to them, to get them to observe and respect our age-old principles. We've even managed to marry them within our community. That's important, as that's how we'll avoid problems getting them to come back home with us."

Raising his arms to the sky, he suddenly cried, "But woe to us parents, if we wait a few years more, we'll lose them! For the day will come when we can no longer stop them from marrying a girl or a boy outside of our community! If that happens these children won't want to follow us and we'll be torn apart; the unbearable separations will see the father in one country and his child in another. We have to act quickly and demand to be repatriated," concluded Quát. "It's in the interest of the whole community."

The audience were convinced by Quát's argument and nodded approvingly. They immediately set about writing the petition they would send to the authorities.

"Obviously those who wish to stay on the island will be completely free to do so," Bát stated.

Lan, standing silent next to Liên, was thinking about her son Hồng, who, according to tradition should already have been married for two years, so that his wife could help Lan with all her work in the shop and at home, and especially so that she could produce a new generation. But Hồng, who had very firm ideas on the subject, had always managed to convince his parents to give him a few more years of freedom.

"I'll get married when I'm twenty," he promised.

In these tricky situations Minh remembered clearly the painful problems he had had with his own parents, which had forced him to flee in desperation to this far-flung island! He had always wanted to give Hồng a degree of freedom, as the image of his father suffering and ill after he had fled, had never left him-pursuing and tormenting him for nearly twenty years. He didn't want the same misfortune to occur again.

Liên was helping the men in the feverish search for the appropriate terms and the precise reasons to give their demands the best chance of success.

"Hồng's an only child and is very lucky to have such an understanding father," murmured Lan. She was happy for her grown-up boy, content to see him live free and without a care. Still leaning against the wall, Lan turned her head to the left. At that moment her eyes met those of a very young woman who was standing behind the glass counter of the shop. The young woman looked naive and downtrodden. She was holding a newborn in her tiny arms, while, at the same time, attending to the few remaining customers at this late hour of the evening. Another child, aged about a year and a half, was pressing up between her legs, running her dirty little hands over the glass which was already smeared with saliva.

Lan felt sorry for her, "If you didn't know her, you'd think she was a young girl looking after her little sisters!"

But Lan knew this young mother's story. She remembered two years earlier when Tý, who had just turned fourteen, was called one evening before her parents, Monsieur and Madame Bát.

"My daughter, this is Madame Ánh," her father said.

Tý knew this woman and observed her with some distrust.

"She's a meddling gossip," she said to herself, "the kind of woman who wants to put her nose into everyone's business."

Tý didn't like Madame Ánh's malicious eyes, nor her hypocritical smile. Her thick lips, ravaged by lime and betel which she chewed all day, scared the young girl even more.

"And here's Đức who's come to visit us and . . . to meet you."

The young fourteen-year-old girl pricked up her ears; she was afraid: an obscure inexplicable fear, like when she was alone and awake in the dark of night.

Tý glanced rapidly at the stranger, then lowered her head immediately, expecting the worst. She had had the time to realise that the man opposite her was as old as her father! And his hair thickly coated in brilliantine shone unnaturally in the harsh light of the electric light bulb. To the young girl it looked as if this frightening individual was wearing a jacket on his frail shoulders for the first time in his life. Under this jacket he wore a grubby white shirt with sleeves that were too long for him and almost covered his fingers with their dirty, unkempt nails.

"He looks like a man disguised for a fancy-dress party, like the Europeans sometimes do," thought Tý, not daring to burst out laughing, although she felt like it.

Bát spoke solemnly, "My dear girl, you're grown up now. I know you're a good girl who always obeys her parents' orders."

"What do they want from me?" Tý wondered, staring at the ground with irritation. She felt embarrassed by these unusual compliments.

She heard her father's gushing voice again. "I'm sure you'll continue to listen to the advice of your father who has nothing but your welfare at heart!" Bát stopped for a moment, looked over first at Đức, then at Madame Ánh, then, observing his daughter he continued.

"Madame Ánh is the intermediary for our dear Đức. She's come to ask for your hand in marriage on behalf of this . . . young man."

Tý lifted her head briefly, her eyes blank, as if she had just woken from a bad dream. Then she looked in panic over at her mother who remained impassive as she continued to knit a jumper for her shop. Big tears rolled down the child's cheeks.

"Father, mother, I'm still too young. I only turned fourteen two weeks ago!"

His face tense and furious at this answer, Bát said cuttingly, "Where we come from girls can marry at thirteen!"

Then, turning towards the visitors he reassured them with a stupid smile, "Don't worry. My daughter's a little tired tonight but everything will be fine. You don't need to worry about it . . . Come back and see us in two weeks as we arranged."

After interminable polite exchanges, where they all wanted to appear as friendly as each other, the odd couple finally left.

Alone with her parents, the young girl begged them again, "Father, mother, have pity on your child . . . on your daughter who has always obeyed you without ever daring to protest or refuse an order, but this time, I appeal to your goodness. Please let me continue to live with you. I'm only a child . . . I still need you. Give me a year or two longer to live with my family, and then I'll obey you. I'll marry whoever you think would be a good husband for me."

She hesitated for a moment, then, unable to hold back any longer, cried out in rage, "This man's too old. He's even older than you, father . . . have pity on your poor daughter, father!"

Then she burst into tears, like a desperate child.

Her father was angry. "I'm not used to my children telling me what to do. I will not change my decision. You will marry Đức! He may be my age, but he's brave, hardworking and honest. I met him when we were working together at the mine. He'll be a good husband, you'll see! And anyway, we need a fellow like him to help us with the work in the shop. Your two brothers are still too young!"

Monsieur Bát continued more gently in the hope of convincing her.

"You'll still be with your parents, don't worry about that! I'll arrange a room for you behind the shop and that way you'll live together with us as a family!"

Tý realised that she was forced to go through with this marriage in the interests of her family. From that moment, she understood that nothing could shake her father's decision. She cried for a long time that night, then she began to detest this stranger, this old man. For the first time in her life she also started to detest her parents. She wanted to die. Tý cried until she had no tears left, and then she lay still, her eyes open in the darkness of night, in the darkness of her life. . .

Toán

A few days had passed and life continued as usual. Every morning after Mass Toán visited the Minh family.

"Uncle Toán! You're not talking much this morning; you seem upset!" Hồng said.

"I didn't sleep a wink last night. I waited impatiently for the sun to rise so that I could get to church before coming to see you. That did bring me some relief!"

They were all sitting around the table having breakfast. Toán sat down on one of the chairs.

"You seem tired and preoccupied," remarked Lan.

"Well, you see, I had a fight with Thường yesterday evening. He came to see me in my garden as he wanted to buy lettuces for his shop. It's a beautiful shop, a great success . . . he's a rich man now, but unfortunately, he's now convinced that because of it he's allowed to do whatever he likes. He's the kind of guy who imagines that because he has money, he must know everything."

Toán was out of breath and stopped for a moment, then continued his story.

"He told me we're all idiots, we're delusional. The French government will never listen to our demands. 'Go back to Tonkin if you want to! You're all idiots,' he repeated."

Even though he had been to morning Mass, Toán was agitated and irritated. "That was too much," he said. "I was outraged. At one point I thought my heart was going to shatter into pieces. I didn't feel very well, but my strength came back to me quite quickly and I told him that from then on I wouldn't provide him with vegetables . . . before he could leave I held him back and said this: 'I've put up with you so far Thường, in spite of your bragging about all your money. But try not to ever forget what I'm about to say to you. Do you remember the conditions you lived in back home? Didn't you once tell me, when you were still a worker like me, that you were very poor then. That, as you had nothing else to wear, you had to strip naked so you could wash your rags in a pond? You couldn't bear the smells coming from the rags which were seeping into your body and you absolutely had to wash them! Do you remember that this poisoned the fish in the pond? You see, Thường, unlike you, I have a very good memory and I'm shocked by people like you. You're like the butterfly in one of our legends. Maybe you don't know it. . .

'The butterfly was superb, proud of its brilliant colours, happy to fly around effortlessly in the blue sky. One morning it met a caterpillar moving laboriously along a small branch. The butterfly landed near the caterpillar, the better to observe it and said mockingly, "How ugly you are! How disgusting! I wonder how nature could produce something like you. Look at me! Admire my beauty and elegance. Aren't I one of the most beautiful creatures on earth?"

'"You are indeed magnificent, extraordinary," replied the caterpillar with irritation. "But I pity you, my friend. Your memory is very short. Before you became a beautiful butterfly, you too were a disgusting caterpillar!'

"When Thường heard these words," continued Toán, "he turned bright red and left quickly without a word, as if someone were chasing him . . . just like the butterfly in the fable."

Toán was quiet after this story, his face pale. He closed his eyes as if to help him get over it.

"You defended yourself well. Why are you still angry this morning?" asked Minh.

"I don't know, I don't feel very well. The smallest thing bothers me and exhausts me. . ." answered Toán looking more and more pale and tense. "I wonder if I'll ever be able to go back home in time," he stammered breathlessly. "I have the impression I'll never see my country again!"

"Don't say such things, Toán, please," protested Lan.

"What's the matter Uncle Toán? You look strange," Hồng asked.

"I'm wondering if I should really go back home," Toán continued, his eyes hollow, as if talking to himself. "My wife's dead and so are my children, all dead . . . Thuý, my terrible brother, is the only one still alive. Is it still worth it? I'm afraid I might commit a sin, or even a crime if I see Thuý again!"

"Uncle Toán, you're so pale. Father, I think Uncle Toán's unwell!"

"My heart . . . I'm suffocating. . ."

Toán's strength abandoned him and, a rosary in his hands, he fell to the tiled floor before Hồng could make a single move.

"Let's get him to hospital quickly!" cried Minh. "I think it's serious," he added.

Lan and Hồng took turns every day at his bedside as Toán grew weaker. Minh came to replace them at nightfall.

But it was hopeless. Toán drew his last breath one morning at the first light of dawn. Minh had fallen asleep on the chair next to his friend and when he woke up, Toán's face was so relaxed that it seemed that he was resting, his rosary between his fingers. An angel had no doubt come to fetch him at the end of his last prayer in the dark of night. Toán would never see his country again.

Phúc

June 1960

Minh and Lan were putting things on the shelves in their shop when Phúc suddenly burst in.

"Good news, my friends," he cried, his face shining. "Good news! We've just received the answer from the governor. It's a victory for us! The French government has chartered a ship to take us all home! All those who want to leave, that is."

"Excellent news!" exclaimed Minh.

"We'll all leave, at least three-quarters of the community will," cried Lan, smiling with joy.

Hồng who had heard everything, suddenly left his workbench which was in a room next to the shop. For some time now he had been repairing radios, gramophones and recorders for clients and friends. Hồng joined the small group who were now ecstatic.

"When's the departure date?" he asked unenthusiastically.

"The first departure is for December this year. That means we have exactly six months to settle our affairs and prepare our suitcases," replied Phúc excitedly.

Hồng went back to his workshop without a word.

"Hồng doesn't appear to share our joy!" remarked Phúc.

Minh and Lan were overcome with happiness and took no notice of their friend's observation.

"I'll leave you to it, dear Minh and Lan. I have to go and inform our countrymen in other districts of the good news! Then they'll let the Vietnamese community know, in the town and then all over the country. Goodbye, see you soon!"

Phúc left the room as quickly as he had come. He jumped nimbly into his car. With a roar of the motor and the screech of tyres on the asphalt, the car disappeared around the street corner. Suddenly Minh and Lan heard a violent crash followed by a terrible noise of metal being ripped apart. All three of them rushed out of the shop. A nightmare vision greeted them.

"Uncle Phúc! Uncle Phúc!" yelled Hồng, holding back his mother who fainted before falling to the ground.

Minh rushed like a madman toward what remained of his friend's car which had crashed into an enormous truck. With the help of some bystanders who had helplessly witnessed the terrible scene, they managed, with a crowbar, to remove Phúc's broken, bloody body.

Minh refused to admit the painful truth.

"No!" he said. "No! It's impossible. This is a nightmare! Phúc, my friend. Phúc!" he cried, making a huge effort not to break down and cry in front of all these strangers huddled around the dying man.

A tall strong man, with dark skin and frizzy hair went up to Minh.

"I'm the truck driver," he said, his face haggard. Looking at Phúc who was lying on the road he continued, "He missed the turning. He was going too fast . . . and drove under my truck. There was nothing I could do to avoid him."

He kneeled down and looked at the wounded man, then he turned towards Minh despondently and said, "He's not breathing . . . I'll call an ambulance, but I think there's nothing more we can do . . . he's dead."

Shattered, Minh remained crouching near the lifeless body. This time, he was unable to stop the tears streaming down his face.

"My poor Phúc, my friend! You'll never see our country again either! You were so keen to entrust your body to your native village at the end of your life! You fought so hard to reach this goal . . . the day of victory, your victory, has finally arrived and you've gone, leaving us to benefit from your struggle!"

Minh got up, dazed, as if he were alone, lost amongst all these curious onlookers who had formed a tight circle around them.

"Last year, it was Toán, today, it's Phúc. My best friends. What about me—will I ever be able to see my country again?" he asked himself in dismay.

The Returned

October 1960

Liên continued to work relentlessly, and her restaurant was still just as successful. But money didn't interest her; indeed, nothing interested her. She worked hard to forget and to avoid feeling sorry for herself. She realised that only through hard physical work could she manage not to think of anything and just wait for the boat which would take her back to see her parents.

Phúc's death had of course upset her. But gradually she realised with dismay that, after twenty years of living with Phúc, she no longer thought about him, at least not as much as she should.

Liên often blamed herself for her incomprehensible lack of grieving and, at these moments, she regretted never having had a child with him. Sometimes, in the dark of night, alone in her big bed, she had promised herself that she would never accept another man for the rest of her days. Liên seethed with rage, reproaching life, or God if he existed, or all gods, for that matter, for being so unfair towards a woman, a weak and fragile creature.

One day, during lunch, one of her waitresses came looking for her in the kitchen.

"Madame, there's a customer in the restaurant, from your country, I think, who doesn't want a whole meal! He asked me for just a simple snack and a bowl of tea." The young girl added, "He's bizarre, he seems dazed amidst our customers. In truth, Madame, I'm afraid of him. That's why I've dared to come and tell you about it."

Liên was intrigued by the waitress' unusual reaction. She decided to check on the customer and take the order over to him herself. But when she got near him, she froze, as if petrified.

She thought she had seen this man, this profile, somewhere, despite his short hair. But Liên couldn't put a name to this sad, serious face. And she was even more troubled when she placed the tray on the small table.

During this time, the man observed the happy customers chatting with irritation. As Liên was still speechless in front of him, he raised his downcast eyes towards her. Then he too stared at her, surprised, unable to utter a single word. He looked at Liên for a long time as if he didn't dare believe what he saw. Then he pulled himself together and finally stammered, "Liên! Is it you? What are you doing here?"

"Thắng! Is it you?" cried Liên, her eyes wide open in shock.

"You haven't changed . . . you're still the same. As for me, I'm unrecognisable," he said softly.

"No, Thắng you haven't changed that much. We've grown older, that's all!"

Thắng was still, looking at her intently. Liên was crying silently. Too many memories had suddenly flooded into her heart and her mind.

"I knew that you were there, on the other side of the island, but I didn't dare visit you, I didn't have the right to," murmured Liên slowly, as if she had committed a serious mistake.

Then she added, "But from time to time, for festivals you received parcels, food, and. . ."

Thắng's face lit up and putting his hand out towards Liên he said, "So it was you! During all these years, you. . . ?"

Liên nodded slowly, "Yes, Thắng . . . it was me."

With her right hand Liên wiped away the tears streaming down her cheeks. Her eyes were red as she murmured with a shy smile, "I suppose you must be free now since you're here."

"Yes, they freed me about an hour ago. I'll be on the ship home in a few months . . . as I was walking past this restaurant I came in, but I didn't know who the owner was. Is it yours?"

Liên nodded, looking down at the ground.

"I know what happened, Liên . . . I'm really sorry for you."

Then they stopped talking, not knowing what to do. Liên was oblivious to what was going on around her. She didn't even hear the noisy, laughing customers anymore. She managed to control her emotions and stood up saying, "Don't eat that piece of bread. I'll make you some good food. Yes, yes, you need it!" Liên made her way quickly towards the kitchen. At that moment it seemed to her that the world was beautiful again and life was brighter, sweeter.

"Everything you have now, Liên, was obtained thanks to the labour of your poor husband," she said to herself. But this pious thought soon disappeared from her mind. She had been shaken up by the very real person sitting over at the table at the back of the room.

Liên went back into the room a moment later, smiling as she carried a tray loaded with piping hot dishes from which a thick white steam rose up to the ceiling. But, to her extreme disappointment, she found the table empty. Thắng had disappeared. All that was left on the checked tablecloth was the untouched piece of bread and a scrap of paper. She grabbed it nervously and read the few words which had been scribbled in haste: "Forgive me for bothering you." Liên dropped down onto the chair in despair.

She had thought she had found life again or at least the friendship of the person she had been unable to forget, and whom she had always loved from the bottom of her heart. From that moment she realised that she was truly alone.

The Return

The ship had finally come. After the Christmas festivities the first convoy of passengers began the journey they had waited so long for—the journey back home.

Those who had been away the longest were filled with joy to be on board. They were leaving with many children. Minh, Lan and Liên had found buyers for their businesses and, following a tacit agreement between the interested parties, the new owners would only take possession at the end of January when the second departure was scheduled.

Enthusiastically, Minh and Lan prepared their baggage and Hồng helped Liên with hers.

Thắng had come several times to visit his friends, each time getting to know Hồng better. But the rest of the time he preferred to keep to himself, hiding in a tiny dark room he had rented from a gardener who lived outside the town.

Minh often thought of Thắng and he remembered in particular a conversation he had had with his friend one day. He was criticising Thắng's cold, unfriendly attitude towards Liên.

"Don't be so hard, Thắng. She needs you. Despite the respect and affection she owes her deceased husband, Liên has always loved you, you know. And since you last met, she's been more upset than ever!"

"I must confess," Thắng replied, "that I've never been able to forget Liên either. I still love her as much as when we first met . . . Despite all those years of prison I'm sure I'll always love her. Until the day I die."

Thắng stopped talking and looked fixedly at Minh before continuing. "But you're sensible Minh, and you'll understand. What have I done over the past years? I've been a rebel, an outsider. I've lived for over twenty years on the fringes of a society that I'm now discovering, and which scares me. Everything has changed. Liên's had a husband and she has money now. And what have I done? What have I been able to achieve all this time? Nothing! Nothing! I was squatting in a cell. No, I don't deserve her love. I don't have the right to come into her life for a second time. I've been a prisoner and I'll be a miserable failure for the rest of my days."

"No!" protested Minh vehemently. "The way you think and talk is proof enough that you've stayed the same, a normal man like me, like all of us here. You don't have to. . ."

Minh couldn't finish his sentence as Thắng had disappeared. He had escaped to avoid having to listen to common sense and reason.

***

Preparations for the departure were in full swing.

"You should be packing your things, my son," said Minh who had just piled a large quantity of clothes into a crate. Hồng, looking glum, did not reply.

"Didn't you hear what I just said to you, Hồng?"

"Yes! I heard very well, father!"

"What's the matter? You don't look very happy."

Hồng's face was pale, and he was silent.

"Is there a problem?" Minh asked.

The young man did not reply. With his head lowered, he continued tidying up his parents' things.

"I'm worried about you. What's going on, Hồng?"

Then, turning to Lan who was doing a mountain of ironing at the back of the shop, he said, "Can you come here, Lan? Hồng seems to have some problems. Maybe you could help him resolve them better than I can."

When Lan came over, Hồng stammered, "I need to talk to you."

He was embarrassed and didn't dare raise his head, as if he was afraid to look at his parents.

"Is it serious?" Lan asked, looking concerned.

The young man nodded. His parents looked at each other in bewilderment, disconcerted to see their son in this state.

"We're listening, Hồng, you can speak without fear, we're your parents." Minh said.

"But please, hurry up. We're deeply troubled by this," Lan added anxiously.

"Come into my room then . . . I'll feel a little more at ease there."

Minh followed his son in silence, his face tense, while Lan, shaking all over, waited for the worst.

"Father, mother," said Hồng, once they were in his room, his pale face grave, "Please forgive me. . ."

"Why must we forgive you?" his mother asked. "What have you done?"

"Nothing mother, nothing serious."

"Why so much mystery? Tell us for heaven's sake. We're very worried by your attitude."

Hồng gathered all his energy, breathed deeply, then said at last, "Father, mother, I'm asking your permission to stay here."

"What do you mean—stay where?" interrupted Minh suddenly frowning, as he hadn't really understood what his son meant.

"I'm asking your permission not to leave . . . to stay in New Caledonia."

"What are you saying? Have you gone mad?" yelled Hồng's father, beside himself with rage.

Lan hid her face in her hands to hide her distress.

"I hope you're not serious and that it's a joke. If so, I can tell you straight away it's a very bad joke."

"Father, I'm deadly serious, and I've thought about it a lot before coming to this decision."

Lan came over to sit on the bed, near her son, then she put her head on his shoulder, saying, "No, my child. I beg you, don't abandon us. You're everything to us. You're our hope, our joy, our son! Don't you understand?" Then she burst into tears.

"Give me your reason for this sudden decision," said Minh calmly, as if he refused to believe or even consider what Hồng had just announced.

"I love this country . . . it's where I was born . . . I love the people. It's a magnificent country, and life is good here."

"If those are your reasons, I can tell you that our country is beautiful too. You'll see our green rice fields all along the roads, our countryside is one of the most beautiful in the world. Halong Bay is even considered to be one of the Seven Wonders of the World."

Minh added suspiciously, "I suspect those are not your only reasons."

". . ."

"Is that really all?"

"No father. I'm in love with a girl. . ."

"Ah! So that's it. Monsieur is in love! I don't understand you young people," said Minh, somewhat relieved by this surprising revelation. "We've already asked you several times if you wanted to get married and you've always answered 'No, father, no, mother. I'm still too young.' Now, today, suddenly, you want to get married. Nothing could be simpler! We've never been against your marrying, indeed we're happy to accept it. And I can't see what, in all this, might prevent you leaving." He continued, "Introduce your fiancée to us! You should've done so a long time ago."

Minh seemed delighted with this pleasant prospect.

"But none of this is important," he said. "Bring your fiancée to meet us and we'll arrange everything with her parents and with her too, of course! But I must say this is bad timing. It's a little late now to get married three weeks before we leave!" He thought for a few moments, then cried, "It doesn't really matter, you can get married in Vietnam. That'll be wonderful! The first marriage back home of a Vietnamese from Caledonia, as soon as we get there! Imagine that!"

But, unexpectedly, Hồng was turning even paler.

"You're not saying anything. Doesn't that suit you?" asked Lan standing up.

"Well, the thing is . . . she's a different nationality . . . she's Caledonian," Hồng stammered.

"She can't come to our country yet. Our country has just been through a war and it'll take a few more years. . ."

Minh and Lan were aghast. They looked at their son incredulously, not daring to believe what they had just heard. Lan was so despondent that she dropped to the bed sobbing, as she hadn't done for a long time. Minh, disoriented and upset, was as pale as his son. All the same, he said solemnly, "Until today we've always acted in your best interests. Today I see with regret that it seems I have to be a bit stricter with you. From now on you'll do as I see fit. I will not allow a single digression from this until we leave!"

Then he added even more harshly, "Now I'm giving you an order. Get your things ready and tell this girl that, for us, the child, especially the oldest child, owes obedience to his parents! He has to live with them and take care of them throughout their life. He doesn't have the right to fail in this sacred duty."

Exasperated, Minh left the room saying, "You can say goodbye to her. That'll be the end of it and I don't want to hear about this girl ever again!"

Hồng looked haggard; he was lost in the face of this terrible unsolvable dilemma: duty or love.

Lan looked sorrowfully at her son. Then she got up and asked him in a voice that was both affectionate and pained, "Who is this girl?"

"You know her well," replied Hồng. "Her father worked at Tenep with us. They've been living in Nouméa for a year."

"What's her name?"

"Darrette! Ghislaine Darrette!"

"Ah! I see. Her father was one of the foremen at the mine," murmured Lan. "But why haven't you ever spoken to us about this girl? And how long have you been in love?"

"I met Ghislaine at the beach two weeks after she arrived in Nouméa. As I always knew you wanted to leave, that going back home was all you wanted, I didn't want to tell you until I had made a decision myself."

Lifting his head, he looked at his mother and said, "I'm sorry, mother, to cause you so much grief, but I love Ghislaine! We're in love, mother! You've loved father for so many years, so you should understand us!"

Hồng hesitated for a moment and then said fearfully, "Couldn't you, wouldn't you stay here . . . with us?'

Lan, outraged, turned bright red. "No! We have to go back to the land of our ancestors! It's useless to try to discuss it any further. Make sure you don't forget what your father has just said! You have to obey us!"

She left upset; her body seeming to float in the air, so jerky and disjointed was her gait.

Sadness and silence now pervaded this family which had been so close before. Lan suffered intensely. She took pity on her son.

"My poor boy," she often murmured. "He must have sacrificed his happiness and his love for us. Ghislaine must be a wonderful girl for him to be so attached to her. I remember her. They used to play together when they were little."

Lan's face softened at this innocent memory, then she murmured pensively, "How times have changed. Who could've imagined that one day my son would marry the daughter of a foreman? A boss at the mine?"

A sad thought crossed her mind and her features were drawn. "How complicated life is! We're going to leave a part of our hearts, a part of ourselves in this country."

As for Minh, he had lost the joy and wisdom which had always been present in his life until then. He felt guilty for his brutal egoistic attitude.

"I'm behaving just like my father twenty years ago. I'm forcing my son to obey and respect our customs. I'm ashamed of myself. Didn't I flee to escape these traditions which I thought were so backward? Today at the end of the twentieth century I'm reacting exactly the same way, not allowing my son any alternative."

As for Hồng, he managed, with an iron will, to put on a calm face in front of the parents he loved and respected in spite of everything. But he knew that his broken heart would never be happy again. So as not to hurt his parents further, he avoided turning up in the company of the young girl, with whom he had had a difficult conversation. Ghislaine was unhappy, as unhappy as Hồng, perhaps even more so.

"Times have changed," she protested. Then she had added wearily, "I don't know if I'll be able to keep on living when you're far away from me . . ."

The days and nights slipped past with frightening speed.

The big day came.

Lan and Minh got up at dawn and, with some sadness, prepared their last breakfast on this land which had kept them for so long and that they had come to love in spite of everything. When everything was ready on the table, Lan went to knock on one of the doors.

"Wake up Hồng. It's time to get up. You'll have plenty of time to sleep on board, my son!"

But her calls were met with a worrying silence. Intrigued, Lan opened the door. The room was empty. A quick glance told her that Hồng had not spent the night in his bed. A piece of paper lay on the small table. She rushed over and grabbed it, to find the following words:

"Forgive me! Forgive your unworthy son, I love you so much!"

Lan ran to her husband. In tears, she handed him the message. "We have to call the police," she cried desperately. "We have to find him. My son! My son!"

Minh nodded at first, then thought for a moment before refusing. "No! No, we mustn't!"

"Well in that case, we'll stay. Let's drop everything! Even all our possessions which are now on board," screamed the unhappy mother, still weeping uncontrollably.

"No," said Minh in a tired voice. "Let's go back home. Hồng has the right to live here. He has the right to be happy, we mustn't stop him. We must not," he repeated mechanically. His eyes were hollow and his face devastated by his deep sorrow.

"He'll come to see us one day. I'm sure of it. He's a good boy. . . . Let's go, it's time to leave," he said sadly as he stood up.

When they finally got to the port, Minh and Lan felt as if they had aged twenty years. Their bodies were bent over, stooped like two old people, they had difficulty moving.

"Goodbye New Caledonia, I'm trusting you to look after my son. Goodbye!" murmured Minh softly, squeezing his wife's hand.

Liên had arrived before her friends and was standing next to her hand luggage.

"I'm going to have a lot of trouble trying to get on board with all this," she murmured.

She was looking at all of her bags and then at the raised bridge of the ship when suddenly she felt a presence. Two strong hands grabbed her belongings and she followed Thắng as he climbed up the gangway with his arms completely full.

Liên seemed young again. She was smiling at life as she thought, "This is exactly how it was twenty years ago. The two of us boarding the ship together like this in Hải-Phòng!"

All of a sudden Liên realised that life was still worth living.

Minh, on the quay swarming with people, noticed a little boy selling flowers. "He must be about fifteen," he murmured. "He looks just like my son at that age." Without thinking he went up to the boy and gave him the few coins he had left in his pocket. To thank him the boy gave him a flower, but Minh could not accept it, so great was his sorrow. The young boy, with a grateful smile, put it in one of the bags Minh was holding. Then Minh helped his wife board the ship. The sun was dazzling, but they descended immediately to the holds which had been turned into dormitories. Lan was so exhausted that she had to be lain on a bed. Minh stood still near her; he had the face of a sixty-year-old.

"There's just one thing we have to do now," he said to console himself. "We're now going home to participate in the reconstruction of our homeland. We owe it to the country, and we also have to bring purpose to our lives, for the rest of our lives."

"And we'll try to find our parents," added Lan.

"Yes, of course, that goes without saying."

Early that afternoon, the ship cast off and left the quay.

Minh was exhausted, dazed. He went to one of the portholes, and then, putting his hand out, he let it hang for a moment above the dark water in the port. A small object slipped between his fingers and fell into the sea. A tiny thing, immediately swirled around by the waves, lost for ever. It was a rose. In Vietnamese "Hồng" means "rose."

With distress Minh watched first the port recede, then, the whole town. "My son's somewhere in one of those houses. He didn't even dare to come and say goodbye," he murmured in despair, "not even to say goodbye!"

Minh's grief was so profound that it felt as if all the sadness in the world had suddenly fallen on his shoulders. In that instant he understood better his father's distress when, one morning, he had fled like a thief. He realised that it was now his turn to suffer, just as his parents had suffered. However, Minh was convinced, at least he hoped, that his son would come back to him one day.

"We just have to be patient," he said to himself.

Patience and hope, he had always had both and was certain he would still have them, until the last hour, the last minute of his life.

Index

D

E

F

G

H

I

J

K

L

M

N

P

R

S

T

U

V

W

Y

Biography

Tess Do is Lecturer in French Studies in the School of Languages and Linguistics at the University of Melbourne, Australia. Her teaching and research interests lie in the field of Francophone literature and deal with issues related to colonisation and decolonisation, exile and migration, cultural identity and the relations between migrants and their homeland. Focusing in particular on Indochina and the areas of food, memory and cultural heritage, her main publications include articles and book chapters on Francophone writers of Vietnamese origin.

Kathryn Lay-Chenchabi is a scholar in Francophone post-colonial studies and a NAATI-accredited French and English translator. She has a particular interest in questions of cultural and linguistic identity and has published in the field of French writers of North African descent. She has taught French language and culture in the French Studies program at the University of Melbourne and translation theory and practice in the Master of Translation and Interpreting program at the Royal Melbourne Institute of Technology.

www.ingramcontent.com/pod-product-compliance
Lightning Source LLC
Chambersburg PA
CBHW040925050726
47507CB00023B/351
* 9 7 8 0 6 4 5 3 7 1 3 0 7 *